# TESLANAUTS

Matthew Donald

*To my parents Don and Barbara, who helped build this book and electrify its prospects*

TESLANAUTS

Author photo by Malle Malia Zablan



For questions and feedback contact:
**mattd@matthewdonaldcreator.com**

ISBN: 9798986024806

First Edition: August 2022

10 9 8 7 6 5 4 3 2 1

**ALSO BY MATTHEW DONALD**

Megazoic

Megazoic: The Primeval Power

Megazoic: The Hunted Ones

Megazoic: An Era's End

Check out Matthew Donald's website,

**www.matthewdonaldcreator.com**

for more information, links to his Patreon, and his two podcasts, The Writ Wit (all about writing tips and tricks), and Paleo Bites (all about various prehistoric animals)

# Chapter One

RAYMOND CALVERT was an unusual kid. While other seventeen-year-olds went out dancing, caught the latest Charlie Chaplin flick, or watched in awe as Babe Ruth hit yet another home run, Raymond focused more on studying the workings of electromagnetic technology, or at least the blueprints of which he had access to in his house. He did this not for any scientific or technological benefit to society, but to search for clues. His father had been missing for years, and these were the breadcrumbs left to him. When talking to others, he hadn't the slightest care about the magazines or movies or other social conversation starters; instead, schematics of devices others would deem impossible with modern science piqued his interest.

He had a mission. His father couldn't wait. *He* couldn't wait.

In the decade before, the world was in the midst of a great war. *The* Great War, as it was called. The War to End All Wars. All the imperfections of humanity shone bright and proud, proving to everyone just how ruthless and despicable man could truly be. Centuries of rivalries, petty disagreements, technological advancements, and a desire to destroy all culminated in a terrible struggle that civilization had never seen the likes of before, resulting in the deaths of millions and a stark reevaluation about the advancement of society. Were people truly better than they were thousands of years ago when they hit each other with rocks and sticks? Eventually though, it ended with the signing of the armistices, resulting in the surrender of German, Hungarian, Ottoman, and other Central Power forces.

A year before these historic agreements were signed, though, Raymond was a naïve twelve-year-old boy, blissfully ignorant of the horrors overseas. He played and matured in his Brooklyn home, without fear of gasses or bullets or any other terrible instrument of war. His mother took care of him, got him to school, and kept him in shape, helping him grow from a boy to a man.

His father, however, had a very different life, of which Raymond still did not truly know all the details. He worked with the same technology his son dabbled with now, in fact much more of it. He had a secret employer that he could not tell his family about, and often spent many weeks away from his family home. Occasionally, Raymond heard mumblings of a man named Tesla, and occasionally snuck a peek at the telegrams summoning his father away to work. Even though he could barely comprehend the technical language, it all seemed so fascinating to the young boy. His father was like one of those heroes in his books! He could fight anything, and perform feats beyond that of normal men.

At least, that was how it seemed. One day, though, in the cold snowy months of December 1917, uniformed men came to Raymond's mother and told her the worst thing a family could learn: her husband would not be coming back home. Such a tragedy was one many families knew all too well throughout the war, but that never made it an easy one to hear. But was there more to the story?

Now, in the spring of 1922, Raymond was on the cusp of becoming a man. His jaw shaped into more square-like proportions, and dark hair started popping out on his arms and chest. As he grew, he studied all he could about what his father had done, and recovered documents once thought lost. That was when he started dabbling with electromagnetic schematics, after he had found numerous designs signed by his father. He had to know what happened. He had to learn.

And now, it seemed he would finally get an answer.

"Right this way, Mr. Calvert," a government worker told him, leading him to a black car. He and another worker escorted Raymond out the back door of the office he had barged into demanding answers, and where exactly they were taking him remained unclear. One of them had a big handlebar mustache, while the other remained clean-shaven, but otherwise the two seemed identical in their medium build and angular faces. Dressed in fine gray suits with distinctive silver cufflinks, and the blackest pair of bowler hats Raymond had ever seen, the two men leading Raymond had a fancy yet unusual presence to them, and all the good feelings of a rusty knife. If their job was to make Raymond feel uneasy, they succeeded admirably.

Several months ago, when rummaging through old unopened mail addressed to his father, he had found a summons from his father's employer with a peculiar encryption, keeping the contents classified to any unknowing eyes like Raymond's. However, one thing remained unconcealed: the schematics. Presumably, his employer thought no one other than Raymond's father would dabble with the required components.

Yet, after fiddling with the technology specs for several weeks, Raymond learned what device the schematics were for: a gun, but unlike any Raymond had ever heard of before. Rather than a standard bullet and magazine, it seemed to fire light particles in a concentrated beam. While Raymond hadn't the necessary equipment to complete the schematic, it still motivated him to run to the city hall and ask what the blazes was going on. Was his father some kind of highly specialized arms-dealer? Did someone murder him to get a hold of this equipment?

Raymond had to know. Once he arrived at New York City Hall and showed them the schematics, while telling him his father worked for some secret "Tesla" organization, the men at the office told him to wait in the back for government officials to answer his question. And that's when these two officials seized Raymond, getting him in the back of a car and driving him to God-knows-where.

"Sit still, and keep quiet," the clean-shaven official told Raymond as they drove.

"I haven't said anything yet, sir," Raymond muttered in the back.

"Yes, and let's keep it that way," the mustached one said from the shotgun seat. "Now, how did a fellow like you even learn about this Tesla company?"

Raymond didn't say a word. The worker glared back at the seventeen-year-old and waved his hand around. "Speak up, son! Where did you learn of this?!"

"You told me to keep quiet!" Raymond shot back. "Would you mind being consistent?"

"Perhaps we should take him back," the first official said to the other while turning to another street. "Maybe he'll keep quiet if given a threat of force."

"We don't threaten our fellow American citizens. Unless they're lawyers or loan sharks. You're not a loan shark, are you?"

"Yes, I swim in people's debt," Raymond grumbled, not bothering to hide his sarcasm. "My fin constantly pokes out of the pools of cash. Does that answer your question, sir?"

"Clearly, this young man is not a loan shark," the mustached official said.

After a very tense half-hour drive, the three of them arrived at a worn-down apartment building, halfway to rejoining the earth. With bundles of dislodged wooden planks, wads of cobwebs, and an overabundance of grime, it looked only slightly more inviting than the trenches of no man's land in the thick of the war. As they waited by the building, Raymond's brow lowered. He wondered why they picked this particular spot. Surely this ruined residential structure held no particular significance to anyone but vermin, right?

"We have arrived," the mustached official said, exiting the car and motioning Raymond to get out as well. "Now, Mr. Calvert, explain to us how you have heard of this Tesla company."

Raymond did not particularly feel like explaining his life story to these seemingly unscrupulous characters in such an uninviting location, yet he knew if he did nothing, he would never learn what exactly happened to his father. Shrugging, he decided to comply with their demands.

"My father was a government worker, sir, but he never told us precisely where. He was declared missing in action five years ago on a mission during the war, and was presumed dead. However, he left behind some blueprints with a code I could not decipher, but after studying it further, I understood the components within the schematic well enough. They were for a weapon unlike anything I have ever seen, using particle beams as ammunition rather than bullets. Add to the fact that I overheard my father murmur the name 'Tesla' sometimes when I was a kid, and it's not hard to put two and two together."

"Your father could have simply worked in an experimental military sector," the clean-shaven official said. "And his murmuring of Tesla could just be unrelated jabbering. What makes you so sure they're connected?"

"I've heard of Nikola Tesla, sir. A brilliant Serbian electrician living here in New York. A great 'wizard', as I've heard him called. He's been laying low for the last few years, socially distant and reclusive, but he's got a swinging portfolio. This kind of schematic fits right into what I have read about Tesla's more outlandish experiments."

"Which is?"

"Nothing but ideas, really. Autonomous machines, electromagnetic manipulators, wireless technology, and maybe a big tower or two controlling it all. He never built any of it, as far as I know, but the man sure could dream big."

The men looked at each other, before looking back at Raymond. Their thick eyebrows furrowed, as they clearly contemplated whether to press the issue further. Raymond stared blankly at them, wondering what these fine folks were hiding from him. One could cut the tension of the moment with a nail file.

"How much do you want to know what happened to your father?" the mustached official asked.

"I won't stop until I know, sir."

"How good are you at keeping secrets?"

"Depends on the secret."

"Well, if you want to know what happened, Mr. Calvert, you best be keeping your lips sealed. We're talking about global-conspiracy-level information."

Raymond blinked at their words, rather unsure of how to take their statement. Had he gone in too deep? Would he be detained for the rest of his life, away from his mother who struggled to take care of them both and constantly worried about him? The first government official's earlier question rang in his ears: how much did he *really* want to know what happened to his father?

More than anything. That's how much he wanted to know. It was a missing piece in his life that needed filling. It drove him crazy. It interfered with his school, his work, and his sleep. Not knowing would be far worse than anything they could throw his way. Still, he knew it best to exercise caution.

"Is there any going back?" Raymond finally asked.

"No," the clean-shaven official said. "Once you know, there's no going back. You can write home, and you can even visit home, but you'll be on constant government watch to ensure you're not spilling any secrets. Sometimes there are questions best left unanswered, even the ones you want answered most. The world is undergoing a regression of idealism. The haunting memories of the war, the battle between science and fundamentalism, the rampant greed, the political turmoil; all of it is washing away the simple romance and chivalry folks long for. Do you *really* want your question answered in a world like this one?"

"It's the nineteen-twenties," Raymond said, shrugging. "Things aren't so bad. Granted, I was looking forward to a good shot of bourbon when I got older, but I'll take prohibition over war any day."

"Think about what you're doing, son," the mustached official said. "Think about all you're throwing away. You're still young; you could go to college and get an education. You could get a job, a wife, and a child or two, like any other upstanding gentleman. If you do this, you're throwing all that away. You got a sweetheart of your own, I reckon. Why disappoint her like this?"

"I don't have a sweetheart," Raymond said dully. "You might find this hard to believe, but my rampant obsession over unresolved father issues tends to drive the ladies away. I'm ready."

"Going once."

"I'm ready."

"Going twice!"

"Still ready. Please, can you just be straight with-*ow*!"

Whipping out a device looking suspiciously like a cattle prod, the mustached official zapped Raymond's hand with a small yet jarringly annoying jolt of electricity. The current flowed through his body, rattling his bones and organs for a few seconds, before it finally gave way, leaving only a sharp tingling in his fingers.

"What was that for?" Raymond demanded.

"All in due time," the clean-shaven official said, smiling mysteriously. "Now, follow us, Mr. Calvert. Your future begins."

The two men then walked to the main door of the building, motioning Raymond to follow. The mustached official tried to open the door, but the knob wouldn't move, which made Raymond smirk. Maybe this was the wrong address after all. However, after a few seconds, a sharp *zap* came from his wrist and onto the door, somehow allowing it to open at last. A nifty little gadget, for sure.

The door led to an empty hallway, with cobwebs on every corner and not a light to be found. Raymond and the workers slowly trudged through the hallway, with each step making a creaking sound in the floor. As they made their way through this thoroughly dreary place, Raymond couldn't help but wonder what the significance of this place was, or why it was kept in such a repugnant state. It was a miracle the city hadn't torn this place down yet.

A miracle... or maybe a multimillion-dollar cover-up effort involving the bribing of civic officials and the shushing of any questioning passerby. Who would make such an effort, though, and for what reason? Whatever it was, Raymond figured he was about to find out.

"It's rather domestic," the young Brooklyn man noted. "Maybe a bit too much. Is this the base of your secret Tesla company?"

"You caught us," the clean-shaven official sarcastically replied. "Welcome to Teslanaut HQ, Mr. Calvert."

"Teslanaut? What does that mean?"

"You ask too many questions. It's gotten you into a lot of trouble already, son. Don't let it get you into any further."

After a quick trot through the dark and dusty hallway, they finally reached another door, this time with no door handle. The mustached worker knocked four times, paused for a moment, then knocked a fifth. This caused the peephole to open up, revealing two white eyes that seemed to glow like little light bulbs.

"Password?" a barely audible voice said through static, almost like it came from a recording.

"Oh, so this is a speakeasy!" Raymond said. "Maybe I *will* get that shot of bourbon after all."

"Why don't you have a go with the password, Mr. Calvert?" the clean-shaven official asked. "Since you know so much, apparently."

"Alfred Wegener," Raymond guessed with a shrug, saying the name of the first out-there scientist he could think of other than Nikola Tesla.

"Good try, but no," the official said with a chuckle, before turning back to the door. "Westinghouse," he told the glowing eyes.

The peephole closed, and the door opened, revealing an empty room only slightly larger than a closet. The owner of those strange eyes was nowhere to be seen, but once they entered the room, Raymond looked back and saw that the door on the other end had a series of metal boxes with gears and wires attached where the peephole should be. That was not a man behind the door, but a machine.

The mustached official gripped Raymond's forearm and moved him to a specific location in the room. Once the three of them stood together, the clean-shaven one pulled a hidden lever under the peeled-off wallpaper at his side. With a sudden jolt, the square floor panel they stood on lowered, revealing it as a secret open elevator.

"Fascinating," Raymond murmured.

"It's just a lift, kid," the mustached official said. "You haven't seen anything yet."

"What, are you going to poke me with that cattle prod again?"

"That wasn't a cattle prod, and no, I'm not."

Raymond shrugged and just waited in silence as the elevator continued to descend. He did not appreciate the lack of answers from these gentlemen, but he knew he could do little to get anything more from them. Darkness was all that greeted them as they plunged down the lift, until after a hundred feet or so when hand-sized light bulbs finally began lining the walls.

Once they reached the bottom, they found themselves within a long stone tunnel with a clear channel of water flowing through like a river. Fluorescent lights barely lit the roof, and water from leaky pipes dripped from up above. Raymond expected the rancid smell of a sewer when they arrived, but there was none. Indeed, the water had a different fragrance to it, one more salty in nature.

"Are you ready to witness something truly remarkable, Mr. Calvert?" the clean-shaven official asked.

"Is my father hidden somewhere, tied to a chair?" Raymond asked flatly, looking around the tunnels with mocking expectancy.

The man ignored him, and pulled a switch on the stone wall. A flash of light illuminated the room, like they had just gotten their picture taken, before the water stirred in the channel to their side. A wave of a most foul aroma briefly overtook their noses, prompting Raymond to cover his nose and hold his breath. Clearly, the sewer smell just needed a little time before unleashing itself.

Before he could angrily let out another sarcastic quip, the flowing water carried something else their way. A metallic submersible, no bigger than a rowboat with a round dome cockpit at the front and a multitude of turbines at the back, drifted down the tunnel and stopped by where they stood. The second worker pulled a door open at the top, and the three men climbed inside, Raymond more reluctantly.

"Impressed yet?" the mustached official said.

"Who are you?" Raymond demanded, his curiosity about what exactly these folks were hiding getting the better of him.

"I'm Agent Zero, and that's Agent Null," the clean-shaved one said. "We're what you could call recruitment officers for our organization."

"Do you have actual names?"

"As far as you're concerned, Mr. Calvert, those *are* our actual names."

"What about that blinding flash of light back in the tunnel? Would you care to explain that?"

"That was our scanning equipment," the clean-shaven worker, Agent Zero, explained. "When the lever is pulled, electromagnetic sensors within that light check for a specific electrical signature in the room. If the proper signature is detected, the submersible is released."

"What signature?"

"The one from the 'cattle prod', as you called it," Agent Null said, his smile sullied by a hint of mischief. "It's part of the initiation procedure for our agents. The signature will remain within your nervous system until you die, so don't worry, you won't have to endure another exposure."

"Well, that's a relief!" Raymond laughed at first, before the hairs on the back of his neck went up after processing exactly what the agent had said. Initiation procedure? *Agent* initiation procedure? All he did was ask the whereabouts of his missing and presumed dead father, mentioning an unusual Tesla weapon and a potential secret organization behind it, and now he got recruited? What kind of operation did these agents have here?

The submersible flowed down the tunnel, until it submerged into the water. After a few minutes, they reached the Hudson River to the west of Manhattan Island, with the surface a dozen yards above. Lights switched on at the front, but they did little to increase visibility beyond a few feet forward. What particularly astounded Raymond, however, was the lack of piloting from the two agents. The submersible drove itself through the water, turning and descending through the water in controlled motions, yet without any person seeming to do the controlling. The surprises today seemed to never end.

"Tare-Nan Cast, do you read?" Agent Zero said through a radio on the submersible dashboard. "This is Agents Null and Zero, transporting new personnel. We're calling upon the Suspicion Permittance protocol, code Sail-Pup. Over?"

"Roger, agents," a voice on the other end of the radio said. "Proceed to Tare-Nan Cast."

"That's the U.S. Air Service alphabet you're using, right?" Raymond asked. "I recognize that from overhearing my father's reports in his office."

"You're a smart kid," Agent Null said.

"Or your house had thin walls," Agent Zero noted. "Sounds like your father should have kept his voice down."

The submersible continued through the gloomy depths, until it reached a circle-shaped series of lights illuminating the side of an oddly prominent dome, much too high and symmetrical to be a simple mound on the seafloor. On the far side stood a cylindrical tower, with a sphere at the tip and circular ridges ringing the sides, that gradually faded and brightened in a cyclical motion. The lights came from underneath, keeping them from piercing the water and alerting the surface of their presence. Raymond had never seen such a tower before, except for maybe at Coney Island.

A vault door slowly creaked open on the end of the dome, which the submersible promptly drove through to enter. It rose up to the surface, now only a few yards above, revealing a docking station at the end of a base. Agents Null and Zero opened the doors and helped Raymond out of the sub, clanking their dress shoes onto the metal grating of the dock. Their vehicle automatically submerged and drove out of sight, presumably to a loading bay further inside the dome.

"Welcome to Teslanaut HQ, Mr. Calvert," Agent Null said, a smile creeping under his mustache. "For real this time."

"Get those mech blueprints to the factory, stat!" a voice shouted.

"Our agents have received the coordinates from the French Volt Knights of the enemy base near the southern German border," another voice reported. "Shall we send more men to assist right away?"

"Let the boss know this. He needs to approve these gadget designs!" a third voice demanded.

Just ten yards away from the dock, without a wall or gate to block it, was a sight that Raymond would never forget. Amidst a forest of gears, pipes, and zapping coils lay a control hub of hundreds of workers, scurrying about with papers, supplies, and a slew of shouted orders. Some of them were stationed at their control ports, turning valves on the panels, typing commands on a typewriter, flicking switches to control power, and a wide assortment of other tasks that Raymond could hardly fathom. As well as people, mechanized automatons big and small darted all around, whether walking on legs, rolling on wheels, or flying with miniaturized airplane propellers, somehow acting completely independently of human control.

"The Electrocracy has ordered further reinforcements to aid the Volt Knights with their infiltration," someone shouted, holding his ear to a telephone speaker after receiving orders from someone on the other end. "Coordinates are forty-eight point six degrees north, seven point seven degrees east."

"Send fifty more field agents and a squad of new recruits," a commander ordered. "We will support our allies overseas."

"Can someone please rewire this hover-head and make it stop following me?!" another man asked, hurriedly backing away from one of the smaller flying automatons that constantly buzzed its propellers toward him.

"Still need the boss to approve these gadget designs!" the same man from earlier reminded everyone. "Any day now!"

Raymond felt his mind growing increasingly numb with shock by the second, and his eyes growing wider with each revelation he beheld. It was all so incredible, witnessing such mechanical wonder, as well as such casual acknowledgement of it from everyone present, like the flying metal men and the supplying of "shocker" tanks happened so often they almost grew weary of it. The constant commotion, the technological treasures, and the perpetual power seemed unfathomable to Raymond or anyone else he knew, and yet here they all were, basking in such advanced glory.

Raymond already grew overwhelmed from seeing it all, and he had still not yet looked up. Once his gaze went from the workers below to the walls above, his eyes managed to widen even further.

"Rally, workers," a skinny, six-foot, dark-haired man commanded from a balcony overlooking the control hub. "We will help our friends in Europe, but we must be prepared for any eventuality we might come across."

Raymond couldn't believe it. Standing up there, guiding the workers and leading them to their tasks, was

Nikola Tesla himself. Clad in a silver vest and copper-colored jacket, he watched the workers with an inquisitive regard, studying their movements like dust mites under a microscope. Sporting sleek dark gray hair and a groomed mustache, he looked rather dashing for his age of sixty-five, helped by his lean frame and fine attire. Yet, within the focused gaze of his eyes, Raymond could see a hundred other plans forming inside his mind, his brain firing on all cylinders at every moment.

Was this great man who Raymond's father worked for? Did he actually report to this incredible inventor, this brilliant mind seemingly centuries ahead of his time? Raymond had no idea, but he reckoned he was about to find out.

"Excuse me, boss?" a smaller, scrawnier looking young man said to Tesla, holding several pieces of paper similar to the schematic Raymond found in his father's mail. "My, uh, team in the factory has completed our latest attempt at the, uh, auto-mech project."

"Let us hope this mech lasts a couple seconds longer than the last attempt!" Tesla chuckled. "Brilliant job, Mr. Worthington."

As the young man escorted Tesla away from the balcony to another room behind the wall, Agents Null and Zero took Raymond through a door to the left of the control hub, isolated from the frenetic energy of the headquarters. Through the door sat what might have been an interrogation room if it weren't for the lack of a one-way window. Yet the single desk with two simple chairs did little to ease Raymond of the implications.

"Wait here," Agent Zero said, pushing Raymond inside and shutting the door. Impulsively, Raymond clutched the doorknob to find that, of course, it was now locked. With a huff, the teenager sat on the chair and thought about all he had seen and all he had learned in the last half hour. A secret organization, equipped with technology beyond anything he had ever seen, headed by the legendary Nikola Tesla himself? A potential answer for the mystery of what happened to his father, as well as a glimpse into the life he lived outside his family? An abduction by the government and an unwanted recruitment after prying too much into matters a seventeen-year-old perhaps should not know?

What had Raymond gotten himself into?

# Chapter Two

HELEN BRIMSBY held her rifle firmly in her gloves, blinking to get the dirt from her lime eyes. She stood with a squad of a dozen others in a trench outside Strasbourg, France, one that garnered plenty of use during the Great War. With all the explosive ordinance and poison that had plagued this land and defiled the earth, the harrowing experiences the soldiers had to brave here still haunted the air, and the screams of dying men could still be heard amidst the breeze and the buzzing insects. To this day, the general public breathed a sigh of relief that the war finally ended four years earlier.

At least, they were told it had ended then, and to be fair, they were mostly right. With the signing of the various armistices, and the efforts of major political figures including Woodrow Wilson and Ferdinand Foch, the fighting on the Western Front had mercifully come to an end. Yet, there was another front where the battle persisted, one beyond the eyes of the common world.

The conflict of volt-tech had been going on for over a decade. The Great War had escalated it, prolonged it, and amplified it to previously unimaginable levels. And now still, even after the armistice, it dragged on. Yet the soldiers that fought on this front were not soldiers at all, strictly speaking. The Teslanauts did not employ "soldiers," for Tesla himself was no advocate of war, even if he was forced to fight it occasionally. Thus, these combatants were known as "agents." They carried various gadgets along with their rifles, and worked to resolve conflicts rather than escalate them.

Yes, agents were what they were. And that's what Helen was.

"Their factories are a couple miles ahead," Helen told her accompanying agents, her posh British accent unique among her mostly American companions. Strands of her wavy auburn hair dropped onto her round face; the rest kept in a bun underneath her helmet. "Be on the lookout for patrols and the like."

"Don't you worry, we've got this under control," one of the agents said, chuckling. "Don't need no girls telling me what to do."

"Mind you, girls can now vote in your country," Helen chortled, shrugging off the agent's casual dismissal of her. "About bloody time they get a say in things, I reckon. Maybe next time America won't be so late for the war."

"Our air recon have caught glimpses of an unusual machine patrolling the area," the marshal leading the squad of agents reported, wanting to keep the infighting to a minimum. "Keep your rifles at hand as we move in."

"Yes sir!" another agent barked obediently, saluting the marshal.

Helen nodded at their leader, grateful for his aid getting her in the fight. A daughter of a famed British general, Helen knew first-hand both the glories and horrors of war. Her older brothers had served in the trenches years ago, one of them giving his life for king and country. As a young woman, Helen would normally never get the chance to fight alongside her countrymen; she would instead get delegated as a nurse or support technician. Yet, she sure wanted to fight. She wanted to make her family and country proud just like her forebears, and yearned to avenge her fallen brother.

Thankfully, Nikola Tesla focused more on skill and talent when recruiting new agents for his organization, whether in the foundries or on the field. Thus, Helen gleefully seized the opportunity once she turned sixteen to enlist in the Teslanauts as a field agent, the only opportunity she knew she would get. She didn't care that their gadgets and weapons were beyond what her family knew. She just wanted to serve. It was what her family had always done, and she would be no different. She passed the boot camp and gadgetry training courses with flying colors, and here she was.

Of course, admittance was one thing, but acceptance was quite another. Even with Tesla's valuing of qualifications over labels, women and people of color remained rare in this field. That's why Helen appreciated Marshal Gabriel Morales immediately standing up for her and keeping the unit working together, whatever gender the cogs in their machine. As a Puerto Rican, he understood what she had to go through and sympathized with her plight. A tall, burly thirtysomething, Morales had served in the Great War both on the volt-tech and non-volt-tech fronts, and had an honorable track record as a soldier and a hero.

"I'm picking up some electromagnetic disturbances," Morales stated, holding a toaster-sized machine with an antenna. "I think our enemy has upped their game since last time."

"Fringe groups, nothing more," an agent said, snickering. "They haven't pulled out the big guns since the war."

"Don't get too complacent. Things can change overnight!"

"Our guns are bigger than theirs, anyway!" another agent said. "Especially mine! I can destroy any of you folks whenever I want."

"You ain't seen anything yet," the first agent laughed, holding up his rifle proudly. "This baby can wreck all of ya, and I have the skills to do it, too!"

"If you chaps are done measuring your weapons, we best keep a wary eye out," Helen said. "Our days of fighting fringe groups appear to be behind us, so let's not get too focused on who can blow up whom, shall we? And by the way, my gun is clearly the biggest."

"Relatively, anyway," Morales noted with a smirk. "But Brimsby's right, agents. Keep your eyes open for movement. We don't know what exactly is heading our way, so we must remain-"

An explosion of dirt and brick came from underneath one of Strasbourg's outer buildings, destroying the lively mood in a flash. The building, thankfully long abandoned, tumbled into the dirt, while three metal extremities clawed their way out of the rubble. A harsh grinding sound nearly ruptured the eardrums of the Teslanauts, as gears whirred into overdrive within an unseen machine.

"Contact, contact!" an agent shrieked.

"Gadgets at hand, agents!" Helen told her companions. "Arm up and crack on!"

Rising from the bricks of the fallen building, a fifty-foot-tall machine leered at the trenches, accompanied by electric sparks and the overpowering stench of diesel. Standing on three rod-like legs, the metal creature kept its weaponry locked within a spherical body, with only the edges of gun barrels peeking out from openings along its center. Hooks drooped off the sides of its body, connected to thick cables reeled inside its iron carapace. While it seemed automated, the receiver antennae atop its body and cameras lining its center showed that someone unseen controlled this machine remotely. Rugged and ruthless, the three-legged monster stomped toward the Teslanauts, ruthlessly charging at a pace beyond what its size would suggest.

"What is that thing?!" another agent demanded.

"A bit Wellsian, I must say!" Helen noted.

"Get to cover!" Morales ordered, running deeper into the trench with his rifle at hand. "Don't get caught out!"

The machine reached the Teslanauts within seconds, standing above the trenches and looming over the agents. Before they could react, its cable-connected hooks shot down toward their position like a predator's claws, just barely missing most of them but managing to latch onto one poor man. The cables reeled him upward, with gears churning loudly and excitedly within its iron belly, as the agent struggled mightily to break free. Just before he managed to remove himself from the machine's grasp, its center-mounted guns shot him repeatedly in the chest, not missing a shot with him reeled in so close. The agent's lifeless body fell into the trench, barely missing Helen and Morales as they scrambled out of the way.

"No!" Helen shouted.

"Bring it down!" Morales demanded, knowing the only way to keep the situation from further escalating would be to destroy this machine. They had already lost one of their own, and he would ensure they would not lose anyone else. "Agents, deploy your weapons!"

As one, the agents took the rifles off the straps on their backs and fired at the three-legged machine. But the projectiles that came from their barrels were not of the metal or lead variety. Over the years, Nikola Tesla had worked on a disintegrating energy beam that would surpass every other weapon on the battlefield, not to escalate wars, but to end them. Weapons like these would surely render the fight meaningless, and thus he equipped all his agents with guns armed with such disintegrators.

These beams, as intended, revolutionized battle, but alas, they did not end it. Eventually their enemies figured out how to block and counter the Teslanauts' energy beams, and eventually even how to replicate them; thus, they rendered the war properly escalated. Still, Tesla was a stubborn man and would do everything in his power to keep people from reigniting the conflict they so fervently and obviously desired. The world would always remain imperfect, but that did not mean Tesla would not fight to perfect it.

Helen's, Morales's, and every other agent's energy beams sliced through the air, blasting the machine and sending parts flying. In response, the three-legged mechanoid reeled out two of its cables and deployed them to the front. Channeling its inner voltage, a rectangular shield of lightning bolts activated between the cables, using built-in coils to channel electrical power and block the Teslanauts' energy beams.

"Oh, brilliant!" Helen snapped.

"Flank it!" Morales ordered. "Keep it pinned down while I deploy the Peacemaker!"

The agents moved back down into the trenches, keeping their heads low to avoid the machine's rampant fire. Lifting one of its three mechanical legs upwards, the machine pulled its rod-like foot out of the dirt, revealing a sharpened spear that dug into the ground with each step. The spear, at eight feet long, could easily skewer any of the agents that got caught underfoot, making yet another thing for the Teslanauts to avoid when facing this mechanized nightmare. Keeping its other two legs firmly in place in the dirt, the machine started poking the ground with its sharp spear-like foot, just barely missing the agents as they rushed to flank their target.

"Open fire!" an agent on the trench opposite of Helen ordered. A flurry of blinding white energy beams burst from their rifles and onto the machine's hull, tearing off a few bits of metal plating before it used its cables to form a lightning shield again. As the agents kept holding the machine's attention, Helen and the other agents on her side fired their own beams, forcing it to deal with attacks on two fronts.

"That's it, boys!" Helen shouted, encouraging her companions. "Give this machine a kicking! Keep-"

"Look out!" a nearby agent shouted.

Another cable whipped its way down towards Helen, wrapping around her ankle and pulling her up. Helen grunted fearfully and fired repeatedly at the cable, trying to keep the machine from shooting her up close and losing the brigade another fine agent. The others on the ground followed suit, blasting at the cable holding Helen with energy beams left and right. Just before she got pulled within range of the machine's center-mounted guns, the cable finally snapped from the relentless firepower, causing her to freely fall toward the ground a dozen yards below.

"Brimsby!" the agent hollered.

"I've got this!" Helen assured him, dislodging the disconnected cable from her ankle and throwing it at one of the machine's legs. Just before she hit the ground and shattered some bones, the cable wrapped around the upper parts of the machine's rod-like legs, causing Helen to swing forward with an excited cheer. Holding out her rifle, she fired several beams at the center-mounted guns, destroying them and keeping the machine from killing anyone else with them.

"Nice job, Brimsby!" another agent cheered.

Helen let go of the cable and gracefully landed onto the ground, smiling triumphantly at her maneuver.

The machine's cogs churned loudly in response, rattling the whole contraption almost as if it roared with fury. Lurching forward, its three legs stomped furiously toward Helen, hoping to skewer the annoying little agent who dared face off against it.

"Stand back!" Morales yelled from behind, grunting at a burly weight. "Peacemaker is now deployed!"

The machine paid no attention to the leader of their brigade, instead raising one of its spiny legs over Helen in hopes of turning her into a shish kebab. Before it lowered its foot to strike, however, its leg promptly got sliced in half, causing the machine to lose balance and topple onto the ground with a series of angry gear grindings.

Breathing heavily, Morales swung the Peacemaker back upright, straining from the weight even with his muscular arms. This incredible weapon was a seven-foot sword made of dirigible propeller blades, so heavy and awkward that it needed tiny rockets lining its flat to allow the wielder to swing it. Its parts unfolded from a base cube form, which could split into three pieces for three different agents to carry in their packs when not in use. Thousands of volts transmitted from faraway generators energized the rockets, and also added a bit of an electrical punch to the sword's attacks.

While such an immense and unwieldy weapon might have seemed less practical than it was worth, the Peacemaker excelled in one very important task: destroying heavy machines. With a strong wielder and the propulsion of its rockets, it could deploy slow but *very* destructive strikes at any enemy contraption unlucky enough to get in its way, as this three-legged machine had just learned.

"Good show, Marshal!" Helen cheered, grinning.

"It's not over yet!" Morales boomed, pulling the Peacemaker back before heaving it forward.

The machine fired more guns Morales's way, but as the cameras guiding the remote pilot had been damaged in the fall, it could not manage to land a hit. With a heavy swing, Morales pulverized the spherical body of the machine, rendering it fully out of commission. Exhaling heavily, Morales retracted the sword and split its parts into three cubes once again, putting one cube in his pack while two other agents came forth to carry the others. Smoke and diesel spewed out of the machine's corpse, and gears and wires sprawled out of its broken metal body. The rest of the

Teslanauts gathered around the wreckage and caught their breath, coughing occasionally from the smoke.

"What was that thing?" one agent asked. "We haven't seen a machine that size since the war!"

"Our air recon reported that this machine made its way from the German border," Morales told the rest of the brigade. "Perhaps it was created by some enemy organization based in the country, one with plenty of volt-tech and yet not affiliated with the Electrocracy."

"The Germans declared peace after the armistice!" Helen said. "Why would they risk ruining relations so soon after the war?"

"Fringe groups, I'm telling ya!" the agent from earlier said. "Or at least fringe organizations."

"You might not be wrong," Morales replied. "Regardless, I'm not concerned about its origin, but rather its purpose. What was this thing designed to do, and why send it after us? Surely this organization's reconnaissance would find Teslanaut agents in the area, and would know we would dispose of it. So why waste such a finely-built piece of hardware?"

"When my brothers and I were younger back in England, we'd often play tag in the garden," Helen informed her fellow agents. "The boys would usually gang up on me, and they'd work together to ensure they caught me. One of them would make a big show of himself and keep my focus on him, while the other would sneak in from behind when I wasn't paying attention."

"Hey, lady, we all appreciate a good childhood story, but this is important here!" one of the other agents snapped.

"Wait, Brimsby, are you suggesting this machine was meant as a diversion?" Morales asked, ignoring the agent and ensuring Helen knew how seriously he took her story. Helen smiled inwardly at this, once again appreciating the marshal standing up for her.

"It's possible," she said. "Perhaps we'll need to contact HQ and tell them to keep a lookout for any suspicious activity near here, or see if anything happened while we were busy with this bugger."

"I will file a report to the Electrocracy at once. For now, we must continue our patrols and watch out for more machines."

Their game plan set, the Teslanaut agents hid in the trenches and restocked their supplies, while taking a quick lunch break with some beans and vegetables they had brought along with them. After performing a swift memorial for their fallen agent, they made their way further along the border and kept watch for any more mysterious opposition. The Great War might have officially ended, but the war on the volt-tech front trudged on, and the Teslanauts would do everything they could to keep it from escalating any further.

With a potential new enemy organization to fight, though, who knew what might happen?

# Chapter Three

"CAN'T I at least have a quick glance at the newspaper while I'm sitting here?" Raymond shouted at the door, still waiting impatiently in the lonely room within the confines of Teslanaut HQ. "I'd like to see if the Dodgers won!"

No one answered, and to be fair, Raymond didn't expect anyone to. He also didn't care one way or another about how his home Brooklyn team did; baseball was never his forte. He was just aggravated by the lack of answers, and the addition of so many new questions after being introduced to this fancy place. Other than those Agents Zero and Null, he hadn't the chance to talk to anyone in the last few hours. And to think, all this was due to him storming into city hall with a mysterious envelope and having the gall to wonder what the heck it was!

"How about just the crossword puzzle?" Raymond yelled out to nobody. "I've heard a lot about those lately, and I want to see what I'm missing!"

Sighing, Raymond leaned back on his little wooden chair, placing his feet on the table and crossing his arms. It must have been an hour since the agents left him in here, and frankly, it started looking like he would stay here forever. Whatever wonder he felt about such an advanced clandestine organization under the depths of the Hudson quickly turned to frustration. He still heard them working on the other side of the wall, with muffled commotion and churning engines still sounding off to his left. They could not show him something like that and then wall him off somewhere else without answers! And yet apparently, that's exactly what they planned for him.

Finally, after what seemed like an eternity, the door creaked open. "About time," Raymond grunted, removing his feet from the table and sitting back upright. "I was just about to donate a healthy sum to Edison just to spite you!"

"Oh yes, I'm sure he would put that money to good use in his camping trips with Henry Ford."

Raymond immediately shut up hearing that voice, feeling great shame at his outburst. Nikola Tesla himself walked into the room and relocked the door, straightening his vest and tapping his boots on the floor with each step. His hair and mustache, dark gray with silver linings, were well groomed and combed, as if he took as much care in his appearance as he did his science. As well as this, his eyes betrayed a passion and attentive detail in other manners, as if he constantly calculated equations and designed electromagnetic equipment in his head. Truly, this man's mind stretched far beyond the confines of ordinary men.

"Please excuse the wait, Mr. Calvert," Tesla said, sitting down on the chair opposite of Raymond at the table. "I was working with my agents on some projects. Although, if you really want to send a donation to my old employer, perhaps I should have made you wait longer." His demeanor was calm and subdued, and his tone barely changed between words, yet there was a subtle assertiveness to his words that made him seem bolder than he might otherwise.

"I'm sorry," Raymond said meekly. "I've been trapped in the world's fanciest speakeasy for the last hour, and my temper got the better of me."

"This is no speakeasy," Tesla informed his guest. "There's no alcohol to be found in my headquarters. It severely hinders people's work. Once they're done for the day, though, they are free to party however they choose, as long as they're sober by the next morning of course."

"Well, why else have all the secrecy? I can't imagine hiding all of this."

"I agree, but sadly, the world is not ready. All my life, Mr. Calvert, I've fought to advance humanity. I've struggled through many hardships along the way, with the worst being the continued stubbornness of society. I wanted nothing more than for the common folk to have what the Teslanauts have at their disposal, and yet my resources keep getting into the hands of vile people. The Great War brought out the worst of humanity, and until they refuse to use this technology for violence and conflict, we must act as a counterbalance to rein them in."

"You've done this all your life?"

"My experiments, yes. On this scale, though, only for the last eighteen years. Most people think I've been lying low recently, however, and until the world is ready I plan to keep it that way. I won't go into the details now; we'll save that for another time, Mr. Calvert."

Raymond nodded slowly, slowly starting to understand the importance of this place and their purpose, at least as much as he could in such a short time after learning of it. "How do you know my name?" the seventeen-year-old asked.

"I know your father. You're the son of Francis Calvert, are you not?"

"Yes, is he here? Does he work here?!"

"Years ago, yes. Francis was one of our greatest engineers, able to build from whatever blueprint my inventors could concoct. No matter how far-reaching such an invention might come across, he would figure out exactly how to construct it, and how to make it function properly and effectively. His gift with the science was second only to my own, and his gift with the mechanical was beyond anyone else I know. Truly, he was one of the most talented men I have ever had the pleasure of knowing."

Raymond fell back into his chair after hearing him say these words, his heart lifting almost as much as his eyebrows. He could barely believe it. To hear the great Tesla give out such praise about his father made Raymond feel very proud indeed of his old man, and wonder what kind of adventurous career he must have had here with the Teslanauts. He always knew his father was a hero, he just knew it! And still, the feats he must have accomplished were apparently beyond anything he could have imagined.

Yet even with this incredible new information, one major question still remained. "What happened to him?" Raymond asked, his words dry in his throat.

"It's a long story."

"I've got time. Please, I've been waiting nearly five years. I have to know."

"I understand you are eager to learn the whereabouts of your father, but I do not think you are ready."

"Alive or dead? That's all I want to know!"

"Mr. Calvert-"

"*Answer me*!"

"I will *not* tolerate this tone from you, Raymond," Tesla snapped as he stood back up, his sudden outburst causing Raymond to recoil in his seat. Even now, Tesla's voice didn't rise much, but anything beyond his normal monotone was shocking. "Trust me when I say that you *will* learn when the time is right. We did not bring you here to hide the truth from you. We wanted to *show* it to you. And we will in time, but for now, while you're staying here with us, you'd best mind your manners and treat your superiors with respect."

Raymond fell back in his chair, realizing he should probably learn to control his temper. Put back in his place for the second time in five minutes, he nodded quickly, looking back at the great scientist with a hint of humility. It seemed he would have to wait before he got an answer, but he had waited for years already. At least the prospect of one was now on the horizon. He could wait a little longer for it.

"I won't let it happen again," he said, his words quiet and subdued. "Now, if you don't mind me asking, why *did* you bring me here?"

Tesla nodded, straightening his vest again and heading back to the door. By simply touching the doorknob, he sent a bolt of electricity into it from a hidden metallic wristband, which must have been the same device Agent Null had at the lot entrance. The door opened at once, while Tesla turned his gaze back to the newcomer.

"Your father had one last message to you before he left," he said. "It was in that schematic you brought to the city hall. We already know what it means, but for you to know, we must decode it for you. Come and join me in the factory, Mr. Calvert."

Deeper still in the secret Teslanaut headquarters underneath the Hudson, Raymond Calvert and Nikola Tesla made their way down a grated staircase on the other side of the control hub, the dark corridor lit by groves of fluorescent lightbulbs. As they descended, the first difference Raymond noticed was the temperature; waves of heat began to pelt him from underneath, making his clothes stick to his skin from the sweat. The teenager wiped his brow as they reached the bottom, while Tesla turned the circular handle on the vault door to open it. Once he did, another wave of heat bombarded the two of them, along with a cloud of smoke and the smell of sulfur.

Yet, the magnificent sights that befell Raymond on the other side of the door pushed aside any discomfort. Instead, he gazed in awe at all that lay ahead.

In a room larger than a football stadium, engineers, electricians, and mechanics worked by the hundreds, scurrying to and fro amid equipment, wires, and tubes. Sparks flew like waves in an ocean as welders built great machines, taller than any bus or large vehicle Raymond had ever seen, that moved like giant metal men as pilots within their metal chests controlled their movements. Occasional flashes of electricity zapped through the air, while pipes, gears, and clockwork lined every square foot of the walls, constantly churning, writhing, and making the whole room seem like a gigantic, perpetually running engine. As well as the mighty metal men, the engineers worked with tanks, biplanes, automobiles, and other more standard vehicles and refitted them with new Teslanaut equipment.

Everywhere Raymond looked, people constantly drummed away at technology he could never even fathom before, using tools he could never understand. Despite all the soot and grime, the room's glory shone like a broad lightbulb, as magnificent and divine as the forges of Olympus where Hephaestus made weapons for the gods.

"Welcome to the main factory," Tesla proclaimed. "Here is where all of my ideas and the ideas of my workers come to fruition. Every inventor's dream, every welder's vision, every electrician's revelation, and every engineer's fantasy flows through this room, and they all emerge as real and clear as the grass and sky."

"It's incredible," Raymond gasped. "How can you afford this operation?"

"My old friend George Westinghouse founded the Teslanauts with me in 1904. He was much more business-orientated than myself, and aided the organization in that regard. He is not with us here anymore, but his efforts propelled us throughout those hard times. Now, I have accountants that deal with the finances along with the government grants, so I can focus more on aiding my agents."

"I'm bringing this beautiful machine's arm down twelve degrees, people. Twelve degrees!"

"Careful with that disintegrator, uh, thing! It's very volatile!"

"Did you seriously say 'disintegrator, uh, thing'? All those book smarts, and nonsense like that is what comes out of your trap?!"

"Shock me, shock me some more! I need the jolt, man, the *jolt*!"

Near a flurry of sparks surrounding a half-built giant of metal, four factory workers tinkered with machinery while bickering among themselves about how to get it done. They all looked about Raymond's age, give or take a few years, and yet the intricate manner in which they manipulated their wrenches, wires, and metalcraft made them seem like they had decades of experience. A bulky meathead-looking type pushed up the metal giant's head with his muscular arms, his slow and articulate manner of updating the workers of the giant's position suggesting a higher intelligence than his outwardly brawny appearance might have implied. A pale, scrawny adolescent boy with big glasses and unusually lengthy fingers fiddled with the innards of the giant's central body without concern or hesitation, meticulously taking apart tiny bolts and cords and rearranging them like an artist playing with colors. A muscular copper-skinned girl with thick hair and overalls held a cable with one hand to keep the giant's arm in place, while using the other hand to weld panels onto its metal muscles. Finally, a thin, tanned teenager with thick arm muscles and crazy hair that pointed in all directions worked with the electricity that powered the giant, occasionally grasping a wire and intentionally zapping himself.

"Good work, foundrymen," Tesla said, nodding at the four young ones working on the giant. "What improvements are you making to that mech?"

"I'm hoping the new electromagnetic receivers and power transformers permit this machine to function autonomously for a longer duration than previously possible," the scrawny, glasses-wearing boy replied. "It's, uh, interior workings are exponentially more complicated than the other automated machines we've constructed, such as the hover-heads, but I have confidence with the right mechanical adjustments, we can, uh, you know..."

"...make it work?" the muscular girl asked, smirking at his stammering despite his obvious brilliance.

"Yes, uh, make it work."

"The electrical surges within it are working just fine!" the crazy-haired boy exclaimed, grabbing another wire and jumping in place. "So, *so* fine!"

"You'd best stop clutching those wires, you oaf," the girl said. "All that electricity is making you not right in the head."

"It's making everything sharper! I see things, I perceive things! Everything's so, so clear!"

"Golly, prohibition hit you hard, didn't it?"

"This machine speaks to me," the meathead-looking type said, caressing the metal plating of the giant after placing a piece on top of the exposed wires. "We have a kindred spirit, she and I."

"Why, because you're both big lugs?" the girl asked.

"We both share an affinity for measuring strength. We have power, but we must learn to be gentle with it as well as hardy."

"I once knew a boxer like that," the girl said. "He was this sizeable Russian man like yourself. Very strong, but alas, he couldn't control his power and killed someone during a match. However, that someone's son then went on to avenge his father and kick that piece of meat to the curb! It was a very inspiring story."

"It sounds like you all are working very hard, then," Tesla noted, although his tone was perfunctory enough that Raymond couldn't tell if he meant to convey any sarcasm. "Keep at it. The hands of progress shall never be disarmed."

After his brief words of encouragement to his peculiar crew of workers, Tesla kept leading Raymond forward, until the two reached a far less exciting section of the factory at the very back, behind all the mechs and thrusters and electrified weaponry and other advanced technological shenanigans. Here, what looked like an antique collection of parts and broken pieces lay before them, sorted into boxes by size and type and stored onto metal shelves. At the back of this little section, though, sat a projector, but with clear modifications to its mainframe, including extra tubes and wires as well as additional clockwork gears.

"The schematic, if you please," Tesla said.

Raymond pulled the schematic of the particle gun out of his pants pocket and handed it to Tesla, wondering what exact kind of message his father could have left. Tesla placed the piece of paper underneath the projector and pulled down a curtain to display the schematic. He then flicked a few switches on the projector's modifications, which bit by bit revealed hidden images on the paper while hiding the schematic itself.

"Invisible ink?" Raymond asked, intrigued.

"No, that's far too pedestrian for my tastes," Tesla said matter-of-factly. "For our classified material, we tend to use specialized print that can only be read by machines that alter the wavelengths of light particles, making it much harder for any potential spies to crack."

"That's impossible!"

"Nothing is impossible. Vision, imagination, ambition, technology: they all have no boundaries. All you need is just a bit of time, intellect, and on occasion, money."

Eventually, after another bout of switch-flicking, the projector showed the letter in full, while hiding the schematics themselves. At last, words from Raymond's father! His slightly messy handwriting with oversized serifs; it was so good to see it all again! The scorching heat, the sounds of steam and ironworking, the smell of diesel; all of it faded away as Raymond studied the letter, smiling with misty eyes at all the fond memories it brought. After a couple of seconds, though, he realized he could not just stare blankly at the letter and reminisce. He actually had to read the thing.

And so, he did.

# Matthew Donald

Dear Raymond,

It pains me to write this, but I must leave. As you have already found out, I work at a clandestine organization called the Teslanauts, whose factory you're now standing in. I've labored here since you were eight years old, using my knowledge in schematic design and technological workmanship to help the organization fight in the shadows of the war. My skills are nearly unparalleled, Mr. Tesla has said, only second to his own. Yet this skill has made me a very dangerous man to my enemies. Therefore, to protect you and your mother, I'm heading to a secret bunker in Europe, continuing projects for the Teslanauts abroad. I do not know when I will return.

Know that you will be well off. The Teslanauts have agreed to partially subsidize your mother's work, allowing her to remain at the clothes factory while still having enough hours to take care of you at home. You'll have many years of confusion, sadness, and even anger, but for your own protection, you will not be shown this until your eighteenth birthday, at which point you will make the choice of joining the Teslanauts alongside me, or working elsewhere while maintaining the secret. Whatever choice you make, I know I'll be proud of you, and of the man you have now become.

I love you, son. I hope you can forgive me. We will see each other again, I promise.

Francis Calvert

Lead Teslanaut Foundryman and Technician Officer

December 12th, 1917

Raymond's heart swelled when he started the letter, but once he finished it, it had sunk once more. He missed his father. He felt like he was nothing without him. He felt like he could never escape his shadow. Everywhere he went, people asked him what had happened to his old pop. And every time, he never had a fulfilling answer.

Now, he might have gotten one. But what to do with it?

"Don't feel obligated to make any formal decisions yet," Tesla assured the overwhelmed teenager. "I'm sure there are a lot of questions burning within your mind. However, with the recent orders from the Electrocracy to aid the Volt Knights in France, I request an answer within two days."

"The letter's a bit early," Raymond said meekly. "Apparently I wasn't supposed to see this until my eighteenth birthday."

"And?"

"That's not until October, a whole six months away."

"So, your mother was not the one who sent you here, then. You discovered this place yourself. I must say, I quite admire your resourcefulness. It is a valuable quality for a Teslanaut. You are your father's son, it appears."

"Where is that bunker? Is he still there?"

"You read his letter, it's a secret. As for if he's there, we cannot tell you yet."

Raymond sighed angrily, hating the severe lack of transparency. But as a classified government organization, of course they would have their secrets, even to those already in the know of the organization's existence in the first place. In order to find out the answer, it seemed he had no choice but to join the Teslanauts.

Not that he wouldn't want to otherwise, though. From the little he had seen so far, this place had all the intrigue of a good novel and all the dazzling showmanship of an old P.T. Barnum circus. This organization seemed like the best place for a rollicking adventure, and with the mundane dreariness of the last five years of Raymond's life, that might be exactly what he needed. Finding out the whereabouts of his missing father was just the spark that ignited the furnace.

"Count me in," Raymond finally said.

"Are you certain?"

"Absolutely. What's the best position here to get me to my father?"

"Don't get too ahead of yourself, boy. You still have to go through the proper training procedures. You'll perform a written test before you return, then begin field training on the way to France. If you pass, then we can consider having you work in the proper position."

"Which is?"

"A field agent, Mr. Calvert."

# Chapter Four

RAYMOND RETURNED home that night after another ride on the driverless submarine, this time without the presence of Agents Zero and Null but with a sealed envelope holding the initiation test he would take before returning. After leaving the abandoned Bronx neighborhood and returning to a more public sidewalk, the seventeen-year-old walked idly on the streets, seeing all the unaware people carelessly making their way home from work. Paperboys sold the last copies of the day's *New York Times* for two cents apiece, which presumably reported the usual mundane things. The continued booming of the stock market, the occasional round of political nonsense, articles on whatever new dance trends the young ones were into nowadays; that sort of substandard drivel.

Now though, Raymond knew one big thing the papers left out, one that lay hidden from every regular eye in this whole city. No one had the faintest clue about the technological wonders that lay so near, ones that would reshape their whole perception of reality. It had certainly reshaped Raymond's!

How could he return to this mediocrity after all he had seen? He couldn't. That was all there was to it. Unfortunately, though, he still had someone he had to inform about his decision.

A few bus trips later, Raymond reached his apartment complex in Brooklyn, nodding at the greeter by the entrance and taking the elevator to the fourth story. Once he knocked on the door, he did not have to wait even two seconds before his mother frantically opened it.

"Good God, Ray, don't you scare me like that!" Martha Calvert shouted, hugging her son tight and letting him into their flat. "I've been wondering where you went running off to for hours!" A fortysomething woman with frizzy, slightly graying hair, she wore a simple yet pretty blue dress with yellow trimmings. As someone who worked long hours as a seamstress, she knew the tricks of the trade of good fashion. However, her normally warm demeanor and comforting blue eyes were currently replaced by rigid fright and sheer panic.

"Mom-"

"I was thinking about calling the police for a good while there, but I kept thinking 'oh, he's fine, he'll be back soon!' But the evening kept going on and on, and I felt like I couldn't-"

"I'm here, Mom, all right?" Raymond said, chuckling while patting Martha on the shoulder. "Don't you worry about me. I can explain later."

"I can't *not* worry about you, Raymond! Not after what happened to your father. I'm not gonna lose you, too."

"I know, I know, but I'm all right, I promise. I'm here now, and that's all that matters."

Martha slowly loosened her tense posture, realizing what her son had said. "You're right. You're here now, and I thank the Lord for it. I still expect you to tell me where you've been, though! I saved some dinner for you, by the way. Meatloaf, in the ice box."

"Sounds great."

Raymond walked into their homely little apartment and put his coat on the rack by the door, before getting the plateful of meatloaf from the ice box and sitting down with it at the table. Once he put a bite of the ground beef, soft grains, and sweet tomato sauce in his mouth, he remembered exactly how hungry he was, after spending most of the day flabbergasted at the unbelievable series of events and unperturbed about the status of his stomach. He finished his dinner in just over a minute, prompting a quizzical rise of his mother's eyebrows

"So, where've you been?" Martha asked.

Raymond wiped his lips while staring absently at the ceiling, trying to piece together how to inform his mother of his recent whereabouts while also maintaining the secrecy of the Teslanaut organization. Then again, Francis's letter stated that Tesla subsidized Martha to help her better take care of her son. Maybe she already knew? It was hard to tell, and would be hard to figure out. If she did, she certainly wouldn't have expected Raymond to know, and vice versa. And the secret, according to Tesla, had to be maintained.

"How much do you know?" Raymond finally asked.

"That's a vague question, Ray. You talking stocks, or sports, or world history?"

"Familial history. Recent familial history, in fact. How much do you know about Dad?"

"If I knew, I would have told you."

"Not what happened to him. I mean what he did. Do you know what exactly he did to make a living?"

"He worked for the government, but on top-secret projects. I know certain details, but most of it had to be kept secret. Why?"

Raymond swallowed the last bit of meatloaf, hoping that a way to tell her without accidentally spilling classified information would surface in his mind, but alas, he drew a blank. At this point, it remained unclear whether she knew about the Teslanauts' existence or not, so he would have to find a creative method to inform her of his decision, without making her go into another frenzy of worrying sick about her only child. That last part, he realized, would be about as difficult as Tesla's tireless attempts to make alternating current the accepted norm, rather than Edison and his more business-friendly direct current. After the departure of her husband, his mother had no one to take care of except Raymond. She would not let him go lightly.

"I found Dad's employer," he proclaimed. "I found this top-secret government project. And apparently Dad wanted me to join it, too."

"How did you know your father and I discussed this?" Martha demanded. "And how did you possibly find this project?"

"Long story. Point is, they need me in two days."

"Well, you must have missed the part where I put my foot down and told Francis that my boy wasn't going to join any dangerous government program on my watch. And when news came of his death, my foot dug further into the ground."

"That's the thing, though," Raymond said. "He might not be dead after all."

"Don't you play that kind of game with me, Ray."

"I'm serious! When I was at the secret government place-"

"I'm not going to stand here and listen to you spout on about things you're too young to understand! You've got school to finish, and then you'll work and make a decent living away from all the dangers and horrors your father dealt with. The war's over, Ray, and it's not coming back, so there's no purpose in risking your life when there's nothing to fight over. You're not going to needlessly lose your life like your father did!"

"Mom-"

"Good night, Raymond. We're not having this discussion again."

Raymond groaned and carried his plate over to the sink, before letting loose a few angry stomps towards his room. He placed his hand on the doorknob, but didn't turn, his mind racing with idea after idea on what to say. The words were fleeting, like a kite loose in the wind, but he could *feel* what he had to say rather than articulate it. His eyes closed, and he let out a guttural sigh. He didn't know if what he was about to say would help anything, but he didn't know what else to do.

"The world is bigger than this," he said. "Everywhere I go, I'm told that we live in the greatest city on Earth. But there's a whole lotta cities out there. There's a whole lotta people. Some places might be better than here, and some might be worse. And some people, without anybody knowing, work hard to make every place better. That's what Dad did. And that's what I plan to do by saving him. I need to take this opportunity, Mom. The world needs him back."

Martha didn't respond, so Raymond went into his room and shut the door, sitting on the bed and staring at the ugly yellow wallpaper. The minutes passed, and Martha didn't bother to follow, while Raymond turned his gaze to the simple wooden door as he waited for her response. He studied the scratched paint, and the simple hinges, while thinking about the different ways the Teslanauts could improve it. Maybe add an automated locking mechanism, or a self-powered light, or even a scanning device that took note of who entered or approached the room. All the while, he thought about what he just said and all those the words applied to. It wasn't just his father. It was Nikola Tesla. It was the whole organization. It was every man, woman, or child who had an idea to aid a cause and aid society, in whatever amount.

It was a cause his father obviously believed in, and applied every day during his time as a Teslanaut. Based on what Tesla told him, however, there were plenty of people who wanted to use these ideas not to aid, but to exploit. Not to benefit, but to corrupt. The Teslanauts had to rein them in, until one day, people would be ready. It could take a year, ten years, or a whole century, but Tesla would fight to make sure he could advance civilization. And Raymond's father was at his side the whole way.

There was no more thinking to do. Raymond couldn't leave his father. He had to save him. That was *his* way to contribute.

He stood back up and headed to the door, ready to confront his mother about the issue once again. This time, though, before he reached the knob, Martha opened it herself, her gray eyes moist as she looked up at her son.

"You understand where I'm coming from, right?" she asked.

"Of course I do," Raymond said gently. "Believe me, I'm glad I was too young to get drafted. I don't want my life in danger any more than you do."

"Then why are you-"

"Because I have to know. Dad's disappearance was too sudden. His work is unfinished. If there's even the slightest chance he could still be alive, I have to try and find him. He deserves to come back."

"Promise me *you'll* come back," Martha said sharply. "With or without your father."

"I promise," Raymond declared.

Martha sighed, her eyes starting to dry finally, as she realized how determined her son actually was, and maybe, even a little bit herself, getting caught up in the fantasy that she could see Francis again. Her decision made at last, she hugged her son tight yet again.

"I want you back in a few months' time," she said.

"Of course," Raymond said.

"Also, you're not leaving until tomorrow night."

"Deal."

# Chapter Five

WITH A chorus of exhausted groans, the Teslanaut squad reached their targeted location north of Strasbourg while remaining near the brooks of the Rhine, staying hidden behind some trees to keep enemy air scouts from spotting the suspicious cluster of agents so close to German soil. A grove of pines, eighty to a hundred feet tall apiece, provided ample cover. Drained from their long march, the agents sat down by the trees and rested their backs on the trunks, some of them reaching into their packs and prepping their breakfast.

"You'd think… with the airpower at the Teslanauts' disposal… we could have hitched a ride on a dirigible," an agent panted out.

"Indeed, we could have," Morales replied while wiping the sweat off his black locks, taking a knee to rest without fully committing to a proper sit-down. "While we're at it, we could have fired the dirigible's howitzers in all directions while dancing the Charleston on the deck. This is a covert mission, team. We'll save the more flamboyant maneuvers for our ride home."

"When are the rest of the lads joining us?" Helen asked, scooping up some of the last bites from her veggie can. "The Electrocracy is sending us reinforcements, right?"

"Our fellow Teslanauts will be here in a few days. However, agents from the Knights will rendezvous at our position within the hour."

"The French Volt Knights?" another agent asked.

"Yes, they will be here shortly, so I expect everyone to give them a warm welcome. How's your French, agents?"

"*Piétre* at best, but I'll manage," Helen sighed with feigned dismay. "So, are we really expected to wait here for a few days without going in?"

"I'm sure that mysterious organization will send more of their mechs our way soon enough," Morales sighed. "In the meantime, we can set up a base and establish radio communications. Perhaps we can intercept enemy transmissions and uncover their plans after decoding their encryptions. We cannot rush in without the proper preparations, Brimsby, so we must pick up whatever resources we can."

"Sounds like a good time, Marshal. Crack on."

The agents proceeded to open their packs and take out more cube-shaped mechanical pieces like the ones that made Morales's Peacemaker, placing them on the ground and unfolding them into makeshift comm stations, power receivers, and volt-tech rechargers. The cubes that agents brought along had many different modes, and the Teslanauts designed them to be flexible and adaptive to whatever the mission at hand. Such gadgets allowed the Teslanauts to minimize the load when packing for missions, while simultaneously giving them the proper resources and equipment for a wide variety of assignments.

"Power cells are charging at an excessive rate," an agent noted, seeing the gauges on the side of the radio stations rise after plugging it into the power receivers. "How many transmitters are within range?"

"They're all over," Morales answered. "The Electrocracy constructed transmitter towers all over the continent, and they're building more all the time. France, Belgium, Serbia, Spain, and even the Ottomans have such towers, and those are just some of the ones within range. In fact, France has five transmitter towers alone."

"Isn't one of them the Eiffel Tower?" Helen asked.

"Well, Tesla met with Gustave Eiffel and Thomas Edison at the top of the tower back in 1889, but that was well before the founding of the Electrocracy. Maybe there is some sort of transmitter up there, but I assume if there was, it would remain proprietary information."

"Marshal, I'm picking up something," an agent by their makeshift comm stations reported, holding the headphones to his ears while moving some dials to adjust the frequency and clear up the signal. "Encrypted transmissions using German frequencies. The exact coordinates are still being configured."

"What is it?" Morales demanded.

"We're writing down the code," a second comm station agent said, as he and a few others used typewriters to enter what they could onto a report. "The accents definitely sound German, with a hint of Hungarian and Austrian, as well."

"The war brought down the Austro-Hungarian Empire!" Helen exclaimed. "Why would they reform?"

"See what I mean about fringe groups?" the agent who suggested the idea earlier said. "They're probably just some folks who can't get over their defeat and keep fighting for a lost cause."

"Wait… there's another voice talking alongside them," the first comm station agent noted. "It sounds… American!"

"A diplomat?"

"Or a traitor."

"That ain't no American!" another agent snarled. "No true American would stand alongside the Kaiser!"

"You Yanks are something else," Helen chortled while shaking her head. "The lot of you aren't always heroes, you know. Some of you have the potential to be as evil as anyone else. It might not sound patriotic, but it's realistic. England's the same way, as is any country. It's the unfortunate truth about the world, but it's also a good thing. No one's defined by where they come from, only by what they do."

"Pinpoint the location of the signal," Morales ordered, pointing a stern, stubby finger at the comm station agents. "Once reinforcements arrive, we're moving in."

"Speak of the devil," Helen said, nodding back to the forest. "Looks like our Volt Knight friends have arrived."

Stepping out of the shade of the pines marched a squad of twenty armored agents, with helmets that covered their faces and shields and lances akin to a medieval knight, albeit ones with a volt-tech edge. On their armors' backs sat square-shaped panels, spanning from shoulder blade to shoulder blade and reaching all the way to the lower spine, that received electricity from the transmitter towers that powered their equipment. A ways behind the Volt Knight agents, the Teslanauts caught a glance of a fleet of dirigibles slightly larger than train carriages flying off, heading back into French territory after dropping off their passengers.

"*Bonjour, représentants,*" Helen said, lowering her head to the Volt Knights as they stepped forward.

"*Bonjour,* madam," the lead Volt Knight said after lifting his helmet's visor, nodding respectfully at Helen. A dark-haired Frenchman in his early thirties, his strong cheekbones proudly bore several scars from bullets that had grazed his face, showing his long history of battle without diminishing his rugged good looks. His most notable feature, though, was his right arm; namely the lack of one. From the elbow down his arm was completely gone, replaced with his lance that he could detach whenever he went off duty.

"*Le capitaine* Jean Michel du Foudre of ze French Volt Knights, at your service," the lead agent said proudly. "First Commanding Officer of ze Eleventh Regiment. Zis is a wonderful day for a battle, is it not?"

"Du Foudre," Helen said with a smile. "It's French for... 'of the Foudre'."

"I've never actually worked with the Volt Knights before," another Teslanaut agent admitted. "Is there any reason why they look like they're off to rescue a princess from a dark castle?"

"The Great War hit many countries, but France was among those hit the hardest," Morales explained. "To distance themselves from such recent wounds and instead celebrate a more romanticized time, the Volt Knights style their gear to be like those of early Renaissance soldiers, with their volt-tech enhancing their equipment enough to stand parallel with other agents."

"In many ways, actually, zis gear is even better," Captain du Foudre proclaimed, holding out his shield and pressing a button embedded in it. This made the shield split apart into four panels, with electricity sizzling between each piece allowing it to absorb enemy fire. As he crouched down and held his shield in front him, he activated another switch on his lance, causing the end to peel back and reveal the barrel of a disintegrating energy gun. How he could fire it without a hand remained unclear, but the Teslanauts assumed some hidden mechanism.

"Your attire is certainly impressive, Captain," Morales said, nodding with appreciation at the Frenchman's battle gear.

"As well as zis, we have modern armor underneath chrome-steel outer plating," Foudre said, pulling back his lance and deactivating his shield. "All zis gives us much more defensive power zan you silly Americans. Ze enemy could throw a tank our way and we would still march forward without fear!"

"For what it's worth, I'm not a silly American," Helen told the new agents. "I'm a silly Brit."

"*Oui*, zat is so much better."

"May I inquire, Foudre," Morales said slowly, trying to remain tactful, "about your… umm-"

"Lack of a right appendage?" Foudre laughed. "Oh, zat happened during ze war. A grenade came careening to our position and I leapt like a hero onto it to save my *comarades*. Granted, I missed and landed a meter to ze left, meaning zat my arm took ze brunt of ze damage, but I still saved my men and lived to fight another day, so it ended up being a blessing!"

"How very noble, sir," Helen said with a smile. She wasn't entirely sure how much of that story was true, but she appreciated his enthusiasm regardless. In any case, missing an arm clearly troubled him little, and he could still somehow wield a lance that doubled as a disintegrator gun, so she figured it did not particularly matter to question him further.

"Well, now that the Knights are here, we just have to wait for the rest of the Teslanauts to arrive," Morales told the gathering agents. "It will still be a couple of days, so we should set up our resting quarters. Stay within the trees, though. We don't want the Germans to know we're snooping about, do we?"

***

Deeper inside German territory, there sat a fortress. Perched within a valley in the Alps near Berchtesgaden, a structure of stone and steel stood tall like a metal mountain, built atop the base of an old castle and specifically designed to retain the medieval look even so many hundreds of feet above it. Yet within such an archaic aesthetic stood material of a more modern age, with a far more futuristic feel, and yet with a purpose as barbaric as the battles of old.

After the Great War, much of Central and Eastern Europe remained in shambles. The Ottomans became a shell of their former glory. Russia dealt with the ramifications of their revolution. The Austro-Hungarian Empire completely collapsed. And the Germans had nothing left. No currency, no structure, no glory. There was defeat, and then there was what *they* dealt with. The Allied Powers utterly broke them as countries, and those powers seemed to have no intention of forgiving them anytime soon.

Most of their civilians remained content to lick their wounds and try to move on with their lives. But for some of the victims of this abominable failure, they refused to call it quits. And within their hearts burned not remorse, nor sorrow, but pure, unadulterated fury. They would respond in kind, in some form or another. They would form new powers and regimes, ones intending to return their countries to their original greatness that they had been so vehemently denied.

One such power had already begun to form, even so soon after the end of the war. Within this fortress stood an alliance of thousands of Germans, Hungarians, Austrians, and others, forming a new power known as the Oberschock Federation. They would use volt-tech to finish what those in the war could not. And the best part? No one else knew of their existence, not even the Electrocracy. So far, other than the tripod mech the Teslanauts fought, they managed to remain completely in the shadows, and the Teslanauts hadn't the slightest clue where that mech came from in the first place.

If other countries found out about the Oberschock Federation, war could spark once again. Even though the fight at the volt-tech front remained hidden from the average civilian, the Electrocracy had representatives from many countries, each from secret sectors of their respective governments. That's why the people running Oberschock needed to wait until they finalized their plans before they risked exposure, and so they would.

Within the stone and steel walls of the fortress, dubbed the Eisenzentrum by its occupants, this new power labored on. Hundreds of factory workers forged dozens of new mechanical automatons in the main hall, while others worked on making equipment for their agents to wield in the inevitable confrontations. In the depths of the chambers below, a thousand hands worked on the bigger stuff; giant electric generators able to enhance the energy output of devices, vehicles, and most importantly, weapons.

Overseeing it all, a fifty-year-old German man with a scarred face and a brow wrinkled with hate observed the laborers from his balcony, his arms folded behind his back. Clad in a general's uniform that had seemingly never been taken off, he was a highly decorated veteran of the Great War, having fought many battles on multiple continents. While he had predominantly been on the main front, he now had a new office in the volt-tech field, having been made aware of it by Oberschock's main benefactor.

"General Boltzmann, our electro-scans have been completed," the lead Oberschock technician said to the scarred old man. "It seems the tripod ve sent out has been dismantled." A thin yet muscular Austrian man of twenty-seven, with a hawk-like nose, unkempt brown hair, and a face perpetually covered in soot, he looked like someone who never left the factory even for a moment's rest. Such an image was enhanced by his special volt-tech apparel; he wore a self-built backpack with three spindly mechanical arms, one on each side and one over his left shoulder, that allowed him to partake in more complicated labor. These arms were working diligently even as he himself spoke to his general, forging complicated machinery like an assembly line worker.

"Our reconnaissance shows a brigade of Teslanaut agents near ze French border," the technician said. "Vhat do you suggest ve do?"

"Ve shall keep zem distracted, Mr. Ziegler," the officer replied. "Continue your vork on ze machines to be loaded on ze trains. I vant zem heading toward Paris vithin a few veeks' time."

"Of course, sir. Also, your American friend is vaiting for you in your office."

"What for?"

"He's thinking about altering ze deal."

Boltzmann grunted and stormed off to his office, holding his gloved hand to his face when passing a flurry of sparks from a welder hard at work. He had worked too hard with this new organization to let some foreign benefactor unaware of his country's plight to meddle with his plans. The Allied Powers ruined them, and they would have vengeance, in one form or another.

Bursting through the door leading to his office, he saw a thirty-two-year-old man thumbing through his display case, looking at Boltzmann's medals and various trinkets gathered on the battlefield. A handsome, light-haired man with striking blue eyes and a robust chin, as well as an expensive-looking suit and bowler hat, he looked as picturesque an example of the assumed superior man as anyone else, one accustomed to dominate others beneath him. However, Boltzmann refused to let this man stand above him. These were *his* people, not this American's.

"Ah, Heinrich!" the man laughed, twirling towards Boltzmann with his head held back smugly. "How's my favorite officer doing, huh?"

"I am indeed an officer, Stonewell," Boltzmann snapped, his brow constricting at this intruder. "Zerefore, you best address me by my official ranking."

"My apologies, General Boltzmann," the man said, taking off his hat and putting it to his chest while bowing mockingly. "I thought our relationship had become more amicable in these last few months, after all the accomplishments we have made together."

"Vhat is zis matter of you altering our deal?"

"Really? No 'how was your trip' or 'isn't the weather nice?' It's a lovely day, Officer Boltzmann, isn't it?"

"Get to ze point, *Robert*, now!"

"Of course, of course. I'm concerned that the threat of the Electrocracy is growing stronger. The longer we lurk in the shadows, the more likely we'll get caught, and the less ready we will be. I think we should double our production rate to make sure the task gets done in a timely manner."

Boltzmann rarely felt even a semblance of good emotions lately, but the arrogant words coming out of Stonewell's mouth made him positively fume. "If ve vant zis to be done, ve need it to be done *right*! Ve can't afford rushing production!"

"Don't you want to help your people, General?"

"More zan you know! The war left us vith nothing! Ve must avenge our fallen brothers and return our country to ze glory it once had!"

"Ah yes, the glory of your country," Stonewell chuckled, looking back at all the medals Boltzmann had on display and caressing them with his fingers. "The glory it once had. But what about the other countries? What about their glory? The truth is, the so-called 'Great' War was nothing but a dozen countries on this blasted continent jumping at the chance to squabble with each other like rabid dogs while feigning their superiority. A British brigade fought Hungarian soldiers in Bulgarian territory as the Germans attacked Belgium on their way to France because a Serbian killed an Austrian in Bosnia. It's utter nonsense."

"Vhat are you saying?"

"I'm saying, the world needs order returned to it. The common people need reminding of their place. And this volt-tech I've granted you is the way to do it. Even though the war's over, everyone's gearing up for round two. You can feel it in the air. We need to keep things together by showing them true power, before anyone has a chance to respond. And only *my* way of planning can get that done properly. If we don't do this the way *I* think it should be done, General, I'll pull all my funding and leave your people wallowing back in the scraps I found all of you in."

"You can't do zat!"

"Oh, what are *you* going to do about it?"

With a smirk and a slight bow of the head, Stonewell brushed past Boltzmann and left his office, happily sniffing the smoke fumes and the diesel of the factory before making his way out of the fortress. "It's a decent bunch of workers you got here," he said, cavorting down the stairs leading to the main hall. "None as good as our previous asset, though, but I'm sure you've been able to manage just fine. Oh, by the way, Emil told me he completed your Panzerwurm project."

"He *vhat*?!"

"Yeah, he managed to get it built. It's ready to go, whenever you give the word."

"Vhy didn't you tell me zis, Ziegler?!" Boltzmann demanded, swiftly turning to the lead technician with a piercing glare.

"Forgive me, General," Emil Ziegler said with a shrug, his mechanical arms having finished the last machinery part and moving on to the next. "I go through zese projects like clockwork. Mr. Stonewell vas simply ze one in ze room vhen I completed ze Panzerwurm."

"Vell, zis certainly changes things," Boltzmann murmured, stroking his chin with the faintest trace of a smile. "Such an unstoppable machine on our side… perhaps ve *can* do this in ze time you vould prefer."

"I knew you'd see things my way!" Stonewell laughed, walking out of the fortress.

# Chapter Six

IN UPSTATE New York at the crack of dawn, a convoy of trucks gathered at a seemingly empty set of hangars, escorting Teslanaut agents to this secret base before dropping them off and returning to base. Hundreds of agents gathered outside the hangars, each with all the supplies and gadgets they needed for the upcoming mission. The buildings looked big enough to hold whole squadrons of biplanes, but was that how they would get all the way to France? Surely not! No one had ever done a nonstop flight from New York to Paris before. The Orteig Prize, the reward offering twenty-five thousand dollars to the first aviator successfully making such a trip, had not yet been claimed. Then again, if anyone could do it, the Teslanauts could.

With his backpack strapped tight to his shoulders, Raymond got out of the truck and absently followed the other agents, having no idea what to do other than remain close behind the others. He had his completed test at hand, now back in the envelope and ready to hand over. The test involved naming the compartments of gadgets, calculating the required wattage for specific projects, and more abstract things like his favorite shade of blue or what number made him the most comfortable. He had no idea what any of it meant, but for the technical parts, he used what he had learned when looking at his father's blueprints he had left in his office, and he hoped it would help him get a passing grade. Truthfully though, he had no idea how he did, or what he was doing now. He sure hoped he wasn't the only first-timer present, so he could join a group of other new recruits and they could all be confused together. That sounded nice. Less lonely.

"Halt, agents," a man at the front snapped as they reached the entryway of the first hangar. After glancing at him for a bit, Raymond recognized the man as Agent Zero, one of the 'recruitment agents' for the Teslanauts. "Before we enter the facility, we need to perform a scan of everyone present. If everyone could stand behind that line here so we can keep moving, that would be great."

The crowd stumbled back as they herded behind a line painted a couple of yards before the front door, while Agent Zero walked to a panel on the side of the building and operated what looked like a miniature crane above the door. After a few seconds of mechanical whirring and fumbling machinery, a series of sparks burst before the group from the end of the crane. A second later, the door to the hangar opened.

"Very good, agents," Agent Zero said. "Now, follow me."

The vast majority of everyone present made their way inside the hangar, while a couple of others just stood still, seemingly not noticing what everyone else was doing. Agent Zero and a few others stayed behind and took the hands of the still people to return them to the trucks, which Raymond couldn't help but find rather suspect.

"What's with them?" he asked Agent Zero.

"Oh, you decided to join us, Mr. Calvert?" Agent Zero replied, smirking at the familiar teenager as he helped an apparently dazed man into the back seat of a truck. "That's good. It certainly keeps the Cleanup Squad less busy."

"Cleanup Squad?"

"The great secret must be kept until the Electrocracy votes otherwise. These folks here are stowaways, perhaps government workers who accidentally got in the wrong truck, or maybe even rogue agents from somewhere more malevolent. The scan sends a wave of electromagnetic energy that temporarily stuns the brains of anyone not possessing the Teslanauts' signature."

"The signature from the cattle prod, right?"

"Yes, the 'cattle prod,' as you keep calling it. The signature allows the particles in the wave to flow through unaffected, but these people don't have it, so their memories of the last hour have been erased. They'll wake up in the truck thinking they just dozed off. This is repackaged technology from the volt-tech Cleanup Squad, who will return them to the city and make a cover story, so in the end, they won't suspect a thing."

"I'm not sure how I feel about messing with the minds of innocent men, sir."

"Well then, it's a good thing it isn't your problem, Mr. Calvert."

The other agents beside Agent Zero took the trucks with the dazzled men and drove them back to New York, while Agent Zero himself led Raymond inside the hangar. The possibilities of what marvelous transportive contraption lay inside sent Raymond's imagination into a frenzy. How could they get to Europe in time to aid the French Volt Knights? Would it be a fleet of dirigibles? No, that would surely take too long. Maybe a giant plane that would stop at several islands across the Atlantic to refuel? Possibly, although that seemed rather mundane for the Teslanauts based on what Raymond had seen so far.

What he didn't expect, though, was an entire building stretching many levels downward without a mode of aerial transport to be found, and yet, that was exactly what lay before his eyes. On the top level, a forge similar to the one at Teslanaut HQ sat in one corner, with wires and spinning gears beckoning factory workers to come in and get their hands dirty. In the opposite corner sat a series of control and comm stations, with a small squadron of hover-heads lying deactivated at each desk and ready to serve the whims of the stationed workers. Stairs and elevators led to many other levels, and how deep exactly it all went remained a mystery.

The most unusual feature, however, lined the sides of the building. Like a picket fence, yellow spherical receivers blanketed each wall, with a much larger one at each corner. Wires meshed and coiled around each receiver, connecting them all together while simultaneously transferring the power to the whole building. The amount of electrical energy those receivers could channel seemed insurmountable, certainly many times more than necessary for a building such as this. What manner of Teslanaut technology required so much power?

"Welcome to Teslanaut Mobile Field HQ Fox-Dock 17," Agent Zero said, ushering the crowd down a flight of stairs attached to their end of the wall. "Or as we've nicknamed this station, 'Freckle Dump.' It's a long story, one I'd rather not get into right now. Factory workers, set up your stations. Field agents, check your equipment. New recruits, hold your positions."

"Ooh, I love this place!" a familiar voice laughed. "So much electricity, so much shocking. We're gonna get zapped to Europe soon, haha! We're gonna get *overloaded* with electricity!"

"This place is your heaven, isn't it, Watson?" another familiar voice chuckled. "You right oaf, you?"

Raymond looked ahead and, to his surprise, saw the four teenage factory workers he and Tesla had stopped and talked to during his first visit at Teslanaut HQ. The big and wise one, the thick-haired and well-humored one, the scrawny and spectacled one, and the wiry and rather manic one. They seemed like a little team of friendlies; potentially some people Raymond should get to know on their European adventure. He wished he knew their names, although apparently the wiry and shock-obsessed one was named Watson. But was that his first or last name?

Of course, Raymond felt more concerned about what this Watson character just described. Zapped to Europe? Overloaded with electricity? What did any of that mean? Whatever it was, Raymond did not like any of it one bit.

"Get us to the first station point on the way to Europe, double-time!" Agent Zero commanded.

At his order, roughly seventy people manned the building's control station, pushing buttons and pulling levers from a hundred different panels. With each action, the receivers lining the walls of the building sparked with electricity, forming a barrier of electrical coils that intensified by the second.

"Activate all transformers and radioelectric receiver ports!" Agent Zero ordered, pointing to various workers as he paced along the aisles of the control station. "Bring energy input levers up fifty degrees and stabilize energy output containment!"

"Accessing power from the New York, Toronto, Chicago, and Baltimore towers," a worker reported from his station. "Levels are at twenty percent... thirty percent... forty-five percent."

Like the innards of a furious tempest, the walls surged with constant flashes of lightning, raging like rapids on an electrical river. The whole building quaked with power, each brick overflowing with energy. Sparks covered the roof like a ceiling of fire. Raymond tightly grasped the railing of the staircase leading down the wall, expecting the building to explode at any moment. In an instant, though, he jerked his hands back, realizing the railing was made of metal.

Yet it seemed the metal didn't conduct any of the electricity. Other people held onto the railing without any problem. Somehow, all the power remained contained within the receivers on the hangar's roof. No one even had frizzy hair. How could that possibly be? Raymond had a feeling he would ask that question a lot over the next couple of months.

"Eighty percent… ninety percent… one hundred percent!" the worker exclaimed. "Power at full capacity! Initiating jump in three… two… one!"

Raymond felt his stomach lurch as soon as the worker said the final number, like someone tugged at him with an invisible rope, and nearly tumbled over the railing of the stairs. Other people similarly struggled, especially the new recruits like Raymond, although Watson simply hollered with glee with his arms held out, basking in all the power. Despite the sudden and obvious movement, nothing seemed to change, and as the seconds ticked on, the electricity on the building's receivers fizzled out.

"Jump successful," the worker stated. "Freckle Dump is now at the station point outside St. John's, Canada."

"Excellent work," Agent Zero said, nodding with approval. "How long until we can initiate another jump?"

"The generators should be fully recharged in seven hours and twelve minutes."

"That would be record time! Oh, the Electrocracy will have to rewrite their history books! See to it we can initiate the next jump by that time!"

"Yes, sir!"

The hangar unfolded above them, opening the building up to the outside area. At that moment, Raymond saw what they meant by 'jump' initiation. No longer did the building sit in a grassy, hilly area just north of New York City. Now, the building sat in the middle of a thick forest, surrounded by spruces and firs taller than any other tree Raymond had seen. Fog clouded the air, making it difficult to see further than a few hundred feet out, although the plethora of trees made that hard anyway. The outside temperature had plummeted, making Raymond hold his hands to his arms to keep warm, although the chill he felt didn't just come from the colder weather.

"How… how did we get here?" he stammered.

"We teleported!" Watson shrieked, looking like he might hyperventilate from his joyous laughter. "We got smothered with electricity like a warm blanket and teleported!"

"Teleported?"

"Teleport," the big meathead-looking factory worker murmured, gently motioning his hand as he explained. "From the Greek prefix *tele*, meaning 'far' such as with telephone, and *port*, as in transport. It is always recommended to educate oneself on a word's etymology."

"We certainly appreciate your vast knowledge, Crankovich," the darker-skinned girl said, gently punching the bigger factory worker on the shoulder.

"It's thanks to our, umm, *countless* hours of work perfecting Tesla's vision," the pale glasses-wearing boy said, fiddling with his thumbs nervously while examining the building. "He had this idea of using electrical energy to transfer atoms from one location to another while, umm, keeping molecular structure completely intact."

"Huh?" Raymond asked, feeling quite dumb.

"Oh boy, you're new here, aren't ya?" the girl giggled. "What's your name?"

"Calvert, miss. Raymond Calvert."

"Wait, you're telling me that you're Francis's son?! Great to have you aboard, Mr. Calvert!"

"Francis shook my hand right after petting a cat once," Watson said, looking up at nothing with a sort of childlike bliss. "It was one of the best jolts of my life."

Raymond sighed sadly, thinking about the last time he remembered being with his father. In truth, he couldn't exactly remember the last time; Francis was gone so much during the war working with the Teslanauts. At some point, he just wasn't there anymore. Raymond needed to know what happened. He had to find out, or none of this, none of this new knowledge, none of this great adventure; none of it would feel satisfactory.

"Who are you folks, then?" he asked.

"I'm Rebecca Greengrass," the muscular, thick-haired girl said, tipping her flat cap. "You can call me Becky. Been working with the Teslanauts for several years now, first as a maid, but then Mr. Tesla noticed how good I was with the foundry equipment and gave me a promotion! I learned from my father, who worked in a garage and used me as an unofficial mechanic's assistant since I was six. I've always been fascinated with the gizmos, the gadgets, the machines... but not in an unhealthy manner like Watson."

"Watty needs his sustenance," Watson said, shivering with delight while looking at a bundle of nearby wires. "Look at all those cables. It looks like such a fire hazard... hehe, I want it, I need it!"

"Watson?" Raymond said. "First or last name?"

"I'm Arthur Worthington, by the way," the pale glasses-wearing boy said as everyone ignored Raymond's question, although whether they didn't want to tell him or they didn't know themselves remained unclear. "I work with the, uhh, you know, highly advanced technical aspects of the machines. Not just how it works, but how it, uhh, *performs.* If it isn't at a satisfactory level, then it has to be recalibrated. Mr. Tesla recruited me a little over a year ago after I graduated from the School of Civil Engineering and Architecture at New York University."

"A year ago?" Raymond demanded, astounded by Arthur's claim. "You look younger than me and you've already graduated college?"

"Uhh, yes," Arthur said with a shrug, pushing his glasses up in the smuggest manner an awkward and skinny adolescent could. "Class of 1920 with a double degree in Physics and Mechanical Engineering and minor degrees in Chemistry, Mathematics, Electrical Engineering, Industrial-"

"All right, I get it."

"Yes, please tell us about your fine resume," Becky chortled. "We're all very impressed."

"I can tell how machines work," the giant meathead-looking one said, caressing a panel in the factory. "Or more accurately, they tell *me*. I commune with them, and they speak to me. There's a dialogue between us, and it's beautiful."

"Sometimes I ain't knowing who here's crazier: Ivan or Watson," Becky sighed. "But good ol' Ivan Crankovich's methods, as oddball as they seem, somehow yield results, so we keep him on our team for now. His family fled from Russia after their revolution and immigrated to America, and Ivan joined the Teslanauts after having worked at the Watt Cossacks."

"Watt Cossacks?"

"Russian volt-tech," Ivan explained, his head lowered and his shoulders folded in. Clearly he held memories of his home country he would rather forget.

"New recruits, gather at the training center!" the voice of an elderly yet fiery lady barked out as the remaining workers coalesced. "We're going to whip you kids into shape!"

"That's me," Raymond realized, straightening his hat and readying himself for the initiation procedure. "I'm off to become a Teslanaut."

"See you around, Raymond!" Becky shouted, waving at the new recruit as she and the others started making their way to the factory.

"Oh, would you mind making me this?"

Pulling the schematic with his dad's message out of his pocket, Raymond handed it to Becky with hopeful eyes. She studied the schematic thoroughly, turning it on its side several times as if trying to piece together what was so important about it.

"Why do you want this?" she finally asked. "We have hundreds of these in the library downstairs."

"My dad's last message to me is encoded in that piece of paper. He must have meant to give that device to me. Maybe there's something special about it that isn't obvious?"

"Only one way to find out!" Becky laughed, passing the schematic around to her peers.

# Chapter Seven

"THE ELECTROCRACY dictates that only those that can keep its secrets are worthy of its power," Agnes Cobblewood informed the new recruits, pacing back and forth with her arms behind her back. "I know this better than anyone, as I've kept them since its infancy."

A woman in her late seventies, one might think Cobblewood would be the last person to seriously lead a group of recruits in a secret government organization. Yet her appearance betrayed a more rugged and hardy demeanor, and her deep blue eyes shone with the vigor of someone a quarter of her age. She wore overalls and a top that exposed her surprisingly well-toned and muscular arms, and her voluminous gray hair swept past her shoulders. It seemed that age did little to hold her back, and if God willed it, she would work for the Teslanauts till her early hundreds.

"I've been in military and government organizations long before any of you were twinkles in your fathers' eyes," Cobblewood told the recruits. "I've dealt with Confederate, Spanish, German, Russian, and Prussian soldiers over the years, either fighting them directly or tending those wounded by them. The technology may have changed, and the terms of engagement may have changed, but the mission has stayed the same: protect the peace and keep the power from the evil. With the monumental power of volt-tech, nowhere is this mission more important than with the Teslanauts, and with the Electrocracy."

Raymond stood alongside two dozen other recruits listening to Cobblewood's orientation, each recruit instructed to keep their arms behind their back and remain silent unless addressed. After handing in their tests, everyone was given matching jackets and flat caps with the seal of the Teslanauts, or at least, that's what Raymond was told. In truth, he couldn't see any seal or markings or any codes at all on their apparel, and all the hats looked different from one another anyway. How could they bear any Teslanaut seal? It must have been that signature from the prod again.

"Now, before we get started, I will allow you to ask a few questions," Cobblewood stated. "I request intelligent questions only, if you don't mind."

A couple of seconds of awkward silence passed, with the new recruits nervously shuffling while trying to remain composed. What kind of questions would she deem intelligent or important enough? They wanted to make a good first impression for their new agency. Eventually, one of the agents, a muscular Spanish lad with a strong jaw, decided to bite the bullet.

"What's the Electrocracy?" the agent asked.

"Off to a great start," Cobblewood grumbled, which prompted a few laughs. Raymond faked a chuckle himself, but in truth, he had no idea what the Electrocracy was either, even though he had heard the name quite a bit since all this started. He welcomed an explanation.

"The Electrocracy is the collection of government agencies across the world specializing in volt-tech," Cobblewood explained. "The Teslanauts are not the only organization out there that specializes in this technology, but they were the first. Many other countries have their own organization, and some, like us Americans, have more than one. Down in the south the Proton Rangers were founded just last year, while England has the Royal Shock Brigade, France has the Volt Knights, Russia has the Watt Cossacks, China has the Shandianlong, and so on. Nikola Tesla and George Westinghouse founded the Teslanauts in 1904, and their incredible technology sparked these other organizations to form and follow their lead. Four years later, the presence of volt-tech could not be ignored, and with the overall unrest of the European powers, it was decided that an overarching administration was needed to keep all the organizations in line. Thus, the Electrocracy was founded by Tesla, Westinghouse, Roosevelt, and many others in 1908, to keep the technology in check and maintain the secret."

"Why?" another recruit demanded. A young Chinese woman, she stood alongside her brother on the opposite end of the crowd from Raymond. "These machines are all so marvelous, and this technology could have many applications in society. How does the world benefit from hiding it all?"

"Were you asleep the last decade? You've seen the horrific capabilities of your fellow man. As volt-tech has the power to create, so too it has the power to destroy, and until civilization can be trusted with such power, we must keep it hidden and fight those who use it for ill will. You there!"

It took a couple of seconds for Raymond to realize Cobblewood pointed right at him, although his eyes looked back and forth at the other recruits on his sides to see if any of them thought they were addressed instead. "Yes, ma'am?" he finally asked, his voice low and wary.

"You got any older brothers who served during the war?"

"No, I'm an only child."

"Then what good are you now?!"

"My father worked here with the Teslanauts! At least, that's what I learned a couple days ago."

"Unless he stood at the front lines in Strasbourg and witnessed the bodies and shrapnel flying about with his own eyes, that means nothing to me. The point I'm trying to convey is that the world isn't ready for mass consumption of volt-tech. We knew it before the war, and we sure as hell knew it after. Consider it a privilege that we get to use it to aid the world in the shadows. Now, that's enough ignorant questions from the lot of you. Let's continue our orientation, shall we?"

Cobblewood held out her hand and showed off her right wrist, which everyone now realized had a metallic band on it. "See this? This is an ignition band, and every Teslanaut has one. All Teslanaut gadgets, vehicles, and weapons require incredible amounts of electricity, which is generated from power plants across the world and transmitted from hundreds of towers constructed all over by the Electrocracy. The power is alternating current, and it can wirelessly send energy to anything within range with the proper receiver. These bands, though, are what initially activate the equipment, which keeps it from being hijacked by the enemy; something I'm sure you will all come to appreciate. We'll fashion these bands for each of you, and then we can commence equipment training for you sorry lots."

"We won't let you down!" Raymond shouted.

A couple of other recruits laughed at his enthusiasm.

"The day is far from over, Calvert," Cobblewood sighed, causing Raymond to wince. He certainly did not expect her to already know his name. "You still have plenty of chances."

"All power levels have been restored!" a worker from the control station reported. "Initiating second jump in three... two..."

Two days later, the Freckle Dump station had teleported three more times on its journey to France, first further up north in Canada, then to Greenland, and then from Greenland to Iceland. At this point, the station rested in a bitterly cold field of ice and volcanic ash, far away from any town to avoid detection. Under the shadow of a mighty frozen mountain, the Teslanauts prepared, via the armor workers' forging, the control station's power managing, and, on a white glacier blackened with soot, the new recruits' training.

After Cobblewood's orientation, the new agents were served breakfast and then given their ignition bands, beginning day one of a full week of training, coinciding with the time of the trip to France. The Teslanauts forged each band to the individual, and snapped them onto the wrists of each recruit. Once Raymond's band clicked together on his left wrist—his dominant hand—he felt a tiny jolt similar to the one that Agent Null had zapped into him, only not nearly as intense. Rubbing his wrist and thinking about what this implied, he realized the band and the signature within his system had linked, allowing him to use the power within and the power from transmitter towers together to activate equipment. All he had to do now to turn on any volt-tech device was touch it.

Now sporting their fresh new bands, the agents were taught by Cobblewood how to properly handle the equipment. In the first day they started simple, using tesla-coil gauntlets to turn on lightbulbs in between their hands, but as the moments charged onward, the manner of gadgets used went from mundane to meticulous to borderline maddening. They went from a suit powered by lightning, to a suit that *made* lightning, to a rod that used electricity to increase density and discharge lightning, to many, many more.

As well as devices, Cobblewood demonstrated the various mechanical automatons sustained by electromagnetic currents, able to move and walk and even fly on their own without pilots or remote control. The most diminutive of these automated machines were the hover-heads: football-sized mechanisms with boxy, semicircle heads and two arms ending with fingers that could transform into many different tools like torches, fuses, and grips. They flew using internal propellers that could only be seen if looking from below, and considering how alive these automatons seemed, Raymond assumed they would consider looking at them from such an angle quite offensive.

The Teslanauts used the hover-heads for a variety of purposes, but often they helped with the construction of even bigger machines, some the size of houses. At this size they were all piloted, as the complexity of the machinery also complicated the process of automation. Apparently, though, Arthur and his team of factory workers were attempting to make some of these larger tanks, mechs, and vehicles as self-driven as the hover-heads. None of their attempts had been successful thus far, but Arthur knew it could be done, and would not stop until they found a way.

All the feats the Teslanauts could do with electricity blew all the fuses of Raymond's mind. They did far more than simply turn on lights or power devices. With their wonders, they could alter the physical state of objects and amplify the range of machines. They enhanced durability, increased velocity, improved functionality, and expanded applicability, all in a myriad of previously inconceivable ways. It seemed like magic, but it was all science, concocted from the imaginations of wizard-like dreamers and perfected by the machinations of scientific practitioners.

Of course, Teslanauts were not just ordinary folks with extraordinary technology. The recruits' training also involved some hard, serious lessons on how they would properly *use* their gear, and have minds and tactics as extraordinary as the equipment they wielded. That was the main focus of their training after they received an overview of the tech they would work with, and that's what the agents learned out in the Icelandic glaciers.

"Bring this thing down!" Cobblewood ordered, piloting a mech that stomped upon the ice. A wondrous amalgamation of gears, pistons, and metal, her twenty-foot-tall machine pounded the ground with four bulky mechanical legs that spread out like a crab as it slowly lumbered. The cockpit, fashioned from parts of a tank and a Ford Model T, could swivel a full three hundred sixty degrees, which Cobblewood used to focus on different recruits as they scurried across the white fields. Each movement of the mech sent columns of smoke out four exhaust pipes behind the cockpit, the machine powered by a fusion of electricity and diesel.

"We ain't got no weapons!" another recruit snapped, quickly tiptoeing across the slippery glacier that buckled under the weight of Cobblewood's mech. "You just gave us these tiny rods! How do you expect us to bring that thing down with these?"

"You're agents, not soldiers!" Cobblewood reminded the careful recruit, pressing a button in the cockpit of her mech to activate another one of its systems. "Think of a method that involves your brains!"

"Boy, I joined the wrong organization," a second recruit grumbled.

The agents' struggles would soon increase exponentially. Unfolding from table-sized compartments behind the cockpit's exhaust pipes, twin disintegrator cannons made themselves known to the new recruits, immediately firing a warning shot onto some ice. The ensuing explosion sent chunks of ice and soot in all directions, further fracturing the glacier upon which they stood. As it covered a valley of ash, there was no water underneath the ice, but the cracks in the frozen turf made the glacier very unstable. Several recruits slipped onto their faces and slid upon the icy surface, while others frantically held their rods out at the mech in the vain hope of shooting out lightning and bringing it down.

"What the hell is *that*?" Raymond demanded, his eyes widening at the caliber of weaponry Cobblewood had at her disposal.

"Set the rods down!" the brother of the Chinese woman from earlier shouted, stabbing his drumstick-sized rod into the ice. "Use them together like coils!"

"They're not doing anything!" a third recruit yelled.

"Not yet they aren't! Put them into place and *then* we can activate them!"

Raymond started to see his idea, but knew Cobblewood would see through their plan and do what she could to disrupt it. As the elderly woman shot more chunks of ice off the ground with her mech's disintegrator cannons, Raymond persuaded a few other recruits to stab their rods into the ice at their feet, while the Chinese siblings did the same on their end. A chasm of cracked ice began to form from Cobblewood's incessant shooting of the glacier, with agents on both ends placing their rods on each end.

"Now what?" a recruit asked.

"We wait until she's between them and grab the rods," the Chinese woman explained. "Our ignition bands will power them!"

"Are you not right in the head? That'd electrocute us! I ain't dying on my first day, thank you!"

Cobblewood shot at the ground by a handful of rods, causing the ice to fracture beneath them and sending them tumbling to the ash fields below. Raymond realized that the recruit had a point, and there was no way Cobblewood would willingly walk her mech into such an obvious trap. Still, he couldn't help but think they were on the right track. She had given them these rods for a reason.

"Calvert!" Cobblewood barked, lumbering her mech in front of Raymond. "You best not stand still too long, or the only thing going through your mind will be my cannon blasts!"

Raymond looked between the four legs of Cobblewood's mech and noticed another set of rods behind her. He looked at his left wrist, where his ignition band gleamed in the faint sunlight. Then he looked at the mech powering its disintegrator cannons, his eyes narrowing with determination.

"Time's up, Calvert!" Cobblewood snapped.

Before the cannons fired, Raymond darted ahead and grasped one of the mech's legs, hugging it with both arms while glaring at the rods behind her. Realizing what Raymond was doing, the Chinese woman repressed any fear of electrocution and grasped the base of one of the rods. Their ignition bands transferring the power, the two formed an electrical current that conducted a bolt of lightning between them, with Cobblewood's mech closing the circuit. Both Raymond and the woman were sent flying back, but the brunt of the electricity flowed between them, minimizing the electric shock they received.

The voltage surged through Cobblewood's mech, overloading the disintegrator cannons and depowering them at once, with only a burst of sparks coming from their barrels. His hair now looking like an explosion frozen in time, Raymond painfully lifted his back off the ice and studied the damage.

"My mech!" Cobblewood cried angrily, pounding the control panel as the weapon systems smoked profusely behind her. "You wrecked it! This thing was expensive, you know!"

"We did as you asked, Ms. Cobblewood!" the Chinese woman protested, her strands of raven hair threatening to burst out of her pin from her own shock. "We brought it down!"

"Eh, I suppose you did. Fine, you all pass this test, I guess."

All the recruits cheered as Cobblewood carefully vacated her mech, slowly climbing down a ladder near the cockpit and keeping her elderly body from slipping and breaking upon the ice. Raymond ran over to try to help up the young woman who helped with the combined attack, but her brother was already on it.

"Sorry about the shock," Raymond said, trying in vain to get his hair back into place. When he imagined sparks flying between him and a girl, he didn't expect it to be so literal.

"Sorry for the idea," the woman giggled. "But we completed our mission, which is most important, wouldn't you agree?"

"Yeah, I'd agree. I'm Raymond, by the way."

"Lei Ying. This is my older brother, Lei Ji. We joined the Teslanauts together after coming to America."

"Try not to get too attached, Ying," Ji chortled, helping his sister with her hair. His own midnight locks were also pointed outwards like spikes, although in his case it looked like the product of gel rather than a charge of several hundred volts. "Raymond here looks pretty naïve in the ways of volt-tech. Who knows how long he'll last?"

"You know more about all this?" Raymond asked, his tone growing a little defensive.

"Our mother and father founded the Shandianlong organization back home; China's own volt-tech faction," Ji explained. "The name means 'Lightning Dragon,' in case you're curious. While they run Shandianlong, we've come to assist the Teslanauts."

"Wow," Raymond breathed, seriously amazed at how widespread the volt-tech factions seemed to be. The Electrocracy must have had stations all around the world, and yet hardly anyone was the wiser! "My father worked here as well. I'm hoping to follow his lead."

"Where is your father now?" Ying asked.

"That's why I'm here. I'm going to find out."

Once the Freckle Dump station reached Oslo following two more jumps, the sun had already disappeared under the horizon, the Teslanauts having shortened the day with their teleporting journey. By this point, the new recruits' fifth day of training had ended, and would pick up again tomorrow before they began their journey to the French front. After dinner, Cobblewood escorted them to the second-lowest level of the station, which held the dormitories. Cots sat in rows all throughout the level, with the walls holding lockers for the stationed agents' personal belongings. The dormitory level also had a shower station, which confused Raymond at first. This was a teleporting headquarters, so how could they have water access? But he then remembered the headquarters only teleported to designated points, which must have connected to local pipe grids that the station snapped onto in predetermined locations. After Cobblewood showed the recruits their assigned lockers, she shut the light off pretty much immediately.

Raymond, however, couldn't sleep from the excitement. His entire world had flipped on its head from the sheer volume of wonders the Electrocracy had graciously revealed this last week. To think of all the things humanity was capable of; all the things science and technology could accomplish! Nikola Tesla was more than an inventor, Raymond realized. He was a dreamer. A *big* dreamer, one whose grandiose visions had seemingly no restraints. Would his technology allow man to soar to the sun? Or was there a limit, and they would burn their wings? Based on the required secrecy the Electrocracy mandated on all their activities, maybe they had already reached that limit. Or maybe, eventually, it would all be figured out.

Raymond tossed and turned in his cot, his mind still racing. There would be no sleeping with his mind in such a state. He had to concentrate on something peaceful, something that would ease his senses. And after inwardly recapping all the events of the last couple of days, he figured out what that was: at long last, he was making progress on solving the mystery of his father's whereabouts. Sometime soon, he would fill in that missing piece. He was on the right track. He was sure of it.

Could he dare to hope?

# Chapter Eight

"HOW DO you think he's doing?" Agent Null asked Agent Zero the next morning, joining his fellow officer at his desk in the Freckle Dump station with a cup of Earl Grey. "He seemed rather… overwhelmed last I saw him."

"Everyone is at first," Agent Zero said, putting some cream in his coffee and stirring it with a spoon. "He's handling it better than most, though. Remember when Agent Void recruited that one poor fellow who went catatonic seeing a mech move and fled right on the spot? That was entertaining, even if it took half the workers on duty to locate him and wipe his memory. I tell you, though, Calvert's determination to find what happened to his father, it could end up being…"

"…exploitable?"

"…dangerous. He's not going to like the answer."

"He's just a kid," Agent Null assured him, sipping his tea. "I doubt he'll react in any way that threatens the organization. Just keep an eye on him and make sure he continues excelling in his training. Mrs.

Cobblewood already has several potential positions for him in the upcoming mission."

"Speaking of which, we should contact HQ," Agent Zero realized, leaving his desk and heading toward the communication station. "Their electrowave scans of the target perimeter should be complete by now."

"Urgent message from New York Headquarters!" a communications worker shouted, taking the piece of paper from his station's telegraph machine to Agent Zero as he arrived. "Looks like something you might want to read, Agent Null."

"I'm Agent Zero, son."

"Really? I can't tell the two of you apart to save my life!"

"We're secretive recruitment agents. We're supposed to be inconspicuous."

"Yes, but I don't think it would hurt to give one of you a brooch or a swanky coat."

"Just hand me the damn letter," Agent Zero sighed, prompting the worker to stay silent for now and pass him the paper. While in the mundane world the concept of telegrams passing over oceans or international borders was unfeasible, the volt-tech telegraph machines used the power of the volt-tech network provided by the widely distributed towers to send and receive messages, increasing the range extensively while eliminating the need for direct wires to transmit the message. Nikola Tesla was a pioneer of wireless technology, and volt-tech made great use of this in their various gizmos and equipment.

Taking the letter back to his office to rejoin his fellow recruitment officer, Agent Zero examined its contents, automatically decoded after arriving at the Freckle Dump station.

SENDER: Nikola Tesla, Head Commander of Teslanauts

RECIPIENT: Teslanaut Mobile Field HQ Fox-Dock 17

SENT: April 27, 1922, 22:45 New York HQ Time

RECEIVED: April 28, 1922, 7:52 Mobile Field HQ Time

New York Teslanaut Headquarters and Paris Volt Knight Headquarters remotely sent 782-megawatt electro-scan from Transmitter Towers FRA-1, FRA-2, FRA-3, FRA-4 SWZ-1, BEL-1, and BEL-2 on

April 26, 1922 at 1:07. Scan radius per tower: 544 miles. Results arrived on April 27th, 1922 at 22:32.

Most cities and locations in the electro-scanned area remain static, with no unusual activity reported. However, there was an anomaly located at Ausgraben, Switzerland. The whole town has altered considerably in state. Building signatures were not received. Population signatures have been decimated. Ausgraben appears to have been destroyed due to unknown circumstances.

Request immediate dispatch of a team to investigate and search for survivors and witnesses.

Agent Zero reread the telegram's contents several times over to make sure he understood it clearly, the wrinkles on his brow contorting while he processed what it meant. During the war, whole towns could be swept with gas, mortar rounds, howitzer shells, and airship carcasses, but now? Four years later?

Something didn't add up. How could a town just disappear off the map? And what could cause such a thing? Tesla was right; they *did* have to dispatch a team. This required thorough investigation. Europe still reeled from the war, and many of its citizens felt like another bout was only a matter of time. Yet, so many millions had died already in the last decade, either from battle, disease, or outright negligence. This could not continue.

"Get a hold of the team at the German border," Agent Null told the other recruitment agent. "They must change course at once."

"But our reinforcements are less than a day away!"

"We'll meet up with them once they've completed their evaluation of the situation in Ausgraben. This is our priority now. Contact the French Volt Knights and tell them the attack on the enemy base in Germany will have to wait."

"You assume that the enemy is responsible?"

"We'll let Morales's team figure that out."

***

"We're seriously redirecting to Switzerland?" Helen demanded sharply. "When we're so close to Germany I can practically smell the bratwurst?"

"Orders are orders, Brimsby," Morales stated, as the Teslanaut agents packed up their comm station cubes and returned them to their backpacks. "Apparently New York's remote electro-scans reported a near complete erasure of a whole town. That doesn't happen with normal artillery or bombs. This has to be volt-tech."

"And it might be what that walker mech was distracting us from," Helen said quietly, the dots starting to connect as she thought about it. "This must be the work of those bloody 'fringe groups' that have been giving us trouble."

"I fear you might be right."

"Are ve to accompany you, Marshal?" Captain du Foudre asked, finishing up some tuneups of his mechanical appendage.

"It might be for the best, Captain. Should we wait for approval from your superiors?"

"Never mind zem, we would just be wasting zeir time!" Foudre laughed, already cavorting ahead of the agents. "In fact, we will provide ze ride so we don't have to make zis journey by foot! Contact ze dirigibles zat dropped us off, and tell zem to turn zeir rudders around!"

"*Oui, monsieur.*" a Volt Knight agent said, pressing a few buttons on his shield to unfold an antenna and transform it into his own comm station.

"Dirigibles?" a Teslanaut agent asked, eyes wide with excitement.

"They're just glorified balloons," Helen chortled. "Don't be daft."

"Not ze Knights'!" Foudre said while puffing out his chest, the prideful effect exemplified further by his chivalrous armor. "We like to command ze sky like aerial royalty! Zere is no better way to transport our agents on zeir missions."

"Won't these 'fringe groups' see us coming, if your ships are so glorious?" Morales asked.

"Not with our stealth systems, zey won't! French Volt Knight airships have specialized panels zat send electro-scans straight through zem. Ze enemy won't be able to see us unless we fly practically right above zem!"

"Such stealth systems *exist*?" the excited Teslanaut agent demanded. "When will the Teslanauts get those, Marshal?"

"When mechs fly," Morales muttered. "Pardon me, Captain, but that sounds frankly unfeasible. I'll believe it when I see it."

"Understood, *monsieur*!" Foudre said, shrugging as he led his agents out of their base camp next to the Rhine. "Now, follow me to ze airship landing point. A squadron of flying mechs shall escort us during ze trip, of course!"

"Of course."

A half-hour of travel later, the Teslanauts and the Volt Knights rendezvoused with the French airships, as they landed in a field outside the forest to pick up their new passengers. They were smaller than some of the massive zeppelins over in Germany, about the length of two train cars, but they had four egg-shaped envelopes rather than one, with a spider web of propellers on each end sitting on rotatable panels that allowed high maneuverability. The metallic supports, pipes, and linings draped the envelopes like moss, more curved and sweeping than the Teslanauts expected, as if aesthetic quality was as much of a deliberate design choice as its performance and functionality. While the cabins lay underneath as expected, walkways and balconies lined every corner, with a ladder on one side that came within reach of the agents as the dirigibles hovered over the grass.

"Behold, gentlemen, ze pride of ze Volt Knight aerial fleet!" Foudre exclaimed, climbing up the ladder before standing on the walkway and facing the Teslanauts with his arms raised boastfully. "We call zem 'Interceptors,' and zey are our finest airships. Zese are not only advanced, but also much faster zan zey look. Zey will get us to Ausgraben within an hour's time!"

"An audacious claim," Helen said, "but quite impressive if true. What do you think, Marshal?"

"I think we need to get to Ausgraben as soon as possible," Morales said, hurriedly climbing up the ladder to join Foudre on his airship. "If these can get us there in a timely manner, then I'll be impressed. Until then, Captain, you are only words."

"You should have more faith in us, Marshal Morales!" Foudre laughed, although judging by his demeanor he was not terribly offended. "Our country survived against ze Germans, after all! I assure you zat we will get to Switzerland in time. Now climb aboard!"

Once all the present agents boarded the Interceptors, Foudre pointed forward with great gusto, although after witnessing every other way the Volt Knight Captain expressed himself the Teslanauts expected nothing less. Immediately, as if driven by his gesture rather than pilots, the airships burst forward, more like a rocket than a dirigible, using a combination of propellers and a series of thrusters on each side for propulsion. It was only a combination of hardened steel restraints and seemingly dumb luck the ships' envelopes didn't dislodge from the sudden acceleration, but somehow the whole rig stayed together. Every agent quickly grabbed hold of the railings, the wind blasting upon their faces like artillery explosions from the war.

"Isn't zis great?!" Foudre roared with delight as they zoomed ahead. "And to think you doubted us, Marshal!"

"We're not gonna die, we're not gonna die, we're not gonna die," a Teslanaut agent murmured, trying to convince himself more than anyone else.

"I sure hope these things stay together!" Morales yelled. "I don't know if I trust French engineering with my life yet."

"Is that really what you've heard about our engineering?" Foudre said, sounding more vexed than normal. "Bite your tongue, *monsieur*! Besides, I could say ze same about British cooking!"

"Hey, our cooking isn't so terrible!" Helen said. "Last week I had a kidney pie that was quite delicious!"

After a trip of roughly forty-five minutes, the Interceptors reached a country road just outside Ausgraben, hiding their fleet behind a grove of trees as they landed. A convoy of automobiles and crowds gathered on the road leading out of Ausgraben, made of hundreds of people hurriedly moving without looking back. The way they bolted, the looks in their eyes; all of it conveyed a notion of panic the agents hadn't seen since before the signing of the armistices.

"Hold your positions," Morales ordered, climbing out of his Interceptor and moving out of the grove. "I'll check with the crowd and see what happened."

"You don't think I should go out and converse with zem?" Foudre asked.

"You have a mechanical arm and electrified medieval armor. You're not showing yourself to civilians, Captain."

"I know, zat was a test," Foudre chortled, "and you passed! Good job, Marshal!"

As Morales left their hidden pasture, Helen and the Teslanauts took the time to recollect themselves after their exhilarating and frankly terrifying flight, while Foudre and the agents of the Volt Knights just ate their lunch from their packs as if they finished a pleasant walk in a garden. Helen couldn't help but smirk with appreciation at their French companions' fortitude, especially after losing so much during the war. Though the front extended across many countries, France was right in the thick of it, having lost over a million and a half people. The horrors they endured would render most catatonic, and yet they kept going, with seemingly more vigor than even their American or British friends.

"Why would anyone attack Switzerland?" a Teslanaut asked. "They weren't with the Allied *or* Central Powers. They're as neutral as it gets."

"Perhaps that's exactly why they attacked them," Helen suggested. "They wanted to test some new volt-tech, and so they went for a target that wouldn't spur either side into conflict. It's vile, but strategically it checks out."

"I would have liked to see zem try to attack Paris," Foudre said. "Ze full might of ze Volt Knights would have kept zem from getting even close."

"That would just restart the war, though. Tesla constantly tells us to avoid that at all costs. He hates war."

"A bold stance," Foudre muttered, not bothering to hide his sarcasm. "Ze only ones who like war are ze ones in ze suits and ties at home rather zan guns on ze field. I'm just saying, I would like to see zem *dare* to try and attack. We'd put a stop to it so quickly zey would retreat and never try again."

Morales returned to the group a few moments later, his brow low and his hand to his chin. Hoping to get some answers, the agents tried to get a read on how he took the civilians' response, but the look in his eyes showed a deep confusion they could not deduce.

"Well?" Helen asked, eager to learn what happened. "What did they say?"

"It was difficult to understand," Morales said. "They're still rather panicked, and I'm not the most familiar with German."

"I know a lot of it myself," Foudre admitted. "Zat's why you should have let me do ze talking instead! Oh damn, now *I've* failed ze test."

"They're the sole survivors of an incident unlike any I've heard of," Morales reported. "Ruptured ground, toppling buildings, a whirlpool of metal... I can't imagine such a thing, even with the powers volt-tech is capable of. We have to go to Ausgraben and see for ourselves."

"How far is Ausgraben?" a Volt Knight agent asked.

"Not too far, only about fifteen miles east."

"Good thing we've come prepared, as usual," Foudre chuckled, heading back to the Interceptors. "We'll get us there before you know it."

"You're aware we can't fly those airships of yours so close to civilians, right, Captain?"

"Don't worry, Marshal, we're not going to fly zem. We're going to drive zem. Observe."

Foudre directed his Volt Knight agents to follow his lead, each one standing underneath the Interceptors as they hovered over the ground. Once each agent stood in position, they pulled down a lever from a compartment just within reach under the deck of each airship. With the sound of spinning gears and whirring machinery, each airship began to transform, deflating the balloons and folding up the envelope's supports, while unfolding new compartments and a set of wheels hidden within the bodies of the airships. Like mechanical origami, the Interceptors transformed from one mode to another, in a seemingly never-ending process of shifting tech. In a little less than a minute, the vehicles had changed from a fleet of airships to a caravan of trucks, ones they could easily drive out in the open without arousing suspicion.

"*Voila*!" Foudre exclaimed. "We have our ride, gentlemen. Climb back aboard and let us depart!"

"I'm quite impressed," Helen said, grinning at the Volt Knights' showmanship.

"I have to admit, you make the most dependable of allies," Morales said, motioning the Teslanauts to climb into the back of the trucks. "Are these automated like their airship modes?"

"What, you want everyone to think zere are ghosts driving out on ze road? Of course zey're not automated!"

"Good, that was *my* test, and now *you* passed."

Once everyone loaded inside the ground-based Interceptors, they drove out to the road and honked to let the refugees know they would be sharing the road. The crowd did not stretch on much longer, and they hoped that was more due to Ausgraben being a small town than from a vast number of casualties. As they made their way to the town, the terrain gradually grew grayer and more ruptured, with cracks and risen earth cobwebbing in areas all around them. Even the wildlife grew less numerous as they drove, with the groupings of rats and pigeons slowly petering out to nothing. Clearly, something substantial had happened ahead.

"Stop the car, stop it!" Morales barked a half-hour later, realizing the road came to a sudden stop. The convoy of trucks braked at Morales's command, while the agents got out and saw what lay before them. At once, their jaws dropped, gazing in horror at where the town of Ausgraben once was.

Stretching thousands of feet wide and hundreds of feet deep, a crater was all that was left of the quaint Swiss town. Dirt, rocks, and toppled houses littered the remnants, while smoke and dust choked the air. No people, no livestock, no life at all remained in the rubble, with the hundred or so refugees down the road seemingly the only survivors. Staring at the sunken ground with shock and horror, the agents felt the real dread of the war that had already claimed so many lives starting again, a notion they had assumed foolhardy after the signing of the armistices. Yet, after seeing the lifeless rubble that was once Ausgraben, they knew such a dire prospect was now a frighteningly real possibility.

"My God," Foudre whispered, his loud and boastful demeanor gone after seeing the destruction.

"There's nothing left," Helen gasped. "What could have caused this?"

"I'm not sure," Morales muttered, studying the crater for any clues. "I'm not seeing any ash, so I don't think it was artillery, but what it could have been I have no idea."

"I've got the feeling we're not dealing with 'fringe groups' anymore, if they're capable of something like this," a Teslanaut agent said, shaking his head at the terrible sight.

"Look at zis!" Foudre said, motioning his mechanical arm toward a particularly large area of overturned dirt and rubble.

The agents turned to where Foudre pointed, seeing the piles of ruptured earth congregated in a circular portion of the ruins. Based on the smaller crater surrounding this area, the dirt seemed to block a large tunnel leading deep underground, a tunnel that was surely not a feature of Ausgraben while it still stood.

"It's like something bored through the earth and destroyed the town from underneath," Morales said, his voice low with disbelief at such a prospect. "What kind of terrible machine could do such a thing?"

"Not one zat I look forward to facing," Foudre said with a shudder.

"What do we do, Marshal?" Helen asked Morales. "This is bigger than we thought."

"We must find out who's responsible. Destroying an innocent town is nothing less than an act of war, and we cannot allow these vermin to rekindle the conflict. Set up the comm station, and send a message back to headquarters. We must inform them of-"

"Marshal, look out!"

Seconds after the distant sound of artillery fire, a barrage of seven rockets flew in from the north and blasted the ground, landing near the rim of the crater a couple dozen yards away and rupturing both the dirt and the agents' eardrums. The group ducked behind their trucks and braced themselves for the explosions, and yet none came. The rockets remained completely intact, sticking head-first into the dirt and blanketed by smoke and dust. Nearly twenty feet long apiece, they were larger than any rockets the agents had seen before, and surely with such terrible sizes they would deal incredible damage. But they didn't go off.

"Why aren't they exploding?!" Helen demanded.

"Maybe they're not really rockets," a Teslanaut said hopefully.

"Or maybe they're trying to lull us into thinking they failed," Morales warned. "Captain, cover us with your shields."

"*Oui, monsieur*," Foudre replied, directing his Volt Knights to hold out their electrified shields and protect the agents behind them.

The seconds ticked onward, each one longer and tenser than the last, and yet the rockets just sat there in the ruins of Ausgraben. The agents waited, their hairs rising on their arms, their hearts steadily racing as they readied for any sort of reaction from the rockets.

"What's going on?!" Morales asked. "Why aren't those blasted things-"

At last, the rockets did something, but it was no explosion. A set of four rectangular panels opened up on the sides of each rocket, folding down as jets of steam burst out from the rockets' thrusters. A gangly mechanical limb emerged from each panel, with the lower two planting onto the ground and pushing the rocket out of their area of impact. The upper two panels opened further panels at their ends, with four barrels arranged like a pipe organ on each appendage. Finally, a fifth panel unfolded at the top of the rockets, as a brick-shaped head with a single optic sensor rose between the thrusters.

In the span of thirty seconds, the septet of rockets became a squad of giant mechanical men, standing thirty feet high as they lumbered toward the agents. Holding their steel hands out toward their position, the giants rapidly charged their energy reserves from the surrounding transmitter towers and prepared to open fire.

"What in the devil's name?!" Helen said.

"Take cover!" Morales ordered.

A barrage of disintegrator beams blasted from the giant rocket mens' hands, sending torrents of dirt and fire up from the ground ahead of the agents' convoy. Foudre motioned for everyone to scramble back to the trucks, and once they did they stepped on the gas to evade the giants' fire.

"Giant mechanical men deployed via rockets?" Foudre exclaimed, half with horror and half with begrudging appreciation. "Extraordinary! I wish ze Volt Knights had thought of zat!"

"We can't maneuver with these trucks!" Morales grunted. "Foudre, can the Interceptors return to their airship forms with us inside?"

"Not if you want to get out with all your bones intact! Ze machinery folds onto itself too much as it transforms."

"Why couldn't your airships just be trucks with balloons on top? Why do they have to change in such an unnecessarily complicated manner?"

"We can discuss ze flaws of my country's engineering practices *after* we escape from zis!"

"We will hold ze line for you!" a Volt Knight agent said, as a squad leaped out of the back of the cars and extended their shields, blocking the disintegrator beams and keeping the rocket men's attacks at bay. However, the electricity within their shields sparked profusely from all the fire, with the metal it coated buckling from the intense pushback. They would not be able to protect the agents for long.

"Teslanauts, fire at will!" Morales barked as they pulled over the trucks on the dirt road and leapt out to face the rocket men. "Keep them distracted! The Peacemaker is our only hope!"

As Helen and the other Teslanauts with weapons stood behind the Volt Knight shields and fired at the rocket men, the more gadget-focused agents prepped the metallic cubes that joined together to form Morales's mighty weapon. Foudre, meanwhile, leapt well past his mens' shields and charged forward with a hearty laugh, preparing the lance that made his right hand and puncturing the legs of the lead rocket man. With just a few attacks, his electrified lance pierced through its mechanical ankles, toppling the thirty-foot giant.

"Excellent job, Captain!" Helen cheered.

"It's still not dead, madam!" Foudre reminded her, as the rocket man used its fifteen-foot arms to crawl through the rubble. If they didn't disable it completely, it could fire its disintegrators from a much lower angle than the other rocket men still firing behind it, meaning the Knights would have to block attacks from two different angles. Their shields were not designed to defend such a wide range all at once.

"Where's ze power receivers?!" Foudre grumbled, stabbing the rocket man with his lance at multiple locations. He tried the head, the shoulders, and the heart, each attack creating a splash of sparks, but even with so much ruptured equipment, the machine kept crawling on.

"Just slice its weapons off and focus on the others!" Morales roared, grunting as he dragged the newly unfolded Peacemaker behind him. "Shieldbearers, move forward and cover me!"

Activating the seven-foot sword's rockets to negate a bit of the exertion, Morales bolted toward the rocket man behind the crippled one while staying behind the Volt Knight shields for as long as possible. Once he neared the mechanical giant, the shieldbearers parted and allowed him to move unabated. With a mighty swing of the giant sword, he sliced right through the ankles of the second rocket man in one swoop, and as the machine slowly fell, he kept swinging the sword through it again and again. By the time its head reached the ground, its body had been ruptured into twelve useless pieces.

"Keep at it, Marshal!" Foudre cheered triumphantly. "We can take out ze rest of zem! We'll cut zem like butter while they-"

"More rockets!" Helen shrieked, pointing to the north once again.

Another salvo of artillery fire, and this time twelve rockets blasted the Ausgraben rubble, turning the number of functional enemies from five to seventeen. By this point, the Volt Knights' shields could barely hold any longer, and who knew how many more rockets this mysterious enemy would fire their way.

"What do we do, Marshal?!" a Teslanaut agent demanded.

"Keep attacking until reinforcements arrive!" Morales ordered. "They'll have heard about our redirected path and will join us!"

"And if they don't?"

"They *will*! Stand your ground!"

# Chapter Nine

TWO JUMPS later, and the Freckle Dump station had reached a point just outside Paris, France. But with the telegram sent by Tesla earlier, they had to make one additional jump to join the Teslanaut and Volt Knight agents in Switzerland. As they prepared for this final teleportation, Raymond and the rest of the new recruits waited by the center of the station for their training results gathered over the past week, to see if they passed and officially became novice Teslanaut agents.

It was a nerve-wracking moment. The trainees fidgeted their feet and twiddled their thumbs as they waited for the results, knowing if they did not end up qualifying, they would be sent to the Cleanup Squad and have their memories erased before getting shipped home, a prospect that made everyone feel uneasy. No one wanted to lose a whole day of their lives and forget the wondrous technological achievements of the Teslanauts. Some of them felt like they could never go back to their normal lives after this. But the secret had to be maintained.

"We did well, Lei Ying," Ji assured his sister, sitting with her and a dozen other recruits at a table just outside the station's factory. "We will not disappoint our family, don't worry."

"I sure hope I'm not disappointing mine," Raymond muttered, thinking not only of his missing father but also his fearful mother. He would write to her as soon as he got his results, and let her know that, at the very least, he didn't get killed during introductory training.

"There are many professions in the agency," Ying said, looking out at the hundreds of agents working in the foundries and comms and the others waiting to begin field duty. "What are you thinking of doing?"

"I'd like to become a Bolter," Ji replied. "They wear these special suits that halfway feed them into the volt-tech power network and let them run and work at incredible speeds. It sounds intense, but ludicrously thrilling. How about you?"

"I'll probably be a communications specialist. I prefer directing others to do the dirty work. How do you think I kept our family in order all these years, huh?"

"What about you, Ray?" Ji asked Raymond while ignoring Ying's retort, prompting a sly smile from his younger sister. "What are you going to bring to this electrifying enterprise?"

"It's Raymond," Raymond said shortly. "And I'm not sure yet."

"You have many options. You could be an Electro Engineer, a Mech Master, part of the Cleanup Squad, a reconnaissance specialist, a factory worker, or maybe even a janitor if you're lucky. Surely you've got something in mind?"

"I haven't thought about it yet."

"Well, then what are you joining for?"

"I told you, to find out what happened to my father. Everything in the meantime is just getting me to that end goal."

"Leave him be, Ji," Ying said, pushing her brother aside to try and keep things from getting too confrontational. "Everyone has a place in the world of volt-tech. I wish you the best of luck in the search for your father, Raymond."

Raymond shrugged, not really wanting to talk about it right now, but inwardly appreciating her support. He *was* very interested in the rest of the volt-tech world, from the complicated logistics to the most spectacular machines, and he was appropriately wowed at everything he learned. But he had a goal, and he would remain focused on it no matter what.

A hover-head levitated over to Raymond, the soccer ball-sized automaton cocking its head quizzically at the fleshy human. Unlike the others Raymond had seen, it had a few exposed wires on its right side, dangling down its panels like dreadlocks. Raymond chuckled and patted the hover-head with his left hand, his new Teslanaut-forged wristband giving the machine a little jolt. The hover-head wriggled excitedly at its nourishing electric meal, while a tiny spark erupted from its exposed wires. Far from harming the mechanical critter, it only seemed to pep it up more, as it started circling the air with glee at the buzz.

"Excuse me, that hover-head is broken!" a familiar deep voice called out at Raymond's side. "I need to fix it right away!"

Raymond turned and saw Ivan Crankovich, one of the factory workers he had befriended earlier, rush up to the hover-head with his arm stretched out, his footsteps shaking the ground from his sheer bulk. Raymond had not seen him so worried and full of emotion before. His normally stoic eyes were wide and frantic, as his connection to the machines made him especially sensitive to any imperfections.

"Nah, I like him this way," Raymond insisted while patting the hover-head again, this time with his right hand to keep the little machine from shorting out. "Can I keep him?"

"It's not built to standards! It's not supposed to spark!"

"His *sparking* isn't harming anything. Tell you what, I'll keep him away from you so you don't obsess over it. Deal?"

"It's going to bother me," Ivan muttered, the enormous teenager walking away with a bit of an angry pout on his face. "But if you insist, I guess I'll... try and keep it out of mind."

"I appreciate it!" Raymond hollered. He could tell that Ivan didn't believe what he said, but he admired his etiquette. As the aspiring machinery connoisseur lumbered away, Raymond refocused his attention on the hover-head, who looked back at him with its circular optic sensors in a sort of pleading manner.

"You're not supposed to spark, and yet here you are," Raymond told the friendly mechanism, tapping his left hand on the hover-head once again to give it more of the buzz it craved. "I think I'll call you that: Sparks. I'm gonna take good care of you, Sparks."

"You're aware that's a machine and not a mutt, aren't you?" Ji asked. "It's an emotionless contraption that only reacts in predetermined ways. You might as well befriend a toilet."

"I think this one's special," Raymond chortled as Sparks flew off to join the other hover-heads in storage. "It's sure nice being able to make new friends."

"Befriending a robot shouldn't be the ideal," Ji said, narrowing his eyes while watching the hover-head leave.

"Robot?"

"Ever read Čapek? That's what autonomous machines are called now."

"I'll stick to Sparks, thank you."

"Calvert, Raymond!" the bold, angry voice of Cobblewood barked further away.

Raymond nodded and stood back up, ready to hear his results. Ji smirked at Raymond's eagerness, as if anticipating him to be disappointed, but Raymond was not terribly worried. Granted, he needed the Teslanauts' help, but he had seen some of the other recruits who got rejected, and they did far worse than he did in all the performance trials.

Then again, if he *had* somehow failed, the Teslanauts would wipe his memory, and he would be back to where he started, forgetting his father's secret profession and leaving that hole unfilled for the rest of time. Imagining this, Raymond suddenly felt his chest tighten, and his steps toward Cobblewood become more of a labor. He just now realized how much progress he would lose if he could not pull this off.

He had come so far already. He couldn't let this go, not yet. There was still so much more he had to learn, and he needed answers. This was the place to get them, and if he failed, he would never know the truth. By the time he reached Cobblewood, his legs had startled to wobble, although he tried his best to hide it. Maybe Ji's attitude was getting to him, but he felt far more nervous than he had when he started walking to the old trainer.

Cobblewood held a clipboard and marked a few things with her pencil, seemingly paying more attention to it rather than Raymond. She almost didn't appear to notice the anxious teenager standing by her, but eventually, without even turning her gaze, she spoke at last.

"Mr. Calvert," she began. "In field tests, your scores were rather mediocre. You completed all your missions, but your skills with volt-tech leave much to be desired. You got some of the basics figured out, like knowing how to direct a stream of electricity, but your inability to use the tech for advanced problem-solving was a big weakness of yours. When machines needed their components rewired rather than overloaded, you struggled greatly. In addition, you often acted with your gut rather than with your wits, which could endanger your fellow agents in a scuffle."

"Oh boy," Raymond muttered, not liking this so far.

"However, you did excel in one very important category," Cobblewood said. "You kept your focus on the objective and did everything you could to complete it. Your determination is unparalleled, and your drive to finish the mission encouraged the other, more technologically adept agents to follow your lead. While you still have a lot, and I mean a *lot* to learn, you're definitely someone we should keep our eye on as you progress."

"So... I passed?" Raymond asked. "Am I a Teslanaut?"

"Barely. Like, you're the width of a flea's leg away from mediocrity, but you've made it through by the skin of your teeth. So, good job I suppose? Just get to work on improving your skills."

"Yes, ma'am!" Raymond said, feeling the pressure rise off his chest so fast it nearly lifted his whole body like a blimp. "I won't let you down! If I had less shame, I would give you a hug!"

"If you hug me, Mr. Calvert, shame wouldn't be the only thing you'd have less of," Cobblewood grunted, now looking at Raymond but with her eyes pointed down threateningly. "Now, it's time to discuss your position. Mr. Tesla has informed me you wish to be a field agent, but we still need to narrow it down further. Have you given it much thought?"

"Not really, no."

"Of course you haven't. Well, whatever you end up being, we'll need all available agents to aid our allies when we reach Switzerland, which doesn't give you nearly enough time to train for anything specific. This first mission, you'll just be a standard, non-specialized field agent, but as for beyond that... you know, with your excessive drive and determination, you might make a decent Bolter."

"Really?"

"Perhaps, yes. I mean, you're in a suit that does the work for you, so your lacking volt-tech skills wouldn't be much of an issue. That would be good at least for someone like you. Now get away from me, I've got other recruits to grade."

"Of course, Ms. Cobblewood!" Raymond said gleefully, not bothered at all by her grumpy attitude. With how relieved he felt at the moment, Cobblewood could have cursed at him and beat him with a yardstick and he still would have a grin on his face. Making his way back to where Ji and Ying sat, he tipped his flat cap at Ji with a smug smile.

"So, you made it in?" Ji asked, seeming quite surprised.

"Not only that, I might become a Bolter as well," Raymond replied, sitting back down on the bench beside Ji and his sister. "Looks like we'll be seeing quite a lot of each other out in the field."

"Well, as long as you don't slow me down out there. Try to keep up, *Raymond*."

"Lei, Ji!" Cobblewood shouted.

"Time to make my family proud," Ji huffed, standing back up and heading for their trainer. "I'm looking forward to having both the Shandianlong and the Teslanauts on my resume!"

Ying giggled at Ji as he left, leaving her and Raymond alone on the bench, barring the other dozen trainees sitting around them. Waiting for her brother to get out of earshot, Raymond turned back to Ying with a rather furrowed brow.

"What's his deal?" he asked, a bit more sharply than he intended. "Why does he seem so desperate to pick a fight with me?"

"Lei Ji and I have been trained by our mother and father in the applications of volt-tech our whole lives," Ying explained, her tone getting more serious. "It took us a long time to get where we are. Our family has worked diligently at the Shandianlong to prepare us for the Teslanauts. You, though, just learned about this world a week ago, and you're already right here beside us. He feels you haven't earned it yet."

"That's not really my fault."

"It is a consequence of your privilege. All throughout the world, people are told that dreams come true in America, a great melting pot of culture and ideas where everyone has the chance to succeed no matter their background. But the truth isn't so simple. Society still has some people start in positions far ahead of others in the race of life. How hard did the women in your country have to fight just to get an equal say at the voting booth? Or how hard do the women in mine have to fight to get the respect we deserve?"

"Hey, your brother's far ahead of me in many, many areas," Raymond insisted. "He's gonna get much better scores than me, since he's worked so much harder on learning volt-tech than I have. I know I'm an amateur compared to him. I know I've got a lot to learn."

"That's good to hear," Ying said, flashing a hint of a smile. "But I also think there's more to it than that. Ji and I have goals with the Teslanauts. We want to better our people and our country. What about you?"

"I want to find my father."

"Family is very important, yes. So, how are you going to continue your family's legacy?"

"Meaning?"

"What do *you* want to do?"

Raymond fell silent. Truth be told, he never actually thought much about what *he* wanted to do. All he had in mind was finding his father, and solving this mystery once and for all. Then his father could rejoin their family and work to improve the world through the Teslanauts once again. It was that, and only that, that drove him forward. He did not even consider what his own goals with the Teslanauts would be. It had not even crossed his mind.

"Passed with flying colors!" Ji shouted gleefully as he sat back down in between Raymond and Ying and pulled off his flat cap. His spiked hair seemed to share his excitement, as it seemed even pointier than usual. "And I've guaranteed my spot on the Bolter squad!"

"Glad to hear it," Raymond said, now much more genuine than snide after listening to Ying's comments. "I look forward to learning the ropes from you."

"Just don't get in the way so much and you'll be fine," Ji chuckled, his demeanor easing ever so slightly.

Finally, the Freckle Dump station reached its final point just outside Zürich, Switzerland, having completed its journey at last. This station was the nearest to Ausgraben, only about twenty miles away. Further telegrams from the field agents informed the stationed Teslanauts of the severity of their situation. An army of automated machines of unknown origins assaulted their position, with seemingly endless reinforcement capability. The field agents now needed their own reinforcements, and so came the Teslanauts.

"Get into positions!" Cobblewood ordered, now back in her fully repaired mech while standing by a large, currently unopened warehouse door in one corner of the station. "Keep close and march behind me!"

Raymond, Ji, and about a dozen and a half others stood between the legs of Cobblewood's four-legged walker, the only field agents who successfully made it through recruitment training. The rest either stayed at the base to aid them remotely like Ying, or were sent home via a small airship that took off just before the station's final jump, their memories already wiped and altered as they slept aboard the ship. Other agents, known colloquially as the Cleanup Squad, would take them back to their residences and make sure they'd wake up blissfully unaware of the existence of the volt-tech world.

Raymond didn't get a good glimpse of the Cleanup Squad before the airship took off, but not due to a lack of trying; they all wore face-concealing helmets akin to gas masks and, somehow, seemed perpetually blurred all over, like an unclear photograph in the real, physical world. How in the name of Warren G. Harding did *that* work? Lightning and volt-tech were capable of a lot of crazy stuff, but it's not like lightning could do *anything*.

Or maybe it could.

"Final inspection!" the familiar voice of Becky Greengrass shouted, as she and the other factory workers came out with little lights and sensors to check up on the agents' equipment. Each agent had a disintegrator gun, a lightning rod, and a backpack with an as-of-now deactivated hover-head, as well as some more basic tools like wrenches and pliers. A few more experienced agents had those multi-purpose cubes that could unfold into other equipment strapped to their backs, which they would use to make comm stations or nullifiers or many other useful gadgets. Finally, as well as Cobblewood's mech, two other walkers joined the mission, these bipedal and more humanoid in design. Each stood roughly fifteen feet tall and had a crew of two, one controlling the legs and another controlling the arms. As well as the expected metal casing and electrical wiring, these mechs came equipped with cloth flaps on the arms, shoulders, and thighs, looking similar to those found on the first airplanes. These simple gadgets gave the mechs a bit of extra speed through wind power, with each flap functioning as a miniature sail. Not all the Teslanauts' mechanical enhancements came from electricity.

"Clear, clear, clear," Arthur muttered after checking each agents' gear, marking each one off on a clipboard and not making eye contact with anyone as he worked. "Clear, clear, clear, clear, cl-"

"I think they get it, Worthington," Becky said with a chuckle as she examined their mechs. "Just let them know when they're *not* clear."

"Y-yes, of course."

"Hey, this hover-head is all messed up!" Watson shouted, pointing at Sparks attached to Raymond's backpack. Even deactivated, its exposed wires betrayed its imperfect nature. "It could explode in an electrical shower! Not that *I* would mind that, of course, but-"

"He 'likes' it that way," Ivan grumbled, peering at Cobblewood's mech with a flashlight and performing inward calculations to ensure it worked properly. "Don't bother trying to talk him out of using it."

"A broken machine?! This must be *killing* you!"

"Not as much as your enthusiastic reminding me of it is."

"Don't worry, everyone; I'll make sure he's well taken care of," Raymond assured the bickering factory workers. "I've always thought about getting a pet, so Sparks will be in good hands."

"You *named* it?!" Watson demanded, practically shrieking at the prospect. "Don't do that, you'll give it an identity! Next thing you know it'll demand the right to vote or something!"

"Would that be so terrible?" Becky said, rolling her eyes at Watson's rambling.

"Hurry up with your inspections!" Cobblewood demanded. "We've got to get to Ausgraben yesterday!"

"Everything's ready for deployment," Arthur finally said, putting away his clipboard as he and the other factory workers finished their checkup. "Good luck out there and, uh, don't die."

"Inspiring as always, Worthington. Now, *move*! Mech Masters, lead the way!"

Once the door opened, the troops and mechs ran outside and made their way to the rendezvous point, hiding behind hills and trees to conceal their presence to those unaware of volt-tech. As they ducked, rolled, and sprinted across the Swiss landscape, they quickly noticed a collection of smoky arcs at the horizon, with their endpoint being the exact coordinates they were heading toward. Those must have been the rockets that this unknown enemy fired at the field agents, the ones that formed the giant mechanical men detailed in their reports.

"There they are!" Ji shouted, pointing ahead at the crater holding the ruins of Ausgraben. From their vantage point, they could see almost thirty giant mechanical men attacking the Teslanaut and Volt

Knight agents, with a storm of energy beams enveloping both sides. The agents hid wherever they could from the rocket men's attacks and fired from their cover, while two others remained on the front line attacking with their ludicrous weapons. One wielded a lance, the other a sword, both surely much too big to be practical but both slicing through the giant mechanical assaulters with seemingly no problem.

"Ze reinforcements have arrived!" the lance-wielding, armor-clad one proclaimed. With his mighty weapon, Captain Foudre greeted the agents with a salute before returning to enact automaton carnage.

"Gentlemen, it's a wonderful day for some mech fighting, is it not?" the giant sword-wielding one shouted. Marshal Morales wiped the sweat off his almond-skinned brow and performed another mighty swing to slice one of the rocket men in half.

"Don't just stand there like idiots greeting us!" Cobblewood snapped, something that caused Raymond to smirk a little. Clearly any bitter retorts or snide comments from her end were not personal; she just talked that way to everybody. "Give us the updated intel!"

"The city of Ausgraben was destroyed by an unknown mechanism," Morales reported. "Our intel has deduced that it burrowed from underground and destroyed it from underneath. Before we could uncover more, though, these rocket men started attacking us, and they haven't let up."

"They keep reinforcing themselves!" Helen Brimsby said, fighting at Morales's side. "They're sending them in faster than we can dismantle them!"

"Marshal, send half of your agents down to follow the smoke trails of those rockets," Cobblewood ordered. "Half of our reinforcements will join you and split our forces evenly. Everyone else will persist in combat at this location and keep these rocket men contained."

"You lead the forces here; I'll join the agents following the smoke trail."

"Do as you will; I don't care. Agents, I need volunteers to join Marshal Morales!"

"I'll go with you, Marshal," Raymond said.

"I will as well, Marshal!" Helen said.

"I'll stay here and fight those walking rockets!" Ji said proudly. "I *know* rockets! My people invented them! I'll show those big prancing fireworks they're messing with the wrong man!"

"We don't have all blooming day!" Cobblewood roared, stomping her walker toward a rocket man and using its bulky metal hands to grasp the sides of the enemy automaton. "Just pick your side and move!"

Raymond watched in awe as Cobblewood's mech tussled with the thirty-foot rocket man, her vehicle roughly half the height and yet matching the automaton in strength. The straining gears of each opponent's mechanical arms grinded like metallic thunder, their powerful legs pounding the rubble and dirt beneath them and creating craters with each mighty step. The rocket man clutched both of the arms of Cobblewood's mech and leered at the little human in the open cockpit, its lifeless lenses analyzing the old pilot and studying for weaknesses. With an enraged yelp, Cobblewood forced her giant opponent back with a lumbering shove, causing the lanky automaton to lose balance and collapse on the rubble. Grunting, Cobblewood extended the left arm of her mech and fired an energy beam at the rocket man's core, rupturing its internal mechanisms and putting it out of commission at last.

"Holy smokes," Raymond gasped.

"You done wasting time, agents?!" Cobblewood growled, moving toward another rocket man to do it all over again. "Stop gawking and get moving!"

While half the agents remained at the ruins of Ausgraben to contain the rocket men and ensure they did not go out and hurt anyone else, the other half followed the smoke trails like bloodhounds to ensure this mysterious enemy would no longer keep reinforcing their number. The two smaller, faster mechs joined Morales in this hunting party, as their lightly built forms would get crumpled fast by the attacks of the giant rocket men. Based on the size of the rockets' arc, it appeared their point of origin sat roughly a few miles to the north.

A small dirt road led to their target, but the Teslanauts did not use it, instead hiding in the trees and shrubs at the west for cover. In order to further maintain stealth, they did not move at full speed, instead taking slow and careful steps forward. This gave the agents time to converse and strategize, and also a chance to get to know one another. Many new faces now strode together, after all.

"First time field agent, are you?" Helen asked Raymond, noticing the Brooklyn teenager's hands trembling while holding his gadgets.

"It's that obvious, is it?" Raymond muttered.

"Don't worry, everyone's nervous during their first mission. I'm assuming this is the first time you've held a disintegrator gun?"

"This is the first time I've held *any* gun."

"Blimey, an American who isn't a cowboy?" Helen gasped, her tone loud and overdramatic. "They said it couldn't exist, and yet here you are!"

"I didn't even plan to become a Teslanaut," Raymond chortled. "I just sort of got roped along into it. My father was a Teslanaut, you see."

"By any chance, was your father Francis Calvert?"

"How'd you know?"

"You've got his eyes, and his boxy chin. He was the lead Technician Officer when I first joined. He designed Marshal Morales's Peacemaker sword, in fact."

"Wait, how old were you when you joined?" Raymond demanded, not quite understanding the timeline of these allotted events. "Do the Teslanauts employ field agents at the age of twelve or something?"

"What do you mean?"

"I last heard from my father five years ago! They told me he was dead, but I've learned that apparently he was sent to a secret facility in Europe."

"And where do you think I'm from?" Helen laughed. "Where do you think you *are*? This isn't Yank country you're standing in anymore, you dolt. He was here, aiding the Teslanauts stationed in Europe."

"He was *here*?! Where is he now?"

"I don't know. He stopped contacting us a year ago."

Raymond's heart lifted at last, more than when he passed the initial Teslanaut training, more than when he learned of the existence of the Teslanauts in the first place, more than at any point in at least half a decade. At long last, confirmation that, at the very least, his father was alive for four more years beyond when the government said he wouldn't be coming home. How much more of a stretch would it be to assume that he was still alive now, somewhere on this continent, waiting to be reunited with his son after such a long and grueling absence?

Then again, just as his spirits rose, they fell once more with the news that, again, no one seemed to know where his father actually was at the current moment. And this time he was *so close*. Just a year ago, Raymond could have seen his father. But now, he had to keep fighting and ensure he could see him again.

"By the way, I was sixteen when I joined in 1920," Helen told Raymond. "That's the youngest they recruit agents, not bloody twelve."

Raymond nodded slowly, although truthfully he only half heard her. He was too busy wading in his own thoughts. With every revelation, he grew closer to finding out the truth. He had to keep going. He had to learn more.

"Target in sight," Morales said, halting the group and motioning for them to hide in a pocket of nearby trees. Just up ahead, a convoy of trucks gathered in a ditch, their trunks carrying sloped platforms and holding stacks of rockets. Men in gas masks lit the fuses and sent the rockets flying every minute, and behind them a huge stash of the rockets lay piled up and surrounded by armed guards.

"Finally, we meet our opponents at last," a Teslanaut agent said.

"Do you see any identifying marks?" Helen asked Morales as he studied the enemy group with his binoculars. "Who exactly are we dealing with?"

"I'm not seeing anything of note," the Marshal muttered. "But I would be surprised if they'd outright advertise their benefactors on their person. They want to keep it hidden from agents like us."

"So, what do we do?" Raymond asked. "Fire a disintegrator beam at that stash of rockets and blow it up to kingdom come?"

"They're not normal rockets, Calvert," Morales informed the new agent. "They're not built to explode. Their fuses just fire them."

"How do you know my name?"

"I overheard you and Brimsby talking. You should perhaps learn to converse in a quieter fashion, kid."

"I think we should mount our lightning rods onto these walkers and have one of them flank the other side," Helen suggested, motioning to the two humanoid walker mechs accompanying their troop. "We can create an electrical coil in between the walkers and give these rocket-mounted trucks a good lightning bath."

"Sounds like as decent a plan as any. I will need a few of you to cover the walker as it flanks the enemy's position, while the rest of us remain entrenched here to maintain-"

A disintegrator beam blasted a nearby tree, immediately engulfing it in flame and causing the nearby men to scatter. In the ditch, the enemy agents started marching toward the Teslanauts with their disintegrator rifles at hand, while the guards surrounding the rockets crowded closer together to protect the stash.

"They've spotted us!" Helen shouted, grabbing her own rifle and readying for combat.

"Move the walker around in a wider arc!" Morales ordered while unholstering a disintegrator gun. Against human combatants, the Peacemaker sword was far too heavy and cumbersome. "They haven't seen it yet!"

Raymond watched from behind a bush as the fire from both sides took place, with energy beams whizzing past the heads of agents out in the open when not hitting their targets outright. A chill crept and spread through his core like a spindly creature emerging from a burrow, seeing the violence and gunfire perpetuate in front of him at such a close and intimate distance, hearing the ruptured earth and the cries of those who got hit, and smelling the smoke and gunpowder from the enemies armed with more conventional weapons alongside their disintegrator guns.

Having been born in late 1904, Raymond was only nine years old when the Great War started and fourteen when it ended, making him too young to get drafted and fight. He had spent his formative years in the comfortable confines of Brooklyn, with the only brushes with death coming from the great flu pandemic a few years earlier. Now, while the firearms were more advanced and the gadgets more fantastical, this firefight between the agents was the closest he had ever been to experiencing even a fraction of the horror all those men faced in those terrible years, and the rampant, heavy fear grasping his chest from it all made him reassess his whole situation. He had come here to Europe with the Teslanauts to find his father. Now, all he wanted to do was be back home with his mother.

"C'mon, Raymond," he grunted, gripping his own disintegrator gun tight and readying himself to get out of cover and fight. "You can do this. You can fight. You're a Teslanaut now. You're a..."

At once, after futilely attempting to prepare himself for combat, he remembered something specific from the training, something they hammered home to the recruits at every opportunity: the Teslanauts were not soldiers. While combat situations would arise on many occasions in their profession, and they would have to learn how to handle them accordingly, their job was not, in fact, to fight. The Teslanauts were *agents*, first and foremost. They worked to solve conflicts, not escalate them. Maybe there was something else he could do to solve this particular conflict.

"Hey, Sparks," he said to the hover-head still attached to his backpack while awaiting deployment. "You want to feel a *real* buzz? How about you help us close the circuit?"

As the agents continued their assault against each other, Raymond detached Sparks from the holder on his backpack and held out his lightning rod to lure the little machine. Sparks eyed the lightning rod *very* interestedly, its large circular optic sensors gazing upon the rod like a dog at a treat. Then, after staring at the closest truck holding rockets and studying the distance and angle, he prepared himself like he was back at the football tryouts he had failed at in school and threw the rod like a pigskin.

The rod landed just underneath the front tire of the enemy truck, prompting Sparks to dart toward it excitedly. Rather than bring it back, though, it just circled it slowly, bathing in the light electric hum honed from the nearby rockets' internal wiring. Raymond smiled, hoping his little plan would not roast the little automaton so much that it would no longer function, but enough that it would help channel the electricity from the two walker mechs. Without Sparks and the lightning rod, the current might not precisely hit the truck if just channeled from the mechs.

The other walker finally reached the other side and waved its long and lanky mechanical arm to the others to show it reached the intended position. Seeing this, Morales held his hand up to signal to the two walkers.

"Charge the rods in three… two…" the Marshal said.

"Wait, why aren't they stopping the mechs?" Raymond asked, realizing that by this point the enemy agents surely saw the two walkers standing at opposite sides of their truck and would have figured out their plan.

"One!" Morales yelled.

Clutching the rods with their wristband-holding hands, the pilots of the walkers channeled all the electricity from their mechs and the ever-present volt-tech towers and sent a bolt of lightning in between the two of them, with Sparks and the lightning rod directing the bolt down to the trucks. The enemy agents dove for cover, as the energy shocked all around and bathed both the trucks and the stockpile of rockets behind the convoy in raw electrical power. The trucks' tires blew out, and several compartments shattered, but the rockets themselves appeared completely fine.

Better than fine, actually. Now newly replenished with power, every last rocket in their stockpile automatically started to unfold into the giant mechanical men, meaning the enemy agents now had a whole army of colossal reinforcements to aid them in their skirmish against the Teslanauts.

"I think we just made it worse!" Morales grumbled.

"Sorry, I thought it would overwhelm their cogs," Helen said meekly. "I didn't expect-"

"This is why you should've stayed back in England and become a maid or something!" another Teslanaut agent roared. "You girls should leave the serious work to those who can handle it!"

Helen's face turned deep red, and she turned her head away while the others focused their firepower on the newly activated rocket men. Raymond, still hiding behind the bush, watched Helen as she turned away from the giant automatons and covered her face with her hands. Feeling utterly useless in this fight, Raymond dove past the Teslanauts and made his way toward Helen, who didn't bother looking up at him as he approached.

"Don't listen to him," Raymond said gently. "You're fine. We've all made mistakes before."

"Yours is talking to me and not fighting!" Helen snapped.

"I'm just saying, I can relate."

"No, you can't! You can make all the mistakes you want and get away without so much as a slap on the wrist, but when I mess up just once, I may as well bugger off! I'll be fine, I just need a moment. Help the others."

"But-"

"Please, just leave me."

Raymond knew there was nothing more he could say, even though he wanted to keep helping her. But he could tell that now wasn't the time. Groaning, he grabbed his disintegrator gun and once again attempted to begin the assault, this time now aiming at the giant rocket men rather than the enemy agents. He felt he could better clear his conscience if he shot at mechanical automatons rather than human beings. And yet still, for some reason, he could not bring himself to fire the gun. His hands shook. His brow glistened. Somehow, he felt like the second he pulled the trigger, any innocence left in his life would be shattered. It was a threshold he did not feel ready to cross yet.

But he had to. He *had* to.

"C'mon, shoot," Raymond grunted, trying to urge himself to begin the fight. "Just pull the trigger. It's not hard. C'mon, c'mon!"

Alas, even if he had successfully engaged in the combat, the battle against the rocket men would be a lost cause regardless. The giants crowded together into a mobile thirty-foot-high wall, one that slowly enclosed the Teslanauts as they lumbered forward. Morales's sword, the Teslanauts' guns, the walkers' disintegrator guns; none of it cut down the rocket men fast enough. By the time the Teslanauts were completely cased in, with rocket men in front and the thick trees behind, there were still twenty enemy automatons left.

"Get behind me, agents!" Morales ordered harshly, angling the big and heavy Peacemaker sword in front of him to use it as a makeshift shield. "Stay behind and brace for incoming fire!"

Before the rocket men unleashed a firestorm upon the hunkered Teslanaut agents, the entire left portion of them toppled over, having been rammed by something from behind. With a strained grunt, Foudre swung his lance in an arc and tripped the rocket men, while Cobblewood, Ji, and the other agents beside him followed his lead, peppering the giant mechanical men with energy beams and electrical fire.

"Foudre!" Morales said, throwing his fist triumphantly at the Volt Knight Captain.

"We destroyed all zese metal giants on our end, and you stopped zem from reinforcing!" Foudre said, ramming a crumpled rocket man with his electrical shield. "So we've come to aid you here!"

"You're welcome, by the way!" Ji laughed.

"Enough chatting! Finish the job!" Cobblewood snapped.

Raymond heaved a sigh and put his disintegrator gun back into his holster, inwardly kicking himself for not participating in the fight yet feeling relieved all the same. He knew he could not rely on others to carry him in these missions in the future. He had to do it himself, and use that fortitude Cobblewood mentioned that got him in the Teslanauts in the first place.

Once the last of the rocket men had been brought down, Morales surveyed the area and checked if any of his agents needed medical attention, while Raymond and Helen stood with the others after recomposing themselves at last. Behind the piles of broken rocket men, Sparks zoomed around in wide circles, having gotten the buzz of its non-living life from the lightning bolt transmitted by the two walker mechs.

The charge seemed to hardly damage it at all, but rather further reinvigorate its power receptors. It was one happy little machine.

After Morales completed his post-battle inspection, he looked over at the ditch where the convoy of enemy trucks had gathered. At once, he noticed one of the enemy agents struggling to free his leg from under one of the trucks, having been too near the trucks when the lightning bolt busted its tires. Running forward, Morales had several other Teslanauts restrain the enemy agent while he and Foudre lifted the collapsed truck off his leg.

Once the man was free, Cobblewood stomped her mech forward and stood it threateningly in front of the enemy agent. "Talk," she demanded, pointing a disintegrator gun at the man from her mech's open cockpit. "Who are you? Who is it you're working for?"

"*Nem mondok semmit!*" the enemy agent spat.

"Excuse me?"

"He's speaking Hungarian, madam," Foudre informed Cobblewood. "He says he won't say anything."

"If you value your life, you will," Cobblewood snapped, stomping the mech's pillar-like legs to creep even closer to the restrained agent. "Who built these rocket men? Where will they strike next?"

The Hungarian agent's mouth began to foam, and he collapsed in the grip of the agents holding him. Morales held his fingers to the enemy's neck to check for a pulse, and sighed. "Poison," he grunted. "Probably mercury bichloride. Must have taken it when he saw us coming to free him."

"Empty his pockets and study the wreckage!" Cobblewood ordered. "We need to find a lead!"

"If I may, madam, my men can check ze scene," Foudre said. "You can send your new recruits back to your mobile headquarters station to train until we need zem. We'll send you a telegram when we're ready."

"I'll stay and help, along with a few of my own agents," Morales said.

"If you insist," Cobblewood sighed. "Come along, recruits."

While the Volt Knight and veteran Teslanaut agents studied the wreckage and searched the Hungarian man's body, Cobblewood escorted the new Teslanaut recruits back to the station point holding the Freckle Dump headquarters. Looking back at the wreckage, Raymond found it particularly odd that the Teslanauts, with all their fancy technology at their disposal, had never seen anything like the rocket men before. Who was this mysterious enemy that sent them after attacking Ausgraben?

Raymond had a lot of work ahead of him. He would have to learn how to perform his duties as an agent in order to face this new foe and aid the Teslanauts. He couldn't afford to mess up again.

# Chapter Ten

IN THE depths of the Eisenzentrum fortress near Berchtesgaden, Germany, a convoy of trucks that escaped the Teslanauts and Volt Knights returned with their cargo of rockets, bringing them back to the safety of the castle for repairs and storage. Now, the Oberschock Federation had kept their enemies on their toes while still maintaining enough secrecy to keep their base of operations hidden. Of course, any further probing with their new volt-tech toys added considerable risk that, eventually, their position would be discovered. That's why they had to prepare for their primary assault as quickly as possible.

Watching the trucks drive through the entry tunnel from a balcony above, Robert Stonewell and Heinrich Boltzmann studied the state of the trucks and their workers while evaluating the results of their field tests. Their postures and expressions could not be further apart; while Boltzmann's brow and mouth remained furrowed and his hands folded behind his back, Stonewell had an enormous smile, peering over the balcony to look down at the trucks like a child on a hot air balloon.

"Can you believe how well this went?" Stonewell asked. "The Panzerwurm's first field test was an absolute success!"

"Yes, but ve destroyed a whole town in a neutral country," Boltzmann grunted. "Vas such an act necessary?"

"Where else were we gonna test it? If we'd sent the Panzerwurm to Strasbourg, you'd have the Volt Knights breathing down your neck before you know it. By attacking somewhere neutral, you lessen the risk of the Electrocracy retaliating. Besides, no one cares about Switzerland."

"You really are a piece of vork," Boltzmann grumbled. "No vonder you left ze Teslanauts."

"The Teslanauts left *me*, Heinrich. I had to go somewhere that would follow my ideas rather than fight them. You know how that feels, surely. Now, what's next on the schedule?"

"Ze train is preparing to load ze last of ze cargo. It vill be ready to depart for Paris by tomorrow. Is zat enough time, or vould you rather ve rush things and leave now?"

"Is that an option?"

*"Herr Stonevell..."*

"I know you're kidding," Stonewell laughed. "Having the train leave by tomorrow should be fine. I'm assuming you'ill be providing escorts?"

"Until zey reach ze border, yes."

"You need to learn to push things a little further, Heinrich. Those trains will need protection for the whole trip."

"You must understand ze precarious position my country is in, *Robert*!" Boltzmann snapped. "Ze whole vorld is vatching us, ready to strike at any moment ve look too eager to restart ze conflict. If I send a fleet of mechs or flying machines vith ze proper arms blitzing across ze French border, it vould send our enemies into a frenzy against us! Surely even *you* get zat!"

"I'm just saying-"

"Zese are *my* men, *Amerikaner*, not yours! Know your place!"

"You do what you gotta do, I suppose," Stonewell sighed with a shrug, walking away from the balcony. "All I can do is offer suggestions."

Once Stonewell left his frustrated German companion to stew, he made his way through the hallways of the Eisenzentrum fortress, walking down numerous great stairways and decorated halls without paying attention to any of it. The architecture of the place was stunning, with the stonework perfectly rigid and keeping the structural integrity practically pristine even all these centuries after its construction. Many great leaders and warriors of the past had used this castle, keeping them safe from invaders be they Saxon, Prussian, or whomever. The blood of knights and mercenaries alike stained several of its vast chambers, telling heroic yet gruesome stories of great historical conflicts.

And Stonewell couldn't care less. He just used the Oberschock Federation for his own whims.

Finally, deep in a dungeon underneath the rest of the fortress, he reached a chamber holding a chair, a cot, and several work tables, with only a flickering bulb to dimly light the place. Blueprints and scribbled notes covered the tables, with schematics for machines and equipment big and small sketched all over. A true visionary once worked here, fulfilling the orders of the Oberschock Federation. Yet now, the chamber was empty, save for a small leather-bound notebook lying on the floor.

"You left us too soon, Calvert," Stonewell sighed, with the faintest trace of regret. "Think of all you could have accomplished for us."

***

"Wait, you're saying they had *automated* mechs at that size?!" Arthur demanded, the normally stuttering factory worker now quite assertive. "I *knew* it was possible! I've got to work harder at it, or they'll beat us!"

"Sounds like they've already beaten us in that regard," Becky said. "But I'm sure you'll win the next round."

The factory workers gathered around Raymond back at the Freckle Dump station as he told them what had happened in their brief encounter with their mysterious new enemies. He had a few minutes before training started, so he figured he'd relay his experiences to some of the only friends he had made so far. He told them about the ruins of Ausgraben, the rocket men attack, and their skirmish with the agents and automatons at the site of the convoy. The only thing he did not mention, though, was his hesitation in firing the gun. He still felt too much shame. He had to come around, though, if he wanted to succeed as a Teslanaut.

"How'd your pet hover-head do on its first mission?" Watson asked. "Did it explode in a big shower of its namesake sparks?"

"Almost, but he loved it," Raymond chortled, looking back over his shoulder lovingly at the deactivated machine attached to his backpack. "He never looked so alive after getting that big shock."

"Wow, I never thought I'd relate to a lifeless mechanism, but here I am!"

"There's beauty in the art of machinery," Ivan grunted. "Constructing a machine is like painting a picture. There's thought to every piece. They're alive in a way, but only through the symmetry of their predetermined components. Your splintered hover-head is a defilement of that beauty."

"Sheesh, did a broken down Ford Model T kill your grandmother or something?" Becky asked. "Let him have his fun. People can enjoy the same thing in different ways, you know. By the way, Raymond, I might need more time on your special disintegrator gun."

"Oh?" Raymond asked.

"Yeah, it's got an extra component compared to the standard model. I think it might somehow transmit electricity collected from your wristband. A *lot* of it.

Might be useful for overloading the circuitry of machines."

"Or make them more dangerous," Raymond muttered, remembering the incident with the rocket men.

"Hey, Becky, once you're done with that electricity-transmitting gun, do me a favor and shoot me with it a few times," Watson said, his eyes wide and somehow more manic than usual. "You know, for... testing purposes."

"Be careful, or I might actually take you up on that," Becky chuckled.

"Looks like the, uhh, rest of the team is ready for training," Arthur said, lifting his head up to look over Raymond's shoulder and at the other new recruits.

"I should join them," Raymond said, swinging his shoulders back and cranking his neck to prepare himself. "I'm starting Bolter training today, after all. Don't want to be late for my first session!"

As the Teslanaut agents and recruits made their way back into the Freckle Dump base, one of those that came in was one Raymond was not expecting. Helen Brimsby joined with the other agents, taking her army helmet off and replacing it with a ruby red cloche hat from her pack. Trying not to make his movements too obvious, Raymond nudged through the crowd of recruits toward her, the other agents standing still in front of Cobblewood and awaiting instruction.

"Hello, Mr. Calvert," Helen said flatly, still seeming rather short after the incident with the rocket men, although whether her animosity was toward Raymond or herself remained unclear.

"Please, call me Raymond," the Brooklyn teenager insisted. "What are you doing here in training? You've been with the Teslanauts for two years already."

"One can never train too much, I reckon. I figured I'd learn from today's experience and hone my skills further."

"If you think it'll help, I suppose."

"What's that supposed to mean?"

"Nothing!" Raymond said with a wince, realizing too late how badly he worded his response. "What I *meant* to say is, if you think more training is the right thing to do, then go for it. Whatever you need to do to get yourself back into the swing of things."

"That's a little better," Helen chuckled, finally easing up a little. "Sorry, I'm a little defensive by nature. It's built into me from years of being a woman in a man's field. By the way, thank you for trying to help me during that last skirmish. It's nice to know when someone has my back. I hope you find your father; he was a good man."

"I hope so, too," Raymond sighed. "Thanks."

"Trainees, listen up!" Cobblewood shouted in front of the agents, stopping all the agents' conversations at once. "We don't know when the Volt Knights will find a lead from the wreckage and tell us we can move out, so we're on a tight schedule! We need to move double-time! First up is Bolter training!"

"That's me," Raymond told Helen. "Are you joining us in Bolter training, by any chance?"

"No, I'm sticking with standard field training," Helen said. "I'm sure we'll see each other around though, Raymond!"

Motioning at the seven agents interested in becoming Bolters, Cobblewood led them to the factory while the others waited. Hanging on a rack just to the side of where the workers repaired Cobblewood's four-legged mech were seven black leather suits with brass braces on the elbows, ankles, and torsos, reminiscent of flight jackets in design and color. Yellow spheres dotted the back of the arms, legs, and neck, barely bigger than marbles, which Raymond quickly realized were smaller versions of the ones lining the top of the base that collected power for teleportation. The boots connected to the pant legs, and the rubber lining their grooves stretched in layers underneath the leather throughout the entire suit. The rubber, with its natural electrical resistance, kept the wearers safe when conducting the power from the volt-tech towers, and considering how much electricity these suits needed, it was a very necessary addition. Finally, a bronze-colored helmet with a rubber cap underneath completed the outfit, with pilot's goggles to protect the eyes from wind.

"Take these to the locker room and put them on," Cobblewood ordered. "Then meet up on the fields outside. Don't keep me waiting too long!"

Once every agent donned the Bolter suits and stepped outside the station, the sun was just beginning to set, giving enough light to allow the agents to see but not so much as to blow their cover. The group stood out in an open field far away from any roads, with only abandoned farmhouses as the surrounding architecture. Just in case, communication specialists inside the base monitored the surrounding area using the volt-tech towers and tapping into any nearby frequencies. Thus far, they seemed to be in the clear.

"It's tighter than I expected," Raymond gasped, placing his leather glove-bound hand on his stomach while his other hand adjusted his goggles. He had never been in such constrictive clothes before, other than perhaps the suit he wore at his father's funeral years back when he was assumed dead.

"You don't want any loose parts flapping behind you as you run, do you?" Ji said, jogging in place as he readied himself for a heck of a ride. "Besides, this suit makes me look *swell.*"

"All right, recruits, listen up!" Cobblewood snapped. "I'm not a participant of this division, so I'll leave to train the other recruits inside. Instead, I'll let Watson oversee your work today. He's an experienced Bolter, so he'll do a good enough job with you lot, I reckon."

"Watson?" Raymond muttered, wondering if she meant the same person he knew.

Sure enough, the wiry, manic-eyed teenager stepped forward from behind Cobblewood, now also clad in the Bolter suit, with the helmet somehow keeping his long, perpetually spiky hair contained. He shivered with anticipation, quite ready to be smothered with electricity once they activated their suits. Realizing this, Raymond's chest nearly collapsed into itself with panic. Was *that* why Watson was so insane: too many bouts in the Bolter suit? Would they all be next to join him in crazytown?

"Thank you, thank you, dear Agnes," Watson said, kissing Cobblewood's hand gently. Grunting with disgust, the old woman walked back to the Freckle Dump base while shaking her hand in the air to rid it of Watson's dirty mouth particles. Totally unconcerned by Cobblewood's reaction, Watson turned back to the seven recruits with his hands behind his back, swaying back and forth while trying desperately to contain his excitement.

"Some of you may know me as a factory worker," he began, looking directly at Raymond as he said this. "And I am, I am. But I also double as a Bolter from time to time, when working on machines isn't exciting enough, that is! In fact, I first joined the Teslanauts as a Bolter, hoping to get the bountiful amount of shocks I so craved. Unfortunately, the Bolter system is designed *not* to shock its user, but channel them through the electricity itself, which isn't quite as much fun. Still, it provides a good enough thrill!"

"'Channel its user through the electricity itself?'" an agent asked, his eyes widening underneath his goggles. "What does that mean?"

"I'm glad you asked!" Watson said. "There's a lot of technical talk behind its properties, which is admittedly beyond my capability of comprehension, so I'll let Mr. Lei explain this part. He's studied long and hard about how the Bolter suits function, so I've heard."

"Thank you, kind sir!" Ji said, smiling beside Raymond. "The Bolter suits are the culmination of decades of research by Electrocracy scientists led by Mr. Nikola Tesla on the effects of solid particles energized by electrical charges. Once we pull these switches on our wrists, the Bolter suit channels the electricity from the surrounding volt-tech towers. The suit's molecular structure is altered by this, allowing both it and its wearer to flow forward as a partial wave of energized particles rather than as a solid object, in a similar fashion to the teleportation capabilities of your mobile headquarters. While our boots can grip the ground and our gloves can grasp and manipulate objects, we essentially become blurs, able to move at velocities beyond any vehicle or projectile."

"Blah blah blah, you get the idea," Watson sighed, waving his hand around. "All right, we're going to test these suits with a little exercise. Once you turn them on, I want you to run to Paris and pick a flower from a windowsill. Bring it back to me intact and you'll complete this portion of training."

"Paris?" Raymond asked, dumbfounded by the prospect of this exercise.

"Oh, and don't get spotted by any passersby," Watson said, ignoring Raymond. "You're mostly invisible when running, but stand still and you and your somewhat ostentatious suit will be on full display. Also, and this should hopefully be obvious, but don't grab the Eiffel Tower. That thing is the world's biggest lightning rod and you don't want to know what'll happen if you touch it while in your suit. Even *I* think that'd be too much of a shock."

"Wait, you said 'run to Paris'?!" Raymond demanded. "As in, Paris, France?"

"No, I meant Paris, Texas, obviously," Watson said, chuckling. "Yes, Paris, France! I said not to touch the Eiffel Tower, didn't I? How far is Paris; three hundred miles? You should be done in a jiffy! Now, get ready to move, agents!"

"Is he being serious?!" Raymond asked Ji, his tone increasingly shrill at what Watson requested of them. "He wants us to run three hundred miles?!"

"More like six hundred," Ji said. "It's three hundred miles to get there, then another three hundred back."

"What?!"

"Activate your suits, gentlemen!" Watson ordered, holding up his pointer finger in a declarative fashion.

One by one, the agents flicked the switch on their suit's left wrist, with each motion sending a crackling of electrical power through the air around them. Knowing it was too late to question Watson further, Raymond closed his eyes and flicked his suit's own switch, bracing himself for whatever would come.

In an instant, he felt a minor tingle through his body, like a tiny firecracker flowing through his veins, startling at first but oddly pleasing in the end. A low hum buzzed in his ears, with the occasional spark emanating from any of his suit's spherical receptors. While he stood still, parts of his body flowed in place like tiny cyclones of dust particles, yet he felt no pain. On the contrary, he felt like he was floating in a warm bath, but with a bit of effervescence to it, like a tub of carbonated soda rather than water.

"Whoa!" Raymond shouted as he felt the sensations of the suit's activation, but he could barely hear himself. His voice was distorted by the suit's energized particles. He started slowly babbling nonsense to try and adjust his hearing to the change, and after a few seconds, he finally managed to pick noises out clearly, with the caveat of everyone now staring at him like he was an idiot.

"Oh, I can feel the shocking sensations from here," Watson sighed, breathing it in and waving his hand to his face like a chef smelling a fine dish. "Mmm, perfection. Now, head to Paris and get me some flowers. I've got a hot date tonight and I want a bouquet for her. Now, *scram*!"

At Watson's command, the agents disappeared one by one in a flurry of flashes to run toward Paris, leaving only a line of sparks floating in the air behind them for a few seconds. Readying himself, Raymond pointed toward where Paris stood three hundred miles away, and booked it.

Immediately, he nearly tripped from the shock of just how far he went. In three steps he stood near a grove of grapes in a far-off vineyard, something he didn't even know was here in this direction. Looking back, he could barely see the top of the Freckle Dump station out in the field beside Zürich. It must have been at least a mile away. That meant his stride was over a thousand feet. And he ran this distance in *two seconds*.

"Oh, wow!" Raymond said, laughing giddily. "Holy--" he began, proceeding to use some colorful language out of sheer delight. He loved this. He couldn't wait to run further.

And so he did.

Moving across the land like a bolt of grounded lightning, Raymond scorched across the Switzerland fields, running across the French border in less than two minutes. Following a westward road leading through the country, he zapped through Montbéliard, Vesoul, Langres, Chaumont, Troyes, and many other French towns over the next seven minutes, only occasionally pausing to take a quick break and collect himself. His rushing still took exertion, even at such a blistering speed, and like before he had to stop after a few minutes of constant running; the difference being a few minutes of running in the Bolter suit took him over a hundred *miles* rather than a couple thousand feet.

Everything around him barely registered in his brain as he moved. He could vault over rivers, race through trees, and pass town traffic without concern, as the electricity within the suit vibrated his molecules to the point that they could flow through matter rather than collide with it. It was only to a point, though; he couldn't run through a large building or a mountain, but still he marveled at just how easy it was to cavort across hills, meadows, streets, and towns.

The wonders of volt-tech continued to absolutely astound Raymond. The things Tesla and inventors of his ilk could do with electricity threw his whole perspective of the world into a spin. It seemed that truly, anything was possible. No matter how wild the ideas of the grand Electrocracy think tank, they could get it built, and get it done. Even after he found his father, he had no idea if he could ever go back to the mediocrity of the world he had known. The thrill of this hidden world was too consuming, too addicting, and too adventurous.

Eventually, he reached the edge of the Seine River in Paris, having run the three hundred miles in roughly ten minutes. Immediately, he hid under a bridge, knowing that he would be seen and, in his weird suit covered in yellow spherical receptors that made his body vibrate unnaturally, he wouldn't exactly be inconspicuous. Hiding under the stone arch of the bridge, Raymond looked around for a garden or windowsill, so he could get a flower and take it back. Finally, he found one beside a cluster of shops on a nearby footpath, but even with the setting sun and the growing darkness, the foot traffic surrounding it was considerable. There was no way for Raymond to get there without people spotting him and reporting a strange ghostly man clad in a leather and rubber suit lined with golden ping pong balls to the authorities.

"Not a garden, a *windowsill,*" he muttered, remembering Watson's instructions. Looking up at the nearby buildings, he saw several apartments with windowsills, and indeed, they had boxes of flowers. Raymond just about ran up to get one, only to remember that he wore a Bolter suit, and even the tiniest step forward would send him crashing through buildings hundreds of feet ahead.

How could he ever exert such precise control in this thing? Presumably, this was part of the training. He had to figure it out.

"Maybe I can run up the side of a building?" he asked himself. Unfortunately, none of the buildings were tall enough for him to test it and see due to how fast he moved, except for one: the Eiffel Tower. And yet, Watson explicitly warned them *not* to touch it while in the suit; the sheer amount of electrical power the suit discharged would prove fatal to whoever was in it if they contacted such an enormous metal rod.

Raymond knew that wiry, manic factory worker spoke the truth, no matter how tempting a prospect it would be. It was truly the forbidden fruit of building-running test subjects.

"Get it out of your head, get it out of your head," Raymond grumbled, knowing there had to be another answer.

After a few more seconds thinking about it, he remembered one other building potentially tall enough for the test to work, one slightly safer to the touch. Turning a corner, Raymond looked at the great cathedral of Notre Dame, specifically the stone bell towers on the western side. Knowing he had to be precise, Raymond exhaled deeply, and ran toward Notre Dame.

The next second, he was high in the air, having run up the walls of the cathedral well past the bell towers and raced well above them. Screaming, Raymond looked at the Parisian street complex by the bell towers roughly three hundred feet down and closing fast. He tried to run again, but as his feet did not touch the ground, all he did was uncontrollably somersault in midair. By this point, multiple people saw him, and pointed at him while gasping in horror.

Hoping to all goodness this would work, Raymond held his arms out and grasped the sides of the Notre Dame bell tower, his leather gloves digging into the stonework and stopping his fall. Finally able to get a grip at last, Raymond ran down Notre Dame and past the people who saw him, starting to panic at how easily he could lose control and how many people had already spotted him.

After bounding another few steps, he reached a series of apartment complexes on the other side of town, with window boxes full of flowers taunting him to try his maneuver again. His eyes darting around in a series of sharp and frantic turns to check for any witnesses, Raymond finally worked up the courage to run up again, bolting forward just a couple of steps.

He found himself in the air once again, but this time not quite as high, only about a hundred feet. Before he panicked like last time, Raymond noticed that he would fall right past one of the windowsills with a fresh batch of red and purple petunias at arm's reach. An idea springing forth in his mind, he grabbed one of the flowers as he fell and angled his feet to the building's wall. The second his boots made contact with it, he bolted out of Paris with the flower at hand.

"That was close!" Raymond shrieked as he made his way out of the city, his body chock full of adrenaline and chills. "That was *far* too close!"

Once he stood in an open field outside of Paris, he stopped and made sure his prize remained intact. Sure enough, the flower still sat in Raymond's hand, minus a few leaves. Thankfully the Bolter suit came with pants pockets, so he placed it in his left pocket, blossoms down to keep it safe. With his objective complete, Raymond turned southeast and ran back to the station point near Zürich, Switzerland.

It took another ten minutes for him to return, give or take a few seconds of resting and checking the flowers for damage every so often, and when he did, the other trainees had already returned, passing their own flowers to Watson while turning off their suits.

"Thank you, thank you!" Watson said happily, making quite the bouquet out of everyone's gifts. "My date will simply love this! You all completed your mission, so you all passed, I suppose."

"Raymond got spotted!" Ji said, his eyebrows angled furiously downward while pointing at Raymond with a shaking finger. "A whole crowd of people saw him fall off Notre Dame!"

"Wait, what?"

"It wasn't a crowd!" Raymond protested, rather baffled that Ji or any of the other recruits saw him. "It was like six people! I got the flower, so who cares?"

"Who *cares*?" Ji repeated, taken aback at such a notion of apathy. "Every time someone catches us, the Cleanup Squad has to go locate the witnesses and everyone they talked with to alter their memories! Even just finding the right people can take them days, and who knows how many others the witnesses told about your incident in that time?"

"The Cleanup Squad can handle it," Watson insisted, holding his hand out in an effort to calm Ji. "Trust me, they had quite the fun time watching over me and my, well, experiments when I first started here. Many witnesses to the explosive results of those events, let me tell you! Still though, getting spotted *is* an automatic failure, so unfortunately Raymond, you don't actually pass. You're gonna have to try the training again tomorrow."

"Again?!" Raymond asked.

"Yes, I know. I'm quite distraught myself. In fact, I think I'm gonna go to the mech forge in the factory and grab a couple of wires to cheer myself up! Would you like to join me?"

"Uh, no thanks."

# Chapter Eleven

BY THE time the recruits' Bolter training session had ended, it was eight thirty in the evening, and the sun had just dipped below the horizon. The agents hung their suits back on the storage racks at the factory as Cobblewood called the training good for the day. Raymond knew he should keep from kicking himself too much for failing the test, as it was his first ride as a Bolter after only learning of the concept yesterday. But still, he was the only one in the group to have failed. Everyone else seemed to have got the hang of it straight away.

"You're not here for this," Raymond tried to tell himself after dropping off his Bolter suit. "It's perfectly fine if you don't get this right away. You're here to find your father. That's all."

Still, the words from Ji's sister Ying from earlier rang in his ears: "What do *you* want to do?" Regrettably, he still had no answer. He knew that would have to change soon, though, if he wanted to do some good with the Teslanauts. He could not coast on a vague promise forever. There was still a chance this would all lead to a dead end, no matter how badly he yearned for answers.

Since it was Friday night, Cobblewood decided that while waiting for the report from Morales and Foudre the agents could go into town and enjoy the local venues, with the condition of posing as American tourists. Still though, as Switzerland was not one of the countries participating in prohibition, the Cleanup Squad was kept on standby just in case anyone drunkenly revealed the Teslanauts' existence. They could never be too careful.

Raymond joined Becky, Ivan, and Arthur on a tram leading into Zürich, while the other agents would join them later. In contrast to the lightning-fast zipping and zooming of the Bolter suits or the transcontinental teleportation of the Freckle Dump mobile headquarters, the simple electric tram moved at a far more leisurely pace, the dark green carriage gently moseying along the track at the edge of the street. At first, Raymond felt restless and rather bored, wanting volt-tech to take over and strap a rocket or a teleportation rig on this thing to make the ride a real thrill. But after a couple of minutes of feeling the brisk air, relishing the sights of a country he had never been to before, and enjoying the company of some friendly fellows, he realized that this slow, relaxing pace was exactly what he needed. Finally, a moment of peace after all the excitement of the Teslanaut job.

Raymond sat next to Ivan, Arthur, and Becky in the carriage, the latter of whom surprised Raymond. In America, Becky would have been forced to sit in the back carriage due to her black skin, but here she was free to sit with the rest of the white kids. Raymond was glad she was up here, as he had gotten along with Becky perhaps the best of any of the factory workers, and he couldn't help but wonder why his country viewed things differently. Even Tesla, their inspiring leader and founder, was an avid eugenicist, one of his far less admirable qualities. It was honestly a huge step forward that Becky was allowed to work alongside the other Teslanauts at all, but much more could still have been done. Not all progress should be merely technological.

At least the carriage was empty other than the driver, meaning the group could talk about their secret lives as long as they kept their voices low. "You didn't... bring Sparks with you, right?" Arthur said.

"Nah, he's resting with the other hover-heads back at the base," Raymond replied. "He may be my new pet, but he's still proof of the volt-tech world."

"You know, I've been thinking about your strange relationship with that device, and I've learned to approach it in a more interesting manner," Ivan said, the giant teenager's weary eyes revealing he had given up trying to stop Raymond from dabbling with a half-broken machine. "It's a device like any other, responding to actions in preset ways, but you're projecting a part of your own consciousness into those ways, giving it a personality in your eyes when none exists. It's fascinating to analyze this from a psychological perspective."

"Sparks absolutely has a personality," Raymond insisted. "Have you seen how happy he looks when exposed to an electral current? He might as well be like Watson in that regard."

"Speaking of which, uhhh, where is that fellow?" Arthur asked.

"He's got a 'date' tonight, he said. He made us all bring flowers for him during Bolter training."

"That's a bunch of hokum!" Becky shouted, perhaps a bit too loudly, but the driver didn't seem to notice. "That boy has one true love, and that is his last jolt! He's pulling your leg for sure."

"Still, he's not here, so maybe, you know, Raymond's right," Arthur said, pushing his glasses up his nose. "Maybe we'll run into him once we reach town with his, umm, date."

"I bet she's just as screwy as he is," Raymond said. "The two can feed off of each other's manic energy."

"Like vibrating atoms!" Arthur shouted joyfully, as if finally understanding the concept of love for the first time.

"I'm assuming she's actually quite mellow," Ivan said. "The type that remains calm and collected even during the fiercest storm. That way the two will balance each other out."

"Like magnetic poles!" Arthur shouted, equally as joyfully.

"Y'all are full of horsefeathers!" Becky yelled.

After a couple more minutes, the tram reached the street of Bahnhofstrasse, Zürich's downtown and the pinnacle of its high-end lifestyle. A luminous collective of colors dotted the surrounding architecture, from the harsh yellows and whites of the streetlamps, to the blues, reds, and greens of the buildings' arbors and windowsills. Numerous expensive shops and avenues lined the surrounding buildings, including luxury fashion, watchmakers, jewelry stores; the works. Any of them would be lucky to afford any item sold at these venues, despite working for a secret government agency of advanced technological prowess, but just perusing the stores would be enough fun to last them the whole year.

Even this late in the evening, the flurry of activity along the street complex astounded the group. Trams drove to and fro, carrying passengers of all ilks across the city. People crowded the footpaths and the venues, while parties gathered in the cafes and pubs. As Raymond and the others paid for their ride and left the tram, they simply stood in awe on the sidewalk and basked in all the commotion. The lights, the colors, the activity, the exotic location; it lifted their spirits and, temporarily, made them forget the dangerous mission at hand. The war was over. It was the roaring twenties. It was a time of plenty, a time of prosperity, and a time of entertainment. After the hardship and brutality of the last decade, it was times like these that those brave soldiers had fought to protect. It was times like these that made life worth living.

"Quite a ritzy place," Raymond said, whistling appreciatively.

"Ivan and Arthur are getting stuff for us from the chocolate shop," Becky told him, as she pointed to the others walking toward the Confiserie Sprüngli cafe. "You going with them?"

"I'll join them in a moment," Raymond said, looking ahead at the other venues. He wanted to explore some more. "Tell them to save something for me, though!"

"No promises!" Becky laughed.

Raymond ambled along the sidewalk, soaking in all the sights of the people, the luxurious items, and the energetic atmosphere. He had never seen anything like this place. Brooklyn was a great town, with people from all walks of life given opportunities to make a living, but it was also grimy, unfriendly, and full of rats and smoke. Zürich, meanwhile, with all its colors, music, and commotion, looked positively inviting. This might have been a rich folks' corner, but anyone could take a peek, and appreciate the sights and luxuries of what the highest culture had to offer. The Teslanauts may have had the technology, but cities like this had the magic.

After a further stretch of his legs across the street, Raymond went into a watchmaker store, curious to look at the tiny ticking trinkets from his new perspective. After all the advanced volt-tech he had learned of during his adventure with the Teslanauts, brief though it had been so far, surely the conventional mechanical craftwork of the common timepiece would seem rather humble in comparison. Yet, after browsing the shop's collection, with some helpful explanations from its salesmen, he realized the fact that these devices did not zap a target or transform into a miniaturized mech did not take away from the artisanship of its tiny clockwork cogs and its metallic casings. It was a different kind of art. A practical kind. One that, even with future advances, would always be necessary.

"Ze wristvatch has been a godsend for many fine professions, such as sailors, tram drivers, and factory vorkers," a Swiss salesman told Raymond as the young American eyed a particular silver piece. "However, zeir true potential vas realized during ze var. Have you heard of ze creeping barrage?"

"That's a series of artillery strikes, if I recall?" Raymond said. He remembered reading about them in a book once, as part of his intense self-studies trying to figure out what happened to his father.

"Not just zat; a series of strikes designed to follow moving infantry and keep zeir pace. Zey required precise timetables so the artillery gunners would synchronize with zeir targets, and so zey vould use ze wristvatch to perfectly align vith zose timetables. Zis is just one of ze many practical uses of zis humble device, and because of it, every man vorth zeir own has a vatch like zis."

Raymond thanked the salesman for the information and started heading out of the shop, ready to join his friends at the chocolate cafe. There was no way in heck he could afford anything sold in this store, but browsing its selection was an honor in and of itself. If he could, though, he'd happily get something here for his mother. She would love a timepiece like this.

Before he reached the door, however, Raymond ran into an unexpected yet familiar face. He saw Helen at a shelf by the entrance, eyeing a pocket watch in an almost reverent manner. Her eyes a hint moist, she took the watch and studied it, staring at it and seemingly taken back to a long forgotten time. After a few more seconds of mysterious examination, she put the watch back on its display rack.

"I'll never forget you," she said softly.

Raymond sighed watching Helen, recognizing that look and that tone right away. However, he might have stared at her a bit too long, for Helen jolted in place once she noticed Raymond with her peripherals.

"Blimey," she sputtered, rushing away.

"Wait, what's with the-"

"Never you mind!" Helen shouted, her face bright red as she scurried out of the store.

"Helen!" Raymond shouted, rushing out to follow her. But by the time he stood outside, she was already gone. He looked around frantically, but the crowds had already hidden any trace of her.

Shoulders slumping, he stood alone in the crowded street, unaware of what Helen was doing or why she felt so emotional over that watch. He knew the look in her eyes, though. It was the same look he had when first finding out that his father would not come home. Who had *she* lost? What did the watch have to do with it? He wished he could help her, but clearly she would rather deal with it alone. And he supposed until she was ready, he had to respect that.

"You got rejected too, huh?"

Raymond turned around to the familiar voice, having last heard it just a couple of hours ago. Watson stood behind him with a more melancholy look than usual, his usually bright eyes now darkened glumly. Even his hair, pointy and wild as it was, seemed to droop with his sad state. The bouquet was nowhere to be seen, but several flower petals stuck to his vest seemed to indicate it was rudely shoved back at him. Or a shock blasted it back. Or an explosion in the factory.

Or nothing whatsoever. It was hard to tell with all of Watson's quirks.

"Oh no, not your date!" Raymond said, his tone slightly facetious. He honestly still had no clue whether Watson's date actually existed. He didn't even know Watson's last name--or his first name, depending on which was which--so he didn't feel like he could fully trust him yet. He seemed like the kind of fellow who would lie about hanging with some attractive gal.

"It's okay, we can be sad together," Watson sighed. He took one of the blossoms off his vest, a pathetic pink and purple piece, and handed it to Raymond. "Here. This is for you, darling."

"Gee, thanks," Raymond said, placing the flower in his breast pocket with the full intention of forgetting about it later. "But I think you're a bit mistaken. I'm not sad. I didn't get rejected."

"What about what that British doll just did?"

"She and I aren't anything."

"But you could be! Look at the tension between you two! One of you's stuck on the other, I can tell. Don't you give up as I have, dear friend of mine! There's still hope for you yet! You're so young, Raymond. You have your whole life ahead of you!"

"You're *my* age, aren't you?"

"It is better to have loved and lost than to have never loved at all! Shakespeare said that."

"I'm pretty sure that was Tennyson."

"You know, you're a good Bolter," Watson said, placing his arm around Raymond with his face far too close for comfort. "One of the best, I reckon. So what if you got spotted by some sightseer in Paris? You'll get it right soon enough, don't you worry."

"How much have you been drinking?" Raymond asked, gently removing Watson's arm off his shoulders and pushing him away.

"I licked an outlet a few minutes ago. But still, I'm being sincere, Raymond! You've got what it takes! But if I may give one teensy little tip-a-rooney before you go Bolting again? To fully maintain control, you can't keep the suit's powers activated the whole time. You can switch it on and off as many times as you like. That way you can run, turn it off, do something requiring more control, turn it on, repeat. Do it enough and you'll have complete command over your movement!"

"Why are you telling me this? I mean, I appreciate it, but-"

"Because I *believe* in you! I don't want to see you fail as I did! Reach for the stars! Find your destiny!"

"All right, that's enough licked outlets for one night," Raymond said, taking Watson by the arm and leading him off the street. "You can join us at the chocolate shop if you want, otherwise go to bed."

"I don't need sleep!" Watson snapped. "Sleep is for the unilluminated! Who needs sleep to recharge when you have electricity?!"

As Raymond took Watson with him back to the others, he thought about what the manic young man said. Not just the tip about using the Bolter suit, but about Raymond's destiny. It all came back to what Ying asked him again. What did *Raymond* want to do? What *was* his destiny? Fate had brought him to the Teslanauts. Finding his father might have been the catalyst, but for better or worse, he was here, hopefully to stay. He had to figure out what to do once this matter was resolved.

For the moment, though, he went to enjoy the night with his friends, trying not to worry about it too much. In the back of his mind, however, he hoped Helen was somewhere else having a good time on her own. If she had lost someone too, then he knew how she felt. The emptiness could be consuming.

But that didn't mean it couldn't be refilled.

# Chapter Twelve

"I'VE GOT something!" Marshal Morales said at last, having dug through the wires and compartments of the felled rocket men well into the night.

"About time something turned up in zis search!" Captain du Foudre said, groaning from the intense labor.

Ever since Cobblewood and the Teslanaut trainees left, the two leaders of their respective units had been devouring all the evidence they could at the site of their skirmish with the rocket men and enemy agents. Looting the Hungarian agent's person found no leads, while the trucks carrying the rockets suffered too much damage from the battle to get a reading on their make or model. It was only after slicing through the rocket men's metal corpses that they came across something of note, and they had to be *very* thorough.

"What is it you've found?" Foudre asked, his armored boots clanking on the ground with each step as he shuffled to Morales.

"An inscription on a compartment in the rocket's thrusters," Morales said, holding the block-shaped compartment after pulling it out of the rocket. "It's rusted and charred, but I can make out the manufacturer: 'Stonewell Arms and Ammunitions.'"

"How do we know zat isn't simply ze original rocket's manufacturer before zese agents modified it?"

"I remember the name Stonewell. We need to send a telegram to Tesla back in New York. He could fill us in on the details."

The Teslanaut agents still present with the leaders set up their mobile comm stations once again, connecting them to the volt-tech network through the surrounding towers. Once they sent a message to New York about what they found in the inscription, it was a matter of waiting for a response. It would take a couple of hours at least; even with the volt-tech power network, there was a serious lag in covering so much distance, as the necessary voltage to transmit across the volt-tech towers could only go so far with coal as the primary global power source. The energy demands of volt-tech often vastly exceeded the supply, and so working with these limitations were the communications and resource managers' specialty. Not every Teslanaut job involved fieldwork with exciting and exotic gadgets.

"How do you know zat name, Marshal?" Foudre asked at one point while they waited, sitting down by the truck wreckage to take a breather from all the work. In such a heavy suit of armor, any notable exertion could prove arduous. "Have you fought against his weapons before?"

"No, I've fought *with* them, in fact. Stonewell's an American manufacturer, having a sizable share of the western front's ammunition market during the war, both regular and volt-tech. He supplied many guns to the Teslanauts and Proton Rangers back in the day, which were then repurposed. I'm just wondering how these German and Hungarian agents got their hands on them."

"You best be careful with zose who supply ze weapons in war. Zey don't care where zey get zeir money from, only zat zey get it at all."

"We're receiving a response from the boss!" a Teslanaut agent said from his makeshift comms station roughly an hour later, as a paper came from their teleprinter. It took several minutes for the message to fully print; clearly Tesla had a lot to say. Once the telegram finally finished, Morales took the paper and read it over, while Foudre looked over his shoulder and read it from behind.

# Teslanauts

SENDER: Nikola Tesla, Head Commander of Teslanauts

RECIPIENT: Mobile Comms Stations Unit 791-02

SENT: April 28, 1922, 20:24 New York HQ Time

RECEIVED: April 29, 1922, 3:37 Mobile Comms Station Time

During the war, Walter Stonewell was the owner of Stonewell Arms and Ammunitions, and was one of the Teslanauts' main suppliers. I always hated working with him, as he clearly valued profits over progress and human lives, but his products proved valuable after we repurposed them and turned them into volt-tech gadgets. He died of the Spanish flu in 1919, leaving the company in the hands of his son, Robert.

Unlike Walter, who remained mostly hands-off when dealing with us, Robert grew very interested in what the Teslanauts and Proton Rangers did with the weapons from his father's company. He learned much about volt-tech and marveled at its potential. I stood back as he observed us, not seeing the harm in letting him study our technology, but once he suggested that we turn the Teslanauts from a division of covert agents into a military sector, I severed ties with him, and told him the Teslanauts would no longer buy from Stonewell Arms and Ammunitions. I refuse to turn this organization into another platoon of soldiers for the government.

Since then, I haven't heard from him, but I received information a couple of months ago that he's built new factories all across Europe and purchased shares in many others to gain partial ownership. The closest Stonewell factory to you is in Vienna, and the presence of a new one there is something many have found highly suspect so soon after the war and the collapse of the Austro-Hungarian Empire. If these enemy agents are indeed supplied by Stonewell, we must work diligently to ensure they don't try to restart the conflict.

I will perform further electro-scans in the surrounding countries and see if we can find these hostile forces' central hub of operations. In the meantime, I would recommend sending agents to Vienna to check the new Stonewell factory.

"We will prepare ze Interceptors for travel," Foudre declared, the Captain already heading off. "Let us depart for Vienna at once."

"You don't have to join us," Morales assured the French captain. "Stonewell never supplied the Volt Knights. This is Teslanaut business."

"If zey're planning to restart ze war, zis is very much our business as well. You have no idea of ze horrors my country faced during ze conflict. You may have heard of zem, but you never experienced zem as we had. We will not let it happen again; not to anyone, anywhere. Zat is ze solemn oath every Volt Knight has sworn. We will happily join you in your quest."

Morales nodded, grateful for the Volt Knights' support. He also knew Foudre's strategy to investigate the new factory right away would prove quite helpful. The sun was still a few hours away from rising, meaning they had plenty of natural cover in the darkness. They needed to move now.

The Volt Knights' Interceptors transported the team of agents to Austria as the night neared its end, with the black sky gradually turning dark blue as the hours trudged on. By the time the Interceptors reached Vienna, the faintest traces of orange began to peek from the east. They had managed to keep their cover in time.

Even after the collapse of the Austro-Hungarian Empire, Vienna remained a prime example of high culture. With its beautiful palaces, theaters, opera houses, and churches, it held an architectural significance few cities in the world could match, and had been home to numerous important people that would later become massive historical figures. None of the agents could know of any of this, of course, or what any of it could mean. Once they exited the Volt Knights' Interceptors, Foudre had them transform into trucks once again, and they drove down the mostly empty streets searching for the Stonewell factory. By the time they found it, after asking around and combing the city's various districts, the sun had started to rise, and workers beginning their shifts made their way inside.

Covering several acres of land, the factory's industrial presence made it akin to an iron tumor. Great smoke towers rose from all sides, protruding a halo of ebony clouds and increasing the apparent height of the building to a domineering degree. While situated near a grove of trees, their leaves looked withered from the pollution, with the patches of nearby grass brown and prickly. Despite its clashing nature with the splendorous city, the factory clearly employed a large workforce judging by the vast crowds moving inside, which could only be good for the city's economy. But one could only imagine what machinations lurked within its stone and steel walls.

"How do we get inside?" a Teslanaut agent wondered.

"We break in through the front gate, of course!" Foudre shouted, throwing out his fist. "Zis is no time to be polite! We must strike first before zey get ze chance to fight back!"

"Let's not be ostentatious, Captain," Morales said, hoping to keep the Volt Knight's overzealous disposition to a minimum. This was a covert mission, after all. "We'll go through the back door and pick the lock, then gather as much intel as we can. We'll need to be quick, though, so they won't see us."

"If you insist, Marshal," Foudre sighed.

The agents parked the Interceptors on the side of the factory and slowly crept around the line of workers until they reached the back end of the building. A lonely black door was situated in the rear corner, which the agents gingerly made their way toward after thoroughly checking for any enemy eyes.

"This should be easy," Morales muttered, using his Teslanaut wristband and a screwdriver-sized rod to give the doorknob a slight jolt. The electricity overloaded the locking mechanism, causing it to give way and allowing the agents to step inside. A handy device for breaking into more mundane facilities, but most volt-tech operations had better defenses against such an attack.

Such was apparent in the next door, which they found after walking through a tight concrete corridor and making a few random turns. It looked more akin to the door of a bank vault, and the subdued yet constant humming from within confirmed its electric nature. Clearly, this thing was volt-tech, which meant that whatever lay inside would prove useful in learning about their enemy.

"Now, this one could be more of a problem," Morales said, staring at the vault door with weary eyes. "Do you have a plan, Captain?"

"Yes, and it's not one you would like to hear," Foudre warned his Teslanaut companion.

"Does it involve breaking it down with your agents' weapons?"

"And my lance, of course."

"You are aware that they'll easily hear us if we make such a racket?"

"Would you rather turn around without knowing ze details of zis place? We need to figure out what zey're doing here in zis factory."

"I don't suppose anyone has an alternative?" Morales asked, glancing around at their group of Teslanaut and Volt Knight agents crowding the hallway. "I'm open to suggestions."

"Don't look at us," a Teslanaut said with a shrug. "We're just following your lead here."

Morales groaned and looked back at the door, its metal bars and electric hum taunting the agents who had come so far just to get abruptly halted here. Foudre was right; they did need to learn what exactly Stonewell used this new factory for, and if he used volt-tech, he could end up being a very dangerous enemy. Surely, though, this door would prove difficult to breach, and by the time they would make any progress, the factory's entire security team would be on their heads.

However, it seemed they had little choice.

"Foudre, order your shieldbearers to guard the halls," Morales said. "Make sure no one's getting in."

"*Oui*," Foudre replied, quickly barking the commands to his agents in French. At once, they activated their electrified shields and blocked the hallway, meaning anyone wanting to stop them would be met with fierce, electrical resistance.

"Everyone else, ready your weapons," Morales said. "We're breaking through this door in three... two..."

Before they started loudly pounding the door and attracting the attention of every living soul in the factory, it slowly opened from the other side, prompting Morales and the others to lower their weapons and freeze in place. Once it was fully ajar, a lone Austrian worker clad in overalls and a flat cap made his way out, unaware at first of who stood before him. Once he turned his head, his eyes immediately widened at the crowd of intruders.

"Uh..." Morales mumbled, not sure what to do now.

"*Guten tag*!" Foudre said jovially, drawing his lance and raising it high. At once, he bonked the poor worker on the head, knocking him out cold and keeping him from blowing their cover. Morales then dragged the worker into the hallway and leaned him against the wall, while the shieldbearers turned around to follow the others now that their little blockade was no longer needed.

"That was close," Morales said, still tense.

"Bah, we handled it just fine," Foudre chuckled. "He'll assume he imagined all zis once we've departed. Now, lead ze way."

Morales nodded and walked ahead of the agents into the newly open vault door. A set of metal stairs lay just within, heading downward and leading into pure darkness. Once everyone stood inside, Morales closed the door behind them and cut off their only source of light. Clearly, that one worker was the only one inside this room. The group slowly crept down the stairs, clinging onto the safety rails as they still couldn't see a thing, before their boots touched a concrete floor at the bottom. Feeling around the wall, Morales finally managed to find a switch, and flicked it on right away.

Gradually, the lights turned on in the room, revealing it to be a chamber far bigger than any of them had predicted; bigger than a sports field; bigger than the New York Teslanaut HQ; bigger than even an aircraft hangar, with light after light illuminating every section of its massive perimeter.

And every square inch of it was blanketed in volt-tech weapons.

"Good God," Morales gasped.

"By ze powers zat be," Foudre whispered with horror.

It was an arsenal of heavy-duty arms unlike anything the group had ever seen, like the bountiful hoard of a trigger-happy dragon. Thousands of disintegrator guns filled hundreds of rows of shelves, from simple pistols to bulky recoilless rifles, all in every make and model a gun could be. Armies of dormant automatons sat in sorted rows, including hundreds of the tripod machines Morales and Helen had first encountered in Strasbourg, and countless stockpiles of the specialized dual-mode rockets. As well as the familiar, many other types of weapons and vehicles none of them had yet encountered sat in storage here as well, including electric triplanes, spider-legged tanks, humanoid mechs the size of houses; all matters of metal, fire, and lightning for warmongers to make whatever explosive masterpieces they could concoct.

The sheer number of deadly devices in their enemy's hands brought a great deal of concern, but just as unnerving was the notion of what their enemy planned to *do* with such an arsenal. The war was over. Even on the volt-tech front, most of the fighting came from dealing with smaller groups of rogues and insurgents, certainly nothing that warranted this scale of firepower. What was Stonewell doing?

"We've got to warn headquarters," Morales said. "Clearly, our enemy is gearing up for a big fight."

"And if zey've got foundries like zis all over ze continent… I'd hate to see what zey're planning," Foudre added.

"Someone's coming!" a Volt Knight announced sharply, rushing down the stairs. "Quick, under ze staircase!"

The agents wasted no time following that command, scurrying down the catwalk staircase and hiding underneath its metal supports. Once everyone remained still, they could hear a series of footsteps slowly ambling down above them, from a group of workers making their way into the room. They spoke in hushed German, which none of the Teslanauts and hardly any of the Volt Knights understood, but Foudre, being mostly fluent, listened with an attentive ear.

"Zey're saying zey need to finish zeir shipments for the Oberschock Federation to a trainyard in

Berchtesgaden," the Volt Knight Captain quietly relayed to the team. "Zey only have a few more loads of cargo to go before zey can depart for Paris with ze Blitzsturm."

"Blitzsturm?" a Teslanaut agent demanded.

"Oberschock?" another said.

"Berchtesgaden?" a Volt Knight asked, a small smile creeping across his face. "I hear it's lovely zere zis time of year!"

"We need to get moving, now," Morales said, ignoring the last agent's somewhat misplaced optimism. "Apparently this Oberschock Federation is behind the attacks at Ausgraben and Strasbourg. Whatever this 'Blitzsturm' thing of theirs is, it can't be good. As soon as we have an opening, let's-"

"Zhere zey are!" a voice from outside their group shouted. "Zey're ze ones who knocked him out!"

Realizing their cover was blown, the group of agents hurried out from under the staircase and faced the factory workers who had spotted them. The Volt Knight shieldbearers formed ranks and made a wall of electrified metal between the agents and the workers. Clearly outclassed, the workers scattered, but in their place a few of the automatons had begun to take defensive action as the factory's security systems activated.

Three of the tripod machines spurred to life, each controlled by enemy agents remotely, as nine spindly mechanical legs marched toward the intruders. Moving forward, the Volt Knight shieldbearers cleared a path for the others and stood in front of the staircase as the agents clambered up it. Disintegrator beams blasted from both sides, as some from the tripods' end hit the staircase's supports, compromising its integrity and tilting the entire flight of stairs downward.

"Whoa!" a Teslanaut agent gasped as everyone fell forward.

The railings of the stairs kept the agents from falling over, but with a couple more blasts from the tripods they would give way as well. Grunting and holding on to the railings for dear life, Morales and Foudre crawled to the door, while helping other agents make their way up.

"Ze shieldbearers! Zey won't make it!" a Volt Knight cried.

Indeed, the shield-wielding Knights still stood at the base of the stairs blocking any further machines from attacking the others. As Morales worked hard to open the vault door from this end, Foudre did the unthinkable and went back down the increasingly tilted staircase, shoving other agents behind him and joining his fellow agents.

"What are you doing, Captain?!" Morales demanded.

"I'll hold ze line!" Foudre declared, pushing the shieldbearers up the stairs. "Get your men out of here!"

"Foudre!"

"I won't leave until every one of my agents is out safely!"

More automatons and machines started coming to life, but this time they were accompanied by human backup. Enemy Oberschock agents marched from between the tripod's legs, firing their disintegrator guns toward the stairs. Foudre soon reached the base of the angled stairway, and valiantly pushed the shieldbearers behind him.

"Get back up zere!" he said sharply. "You can't protect ze rest of us if you don't make it out of here!"

The shieldbearers deactivated their electrified barriers and carefully made their way up the staircase, now only a couple of fallen supports away from dismembering completely. Morales at last managed to open the vault door, a task considerably easier from this end despite the precarious status of the stairs, and sent all the agents through it and back into the main hallway of the factory. Now, the only one standing inside was Foudre.

"Everyone's through!" Morales informed the stubborn Volt Knight leader. "Hurry, Captain!"

Taking a few disintegrator beams with his own shield, Foudre at last realized the time had come to depart. He turned around and shambled up the stairs, his heavy armor making him slow and cumbersome, while the Oberschock agents and machines blasted at the case's supports. Now, only one steel beam kept them up.

"Come on, Foudre, come on!" Morales roared.

"Get aboard ze Interceptors!" Foudre ordered, so close to the top of the stairs. "Get everyone out of here!"

"You'll be coming with us, Captain! Come-"

The last of the staircase's supports gave way, and Foudre tumbled down with it. Morales held his hand out to try and catch him, but he was already beyond reach. The Volt Knight Captain fell to the concrete floor thirty feet below, landing on his left leg with a painfully audible *snap*.

Foudre cried in pain and fell to his side as the Oberschock agents surrounded him. "Go!" he bellowed, clutching his hurt leg while squirming on the floor. "Get my men to safety!"

Morales punched the wall of the factory's hallway, knowing there was nothing he could do to save him. He didn't know if the Oberschock Federation would kill him or keep him prisoner, but with his injury, he would not be leaving here anytime soon no matter what happened. Distraught at having to leave Foudre behind, Morales ran out of the Stonewell factory with the Teslanauts and Volt Knights and boarded the Interceptors, hurrying out of Vienna one Captain short.

# Chapter Thirteen

THE MORNING sun rose at the Freckle Dump station, still currently situated in Zürich, Switzerland. While the communications operators waited impatiently for the report from their field agents, the rest of the Teslanauts readied themselves up, getting back into their professional modes after a bout of fun in town the night before. For some this was easier than for others, but there was nothing like the sounds of churning machines and sparkling electricity to clear a foggy hangover.

Raymond sat on a bench by the factory where they hung the Bolter suits, waiting for the go-ahead to retake the training and pass it at last. No person joined him, but Sparks the hover-head floated expectantly by his face, ready for another surge of electricity to juice up its circuits, which Raymond was all too happy to oblige. He was not sure if he should wait for Watson or just go out and do it, but he supposed he had to be certified, so wait he would.

Still though, he felt a little concerned about Helen. He had run into her twice this morning--once during breakfast and the second time on his way to the factory--and both times she quickly hurried off, clearly still embarrassed by their encounter at the watch shop. He realized this had to be a personal issue of hers that she needed to deal with in her own time, but still, he would have appreciated at least *some* communication from her end. What did he do wrong? What could he do to fix it? If he needed to give her space, for how long? Right now, he had very little to work with. Then again, people dealt with their own problems in different ways.

"I need to teach you a trick," the Brooklyn teenager said to Sparks, holding out his wristband and letting the electrical energy flow through the tiny machine. "Every good pet does a trick. I mean, reacting to electricity is neat and all, but it's going to get old fast. Maybe you could fetch, or fly through hoops!"

"Or it could chase the propellers on its own backside."

Raymond turned and saw Ji walking up to him, probably to join Raymond for some more Bolter training despite already having passed it. He seemed like the type who would rub his success in Raymond's face. Nevertheless, his lowered shoulders and relaxed gaze calmed Raymond's nerve for the time being. Maybe this time Ji would not be so hostile.

"Hey," Raymond said, awkwardly shrugging his left shoulder.

"Hello," Ji said. "Listen, I wanted to make something clear to you before we hear from the field agents about our next mission."

"I know, Ying told me. You don't think I've earned my place here."

"It's not that," Ji said, sitting down next to Raymond on the bench by the Bolter suits. "It's your attitude."

"I know, it bothers you that I don't know my purpose here yet. Ying told me that too."

"She's told you a lot, huh?"

"Enough, anyways."

"She certainly has an analytical mind. She's looked after our family for a long time. She will make a great communications operator here, and a handy resource for our missions. But it's not just about that. Unless Ying told you more?"

"Nah, that was all she told me."

"Hands off my sister, by the way. We'll find her a nice, honorable man back at home."

"Why does everyone think I've got pretty-eyes for every girl here?!" Raymond asked, a bit perplexed by this recurring pattern. "Your sister is very nice, but that's all there is, I promise."

"I'm just messing with you," Ji chuckled. "Don't worry. Our family would never let her end up with a white boy like you. But seriously, I wanted to clarify something. The mission ahead could be dangerous, and I want us to have each other's backs out there."

"All right," Raymond said, not sure if he was ready for whatever Ji was about to say.

"I quite admire your determination. Your technical skills might be a bit lackluster, but you're clearly trying as best as you can. I think you have amazing potential here. You could be something great."

"But…?"

"Your obsession about finding your father worries me."

"You're not the first to say that."

"I'm aware. But I just want you to promise me that whatever you do, you won't abandon the mission."

"Why would I-?"

"Just promise me that, if the time comes when you could find him or help your fellow Teslanauts, you choose to help us. I've seen how dangerous someone as driven as you can be. My sister and I left our home country for a reason, you know. I don't want to see it again. Plus, you might not realize it, but I *do* like you. I don't want something awful to happen to you."

"What would happen?" Raymond muttered, not really appreciating how personal this talk got.

"You could get killed. You could get someone else killed. Something could happen that you could never take back because, in that most important moment, you floundered. Promise me that won't happen, Raymond, and that you'll choose the mission over your personal pursuit."

"But-"

"*Promise* me."

Raymond sighed, knowing that Ji was probably right, but hating the fact that Ji could dissect Raymond's problems better than he could himself. Clearly Ji shared his sister's analytical mind. After staying silent for a few seconds and only looking at Sparks rather than his fellow human, he finally worked up the energy to say something.

"Okay," he said.

"Say it."

"I promise, all right? God!"

Ji nodded slowly, not particularly happy with how he had to force Raymond to say it, but knowing all he could do now was trust he would keep his word. "Thank you," he said. "I'll hold you to it."

"Attention, all Teslanaut agents!" Cobblewood's voice shouted angrily from the station's loudspeaker; not that she ever shouted in a less hostile manner. "Group up by the station entrance for your mission briefing!"

"All right, Sparks, let's get ready," Raymond said, patting the hover-head behind his optical receptors.

"Wait, Raymond!" Becky called from his left, the factory worker rushing up to him and wiping the sweat off her brow. "Don't you go out there without this, you dumb sack of potatoes!"

In her hands, still blackened with soot from her labor, sat the disintegrator gun from the blueprint Raymond had given her. Modeled after a pistol with miniaturized power receivers on the barrel, connected to the barrel via a pipeline-like framework, it looked unlike any of the others Raymond had seen in his short time here. It was bigger, bulkier; like it had more punch to its shot. But more important than any of that, it was his father's last gift. Raymond took the gun with a soft, bittersweet smile, gazing upon it as his mind drifted to old memories.

"Thank you, Becky," he said.

"Make sure to use it this time," Ji chortled from Raymond's side. "Now c'mon, let's go!"

Even so quickly after Cobblewood's announcement, already dozens of workers and agents readied themselves for the upcoming mission, eager to support their organization and get the job done. There were no half-hearted performers here today. Everyone wanted to give it their all. It was that kind of commitment and perseverance that made a good Teslanaut, and that's what everyone here strove to become.

"We've just received a telegram from Marshal Gabriel Morales," Cobblewood said, brushing her hands together as she began relaying the report. Her long gray hair draped over her shoulders, tangled and knotted, like she hadn't had the chance to brush it before she heard the news. "Our enemy now has a name: the Oberschock Federation. They're sending a train to Paris loaded with dangerous volt-tech from Stonewell factories. Our mission is to derail that train and keep it from reaching its destination. We don't know what they're planning to do, but whatever it is, we can't allow it to happen."

"Where is this train now?" a recruit asked.

"It will leave a station in Berchtesgaden within the hour. We'll meet up with it as it travels through the mountains. It goes through a remote part of the Alps on its journey, allowing us to keep our cover while placing all hands on deck."

"How are we getting there?" another agent said.

"The Volt Knights will lend us their Interceptor airships," Cobblewood explained, "while the Teslanauts stationed in Britain will lend us some Teslaplanes to give us more adequate air support."

"Tesla... planes?" Raymond said with a soft gasp, his voice lowered with awe at such a riveting combination of terms.

"This is an important mission, so we need everyone on board," Cobblewood insisted. "Comms operators, you'll be on a large airship nearby to relay info as fast as possible. Mech Masters, we'll need you to pilot machines able to overcome the steep mountain terrain. Electro Engineers and factory workers, you'll be on standby on the same airship as the comms operators, ready to repair and rejuvenate any volt-tech in the thick of battle. Bolters, you'll use your velocity and agility to run alongside the train and take out key targets. The rest of the field agents will fire from airships or board on the train; however your commanders see fit to use you. And please, listen to your commanders. They know better than you, and they've gone on far more rodeos than any of you."

"Am I-?" Raymond began to ask, but Watson, who appeared out of nowhere by his side, lightly elbowed his ribcage to shut him up. "You'll be out there with the rest of the Bolters," Watson assured him. "Consider this your retaking of the training course."

"Really?" Raymond asked, not expecting this.

"Of course, friend! We need all the help we can get! Just don't die and you'll be fine!"

"Lovely."

"The Volt Knight Interceptors will be at the Freckle Dump station in ten minutes!" Cobblewood told the agents, giving a declarative clap to cap off her speech. "Get ready to depart!"

At her command, the agents scattered to grab their gear and prepare for the mission. Raymond, Watson, Ji, and the rest of the Bolters hurried to their suits and changed into them in the lockers, while the Mech Masters selected the best machines suited for steep terrain movement. The Electro Engineers and factory workers grabbed as many tools and repair equipment as they could carry, while the field agents donned their disintegrator rifles, helmets, and devices.

"Make us proud, darling," Becky told Watson with a teasing chuckle as she ran past him with the other factory workers. "I'll make sure to save any shorted wires for you to play with later."

"I appreciate it!" Watson said as he rushed to put on his Bolter suit, his tone completely sincere.

"Good luck on the field!" Ying told her brother.

"Good luck on the comms," Ji told his sister. "Let's make a name for ourselves here!"

Raymond, now clad in the Bolter suit after fastening its many belts, marched with the others in his group and awaited the Interceptors to land outside the station and pick them up. To his left, the field agents gathered, with both groups in a perfect gridlock stance. Their formation was succinct. No alteration was necessary.

So naturally, both Raymond and Helen realized a bit too late that they stood right next to each other by complete accident.

"Uhh..." Raymond mumbled.

Helen remained rigid, as if not noticing Raymond, but he could tell by her reddening cheeks and frantic eye movements that she did. Raymond did not dare say anything. It was clear that there was nowhere for her to run anymore, but he knew she had to be the one to speak first. He did not want to trap her. Due to the incredible awkwardness of the situation, the Interceptors might as well have been coming to them from Fiji now rather than just a couple miles to the east. Would it be like this forever? Would this uncomfortable stasis ever end? Raymond had no idea.

But then, after roughly thirty seconds of silence that seemed to last forever, Helen finally spoke.

"His name was George," she muttered. "He was my brother. He always wore that type of watch."

A dam breaking after holding an entire bay could not compare to the amount of relief Raymond felt after hearing her speak at last, and finally revealing what had happened. The same could be said for Helen, whose face desaturated after bottling up all her emotions and finally letting them free. The two troubled souls stood silently together a bit longer, as if giving the moment enough time to breathe. A flurry of questions erupted in Raymond's head. Why hide this from him? Why not explain right away? Why did she actively seek out the watch if she knew it would make her sad? However, he realized that pestering her further with unnecessary questions would do nothing to help. When he eventually did respond, it was with what he knew was the only right thing to say.

"I'm sorry," he said softly. "I know what it's like to have lost someone."

"Your father's not lost yet," Helen insisted, her voice nearly breaking, but she managed to hold it together. "If you ever get a chance to bring him back home, you should take it, no matter what. The alternative is too much to bear. George Brimsby is gone, but Francis Calvert doesn't have to be."

Raymond sighed hearing Helen's words, appreciating them in earnest but inwardly feeling more unsure of what to do. That was the exact opposite advice Ji gave him, and it just added to the uncertainty of how to best handle the situation. He knew which one he'd *like* to follow, but he also knew which one he *should*. Ultimately, when the time came, he would have to decide then and there, and hope to all goodness he chose correctly.

"Thank you," Raymond said, turning toward Helen at last after purposely avoiding eye contact this whole time. "Good luck out there on the field."

"You too," Helen said, facing him as well with a soft smile and moist eyes.

"The Interceptors have arrived!" Cobblewood roared, opening the garage bay doors leading out of the Freckle Dump base. "Let's move!"

# Chapter Fourteen

A VOLT-tech-upgraded Prussian Class P8 locomotive hauled the Oberschock Federation's supplies through the German railway, chugging along the mountain ridges in a tumultuous flurry of noise and smoke. Like a marching legion, it commanded the field between the slopes, the sixty-foot, seventy-ton steam engine a general in battle leading his troops of carriages and weapons to the enemy front. Thirty cars in total trailed behind the engine, each reinforced with hardened steel to protect their precious payloads within. But tough exterior platings were not their only defenses.

"Every other car has a disintegrator turret zat our agents can man vhenever ze enemy arrives," Emil Ziegler told General Boltzmann as they made their way through the train. As the executive architect of the train's modifications, he was all too pleased showing off his work to the leader of the Oberschock Federation. "Ze surrounding volt-tech network powers both zem and ze locomotive. Zey've been repurposed from several emplacements built during ze var, and should keep any Teslanauts ve encounter at bay."

"And vhat about further defenses?" Boltzmann asked, his hands linked behind his back. "Vhat vill stop zem should zey get past ze turrets?" Dressed in his old general's uniform, complete with the medals and helmet, he looked like he had stepped right back onto the front from years past. Despite his outward rigidity, the slight wrinkling of his brow betrayed a sense of unease buried deep beneath his stony facade. Clearly, the notion of reentering combat brought back painful memories.

"Zey von't, General."

"But as a precaution?"

"Vell, ve've got troopers stationed in each car, as vell as smaller tripod machines zat can traverse ze tops and crawl on ze sides," the Oberschock engineer informed the general. "Also, should ze need arise, ze train can accelerate explosively for a short time via a controlled energy surge from ze surrounding electrical netvork. Beyond zat-"

"Double ze stations. Ve must get ze contents of zis train to Paris. Anyone not tending to ze engine should be prepared to fight."

"Including you, General?"

"I vill ready my gear for ze conflict, yes."

"Zis train is my masterpiece," Ziegler sighed, brushing the wall with his hands like a beloved trophy. "I've vorked on its modifications since ze moment Mr. Stonevell gave us ze funding. I vould hate to see it destroyed."

"If you've done your job properly, it von't be," Boltzmann declared. "You're a brilliant engineer, Mr. Ziegler. Don't disappoint me."

***

The brisk Alps air blew harshly on the faces of the French Volt Knights and American and British Teslanauts as they rode aboard the Interceptors, the speedy dirigibles weaving through cliffs and ridges while following the train tracks to the Berchtesgaden station. Having picked up the agents from the Freckle Dump station point in Switzerland, they now had the proper tech and manpower to complete their mission: stop the Oberschock train from getting to Paris at any cost. While conducting trips to Vienna and Ausgraben, the airships flew autonomously; however, this time a Volt Knight piloted each ship in order to properly navigate them through the mountains and perform evasive maneuvers should the need arise.

"We're looking for something called the Blitzsturm," Marshal Morales told the agents aboard his airship, briefing them about what they learned on their little excursion to Vienna. Everyone tightly gripped the handrails of the airship's deck as they listened to him, not used to riding airborne vehicles with such velocity and maneuverability. "From what we have learned, it's a device that, should it reach Paris, will have disastrous consequences for us all."

"What is this device?" Helen asked.

"We don't know."

"What does it look like?" Ji asked.

"We don't know."

"What consequences?" Raymond asked.

"We don't know."

"This should be easy, then!" Watson laughed. "No intelligence, no visuals, no concept of the objective. Who needs any of that to complete a mission, huh?"

"Stonewell Arms and Ammunitions has factories all across Europe supplying volt-tech to the Oberschock Federation," Morales said, trying to convey the seriousness of their assignment despite the limited knowledge. "We believe the Blitzsturm will allow them to use that tech to restart the war. The Blitzsturm is on this train, so our mission is to derail it by any means necessary."

"We must be prepared for counter-attack," Ying said through their ship's radio, sitting with the other communications operators on a separate airship. "We're picking up electro-scan signals from further east. They could spot us soon."

"Captain Foudre told me that the Interceptors use special panels that send electro-scan waves right through them," Morales assured her, using the radio communicator in his own ship to talk back. While mobile two-way radio communication was still a year or so away for the common folk, the volt-tech world had used it for at least a decade. "If his claims are true, we should maintain our stealth until we're right at their eyes."

"We'll pinpoint the source of the electro-scan, then," Ying assured the Marshal, turning dials and listening to the static on their headphones to figure out the intensity and direction of the waves. She and the other operators sat a few miles away in a far slower airship that looked more like a traditional zeppelin the Germans would use in this airspace, keeping them safe while also allowing them to give key intelligence during the mission.

"Look alive, agents," Morales told the group aboard his airship as they flew through the mountains. "This is our job, and if there's one thing we Teslanauts know, it's how to get the job done. Steel yourselves."

"Yes, sir," Raymond said with a hushed tone, looking at the disintegrator gun Becky made for him from his father's blueprint that contained the secret message. He closed his eyes and held the weapon back down, thinking hard about what he had to do, and knowing he couldn't screw things up this time. Not when the mission was this important.

Plus, he had a promise to keep to his mother. He would come back to her, with or without his father. If the time came, he would have to use this weapon to defend himself, for his sake and hers.

"Did you really have to bring your pet hover-head with you?" Ji asked, noticing Sparks fastened on the back of Raymond's Bolter suit. Even with its body attached to Raymond, Sparks held out its little mechanical fingers into the air, as if it enjoyed the sensation of the wind as they moved. Odd, considering as a machine it had no sense of touch.

"You never know when he might be needed," Raymond said with a shrug.

"We use those things for factory work and assisting in tasks back at base. Not in combat."

"There's a first for everything. Maybe they're amazing in combat!"

"I think it's adorable you're bringing your hover-head here," Watson said. "If I had a cat or a dog, I would certainly take it along with me on a dangerous mission where it could get shot or zapped or whatnot. That would definitely prove how much I cared about it!"

"Sparks can be rebuilt if he gets destroyed," Raymond pointed out, smiling slyly at his factory worker friend. "A cat can't."

"Nor should it," Watson chuckled.

"There's the train!" Helen shouted, pointing to a section of track a few mountains away. Chugging along the mountainsides with several triplanes and smaller dirigibles to escort it, the locomotive moved fast and true toward its destination, ready to deliver whatever heinous misdeeds it could bestow upon the innocent people of Paris. Even so far away, the Teslanauts could tell the Oberschock Federation had installed some potent modifications to the train, what with the bulkier cars and truck-sized gun emplacements. Said guns spotted the Interceptors almost as quickly as they had spotted them, firing blasts of disintegrator beams their way.

"Hang on!" the Volt Knight piloting Morales' ship shouted, quickly diving aside to avoid the beams as they blasted the mountain rocks behind them.

"Whoa!" Raymond yelped, feeling his stomach lurch at the sudden motion.

"We need to take care of those guns!" Morales said. "We can't get close enough with those things protecting the train!"

"What do you suggest?" Helen asked.

"Bolters!" Morales barked. "I'll need you to get to the train and incapacitate the men manning those gun emplacements!"

"Aye, aye, sir!" Ji said. "Raymond, are you ready to run?"

"Wait, how are we getting from here to there?" Raymond demanded.

"By running, of course!"

"By jumping out of the airship, you mean?!"

"You managed to get your footing back after running up Notre Dame, right? This is just like that!"

"How in the world did you see-"

"Scram, Bolters!" Morales ordered. "Take care of those guns!"

"We've got a train to catch, Raymond!" Watson laughed. "See you aboard!"

Ji, Watson, and the other half-dozen Bolters leapt off the side of the Interceptor facing the mountain, activating their suits mid-fall and zipping down the slope. Raymond grunted and shook his head to ready himself, and after a few seconds of deliberating on whether signing up for this whole thing was worth it, he made the leap and took the plunge at last.

Just before he hit the mountain slope, he flicked the switch on his suit's left wrist, channeling electricity from the surrounding volt-tech network into his body's particles and turning him into a speeding blur once more. Gripping the rocks with his boots, he ran forward just a few steps, his movements already hurtling him from one slope to the next. He turned the suit off once he made it to the track, only to find himself just a hundred feet away from the front of the train barreling toward him.

"Agh!" he snapped under the blaring noise of the train's horn, quickly turning the suit back on to avoid getting run over. Moving beside the track on the train's left, he found himself already behind the last car in a single second, but this was exactly his plan. Remembering how easy it was to traverse the sides of the buildings in Paris due to his velocity countering the effects of gravity long enough for him to move, he barreled forward onto the slope on the train's right, then jumping off and deactivating the suit as he aimed for one of the gun emplacements.

He tumbled onto the top of the car, his sudden appearance causing the Oberschock agent manning the turret to jump in place. Quickly getting onto his feet, Raymond faced the enemy agent head-on, before noticing him pulling out a gun from his side. A real, genuine pistol.

"Oh, God," Raymond gasped, freezing in place as the agent pointed the gun right at his chest.

Before the agent fired, he suddenly got forced onto the ground by seemingly nothing, until Ji appeared in front of Raymond after deactivating his suit. "No hesitations, Raymond!" he told his fellow Bolter, kicking the Oberschock agent on the ground to make sure he was down. "We have to act!"

"You're right," Raymond said, nodding as the chill from facing the barrel of a gun faded away. "Thanks for the save."

"Don't expect it every time!" Ji said, reactivating his suit and zooming away.

Raymond shook his shoulders and tilted his neck back and forth, before activating the suit again and running back onto the mountainside. He bounded from peak to peak, zipping so fast the wind felt like water, before turning back around and aiming for another gun emplacement. As he dove downward from another mountaintop, he held his fist out and turned off his suit, his knuckles moving at about a hundred miles an hour. With that, he slammed the back of another Oberschock agent's head with the force of a tiny bullet, knocking the enemy agent clean out with one strike.

"Yeah!" Raymond cheered, jogging in place. "That's more like it!"

"Heads up!" Watson shouted, running up and down a mountain in his Bolter suit as if to amp himself up for an attack. Once he reached an appropriately excessive speed, he dove down the slope and deactivated his suit just as his hand hit the chest of an Oberschock gunner. The sheer speed of his fist meant the gunner went flying for hundreds of feet, soaring in a long arc before careening into the pine trees between the mountains.

"Ow, I think that move broke a couple of fingers!" Watson groaned, shaking his hand after striking such a blow. "But who cares?! This is just swell!"

Now that the Bolters neutralized those mounting the gun emplacements, the Interceptors could get closer to the Oberschock train. Unfortunately, the enemy planes and airships escorting the train still flew uninterrupted, furiously guarding their masters. One particular airship, the size of a large bus, had a rather nasty weapon at its bow: a trio of circular saws nearly ten feet in diameter apiece, attached to a rotary axle to turn the whole front of the vehicle into a whirling dervish of destruction. The ship seemed to fly rather slowly, however, so the Interceptors' pilots figured they just needed to not get too close.

The triplanes, though, were another story. Immediately their gunners shot upon the Interceptors, their standard machine gun rounds spruced up with the sporadic disintegrator bolt as they fired. The Interceptors' metal framework took most of the hit, but it would only be a matter of time before something more valuable took heat. The planes dove past the Teslanaut air force, before ascending back above the mountains on the other side and preparing to loop back around.

"Shoot those bogeys down!" Morales ordered the agents armed with disintegrator rifles aboard his ship. "Lei Ying, scramble the Teslaplanes!"

"They're already on their way!" Ying told him through their radio. "They'll arrive within a few minutes!"

"That ship with the saws is rising above us," Helen warned the Marshal.

"Don't mind it; their planes are a bigger threat," Morales assured her. "They're coming back for another run, agents! Fire at-"

"Incoming!" Helen shrieked, pointing at the buzzsaw-armed airship. Once it hovered a hundred feet above them, it rapidly deflated its balloon and sharply dove at another Interceptor ahead of Morales and Helen's. With its saws spinning at maximum intensity, it sheared straight through the Volt Knight airship's envelope, sending it and its passengers hurtling toward the trees below. Just before the Oberschock airship hit the trees itself, it re-inflated its balloons almost impossibly fast, angling back to a level pitch within seconds as the Interceptor it attacked crashed onto the ground.

"Sweet mercy," Morales gasped. "Never mind, that ship is the bigger threat! Take aim, Teslanauts!"

While they clashed with the buzzsaw airship and the triplanes, a couple of the Interceptors managed to get close to the train by weaving through the enemy air support. With each airship only a bit longer than the train cars, they could fly abreast even in the tight mountainous terrain. Once these dirigibles hung over Raymond and the other Bolters, the Teslanaut and Volt Knight foot agents slid down ropes and mounted the train, while the Volt Knights operating the Interceptors reeled the ropes back in and moved off to try and fight off the planes.

Helen and Morales remained in their airship, currently to get past the planes and the buzzsaw-ship. The Oberschock triplanes got within range once again, performing another strafing run at the Interceptor's position. This time, their fire brought down another Volt Knight airship, with a few well-aimed disintegrator beams chewing through their envelope and blasting the hydrogen right out.

"Where are those blasted Teslaplanes?!" Morales demanded, not happy with how they were handling the enemy air forces.

"Probably stopping to get a bite to eat," Helen said.

"Zat airship is rising once again!" a Volt Knight said, pointing back up at the buzzsaw-armed ship. "We must perform evasive maneuvers! Hold on!"

As before, the saw-armed airship deflated its balloons and plunged down toward its quarry: this time, the Interceptor carrying Helen and Morales. Their Volt Knight captain swerved their ship to the starboard with haste, sending everyone on board falling to the right and tumbling onto the deck. The buzzsaw airship sliced the air barely a foot to their port bow, which was still close enough to chop off a chunk of the Interceptor's metal casing. Once its passengers got back on their feet from the sudden lurch, the enemy ship swooped back up once again, readying itself for round three.

"We can't avoid that blasted ship forever!" Morales said. "We need to take it out!"

Back on the train, Raymond, Ji, and Watson climbed down the ladders off the gun emplacements and made their way inside the cars to look for the Blitzsturm. Unfortunately, the interior of the train was if anything *more* heavily guarded than its exterior, with dozens of armed Oberschock agents patrolling each car. And if their pointing their pistols, disintegrator rifles, and other assorted weapons right at them was any indication, they did not take kindly to hostiles boarding their train.

"You vill not stop us!" a Hungarian Oberschock agent declared.

Raymond had no choice but to act. Shakily, he took his custom-made pistol out of its holster, and, knowing he could not hesitate any longer, fired. But he did not fire at the enemy agents. Instead, he shot at their feet, not feeling ready yet to take aim at a human even in self-defense. However, due to the special electrical properties of his pistol, the blast sent a small spark of lightning through the floor, zapping a few Oberschock agents where they stood.

"Whoa!" Raymond gasped, not expecting that.

"Lucky devils!" Watson said.

Ji took advantage of the confusion by punching the enemy agents and bringing a few more down, while Raymond turned the corner and scanned the train car he stood in. "What are we looking for?" he asked, rummaging through any supplies and crates he could find. "Surely we don't have time to find the Blitzsturm *and* fight!"

"Raymond, look!" Ji shouted.

Just as the Oberschock agents recovered from Raymond's high voltage attack, Sparks flew at them and grasped their shoulders with its mechanical manipulators, hoping to get some of that precious electrical juice. With a few static discharges still flowing through the agents' bodies, it caused the back of its half-circle head to let out a pleasant shower of its namesake sparks, which it very much seemed to enjoy. The sparks further disoriented the Oberschock agents, giving Raymond the chance to tackle another one and punch him in the head. Having been satisfied with its little shock-snack, Sparks returned to Raymond and reattached to the back of his Bolter suit. By the time Raymond stood back up, Ji and Watson had taken care of the other agents in their car.

"Wow, maybe that hover-head *is* useful in combat!" Watson said, laughing slightly at such a notion.

"Yes, let's just give the lifeless contraption a gun already," Ji grumbled, although based on his raised eyebrows and slightly agape mouth, even he looked impressed at what the little machine was capable of. "Now hurry, there will be more enemy agents coming. We have to find the Blitzsturm."

"Our mission was to stop the train at all costs, right?" Raymond asked. "I think we should focus on that for now. We can look for the Blitzsturm more thoroughly once the train is halted."

"You vant to find ze Blitzsturm, do you? Ve'll see about zat!"

A barbed spear longer than two people sliced through the air, only just missing Ji after he leapt to the side. The spear retracted, revealing itself to be attached to a mechanical limb, with said limb attached to the backpack of an Austrian engineer.

"Ve vill return our countries to zeir former glory!" Emil Ziegler declared, scuttling atop the ceiling like a man-sized spider. "And no Yanks or Chinamen like you vill stop us!"

His backpack, usually equipped with three lengthy mechanical arms, now had ten additional limbs of half the length that allowed him to crawl up the walls and ceiling with his back to them. His original three limbs now hung down around his shoulders, and its graspers had a pointy metal spike that could skewer any of them with one strike. His crawling, combined with his goggles and soot-covered face, made Ziegler appear positively inhuman, and certainly not someone the three Bolters would want to meet in a dark alley. Or even a well-lit one. Yet here they were, meeting this foe in a dimly lit train car.

"Retreat!" Watson shrieked, his pitch so high he threatened to shatter the train windows. Clearly, he was a bit arachnophobic.

"Don't use the suit inside the train!" Ji warned his fellow Bolter. "There's not enough room to-"

Before he could finish, Watson had already disappeared, with only a trail of floating sparks left in his wake. Ji groaned and pulled out his disintegrator gun from his holster, only to have it stabbed and thrown aside right out of his hand by one of Ziegler's mechanical barbs.

"Now, now, you shouldn't bring a gun to a fistfight!" Ziegler chuckled. "Zat isn't fair, you know!"

Ji leapt away and somersaulted on the ground to avoid another strike from Ziegler's metal spears, while the Oberschock engineer moved across the ceiling with the scuttling legs on his suit. His body faced the floor, only crawling up top with his backpack, allowing him to face Ji head-on as he attacked.

Raymond grasped his pistol and shot at Ziegler's mechanical arms, hoping to sever them with the disintegrator beams. Alas, having only fired his first shot less than a hundred seconds ago, his aim was not adequate enough to hit such a narrow and fast-moving target. The beams hit the walls of the train car behind him, each impact creating a ripple of electrical sparks that spread in a web of bolts. Seeing this, Ziegler halted his pursuit of Ji and sniffed the air, before turning back to Raymond with one of his spear-tipped mechanical arms held up like a hook.

"A unique design," the engineer said, his goggle-clad eyes pointed right at Raymond's custom-built pistol. "Fascinating. I simply must take zat for study."

Pouncing toward Raymond so quickly the Brooklyn teenager nearly burst out of his skin, Ziegler swung across the ceiling with two of his mechanical limbs like a crazed primate, pointing the third right at Raymond's disintegrator gun. Wanting very much not to lose his father's last gift, Raymond fell backward to the ground trying to avoid Ziegler's attack and faced the ceiling of the train car as the Austrian engineer zoomed above him. Ziegler missed his first strike, but he quickly turned around and readied for another.

Raymond knew he couldn't hope to take on this opponent and win. Not in such an enclosed space. Suddenly though, an idea struck him like a bolt from a Tesla coil. While still lying on the floor, he turned his body perpendicular to the direction of the train and pressed his boots onto the wall. Then, activating his Bolter suit, he took two small steps up it.

The suit having energized his molecules and making him flow like a wave, he phased straight through the roof of the train car, and now flew several hundred feet above the tracks. Still not used to the feeling of tumbling in midair, he shrieked harshly before seeing the mountain slope on his side. Turning his feet, his boots made contact with the steep and rocky surface before he took another step forward. Having gotten a sense of the Bolter's rough speed and control, he knew how short to keep his stride to get where he wanted. Each step was like an instant shot forward, and he could control the distance better and better with each use.

Now, he stood directly atop the Oberschock train car, holding his arms out to balance himself as it chugged along through the mountains. Deactivating his Bolter suit, he looked around to see any sign of Ji following his suit or Watson coming back, only instead to find the one person from inside he did *not* want following him.

"Very clever," Ziegler said, using his mechanical arms to climb onto the roof from an opening between two train cars. "But zat fancy suit of yours has its limitations."

"Like what?" Raymond demanded, looking at the Oberschock engineer with defiant eyes.

"You can run through small objects, but how about ze mountainside?"

Raymond turned around hearing Ziegler's words and nearly fell off the roof at the sight. The Oberschock train headed toward a narrow tunnel, the tops of the cars barely a foot from the tunnel ceiling. It was coming fast; Raymond had probably six seconds tops before it entered. Turning back, he saw Ziegler hold his three mechanical arms out and activate an electrical field between them, creating a shocking barrier that would overcharge his Bolter suit and destabilize the energy particles. Raymond couldn't get past that, and with Ziegler's inhuman reactions, running to the side was out of the question. And he couldn't use the Bolter suit toward the mountain either; it was so close he'd run into it with a single step, and it was far too thick for him to phase through. The impact of hitting it at such a speed would obliterate his body.

He had one option. Seeing the end of the train car a few yards in the direction of the mountain, he booked toward it at his normal speed, trying to ignore the cliffside getting near his face at an accelerated rate. He had one target, and he had to make it. Behind him, he could feel the energized aura of Ziegler's electrical field closing in. It was a race between the engineer and the cliff on which would splatter Raymond first.

At the last second, Raymond reached the end of the train car and jumped down to the link between it and the next car, feeling the tunnel roof scrape the top of his suit's helmet and cut his forehead. His heart threatening to explode in his chest and take his torso with it, Raymond stood on the cable between the two train cars and took a moment to catch his breath and recollect on how close he came to getting crushed by a million tons of rock. He could not *believe* how close that was.

"Raymond, you okay?"

Raymond didn't respond to Ji's voice for a few seconds behind him, still breathing heavily with his hand to his chest. Finally, he turned and saw his fellow Bolter standing just behind the door leading into the train car, with the lights inside the train being the only thing illuminating the area in the darkness of the mountain tunnel.

"Yeah, I'm okay," Raymond breathed, nodding. "I think I lost that guy."

"I think we lost Watson," Ji chuckled. "It looks like he made it out of the train, but there's no telling where he is now. Now quick, we gotta find the Blitzsturm before-"

"Look out!"

From the darkness to their right, Ziegler leapt in between the cars toward the two Teslanauts, having used his backpack to scuttle on the side of the train after narrowly avoiding the tunnel archway himself. Raymond pushed Ji out of the way, causing Ziegler to miss the two, but one of his lengthy mechanical arms grasped the roof of the train and swung him back in place.

"You can't evade us forever!" Ziegler declared, diving into another car and quickly grabbing a phone with his backpack's smaller spider-like legs attached to the wall behind him. "Engineers!" he screamed into the receptor. "Release ze machines!"

A wave of electrical energy flowed through the train, causing Raymond to instinctively jump despite the rubber in his Bolter suit protecting him from a potential shock. Once the wave passed, the many crates within the inside of the trains began to stir, before a flurry of metal legs burst out of them. Now, the train had an army of automatons to defend itself.

"Oh no," Ji sighed.

Rising up nearly six feet, the Oberschock machines were shaped like giant metal carrots, with four tiny arms at the top holding disintegrator guns and manipulator tools. Three spindly legs carried their mechanical bodies, which could grip surfaces tight enough for them to crawl on the sides of the train with no issue. A trio of circular lights above their little arms acted as their optical sensors, allowing them to see all around and remain fully aware of their surroundings. At first, Raymond assumed their awkward stature meant he could outrun them, but as soon as one of the machines spotted him, it moved toward the young Teslanaut with the speed and ferocity of a cheetah, its three legs propelling it forward with perfect precision.

Raymond turned to the train car the opposite direction and ran from the machine, his heart rate going right back up facing the disturbing pursuer. Unable to use the Bolter suit due to the tight corridors and darkness obstructing his view, he moved as fast as he could, but alas, it wasn't enough. The machine grasped his ankle with one of its three legs, using the mechanical toes as a manipulator, and dragged Raymond down to the floor. Raymond flipped over and took back out his custom-built pistol, shooting the machine in its optical sensor and blasting out its light. He had no problems firing a gun at this particular lifeless machine. For some reason, it felt different than firing at the rocket men.

The mechanical imp tumbled from the blast, before turning its top around to look at Raymond with one of the two circular lights remaining. Still reeling from the machine's monstrous design and movement, Raymond fired his pistol at it over and over again, causing oil and electrical sparks to gush from the contraption with each shot, until it finally fell to the ground.

One down, far too many left to go.

Light shone upon the train once more, as it finally exited the tunnel and chugged along the mountainside track once again. Raymond got out of the train car and climbed up to the roof, ready to use his Bolter suit to get out of here and fast. The Oberschock machines were quick to follow, crawling all over the train cars like beetles on a log in their pursuit of Raymond.

Once Raymond reached the top of the train, his eyes widened at the sheer number of machines. There must have been at least twenty of them scuttling toward him. He couldn't handle them all on his own. He needed backup, and Ji had lost his gun to Ziegler's attack earlier. Where was Watson? Where were the others?

Suddenly, a torrent of machine gun fire blasted six of the machines right off the train, followed by the sound of airplane propellers. His eyes lighting up, Raymond turned away from the mountainside and toward the Interceptors, realizing their reinforcements had arrived at last.

"The Teslaplanes are here!" Ying told Morales through the radio.

Flying over the mountains and diving toward their targets, a squadron of seven Teslanaut biplanes strafed the top of the train, taking out half of the machines that had been creeping toward Raymond. Then they engaged the Oberschock triplanes, using precision maneuvers and superior weaponry to clear them out. Originally based on VE-7 Bluebirds, the Teslanauts took the tried-and-true design of this military aircraft and added some special volt-tech modifications. Their machine guns fired disintegrator beams rather than standard bullets, meaning they never ran out of rounds as long as there was power. The fuel usage was minimal, only used to start the plane or for emergencies; electricity from surrounding transmitter towers kept the propellers spinning otherwise. This greatly reduced the noise from the engines, and thus increased their stealth factor while also making it easier for pilots to hear each other when shouting their attack plans.

But the Teslaplanes used electricity for more than powering their engines. They had a unique heavy-duty weapon, using a spherical output terminal attached to their upper wingpiece. "Target acquired!" one of the pilots shouted while looking at the Oberschock saw-ship, her long gray hair blowing behind her even with her helmet. "Take it out, boys!"

"Cobblewood?!" Raymond exclaimed, his eyes wide as he recognized the voice that came from the plane.

"Moving into position!" another Teslaplane pilot yelled.

"Get ready to attack!" Cobblewood ordered from her cockpit.

As the two planes flew toward the Oberschock airship with the sawblades, Cobblewood increased her plane's altitude while the other plane's pilot decreased his. Then, Cobblewood performed a half-aileron roll, aiming her plane's output terminal toward that of the other's as she flew upside-down. Once the two Teslaplanes flew directly above and below the Oberschock airship, they switched on their power transformers.

A huge bolt of lightning erupted between the two planes, with the enemy airship closing the circuit. It sparked and burst, its panels pulverized by the power surge and its balloons busted by the blow. The airship plummeted, before crashing into the pine trees between the mountain peaks, while Cobblewood completed the aileron roll and swooped back around facing upright.

"Way to go, Teslaplanes!" Ji shouted from beside Raymond.

"Good show!" Helen said from her airship, grinning.

"The opposition is cleared," Morales noted, standing alongside Helen. "Move all Interceptors toward the train, now!"

"We'll cover you from the sky!" Cobblewood shouted as she flew her plane above them. "The Oberschock goons will no doubt send more bogeys our way! We'll make them scram fast!"

The Interceptor pilots maneuvered their airships to fly parallel to the train, then threw down ropes for the agents to climb aboard the train. At last, all but those flying the Volt Knight airships had boarded the Oberschock train. Now, they had the means to complete their mission.

"The Blitzsturm is here somewhere," Morales said. "This train is getting close to the French border. We have to find it soon!"

"We've got more of those machines incoming!" Raymond told the Marshal, pointing to the train cars at the back.

At least twenty of the man-sized crawling machines crawled out of the cars, aiming their disintegrator rifles right at their hearts. With no cover at the top of the trains, the Teslanauts quickly retreated to the spaces between the cars before the machines fired, getting to safety mere milliseconds before the torrent of death rays came their way. A few Teslanauts did not make it in time. That was too many deaths already.

"Those metal buggers are on us!" Helen snapped. "We need to take them out before- aagh!"

Right behind the cowering agents, the last two train cars began to stir. They split in half and folded outward, with only their trolleys remaining intact on the track. Then the pieces of the cars further contorted, with hidden gears and wires making themselves known between the reinforced hulls as they moved. As the pieces transformed, they also combined, folding in together and forming one big machine. Four bulky crab-like legs formed from the mechanical pieces. Two steel-muscled arms split from the base. And in the center of it all, a cockpit revealed itself, open to the air but with thick panels on every side for protection.

These last two carriages had transformed into a new mech, the *Stahlwolf*, hitching a ride on the train but able to move and crawl upon it to its whim. And piloting it was the commander of the Oberschock Federation, Heinrich Boltzmann.

"You've made a powerful enemy!" the German officer roared, stomping on the train cars ahead of him. "Ve shall be oppressed by ze Allied Powers no longer!"

"Agents, focus on the smaller machines!" Morales ordered. "I'll take care of their general!"

Knowing exactly what the Marshal implied, three other Teslanaut agents took off their metal backpacks and unfolded them into Morales's weapon. Raymond, Ji, Helen, and the other agents hurried through the train cars and mopped up as many of the man-sized machines as they could, their legs and eyepieces bursting and piling upon the floor. Even though they fell quickly to their disintegrator pistols, their sheer number and rather unsettling speed meant they had to be careful.

"Agh!" Raymond shrieked as a few of the machines grabbed him with their pincer-like legs, pulling him to the floor and scuttling on him like giant rats. Before they fired their pistols, though, Helen took them out with her trusty rifle.

"You're welcome, Raymond!" the British agent chuckled.

Before she could get too haughty though, another one of the machines leapt onto her shoulders, its legs slightly piercing her skin and causing her to fall with a pained cry. Before more followed, Raymond quickly recovered and shot the machines with his pistol, its electrical punch zapping them and blowing their fuses. This proved too tempting for Sparks, as the hover-head hastily detached from Raymond's back and flew through the Oberschock machines to wash itself in the electrical shower, further dismantling their pieces.

"*You're* welcome, Helen!" Raymond said.

"I'm not sure who to thank more; you or the blooming hover-head!" Helen said, getting back up and brushing her shoulders with her hands. Sparks shook in midair like a dog after a bath, then happily reattached to Raymond's back.

"Gee, I'm getting schooled by a flying toaster," Ji grumbled. "I need my gun back real quick-like. How am I supposed to fight unarmed?"

"You better figure it out fast," Raymond said, eyes widening as he noticed the swarm of Oberschock machines gathering inside the train cars. There must have been almost a hundred of them, their numbers stretching across at least four cars down that direction.

"On three, we fire and bring down as many as we can," Helen told Raymond, cocking her disintegrator rifle. "One… two…"

Before they could fire, every one of the machines exploded seemingly without reason, clouding the air in electrical sparks as they collapsed in sequence. Raymond, Helen, and Ji nearly jumped in place from the sudden event, wondering what the heck caused them all to simultaneously malfunction on the spot. It was like something fast and invisible plowed through them and shattered them like tissue paper.

As it turned out, though, that was exactly what happened. "Ooh, the sparks… the *shivers*!" Watson sighed, his legs quaking underneath him as he suddenly appeared before the three Teslanauts after deactivating his Bolter suit. In his hands was one of the Oberschock machines' severed legs, which he used like a spear as he zoomed through the crowd in the Bolter suit. While the wearers of the suit could phase through small objects like the machines, they could still grip objects, and at least some of the molecules of the object would remain solid if the object was big enough. Watson used that to his advantage, turning himself into a missile-like projectile. It was honestly one of the most spectacular things Raymond had ever seen.

"Where the heck have you been?!" Ji demanded.

"I needed a breather, all right?" Watson said, shrugging. "That man's spidery backpack scared me silly!"

"As opposed to the spidery automatons?" Helen asked.

"I can't explain my emotions!"

"I appreciate the save, Watson," Raymond sighed with relief. "Now c'mon. We have to find that Blitzsturm."

"I'm starting to wonder if it's even here to begin with," Ji said. "Most of this train's supplies seem to be their little army of machines. Perhaps that giant mech outside is the Blitzsturm?"

"Marshal Morales didn't say machine," Helen noted. "He said 'device.' I think there's a key distinction."

"It's gotta be closer to the front," Raymond said. "We haven't gotten there yet. Let's get closer to the locomotive and see what we can-"

The train car they stood in shuddered, as a sharp thud came from outside. The four young Teslanauts nearly lost their balance, quickly holding onto the walls to keep from tumbling.

"Whoa!" Watson said. "That's not the kind of jolt *I* like!"

Helen ran to the end of the train car and peered outside, wanting to see what just happened. To her shock, she saw a Teslaplane rolling down the mountain slope to the side of the train, the wings tearing off the body as the ruined biplane fell. Somehow, the *Stahlwolf* mech Boltzmann piloted had grabbed one of the planes in midair and threw it aside like a wad of trash.

"My people deserve justice for vhat you've done!" Boltzmann boomed. "Ze war vill not end like zis!"

Morales climbed up to the top of the train car, while his three accompanying agents carried their backpack pieces with them. The valiant commander stared at the twenty-foot-tall mech before him, scowling at its pilot with the ferocity of a whole nation scorned.

"You did this," he snapped. "You have your hands on the trigger. You long to restart the conflict. I'm here to end it for good."

At last, the agents finished assembling Morales's weapon, which he heaved with a loud grunt. The Peacemaker, all seven feet of it, was held before its opponent. Then, activating its rockets, Morales swung the heavy weapon toward the mech's stocky iron feet.

Boltzmann stomped the *Stahlwolf* forward to avoid Morales's attack, crawling over the Marshal and moving to the train car ahead. His mech crushed the train cars' hulls with each step, denting and ripping them with its immense weight. Before Boltzmann moved too far away, a squad of Volt Knight agents swung from their Interceptors and landed in front of him, holding out their electrified shields and blocking the Oberschock commander's path.

"Face me, you coward!" Morales roared, running up to the mech as fast as he could while dragging a near eighty-pound weapon. With another long and arduous swing, he chopped off the right hand of Boltzmann's mech, letting the thick pieces tumble to the side of the track.

Boltzmann turned to face Morales, rotating the *Stahlwolf*'s cockpit and arms a hundred and eighty degrees while keeping its legs stationary. He held up his mech's arm and studied the severed metal, before smirking ominously at the little Marshal. With another series of button presses, a nine-foot-long sword unfolded from the mech's digitless arm, longer than the biggest zweihänder but able to be wielded one-handed by the powerful mech.

"You vant to duel, do you?" Boltzmann said with a soft, mocking tone. "I vill oblige."

Morales groaned and hurled his sword forward again, the rockets doing much of the heavy lifting as he swung it toward his opponent. The Peacemaker was a tank-buster, meant for pounding machines with its weight like a sharp and pointed club. Yet Boltzmann actually parried it with his mech's own sword, which somehow remained intact even against the Peacemaker's blunt force. Controlling the arm with levers and wheels in the cockpit, he hurled it forward and pushed Morales back through their swords' contact. Morales's boots skidded across the top of the train car, but he remained upright, knowing if he was pushed down while holding such a heavy weapon, it would be near impossible to get up.

After a quick burst of adrenaline, Morales managed to break their swords' lock and juke to the side, causing Boltzmann's mech to nearly lose its balance. Exhaling deeply, Morales swung the Peacemaker to the right, which Boltzmann swiftly blocked again, the blow so powerful that the ensuing burst of wind caused some rocks on the nearby slope to tumble. The two agents persisted in their duel--the world's biggest and slowest sword fight--while the

Teslaplanes looped back around to attempt another strafing run at the mech.

"We can't lose any more planes!" Cobblewood said. "We have to use our coil attack!"

"The mountain slope makes that impossible!" another pilot said while flying beside Cobblewood. "We can't get the mech in between the two planes!"

"There's a bridge a few miles ahead! Once the train reaches it we'll fly on each side and zap that thing!"

Morales tried again and again to push through Boltzmann's defenses, but the *Stahlwolf* kept blocking and parrying his attacks, stomping aboard the train cars and nearly crushing them under the machine's mechanical girth. With each swing, Morales's muscles ached, and his back panged. Fatigue began to sit in, which only grew with every movement. The Peacemaker was not meant for dueling. As such a heavy and awkward weapon, it was meant for one-and-done attacks, crushing machines and rupturing their parts with one massive strike. Morales could not physically keep up this fight for much longer; the exertion grew too intolerable.

Pushing the levers forward within his cockpit, Boltzmann shoved his mech's sword swiftly into the Peacemaker, causing Morales to lose his grip. The one-of-a-kind, rocket-powered weapon fell, sliding off the side of the train car and tumbling into the trees in the slope below. With that, the Peacemaker was lost.

Morales fell onto his back from the shove, quaking as he lay unarmed before his opponent. Despite his clear victory, Boltzmann's face showed no glee or pride. His lips did not creak into a smile, not even slightly. War had wiped the concept of joy from him forever. He just had a mission to complete.

"Our country vill reclaim its glory," the German officer snarled. "Our defeat did not quell ze fire. It vill be rekindled, hotter and brighter zan ever before!"

"Marshal, I'm picking something up on the electro-scans!" Ying's voice said through Morale's radio. "I think it's another Interceptor!"

"What?!" Morales demanded.

The Volt Knights behind Boltzmann's mech cheered, clearly knowing something that the Teslanauts did not. And behind the cragged Alp peaks, that something revealed itself. Plowing through the sky like a ballista bolt, another of the high-velocity French airships reached the train tracks, with a blast of a disintegrator bolt onto the heart of the *Stahlwolf* coming with it.

"*Liberté, égalité, fraternité*!" Foudre roared proudly.

Jumping off the Interceptor before it even fully decelerated, the Volt Knight Captain smashed into the open cockpit of Boltzmann's mech, his chivalrous armor clashing with the rusted and utilitarian aesthetic of the Oberschock machine. From the airship he had so triumphantly leapt, three other Volt Knights used ropes to scramble down, using teamwork to bring down the enemy mech. After grappling with the cockpit, Foudre got back on his feet, and then stomped his left leg, seemingly no longer hurt without explanation.

But after inspecting the limb further, Morales realized what had occurred. Foudre no longer had a left leg, much like he had no right arm. Using precise and intricate volt-tech engineering, the Volt Knights had amputated the broken leg and replaced it with a mechanical limb to get their captain back in the fight as quickly as possible. And like his artificial arm, his new leg came equipped with some handy accessories. Foudre stomped the ground with his leg, the foot more of a small lance with a pointed end. This lance then fired a blast of electrical energy, frying the Oberschock mech's systems for a precious few seconds.

"We've got him on ze ropes!" a Volt Knight cheered.

"The bridge is just ahead!" Cobblewood shouted while flying her plane past them. "We'll finish it off there!"

"Great!" Morales said, throwing his fist up. "Then we can get the Blitzsturm and get the hell off this train."

"Ze Blitzsturm?" Boltzmann asked, still huddled in the *Stahlwolf*'s cockpit despite the Volt Knights clinging to its sides. "You fools, ze Blitzsturm isn't here. It appears you have been misled."

"What?!" Morales roared, refusing to accept that he gathered everyone and coordinated this attack for nothing. "You're lying! This train is heading to Paris with the Blitzsturm!"

"Ze Blitzsturm vill be in Paris, just not via train. Zis is just preparations. But it did get all your forces here, did it not?"

The train began to ascend slightly up the side of a mountain, leading to a cliff with a wooden bridge about a half-mile ahead. The Interceptors and Teslaplanes circled the locomotive like vultures, and the Volt Knights and Teslanauts flooded the cars, while Boltzmann stood alone in a beaten up mech. Surely the Oberschock had no other card to play.

"My engineer informs me zat our supplies have been relocated to ze front of ze train," Boltzmann said, glowering with smug satisfaction. Having regained control over the mech, he stomped it backward until he stood on the car just behind the locomotive. "Ve must be leaving you now. Ve do have a parting gift, zough. *Auf wiedersehen.*"

With a sudden jolt, the train cars the Teslanauts and Volt Knights occupied slowed way down while climbing the slope. The locomotive and the two carriages behind it had detached from the rest of the train, accelerating explosively from the dropped weight even while still carrying Boltzmann's heavy mech. The bridge led to a tunnel with no end in sight, and just before the German officer went through the tunnel with their supplies, he used a phone in the *Stahlwolf*'s cockpit to call Ziegler for one final order.

"Zey've reached ze attack point," he said. "Release ze Panzerwurm."

The speed of the train cars the agents stood on rapidly diminished after disconnecting from the locomotive, and eventually they coasted to a stop at the middle of the bridge. The locomotive disappeared into the tunnel, leaving the Teslanauts and Volt Knights stalled and stranded. Before the Teslaplanes could fly ahead in a feeble attempt to find where the Oberschock forces would exit the mountain, they noticed the mountains themselves beginning to stir.

Rocks tumbled. Trees fell. Whole slopes of the mountain collapsed in a great avalanche. And beneath the bridge, the ground began to contort, spinning in an unnatural earthy tempest. Something terrible, something utterly demonic, would emerge from beneath the stranded agents, something that leveled the town of Ausgraben and could send countless more cities to the depths of the earth.

"Mary, mother of God," Morales whispered in horror.

From the bowels of the mountain valley, a two-hundred-foot-wide mechanical whirlpool erupted into sight, with arcs of jagged metal spikes lining the circumference and every layer within. Two drills the size of tanks and the strength of bombs revolved counterclockwise on each side, upending stone and earth alike with every movement. The spirals of metal and fire soared effortlessly up to the train cars, revealing more flexuous segments with a series of drills lining them like a giant centipede. Just this section alone made it an impossible machine, but it kept rising, hundreds and hundreds of feet, revealing the serrated whirlpool up top as merely a mouth with hundreds of iron teeth. Its serpentine body stretched for thousands more feet, most of which was still underground. Instead of a pilot, the machine just had fire, its mechanisms beyond reason or any known science of man. This was no contraption. This was a monster from Hell.

This was the Panzerwurm.

At once, the bridge collapsed, the train cars and the agents occupying them plummeting helplessly down the cliffs. At least thirty Teslanauts and Volt Knights were falling to their doom, with the Panzerwurm's rumbling and pirouetting maw ready to consume them all.

# Chapter Fifteen

"PILOTS, INITIATE midair retrieval!" Cobblewood snapped from her cockpit, swooping her Teslaplane toward the falling agents. As she dove, the Volt Knights piloting the Interceptors followed her lead.

"There're too many people!" another pilot shouted. "We can't save all of them!"

"Save as many as you can!" Cobblewood said.

Every Teslanaut and Volt Knight braced for the end as they fell toward the Panzerwurm's gaping mechanical mouth, grasping the train cars to keep from falling freely. Raymond watched with horror as he, Helen, Ji, Arthur, Foudre, Morales, and countless others would soon meet their fate, with no way to escape that his panicking mind could concoct. The fall would last only a few seconds, but it seemed to go on forever, as all of Raymond's short life flashed before his eyes. His heart fell as he did, knowing he had broken his promise to his mother. His father may still be alive, hiding somewhere in Europe away from enemy eyes, but it seemed Raymond, in his brash attempt to try and find him, would perish instead. Quite a cruel irony.

But then, as the fall's duration went from half a second to three-quarters of a second, he realized how the Bolters could escape. He had demonstrated before that his boots only needed to contact a surface for them to enact their speedy run. The tumbling train cars would suffice. That would just save himself, though. What about everyone else?

Once the fall reached the one-second mark, Raymond remembered his initial Bolter training, where they had to bring a flower from Paris to the station point near Zürich. Even though the suit used electricity to turn their molecules into waves, the flower remained intact, flowing as a wave just like the wearer of the suit by contact alone. It would be reasonable to assume that any people carried to safety by the Bolters would do so as well. However, there was just as likely a chance that they would get killed. Or fried. Or phased out of existence.

But with no action at all, they would die anyway. He had to try.

Raymond grasped onto the side of the train car and looked at the nearest non-Bolter agent to him: Helen, who grabbed the same car with him. Breathing deeply and praying to God this would work, Raymond pushed against the train and leapt toward her, wrapping his arms around her and then activating the suit.

"What the-?" Helen gasped, still panicking from her one-and-a-half second free fall.

Raymond wasted no time. With the suit ready to go, he zoomed between the mountains and deactivated it when on the ground, now standing hundreds of feet away from the Panzerwurm. He heard Helen's scream, but only barely, as her voice rippled with the particle waves as she did. Once he reached solid ground, as much as he *really* wanted to make sure Helen survived and have her sing praises about how this brave and dashing young American was her hero, he knew there was little time to waste. He had to try and save the others if he could.

Using the Bolter suit's power once again, he zipped back toward the falling train and ran up the side of the Panzerwurm, before deactivating the suit and aiming his arms toward Morales. He could not waste time keeping the suit powered and just taking people to safety mid-Bolt, as he knew he could never exert that kind of control moving so fast with such little training. Plus, he would presumably just phase through them like any other small object when dashing.

"Hang on, Marshal!" Raymond shouted, taking Morales by the arms.

"Calvert!" Morales screamed.

Raymond ignored the anxiety in the Marshal's voice, hoping it was due to the midair tumbling rather than warning Raymond that this was a terrible idea. Powering on the Bolter suit once more, he rotated back around and took Morales to where he put Helen, turning it back off once he reached the general vicinity. Wasting no time once again, he reactivated the suit and went for another.

Raymond did this again and again, as the fall's duration now reached the four-and-a-half second mark. Like the name of his suit, he moved like a lightning bolt. He even thought like a lightning bolt. He had no time to process anything, or to hesitate, or to think about the physical attributes behind how his actions worked. He just had to move. Raymond did not realize it yet, but by performing as he did, acting on instinct, and using this remarkable technology to solve this seemingly impossible task, he truly became a Teslanaut.

Finally, at the six-second mark, the train cars reached the Panzerwurm's fiery, jagged mouth, rupturing from the impact and grinding by its spiraling teeth. The Teslaplanes and Interceptors completed their dives and looped back around, having pulled up as many Teslanauts and Volt Knights as they could. Raymond turned off the suit and sat in the grass between the mountains, taking a moment to catch his breath and recollect his mind. His head tilted toward the ground, his eyes half-closed while he recovered. After moving so fast, razoring his focus, and trying to save as many people as he could, he needed a quick break.

Then he felt a jagged knife in his heart from the chills, remembering what he had just done and how it could have all gone so, so wrong. Fearing the worst, he slowly and warily raised his head. Helen, Morales, and the six other agents he had saved sat nearby, their eyes wide as they also slowly recovered. They looked frazzled, frightened, and like they had come dangerously close to soiling themselves.

But they were all alive, and all molecularly intact.

"Oh man," Raymond groaned, lying back on the grass with relief.

"Bloody hell," Helen gasped, still shaking.

"What did you do, Calvert?!" Morales demanded.

"He… he saved our lives," Helen said.

Ji and Watson stood by the recovering Teslanauts, having just deactivated their own suits. They stared incredulously at Raymond, their eyes as wide as their agape mouths. Up above, the Teslaplanes descended onto the area between the mountains where they sat, avoiding the forested area behind them and landing in the more open part with the agents. The Interceptors also slowed, holding several Teslanauts and Volt Knights themselves as they coasted to a landing. By the looks of it, while they unfortunately lost a number of agents, a vast majority of them had been saved, whether by their air power or by Raymond.

The Panzerwurm, as an unthinking machine, did not pursue the agents where they rested. Instead, it curved its body around like a giant sea serpent and tunneled back into the ground with a tsunami of dust, leaving the group and presumably awaiting further orders from its Oberschock masters. This meant the Teslanauts and Volt Knights could use this time to take a breather.

"God, Raymond, did you really…?" Ji asked.

"He used the suit to get the others to safety!" Watson said, grinning. "That's a training-passing maneuver if there ever was one!"

"That was a huge risk!" Ji shouted, albeit more bewildered than angry. "I've studied the applications of the Bolter suit for years. There's never a guarantee that anyone in contact not wearing the suit could survive such speeds without their bodies vaporized or turned forever incorporeal. Using the suit that way has never been attempted."

"But it worked," Raymond breathed, even in his exhaustion still having the energy for a bit of smugness. "They're alive."

"Sometimes, in order to save lives, it's worth taking calculated risks," Morales said, nodding with appreciation.

"And if he hadn't done it, we'd have been done for," Helen said, her eyes welling up as she grinned at Raymond with gratitude.

Ji said nothing in response. Instead, he just walked up to Raymond, his footsteps careful and determined. Raymond looked up at the other Bolter, unable to read his expression as he stared down at him. After a few tense seconds, though, Ji put his hand on Raymond's shoulder, smiling with pride at his fellow Teslanaut.

"It seems I was wrong to underestimate you," Ji said, grasping Raymond's shoulder tight. "You did good, Raymond."

Raymond beamed, his heart lifting gratefully hearing Ji's approval. Ji held out his hand and Raymond took it, the Chinese teenager helping the American one off the grass.

"All right, enough of this dreck," Cobblewood grumbled as she climbed out of the cockpit of her Teslaplane, although with her own raised eyebrows Raymond could tell even she was secretly impressed. "We lost the train and we failed to stop those Oberschock fiends from reaching Paris. And now we know they have a machine of unimaginable power at their call. What the blazes do we do now?"

"Zey still have not taken ze Blitzsturm to Paris," Foudre said, exiting his Interceptor with a few Volt Knights accompanying him. "Zey have only taken supplies and workers to secretly prepare for its arrival. Zey will leave with it soon, however, but for now, zere is still time to stop zem."

"How do you know?" Morales asked. "And how are you *here*?!"

"Ze answer to zose questions is two-fold," Foudre chuckled. "Which makes sense, as zose were two questions! After my painful fall, I was taken to ze Obershock's main fortress near Berchtesgaden, zeir hub of operations holding ze factory of all zeir volt-tech. Once zere, I was promptly and painfully interrogated. Naturally, I gave a bunch of false answers, with enough truth to zem zat zey would more likely believe me. Zey threw me into zeir dungeon, which zey had because zeir base is literally built on top of a castle, and I hastily escaped."

"How in the world did you-?"

"Let ze Captain finish!" a Volt Knight said, gleefully enjoying their commander's story.

"Once I broke out of zeir dungeon, I did some investigating. I snuck around zeir fortress and avoided ze guards, which, with a broken leg, was quite an undertaking, let me tell you! And it was zen zat I found ze source of zeir power, a device built by zeir previous engineer zat acts as a generator more powerful zan anything steam or coal could provide."

"The Blitzsturm?" Helen asked.

"*Oui.*"

"But what are they planning to *do* with it?" Morales demanded. "And why are they taking it to Paris?"

"From what I could gather, it all stems from zeir current benefactor, a certain gentleman by ze name of Robert Stonewell. He had inherited an ammunition supply company from his father, and a lot of good zat does during times of peace. So he plans to use ze Blitzsturm to restart ze war, and he knows zat, with volt-tech at ze disposal of every developed country in ze world, any conflict with regular arms would not last long."

"So he plans to take volt-tech out of the equation," Morales said. "How does the Blitzsturm do that?"

"What allows us to use volt-tech? It's all based on what Nikola Tesla provided with his electrical projects. Tesla is the pioneer of wireless technology, and his experiments and all zose inspired by it are all possible with ze help of those transmitter towers zat relay power. Zey must be removed for volt-tech to fail, and dismantling zem one by one would be noticed by ze Electrocracy right away. Zey have to be taken out all at once."

"So they take the Blitzsturm to Paris," Raymond said, trying to connect the dots. "And that somehow makes all the transmitter towers fail? How could-"

"Oh my God," Helen gasped, her eyes wide with horror as she figured it out. "The Eiffel Tower."

"I would love to see it, yes!" Watson laughed, not understanding the implications yet. "Let's go to Paris and do some sightseeing, everybody!"

"Wait, what about our tower?" a Volt Knight asked, the Frenchman not liking the idea of their glorious monument being used against them.

"It's also a transmitter," Helen explained. "Tesla, Edison, and Eiffel met there a few decades ago, presumably to plan out all the transmitter towers' construction. And it's the tallest one of all, hiding in plain sight."

"*Oui*, zat is true," Foudre said. "Ze Volt Knights have relied on ze Eiffel Tower for many of our projects, since it can transmit power over such a wide range. Zat range is why it's perfect for ze Oberschock Federation to use. Once zey have installed ze proper receptors, all ze Blitzsturm has to do is touch it and make it conduct its energy, and zen ze tower turns into a giant electrical coil so powerful it zaps every other transmitter tower in Europe, Africa, and parts of Asia and North America. Zey cannot handle such a charge, and will be overloaded and blown to bits. Volt-tech will suffer a massive blow."

"To reach the Eiffel Tower, they'd have to conduct an all-out attack on Paris," Morales realized. "They'd use every machine they have, every weapon, every agent; everything, including their new giant monster. It would amount to an act of war, and the conflict would start once again."

"If they take out the towers, then their own volt-tech will fail too," Raymond pointed out. "How would they fight in this newly restarted war?"

"Why, only through ze biggest supplier of arms and ammunition on ze whole continent!" Foudre shouted. "Stonewell knows with volt-tech out of ze picture, everyone will have to rely on his company or ze others he has shares in for weapons. And ze Central Powers' remnants would have ready access, as would ze Americans, British, French, Polish, and everyone else. Ze Obershock Federation would end, but zeir countries would be resupplied, zeir glory would be restored, and ze Great War would begin again, with Stonewell raking in all ze profits."

"An evil enemy will burn his own nation to the ground to rule over the ashes," Watson said, finally realizing the severity of the situation despite his electricity-dulled mind. "Jesus said that."

"Actually, that was Sun Tzu," Ji groaned.

"Once I learned of all zis, I found a phone in ze base and called ze Volt Knights to send a squad to rescue me," Foudre explained. "And to give me a new leg. Zat thing was useless to me, so zey lopped it right off and gave me zis wonderful new contraption!"

"We have to call upon the Electrocracy," Morales said, his brow furrowing determinedly hearing all that Foudre revealed. "We have to inform them of this so we can stop Oberschock. If an enemy is going to attack Paris with all their forces, we'll need as many of our own forces to defend it. Doing so out in the open requires approval from the Electrocracy board."

"Is this the end of all the subterfuge, Marshal?" Helen asked. "Are we to reveal the secrets of volt-tech to the world?"

"If there's no other way to stop the Oberschock Federation, and if the Cleanup Squad can only cover up so much, then I'm afraid we must. But getting approval from the Electrocracy isn't going to be easy."

"The Cleanup Squad can handle *anything*," Watson assured the Marshal. "Seriously, you should have seen the stuff they covered up for me back in the day. Still, approval would be nice, I reckon."

"We don't have time for any blasted politics!" Foudre roared, more angrily than his usual jovial shouting. "We have to stop zem before zey reach Paris!"

"We will, Captain Foudre," Morales declared. "I promise you, we will. How much proof did you recover for your claims?"

"I found zis journal in the dungeon," Foudre said, taking a small leather notebook from his armor's side compartments. "It details a lot of zat I've just said. It was from a previous prisoner of zeirs, a man named Francis Calvert."

Raymond's heart stopped hearing his father's name, staring at the journal in Foudre's hand.

"Let me see the journal," Morales said. "I'll need to examine it if we are to show it to the Electro... Calvert!"

Raymond swiped the journal from Foudre and skimmed through the pages, ignoring Foudre's shouts of protest. Morales, however, was a bit louder with his. "You hand that back to me right now, Calvert," the Marshal snapped. "That's an order!"

"One second," Raymond murmured, looking for the last entry.

"Calvert, hand me the journal!"

"Almost there..."

"Calvert!"

"April 2nd, 1922," Raymond whispered, his eyes widening as he found the date of the last entry in his father's journal. "That's less than a month ago! My father's alive, he has to be! Oberschock must be holding him prisoner in their fortress!"

"*Calvert*!" Morales boomed.

"Take it, take it!" Raymond said, passing the journal to Morales. Glaring at the young Teslanaut, Morales took the journal and put it in his breast pocket, his earlier pride from Raymond stepping up to save everyone taking a bit of a hit.

"I'll call Ying's airship and tell her to extract us from here," the Marshal said. "Then we'll be heading to the Electrocracy Headquarters."

"You guys go," Raymond said, looking up at the train tracks on the mountain slope from which they came. "I'll meet you there."

"Calvert, what are you doing?"

"I have to go. I can't leave my father."

"Your father's whereabouts are *irrelevant*!" Morales snapped coldly. "We have bigger problems right now!"

"Raymond, this is exactly what I was talking about," Ji groaned, slumping his shoulders and rolling his head back at Raymond's imbecilic statement. "You're too focused on finding your father, and it's gonna hurt all of us! You can't abandon us when we need everyone at hand to stop Oberschock!"

"I'll be right there!" Raymond insisted. "I have the Bolter suit! I'm going to check out the Oberschock base and be back in an hour!"

"Raymond, don't be an idiot!"

"Your father was not present at ze dungeon," Foudre told the stubborn teenager. "If he was zere three or four weeks ago, he's certainly not zere now. At most, you could find some clues, but you should listen to your superiors and follow zeir lead."

Raymond groaned, hating all this and everyone telling him what to do. He did not care about the war. He did not care about stopping the Oberschock Federation. He had done all this--found the Teslanauts, signed up as an agent, performed dangerous missions--just to find his father. That was the only reason. That was all he gave a damn about. And now he was *so close.* He had proof that his father had been alive a mere four weeks ago! He could not simply leave that alone. It was not even remotely possible for him.

"Helen, you told me if I had a chance to save my father, I should take it," he finally said, looking at the young British agent and staring into her eyes. "You said you couldn't save your brother, but I could still save my father, and I shouldn't forget it. Do you still believe that?"

Helen bit her lip and lowered her head, clearly thinking deeply about how to respond.

"It doesn't matter what Brimsby thinks about this!" Morales snapped. "This is not her place! She is not the one giving orders around here! You are not going to desert us, Calvert!"

"Let him go," Helen said softly.

"Brimsby!"

"I know how he feels. I understand exactly what he's going through. This kind of loss consumes you, but if you have the chance to regain what you've lost and don't take it, trust me, you'll obsess over it. And yes, it's a mistake for him to go to the Oberschock base. But it's his mistake to make. You can't stop him. No one can."

Raymond nodded with conviction at Helen's words. That was all he needed to hear.

"Raymond, you *promised* me you wouldn't do this," Ji harshly reminded the other Teslanaut.

"I promised myself I'd find my father," Raymond said. "I'm sorry. I have to do this."

"You're not sorry."

Raymond closed his eyes and shook his head, trying in vain to quell the fury in his mind. He had no interest in hearing anything these people had to say. He had already made his choice. "You're right," he sighed, opening his eyes and looking where he needed to go. "I'm not."

Activating his Bolter suit, Raymond ran at top speed down the train tracks leading east, determined to find his father and end this.

# Chapter Sixteen

THE TRACKS leading through the mountains curved and lined the slopes in a constant zigzag,' and as Raymond followed these tracks, he came across several junctions, forcing him to try and pick the correct one. With the Bolter suit, he could realize quickly which direction did not lead to Berchtesgaden and instead went farther into the mountains or south into Liechtenstein. Thankfully, one of the gadgets all Teslanauts carried on their person was a compass, which Raymond made good use of as he traveled.

That was, when his mind did not seethe with rage.

"They don't know what I'm going through," he growled as he moved over a thousand miles per hour in his Bolter suit down the tracks, unable to hear himself but in his own thoughts. "They don't know what it's like to lose someone you care about and then have the chance to get them back. This is what I've got to do!"

He understood the importance of stopping the Oberschock Federation, of course. He knew they presented a dire threat to the whole of Europe, and potentially the world at large. But who was he to try and stop something like that? How could he possibly help there? He was not even eighteen yet! Other, more qualified people would focus on stopping Oberschock from turning the Eiffel Tower into a lightning blaster or whatever they planned to do. Not Raymond.

What could Raymond do? Who was Raymond to do anything as big and heroic as that? His father was the big shot. He built machines for the Teslanauts and helped the world with his engineering prowess. He stood shoulder-to-shoulder with Nikola Tesla in the world of volt-tech. He was a great man. Not Raymond.

Raymond was nothing compared to his father. Raymond was nothing *without* his father. He had to find him. He had to get Francis Calvert back into the fray so he could side with the Teslanauts and Volt Knights and save the world from the Oberschock Federation. He would help save the day. Not Raymond.

Not Raymond.

*Not Raymond.*

"This is how I'll help, Marshal!" he snapped, even though Gabriel Morales was at least fifty miles away by this point. "This is what I have to contribute! This is how I'll help the Teslanauts! And shut up, Ying!

'What do *you* want to do?' *This* is what I want to do! This is all I *can* do!"

Raymond moved across southern Germany with the stubbornness and resolution of an electrical charge. He followed the tracks beside mountains, over hills, across bridges, and through tunnels- never stopping, never taking a moment to breathe. Either he would find his father or die trying; no other outcome would be acceptable. He had been denied this for too long.

At last, he reached his destination, slowing down near Berchtesgaden Central Station and hiding behind its brick walls. German citizens gathered here, some trying to make a living however they could, and others attempting to board any train out of the country to get themselves out of the pit it had become since the war ended. For some of them, it mattered little if they had visas; they just needed to leave however they could. Raymond understood that mentality, of feeling helpless and taking any chance of alleviating it, however illegal the methods.

Crouching near a wall leading into the train station, Raymond looked around the small mountain town to find anything like the fortress Captain Foudre had described. The deciduous trees, rolling hills, and mountain backdrops made the town quite the lovely sight. Yet most of the biggest buildings appeared to be churches, or other similar places of worship. The Royal Castle, or Schloss Berchtesgaden, was the closest to Foudre's description, but it appeared far too public to hide a covert base of volt-tech operations like that of the Oberschock Federation. Realizing this, Raymond quickly figured out that this fortress would surely not lie in the middle of this quaint alpine municipality. It had to be somewhere outside it.

Pressing the button on his wrist to activate the Bolter suit, he ran up the surrounding peaks and scouted the area, stopping every few seconds to get a glimpse. If he felt just the tiniest bit above burning rage, he might have been able to enjoy the beautiful vistas and fresh mountain air. The Alps stretched beyond the horizon in every direction, like a carpet of mile-high rocks on the floor of the Earth, so majestic in their scope and appearance. Yet Raymond could not focus on it. He had one goal. Thus, he simply looked all around the mountains from his high vantage point and ignored whatever wonder he would normally feel. He denied himself the pleasure of awe for this mission.

At last, atop a higher mountain a few miles away, Raymond spotted a peculiar shape. Its peak did not slope, but went straight up, before leveling out on top like a brick. It sat far away from the town, hidden by clusters of spruce and oak trees as well as the surrounding cliffs. In a medieval society, it would be the perfect place for a fortress, naturally defended from all angles by the environment. This was no mountain, Raymond realized, but a fortress. The one he was looking for.

"That's it," he said, nodding. "That's their base of operations. Hang on, Dad. I'm coming."

With a streak of sparks in his wake, Raymond zoomed to the fortress in just a few seconds, stopping just at its stone and steel walls. This base, Eisenzentrum, sat near a winding mountain road, with a constant convoy of trucks carrying supplies from Stonewell's weapon factories all across Europe. The road led inside the fortress, with a curved stone arch and a pair of gargoyles flanking the entrance. Watchtowers with spotlights, built onto the framework of the castle, scanned for any intruders, like a certain rogue Teslanaut looking for answers.

"I need to get past those sentries," Raymond muttered to himself. "The Bolter suit should help, but I'm still not sure about my precision. How do I know I won't just phase into a wall?"

Using the surrounding spruce trees as cover, Raymond ran beside the road where the caravan of supply trucks drove. Once he reached a couple of hundred feet away from the entrance, he turned around and looked back at the road leading toward the castle. From this distance, he felt reasonably sure he could use the suit to zoom inside the fortress. He knew only using the Bolter suit would let him get past the guards unnoticed. Of course, he could not use the suit when inside due to the narrow corridors where maneuvering at such high speeds made sneaking through the Oberschock castle a much more difficult task, but he would figure it out as he went along.

"All right, c'mon, you can do this," Raymond whispered. Rapidly breathing in and out to ready himself, he turned the suit on and moved, zooming through trees and trucks on the road as he ran. After less than a second, he turned off the suit, jumping as he found himself mere inches from the stone walls of the castle entry room. He had made it in.

The trucks drove into a supply bay behind him, as workers unloaded the weapons and devices in their holds and took them to the factory. Hundreds of German, Austrian, Hungarian, and Swiss workers toiled in here, all of them focused one hundred percent on the task at hand, be it preparing to attack Paris and restart the war or whatever else the federation needed. Still, surely one of them would notice an unknown American teenager standing by the wall if he did not move quickly.

Hurrying away from the room and into the castle halls, Raymond moved through the interior of the base, tiptoeing to remain stealthy and looking out for any patrols. He had to admit, the sheer scope of this castle was something else, with some of the halls bigger than football fields, and the architecture looked old, perhaps going back to the days of the Holy Roman Empire. The Oberschock Federation simply built upon the castle's foundation to turn it into a modern headquarters of volt-tech operations.

Yet Raymond did not break inside this place to appreciate the sights or the history. He had to find the dungeon. As soon as he found the stairwell, he looked around for any patrols and then, when the coast was clear, headed straight down.

The lights dimmed as he descended, and the distant voices of the Oberschock workers in the supply bay began to fade. Each step Raymond took made his skin progressively clammier, and the silence did little to quell any feelings of unease. In his head, he told himself over and over again that, whenever he wanted, he could use the Bolter suit and attempt to phase through the walls and scram the heck out of here, assuming the walls weren't too thick. He could leave whenever he wanted if that was true. But then again, maybe that would not work. It added to the uncertainty of it all.

Sure enough, after descending the stairs several more levels, he reached the lowest chambers of the castle, with only a locked wooden door between him and the dungeon. Normally Teslanauts would break through the door with their handy wrist-mounted devices zapping their lock, but since this door and subsequently its locking mechanism was made of wood, shocking it would not do a lick of good. Looking through the door's peephole revealed a dark hallway that stretched for a hundred feet, meaning if Raymond timed it *just* right, he could phase through it and get inside. Shrugging and turning on his Bolter suit, he mentally prepared his timing, and then took a few steps forward. He zoomed straight through the door, and almost immediately switched the suit off.

"Ow!" he cried as his nose hit the wall on the other side, having turned off his suit just a *smidgen* too late. While he did not collide with the door at full speed, as that would have definitely killed him, he did hit it just as he turned solid and slowed down. It was akin to being punched by several burly goons at once, and his nose immediately started bleeding from the impact. Raymond shook his head to try and dull the pain, and held his nose, wiping the streams of blood on his sleeve while moving his lips to loosen the muscles. He realized after both this, his near-hit of the wall in the castle entry room, and simply breaking into the castle to begin with, he was starting to act reckless. Maybe the Marshal was right. Maybe this was a mistake.

But it was too late to turn back now. He had to resolve this.

Empty, open cells lay before him in a grid pattern, with only a few small flickering bulbs providing the light. The only sound Raymond could hear came from the faded steps and shouts of the workers above, with Raymond perfectly able to hear his breathing and his heartbeat. He knew he needed a better way to get a glimpse of his surroundings if his travel here would amount to anything, but he did not see any gas lamps or flashlights lying around that he could use.

"Sparks," he said, taking the hover-head still strapped to his back off his suit by unfastening it manually. "Any chance you've got a-"

Before he could finish his sentence, the hover-head's optical sensors turned on, and through incandescent light bulbs and focal lenses, its eyes had become two high-energy spotlights. Raymond chuckled appreciatively at this, taking the hover-head and wrapping its dangling arms underneath its rectangular head around his neck to place the little machine on his head. Sparks did not seem to mind.

Using his new headlights, Raymond looked around the cells to try and find clues. He looked from cell to cell, finding nothing but dirty cots and scratched cement. The minutes trudged onward, and yet nothing. The dungeon currently held no prisoners. Captain Foudre was correct: if his father was here before, he certainly wasn't now.

Raymond stomped the ground, hating the lack of answers. He figured it would have been a longshot regardless, but every new clue he found got him closer and closer to finding out the answer. He was told his father died five years ago. Then it turned out he was just moved to a secret bunker, and was last seen a year prior. Then he was captured by the Oberschock Federation and still alive just a few weeks ago! How much more until he actually, *finally* found him, alive and well, in the present time? It couldn't be much longer, surely.

"I've gotten this far," Raymond grunted, his voice getting increasingly louder with anger. "I know you're out there, Dad! I lost you before, but you've made it this far. You have to be alive! You have to be here somewhere! *You just have to be*!"

"Can I help you, sir?"

Raymond's skin immediately went cold. He had blown his cover. He could not hide anymore; the hover-head lighting the way with its eyes made him a bullseye. And he could not pretend to be part of this organization, for he had shouted boldly and loudly in his American accent.

Yet, he realized something about the man whose voice he just heard. He also had that accent.

"You're looking for your father, you said?" the other American voice asked. "Who was he?"

Raymond took Sparks off his head and fastened it to his back, causing the hover-head to automatically turn off its lights. Then he deeply exhaled, trying to calm his nerves. He knew the smart thing would be to activate the Bolter suit and attempt to phase through the walls and retreat, but he still did not know how thick the walls of this castle were, plus since he stood in a dungeon, he would probably get stuck underground even if he got through the walls.

But that was not the real reason he did not attempt to escape. He knew who this man was, after hearing Foudre's account. And this man was the only person who could lead him to his father.

"I take it you're Robert Stonewell?" he said, slowly and shakily turning around to the voice.

"My reputation precedes me, it seems," the man chortled. "Come along. Let's get you out of here and into the light."

Every fiber in Raymond's being told him that following Stonewell's lead was a horrible idea. He could turn him over to guards, interrogate him, or even flat-out execute him on the spot. But he could not help himself. The prospect of finding his father was too compelling. So, knowing full well he would regret it later, Raymond found himself walking toward the voice. He did not see Stonewell clearly yet, as the darkness shrouded his features, but he saw the man open the door leading out of the dungeon, and hesitantly followed.

The stairwell had more light, and finally Raymond saw Robert Stonewell in the flesh. A light-haired, strong-jawed man a little less than twice his age, clad in a fancy suit and a bowler hat, he studied

Raymond for a few seconds with his striking blue eyes, before widening them at what he realized.

"You're Raymond Calvert," Stonewell said, nodding. "I'd recognize that face from anywhere."

"You know me?"

"I know your face, not you."

"You know my name, apparently."

"I've heard it before. Your father mentions you frequently. Almost every day."

Raymond swallowed hearing that, feeling a wide range of emotions. "Is he... here?" he barely managed to squeak out.

"Oh yes, he certainly is," Stonewell assured him. "He's been here for the last year, helping the Oberschock Federation with projects. I'll take you to him; I'm sure you'd love to see him."

Raymond did not like hearing how casual Stonewell spoke, and the vague way he worded his sentences. But nothing was certain yet. He had no choice but to follow Stonewell. All the while, he hovered his thumb over the button to activate his Bolter suit, telling himself he could leave whenever he wanted. But he had to stay here, just a bit longer, until he found out the truth.

"You're a Teslanaut, I see?" Stonewell said, walking beside Raymond up the stairwell. "So was your father. He had hoped you'd become one."

"I joined the Teslanauts to find him," Raymond admitted. "I learned about them when looking through his study and discovering a volt-tech blueprint."

"I see. I certainly understand the desire to reunite with your father. My own father died three years ago, and I'd give anything to have him back."

"So you know why I'm here, then?"

"Of course I do," Stonewell said. "You've already met your father without realizing it, though. Our machines? Our mechs? The weapons your fellow Teslanauts have fought? Most of them were built by him. He's built a lot of wonderful things for us. His greatest creation, though, will soon be on its way to Paris."

"Is it that giant drilling machine?" Raymond asked, his eyes widening.

"The Panzerwurm?" Stonewell said. His jaw clenched after saying its name. "No, that's… not his. Just come along."

Raymond had no idea what Stonewell meant by that, but he was determined to find out. All the while, his nerves kept building, and the uncertainty of it all added to his anxiety. Here he was, walking with the enemy, who talked so perfunctorily about his father and his work both with and against his forces, while walking through the main fortress of Oberschock operations. Everything about this seemed terribly wrong, and he knew should book it right now to be safe. Turn on the Bolter suit, run through the walls, and reunite with the Teslanauts.

But he couldn't. He knew he should, but he couldn't. Staying here could destroy him, yet here he was.

Stonewell took Raymond back toward the loading bay with all the trucks, but turned a corner into a chamber near the castle's great hall. Inside a door he unlocked with a set of keys in his pocket sat a dark room, the size of a large garage, with all kinds of tools, drawers, and cabinets lining every counter. Chalkboards with equations and schematics drawn upon them covered the walls, with a handwriting Raymond almost immediately identified.

"Is this… my dad's workshop?" he asked, his words caught in his throat.

"It is," Stonewell said, nodding. "Here he planned and built everything we asked him to make for us. His masterpiece, though, is on the main table."

Raymond walked through a maze of shelves and cabinets to reach the more open area of the workshop in the back, with a table like that seen in a war room. Upon this table sat what looked like a combustion engine, but the size of an entire car, reverberating slightly as its gears and grinders churned. Wires lined all sides of it like cobwebs, glowing brightly and heating up the room. The occasional spark flew from the side and lit up the room like a bonfire, but the device kept chugging on, rumbling like a motor. Despite the clear presence of electrical energy within, this device was not plugged in. It made its own power. And based on the size of its sparks, it made a *lot* of it. Raymond could feel the energy with his Bolter suit, the electricity tingling his nerves despite the suit not even running.

"The Blitzsturm," Stonewell said, sighing with what could be called reverence. "The ultimate power source. Plug it into a station and all of Europe would be powered for months. Great for sustained energy… or one big burst."

"My dad," Raymond whispered, his voice low with anxiety. "Where is he?"

"Your father made this for us at Boltzmann's request, and he certainly did deliver. He has helped this operation far more than any of the witless goons with guns that would love to run this place. After this, we gave him one more project to complete for us, and then we would let him free."

"Where is my father?"

"Earlier, we started working on a machine great and terrible. We wanted an ultimate weapon, one that would horrify our enemies and ensure the war would continue as planned. The Panzerwurm. The Biblical Leviathan of the modern age, forged not by God, but by man. It took several years of arduous work by thousands of men, men from countless different labor forces across the world that each worked on only one piece at a time in secret, not knowing it was all part of one machine. All we needed was a way to power it and fit it all together, making it work autonomously and efficiently. But your father refused. He wanted no part of a machine he deemed so horrendous. He stopped working for us right at our greatest time of need, and we had to complete the Panzerwurm using other methods."

"Where the hell is my father, Stonewell?"

"He abandoned us, Raymond. He was of no further use to us."

"Where is he?!"

"Look behind the Blitzsturm."

Raymond, his mind clouded with fury at Stonewell's lack of answers, slowly walked over to the other side of the power generator, feeling every step he took as if his feet were made of dumbbells. Behind the device sat a row of four seats, with wires from the Blitzsturm attached to every plank to turn them into electric chairs.

And on the furthest one to the back was Francis Calvert, his wrists and ankles strapped to the chair. Based on the state of his skin, he had been dead for just over three weeks.

# Chapter Seventeen

"DAD..." RAYMOND whispered, not wanting to believe what he saw.

Francis sat on the chair partially decomposed, his once green eyes now faded and colorless, and his thick brown hair now thinned and grayed. His head leaned on his shoulder with his jaw held open, his gums rotting along with his skin. In spite of these signs of decay, overall, he looked almost exactly as he had when Raymond last saw him, having aged only slightly in the last five years. It was all indicative of the life that had been taken away from him.

Raymond had done it. After half a decade, he had found his father. He had completed his objective. He figured out what had happened at last. And the weight of the answer nearly crushed him.

"No, Dad..." he said softly, kneeling by the chair where his father lay.

"He served us well, Raymond," Stonewell sighed, putting his hand on Raymond's shoulder with feigned sympathy. "After we found him in that bunker, we immediately drafted him and made him work for us.

His engineering prowess helped the Oberschock Federation become the force of unbridled power it is now. Eventually, though, he had enough. He died standing up for what he thought was right, and you should be proud of him for that."

"I could have saved you," Raymond grimaced, closing his eyes as he put his hands on his father's arms. "If only I had found that blueprint... just a bit earlier..."

"He had seen too much. Once we acquired him from his secret bunker, we knew we could only keep him for so long. Eventually he would have been rescued and revealed the truth of our existence before it was time."

"He promised me we'd see each other again. He *promised* me!"

"We could not let him leave with the knowledge he had learned. So, we did what we had to do."

Raymond held his head down in utter defeat, his body trembling as he held his father's arm through the gloves of his Bolter suit. So long he had been left in the dark, and now that the light had come at last, it was darker than ever before. His father was alive just a month earlier, after thinking he was dead *five years* ago.

But he was too late. *Just* too late. All of his efforts had amounted to nothing.

"You... you killed him," he seethed. "You did this."

"We certainly couldn't have let him go after all he'd seen," Stonewell said, shrugging. "What were we supposed to do?"

"Not capture him in the first place!"

"Son, you have no idea what you're talking about. In times of need, you make use of whatever assets you can to stay ahead of the game. Francis was a very valuable asset, so we-"

"He's not an asset! He's my father!"

"He *was.*"

Raymond clenched his fists tighter taking in Stonewell's callous remarks, the rage building in him more furious than any power the Blitzsturm could bring. "You'll pay for what you've done. You'll-"

Before he could attack, Stonewell acted first. He punched Raymond in the stomach and pushed him onto the chair next to his father, strapping him into the metal bolts before he could recover. Raymond struggled to break free, but the bolts fastened tightly to his wrists and ankles.

"What did you think would happen when you came here?" Stonewell demanded. "Did you honestly think you'd find your daddy and then merrily skip out of this fortress hand-in-hand? Your naive idealism would be almost admirable, if it wasn't so pathetic."

Raymond tried to activate his Bolter suit to phase through the chair and run to safety, but the switch to turn it on was on his left wrist, and with his hands strapped to the chair he couldn't flick it with his right hand like he normally did. But maybe, if he could stretch his fingers *just* enough on his left hand...

"How do you think I felt when I lost my own father?" Stonewell asked. "He wasn't the most loving parent, but he taught me an important lesson: use what you're given, every facet of it. And what was I given? A small arms company after the War to End All Wars had ended. And by God, I'm going to use that. Through the Teslanauts, and now the Oberschock Federation, I will make the company more profitable than ever, and maybe from beyond the grave he'll finally be proud."

"*My* father was proud," Raymond snapped. "He told me in a note, meant for when I joined the Teslanauts."

Stonewell lowered his head and glared intensely at Raymond, his heart beating so furiously loud

Raymond thought for sure he could hear it. Then, with a powerful thrust of his arm, he punched Raymond in the face, the impact knocking his head back onto the chair.

"Mind your lip, you little rat," Stonewell hissed.

"You should have minded your business before kidnapping my-"

Another swing, and Stonewell punched Raymond in the face again, the throbbing pain clouding Raymond's mind. Blood once more dripping from his nose, Raymond stared right back at Stonewell, ignoring the pain and focusing on his unbridled hatred for this man.

"You know you're assaulting a child!" he grunted. "I don't turn eighteen until-"

"Shut up!" Stonewell roared, hitting Raymond again before he could finish.

After this last attack though, something remarkable happened, something neither of them certainly expected. Sparks, the thoughtless little machine, somehow sensed its owner was in danger and detached from Raymond's back. With haste, it turned one of its mechanical hands into a blowtorch, a handy tool for hover-heads when helping Teslanauts work with machines. This time, it used the torch to try and drive Stonewell away, waving it in the man's face by swinging the axles of its shoulders up and down.

"Aaagh!" Stonewell raged, grabbing the hover-head and throwing it onto the ground. Before it could use its propellers and tiny thrusters to get back into the air, Stonewell stomped on it and smashed its rectangular body under his boot, sending its tiny pieces all over the floor. Its components and wiring fatally damaged, the lights from Sparks's optical sensors flickered off.

"You killed Sparks *and* my father?!" Raymond shouted, his eyes wide with both surprise and fury. "Oh, you're *really* gonna get it now!"

"Give Francis my regards," Stonewell said coldly, stomping over to the Blitzsturm and flicking every switch to get it to full power. The car-sized machine began to stir, blowing out steam and shaking like an engine that could power a continent. Within its mechanisms, it generated power, through a combination of steam, diesel, and molecular discharges beyond anything the world would see in decades. And all of it was about to flow through Raymond's veins.

"At least you'll die right beside your daddy," Stonewell said, flicking the last switch. "You should be thankful. I'll never have that luxury."

Raymond reached the fingers of his left hand as far as he could with his wrists strapped to the chair, trying desperately to turn on the Bolter suit and scram the heck out of here. With all the Blitzsturm's power switches activated, all Stonewell had to do was go to the control panel and turn on the power circuit connected to Raymond's chair. Then it would be gigawatts of electrical hell for Raymond. He stretched his fingers to the point of his muscles starting to tear, making Raymond inwardly scream while his fingers got ever so close.

Stonewell reached the control panel, and stared venomously at the Brooklyn teenager, one he had trapped and ready to roast like a pig on a spit. With a resentful glare, Stonewell pulled down the lever that activated the power circuits.

A mere instant before he did this, Raymond finally reached the switch to the Bolter suit, and flicked it on at last. But connected to the Blitzsturm's seemingly limitless electrical power, the molecules in his suit supercharged to the *n*th degree. The suit turned Raymond into a wave of charged particles; that was how he could move so fast. The Blitzsturm made that wave expand and flow far beyond normal. He did not just become a wave condensed to the size of a person. His wave encompassed the entire Earth.

Raymond felt like he existed in a reality beyond human comprehension. Through the scattered particles amplified by the Blitzsturm, parts of him flowed all throughout the world. He was simultaneously in Germany, England, China, India, Brazil, New York, and Los Angeles, with every atom that formed his being encircling the planet like a blanket of molecules only nanometers thick. Yet, in his mind, he felt whole. He looked at himself and saw his body, his arms, and his feet solid as normal. The surroundings, however, were a kaleidoscope of every piece of matter on Earth. Every type of soil, every kind of sky, the tiniest pieces of every material object; all of it formed an incomprehensible orb that surrounded Raymond, just as he surrounded the world.

He had no idea if he was alive or dead. He felt like neither, or maybe both. But one thing was for certain: he had to turn off the Bolter suit. He had no idea what would happen, but he could not stay like this for too much longer. His consciousness would become mush.

Raymond moved his right hand over to the switch on his left wrist, the process harder than anything he had ever attempted before. Just moving his arm felt insurmountable, and he watched it gradually drift over to his other wrist like it wasn't his own. Seeing his fingers on the switch, Raymond braced himself in whatever way he could, and flicked it off.

Instantly, his molecules reformed. He fell as a whole body onto a sand dune, slamming into the ground like he had fallen several stories. The sand cushioned him, making the impact not quite as violent as it could have been, but he felt sharp and prolonged pain in practically every muscle. He groaned and rested on the hot yet soft ground, breathing in and out to try and recollect himself.

"Oh man," he gasped, his brain slow to recover after such an experience. He had never felt closer to God than that moment.

Eventually, the heat from the sand grew too painful, and Raymond worked himself to slowly and arduously raise his back off the ground. The blazing sun fried his body almost as badly as that last trip fried his mind. Shaking his head to try and dull the headache, Raymond stood back up and studied his surroundings.

He found himself in a sea of sand, with cragged cliffs and giant boulders dotting the landscape. Hills and mountains kept most of the terrain around him hidden, meaning he had no idea how far out in the wilderness he was. These mountains also provided the only shade, as the sky had not a single cloud in its wide blue expanse. Barring a few leafless and spindly trees between some of the hills further down, there did not appear to be a speck of life, not even buzzing insects or the cries of birds. There were no landmarks, no monuments, nothing to help him figure out where in the world the Bolter suit spat him out.

"Well, I better get out of here," Raymond sighed, flicking the switch to activate the Bolter suit. "Maybe in a few hundred miles I'll find a city or something."

Before he could think about running such a long distance, he heard a tiny click instead of the suit activating. Lowering his brow, Raymond flicked the switch again, only to have the same result. He moved the switch back and forth over and over again, at least twelve times in both directions, but nothing happened. Either the Blitzsturm had fried his suit's systems, or he was out of range of a transmitter tower. Either way was very, very bad.

"C'mon, c'mon!" Raymond growled, hoping to turn the suit on by sheer force of will. "I can't be stuck here! I can't… I can't!"

It was hopeless. His suit was kaput. Raymond was trapped in the middle of nowhere, with no idea where he was, no food or water, no one around to help him, and no one but himself to blame. Everyone was right. His drive to find his father no matter what would become dangerous: his stubbornness would hurt others and himself if he pressed onward. But he could not let it go. He had to find out what happened to Francis Calvert no matter what.

Now, he had found out. And here he was, stranded in the middle of nowhere. Was it worth it?

# Chapter Eighteen

HOURS PASSED, and Raymond still trudged aimlessly in the desert, staying behind cliffs in a desperate attempt to find shade. His skin burned, his throat felt withered, and his muscles further ached with every step he took, but he kept going. He had to keep going.

"Surely there's a well somewhere..." Raymond gasped. "There's gotta be a well or something for wandering travellers... there's gotta be..."

With Sparks smashed to pieces in the Eisenzentrum, he had no one to keep him company. Then again, even if Stonewell hadn't crushed the hover-head under his boot, with no transmitter towers in range there was no guarantee it would work anyway. Every ten minutes Raymond flicked the switch of his Bolter suit to see if he got in range, but to no avail. The suit still had no power. He wanted to take it off so bad. The leather and rubber clung tightly to his sweaty skin, further increasing the temperature of his body and the exhaustion from the heat. But he had no way to carry it, and he needed it to get out of here the *second* he found himself within range of a transmitter tower. That was, unless the Blitzsturm's power surge did indeed fry it. Maybe he should have left the suit behind after all.

"No," Raymond whispered. "I gotta keep this suit. It's my ticket out of here... as soon as I find a tower. There's one just over this hill... just over this hill..."

He walked up the hill, and the hill after that, and the next four hills after that, but he found no tower. Still, he kept walking, telling himself that maybe, behind the *next* cragged peak, there'd be something. Maybe a well full of hot, dirty, delicious water. Maybe a road giving him a direction to go. Maybe even a town with five transmitter towers! He had no idea, but every time he saw a rocky hill obstructing the view ahead, he knew any of those could still be possible, and the only way to find out was to keep going. But he always ended up disappointed.

"I'm sorry, Mom," Raymond grunted, feeling every step like he dragged a crowd of people along with him. "I'm sorry I left home. I shouldn't have looked so hard for Dad. I should've just let it be."

"Come along, son."

Raymond's spirits lifted hearing that voice, and he looked eagerly ahead to see where it came from. Standing between him and the blazing sun was the silhouette of his father, waving eagerly at his son who had spent so long to find him. The sun kept his features from being visible, but Raymond still knew this was Francis Calvert, his father, right there before him.

"Dad... Dad!" Raymond whispered, running faster. "You're not dead! You're right here!"

"Yes, Raymond. You haven't made a mistake looking for me. You did the right thing."

"You really think so?"

"I do, son. I'm so happy to see you now, grown up as a young man."

"We can catch up later, Dad. I just want to hug you! I just want to see your face again!"

Raymond must have been running ahead for a solid two minutes, with his father's silhouette still waving and motioning him to come forward. Yet no matter how far Raymond ran, he never got closer. The delirium brought forth from the heat and the exhaustion made him still run, though, believing with all his heart that, indeed, his father was *right* there. He just had to keep running.

"I'm coming, Dad!" Raymond cried out, tears forming in his eyes. "I'm-"

Just before he thought for sure his father had gotten a bit closer, he tumbled down a steep rocky hill, having not been aware where he was going. He rolled down sand and sharp rocks for what felt like forever, with his aching muscles making the pain ever sharper and more apparent. After seemingly having fallen from the tallest peak in the world, he finally found himself face first in the dirt, every part of his body banged and bruised.

"Oh God…" Raymond groaned, slowly turning his body over and spitting hot sand grits out of his mouth. "Oh, it hurts… everything hurts…"

The futility of it all really started to become clear to Raymond. It did not matter how long he walked. It did not matter what he did. He was stuck in the middle of this hot, mountainous desert, with no end in sight, and no victory to be had. He had no resources. He had no friends to help. His father was dead. His mother was countless miles away. All he had here was himself, and so he had nothing.

However, thinking about it further, he did actually have something. Something that could save him from all this pain and exhaustion. He had his father's custom-built disintegrator gun.

Groaning from the pain of moving his body, he took the gun out of the holster of his Bolter suit and looked at the last gift his father would ever give him. He tilted it, the sleek metallic barrel gleaming in the sun, with the modifications Becky had put in place tucked safely inside its magazine. It was a beautiful little machine, with the added sentimentality of its familial origins. He could study it for hours with his exhausted mind, but he knew he needed it for something else. Knowing he had no other option left, Raymond held the gun up, and fired.

At once, a beam of electrified energy raced up into the air, rising higher and higher until it eventually dissipated in the sky. The electricity from within the beam crackled in the sky; one could witness it from dozens of miles out, at least if there was someone out there to see it.

"That's it..." Raymond breathed, lowering his arm and putting the gun back in his holster. "That's all I've got."

He had no more energy to get up or do anything. With the sun baking his skin, he closed his eyes and fell asleep, having no idea when or if he would get up again. As he lay on the hot and sandy ground, he dreamt of a time he remembered well.

It was a cold Saturday morning in December 1917. Raymond, having turned thirteen just a couple of months ago, finished his breakfast in his Brooklyn apartment and happily put his plate in the sink. Fork in hand, though, he held it up in the air, flying it around while making little shooting noises with his lips.

"Take that, you filthy Germans!" he laughed. "The mighty Francis Calvert will shoot you down! Pew! Pew!"

At this point, all he knew of his father was that he worked in a secret government branch, helping the war through means he could not convey to his family. But the mystery of it made it all the more intriguing for young Raymond. His dad could have been anything: a fighter, a soldier, a pilot, a tank crew member, an engineer, a spy; anything. All he knew for sure was that his dad was a hero, just like in all the good stories. What he did *had* to be something amazing.

It had been a few months since they'd heard from him last. He left for work one day, kissed Martha Calvert on the cheek, and headed off. Little did Raymond know that would be the last he would see of his father. He did not even get a good glimpse of him that day; he felt too invested in whatever adventures the characters in his book went on that he read on the chair by the front door.

But that did not matter. Raymond knew his father would return soon enough. After landing the fork safely on the runway of the kitchen sink, he gasped excitedly as he heard a knock on the door.

"Raymond, honey, can you get that?" his mother's voice called from her sewing room.

"Got it, Mom!" Raymond shouted, heading to the door with a grin. Surely he'd open the door and find his father standing before him, having returned from another big trip with all kinds of stories of which he could only partially tell the details, which made them all the more enticing. Barely feeling his fingers on the door handle, he yanked it open and stared out in the hallway of the apartment building expectantly.

Instead, he found two gentlemen in bowler hats and silver suits standing before him, their hands folded in front of them. Raymond did not know at the time, but looking at this memory through the dream, he realized now this was Agent Null and Agent Zero, the recruitment agents for the Teslanauts. This time, they presented themselves only as government officials, and the way they stared down at young Raymond did not encourage his enthusiasm.

"Is this the Calvert residence?" Agent Zero asked.

"Yes, sir," Raymond said, his smile fading.

"Is your mother home?"

"Mom!" Raymond hollered, turning his head to look back inside. "These people want to talk to you!"

Martha walked up to the two gentlemen at the door, holding her hand to her chest. Some part of her must have known what these men would say, but she did not want to hear it. "Ray, go back inside," she insisted, pulling Raymond away from the door and back into the entry room.

Raymond ran into the apartment, but hid behind the wall leading into the kitchen, peering at the front door while listening intently to what they said. His heart felt like a lump, but he did not know why, beyond just having a bad feeling. Surely he worried too much. These men would bring good news, right?

He thought so hard about what they could say, that he realized he had forgotten to pay attention to what they *did* say. He had missed the initial round of conversation. Now, though, he heard them talking about something else, and with no context Raymond had difficulty discerning what they meant.

"Your husband's organization will help compensate you until your son moves out," Agent Null's voice said. "You'll still need to work, but this way you'll be slightly better off."

"I understand," Martha's voice replied. "Do we tell Raymond the details?"

"We can't inform him," Agent Zero said. "Not legally anyway. Francis's work remains top secret. Just tell him that his father will not be returning home. He'll be able to glean enough from that."

Raymond gasped softly hearing what the agent had said, sliding down to the ground in despair. He folded his legs in, and lowered his face to his knees. From that point on, the rest of the agents' conversation with his mother became unintelligible, just a parade of blahs and umms with all the meaning of a four-dollar bill. All he heard was his own tears, and his muffled breathing.

He could not believe it. He would not believe it.

After anywhere between thirty seconds and five hours, Martha closed the door and sighed softly, clearly bottling up her own emotions. Then her footsteps gradually moved toward the kitchen, before stopping right beside the floor where Raymond sat. Raymond did not bother to look at her; he was far too invested in counting the wrinkles on his pant legs.

"I take it you heard what they said?" Martha asked.

Raymond nodded slowly, still not looking at her.

Martha, realizing she needed to speak to him at eye level, sat on the ground with her son, waiting for whenever he felt ready to speak. After a few minutes of that time not coming, though, she decided she needed to speak first.

"You're too young to really understand, Ray," she began, her tone as soft and gentle as she could muster, "but death isn't the end."

"I know," Raymond muttered. "I hear that every Sunday."

"I'm not talking about your father, or anyone else lost in this terrible war. I'm talking about us. When we lose someone, it may feel like the world is over, but the last thing they would want to leave behind is a person refusing to let them go. We need time to grieve, but then we need to make the world a better place in their absence."

"How can the world be better without Dad?"

"Because we're still here to fill his shoes. He paved the way for us, and it's up to us to continue down that path. One has only truly learned the lesson of their forebears if they can achieve it without them. And that's what your father would have wanted from us."

Raymond wiped some tears off with his arm, still not feeling like talking much after hearing this news. Martha scooched closer to her son, willing to sit with him for as long as he needed.

"I… I don't know if I can do that," Raymond finally said.

"Well, one of these days, you're going to have to. I'm not going to be here forever, either. Let's just take this one day at a time, though. You can learn his lessons another day, whenever you'll need them most."

"Another day…" Raymond muttered, but not so much in the dream. Instead, he found himself murmuring this in real life, his eyes barely starting to open as he regained consciousness. It took some time, but he started to realize that he did not wake in the same position as when he fell asleep. Instead, his back was against a hard surface, and the ground beneath him rumbled, not like an earthquake, but like a gentle rocking. Then, once he smelled the diesel, he realized what had happened. He had been picked up. But by whom?

Before he could wonder too much further, he felt the most wonderful sensation possible: the flow of cool water down his throat. "Rest," a stranger's voice said calmly. "You'll need your energy."

Raymond happily obliged.

Some time later, Raymond's eyes opened, his perception clearer now than it had been in the back of the truck. He sat on a wooden chair in a dimly lit room, with the surrounding oil lamps creating a relaxing, peaceful ambience. Sandstone and marble lined the walls, and despite the hot desert environment, the temperature felt nice and cozy. Then again, based on how long he had probably been out, it was likely nighttime.

"Ah, you're awake," the voice he had heard offering him water earlier said. Walking up to him and sitting in the chair next to him was a man roughly ten years older than Raymond, sporting a thick black mustache and a pendant around his neck with a symbol Raymond had never seen before. His dark eyes looked at Raymond with a fierce, almost eager curiosity, yet with a kindness that put Raymond's uncertainties of his situation slightly at ease.

"My name is Burak," the man said, steadily speaking as if English was not his first language. "What is your name, lonely traveler?"

Raymond swallowed with his newly moist throat, hesitating at first before realizing he needed all the help he could get. "Raymond," he finally said. "Thank you for saving me, Burak."

"You were a stranger in need," Burak said, nodding. "Think nothing of it. Your voice sounds American."

"New York, born and raised. Where am I?"

"You're in a hideout in central Anatolia. Some of the Turkish forces were stationed here, but it seems as if the war will end soon, so this place may no longer be needed."

"War? I thought the war ended years ago."

"The Great War, yes. But smaller wars continue to flare up despite all the armistices. The Ottoman Empire has committed unimaginable atrocities in an attempt to regain the power they lost, and so the revolutionaries led by Kemal Atatürk are attempting to give control back to the Turkish people. I'm afraid here in Anatolia, the war never truly ended."

Raymond sighed and put his hands to his head, hating hearing that peace never came in some parts of the world. Back at home, Americans enjoyed all the largesse and prosperity of the roaring twenties, naively assuming that everywhere else was just dandy. But other places still struggled, and Raymond's place of privilege grew ever more apparent to him.

"May I ask, what is it you are wearing?" Burak asked, looking down at Raymond's suit with a somewhat amused gaze.

"Oh, this?" Raymond said. "Well, uhh… it's kind of proprietary information."

"It's a Bolter suit, is it not?"

Raymond's eyes widened. He certainly did not expect to hear him identify this fancy piece of technology by name. "Yeah," he said, smiling slightly with appreciation. "How'd you know?"

"The volt-tech front extends all across the world, Raymond. We knew you were from a volt-tech organization when we saw the beam you fired. That's how we managed to find you. I assume you are from the Teslanauts?"

Raymond nodded slowly.

"What happened? How did you end up stranded in this desert?"

Getting into the thick of what had happened was admittedly the last thing Raymond wanted to do, but once again, he recognized that in order to get back with the others, he had to let any allies he could find in on whatever information they needed. He had to bring Burak into the fold.

And so, Raymond told his story. And as much as he initially dreaded explaining all that had happened, he found himself talking for almost an hour, starting with his desire to find his father and remaining so stubbornly steadfast to the point of not listening to reason. He went into joining the Teslanauts, learning about all their amazing and advanced technology, finally meeting the great Nikola Tesla, making a lot of friends both human and machine, and how he proceeded to dump all of these good things just because he could not let his fruitless mission go. As he talked, he kept telling himself he would stop in a few minutes. Surely his long and emotional speech grew tiresome to this man. But Raymond kept going, opening up more than he had to anyone since he was a small child. Clearly, he had to let this out, and thankfully Burak listened the whole time.

"And what's the point of it all?" Raymond said to finish it off. "There I was, getting the experience of a lifetime, and I didn't even care. My quest to find my father was for nothing, and now I'm stuck here thousands of miles away from home, from my friends, and from my fellow agents, without a goal or purpose to be found. I still can't answer Ying's question. What do I want to do? In fact now, what *can* I do?"

Burak put his hands together and thought deeply for a moment, contemplating the best way to put into words how he might help this troubled young teenager. Raymond waited patiently for the answer, his eyes tearing after pouring out everything he went through. He needed help. He needed answers. Would Burak provide those answers, when no one else had been able to adequately aid him?

"Have you heard of the Firtina Anka Kusu?" Burak finally said.

Raymond shook his head.

"In English, it means the Storm Phoenixes," Burak explained, removing the pendant from his neck and handing it to Raymond. "It was the Ottoman volt-tech faction, but the Turkish have since taken it over."

Raymond took the pendant and studied it intently, marveling at the beautiful craftsmanship of its brass and silver design. In its center was a great eagle-like bird soaring majestically, like the phoenixes of the old myths. Rather than fire, though, its wings had a constant tempest of lightning in its wake. Nodding with admiration, Raymond handed the pendant back.

"This country has done terrible things," Burak said. "The Ottoman Empire, through the guns of their army and the gadgets of the Storm Phoenixes, have sent many souls to Paradise. They've carried out a campaign against my people, against the Greeks, against the Armenians, and against anyone else who stands in their way. But after gruesome battles, and the actions of brave revolutionaries, we've fought back. We've apprehended their volt-tech. We've taken their cities. The Ottomans are losing their power, and they won't last much longer. We will get our country back and repurpose who we are, putting the atrocities of our previous rulers behind us."

"Meaning?"

"We are not merely defined by where we come from, Raymond, but by what we do. Your father was a great man, supplying machines and other marvels to many forces and assisting countless noble causes in his time. But his time has passed, and through your search for him, he has given you a place among the Teslanauts. You can do whatever you want. Now, what is it you are going to do?"

Raymond had heard this question before, but after listening to Burak's advice, he started thinking about it differently. One way or another, there were a few things he *had* to do. He had to return to his friends. He had to help them stop the Oberschock Federation. He had to earn his place back on the Teslanaut squad.

And he had to bring Robert Stonewell, the man who killed his father, to justice.

He had to do all that. But more importantly, he *could* do all that. It was totally in his control. All he needed was the motivation, and the means to get there.

"I need to rejoin with the rest of the Teslanauts," Raymond finally said. "Any chance you can take me to the main base for the Storm Phoenixes? My suit is broken, and I need it fixed to run back."

"It's not broken," Burak said, studying the sweaty and slightly torn but intact Bolter suit. "There is not enough power in this area. There was barely enough for you to fire your gun. We dismantled the transmitter tower here to keep it from the Ottomans, but we're moving out of this base and regrouping in Constantinople where the Storm Phoenix headquarters is located. From there, your suit should be repowered. We will depart Monday morning."

Raymond nodded. "All right. Soon the Teslanauts will know what I, Raymond Calvert, am capable of. *That's* what I'm going to do."

# Chapter Nineteen

"SO THIS Robert Stonewell is going to attack Paris with an army of volt-tech and restart the war?" Ivan demanded. "And through his company, he'll make sure he gets all the money and power?"

"That's exactly what the world needs," Becky groaned. "Another cracker with a god complex."

The factory workers gathered when the Teslanauts returned and heard about their new information, relayed by Foudre before he departed with the rest of his Volt Knights. After learning about what the Oberschock Federation had planned, they knew they had a lot of work to do to defend Paris and keep them from reaching the Eiffel Tower. They had machines to forge, parts to repair, weapons to arm, and gears to grind, and all of it had to defend against the vast supply of volt-tech machines Stonewell had at his disposal.

As the Teslanauts returned, the four young factory workers received this news from someone they had not met before, but with whom they had a mutual friend. Helen, after hearing from Watson that Raymond knew them well, came up to the group and explained everything, while unsuccessfully trying to mask her guilt at what she told her Brooklyn friend. She hoped with all her heart he would make it back safely, but she realized it was out of their hands now.

"That machine you describe..." Arthur muttered, his eyes wide with fear and yet an odd sort of admiration. "That's... that's impossible. There's no way such a ludicrously complex mechanical system can function, let alone act autonomously."

"I saw the giant bugger with my own eyes," Helen insisted. "I don't know how they accomplished it, but we need to figure out a way to dismantle it. We cannot let that thing attack Paris."

"Imagine the intricacies of such a machine," Ivan murmured, his already deep voice lowered with reverence and a hint of horror. "Imagine the sheer artistry of its design. It's beyond human. It's almost... divine, but twisted. Contorted to the whims of the devil."

"I betcha it'll fall apart easy with some sort of explosive put in the right place," Becky said. "The trick is figuring out that place. And how to get it there. And how big to make the explosive. And how to get ourselves out of there before it blows. Come to think of it, maybe it won't fall apart so easy."

"I trust you'll find a way to get it done," Helen said, nodding at Becky. "We're counting on all of you. You're the ones that helped us make it this far."

"Aw, aren't you sweet!" Becky gushed.

"Any word on Raymond?" Watson asked. "Haven't heard from him since he left us in the Alps."

"Nothing," Helen said, closing her eyes and sighing. "Bloody hell, I hope I didn't make a mistake encouraging him to go. He could get killed."

"Then why'd you do it?"

"Because I know exactly what he's been through. I know how he feels. If he didn't go and find out for himself, he wouldn't be able to focus on the mission. He has to fill that hole in his heart."

"When my family fled Russia... we knew it would be difficult," Ivan said softly, his massive shoulders slumped. "We knew we would struggle leaving behind the country we grew up in for generations. But we also knew it was what we had to do. Most of the time, the best decision is never the easy one."

"Is what you're saying for or against sending Raymond off to the enemy for answers?" Becky asked. "I can't quite tell."

"It is applicable either way," Ivan said gruffly. "Take it as you will."

"Well, that's helpful."

"I just wish I knew where he was," Helen said. "It's been nearly all day. Surely with the Bolter suit he would be able to return shortly."

"I believe I may have found him."

Helen turned to the new voice, soft and gentle, yet resolute. Her shoulders stiff and her spine straight to maintain professionalism, Ying walked up to Helen and briefly bowed, before brushing a strand of her short black hair out of her face. "I'm Lei Ying, and I work in communications."

"Helen Brimsby, field agent," Helen said, bowing back respectfully. "You said you found Raymond?"

"Well, I found where he was last at any rate. I conducted several electro-scans of the surrounding countries using the transmitter tower network, looking for the precise signature of a Bolter suit in action. He's the only one using a Bolter suit, so theoretically its signature would be easy to find. Eventually I managed to track his path by combining a series of graphs from the scans."

"And?"

"He was last seen just outside Berchtesgaden. Afterwards, the signature was blurred. For the scan taken at 2:06 p.m. local time, his signature was all over, like a storm of charged particles. And after that, the signature disappeared. I haven't been able to find him since."

"Some sort of overcharge," Watson said, his eyes and smile widening in sync. "The ultimate shock. Boy, I'm envious. The amount of enlightenment he must have felt… it's like opening your third eye."

"When'd you get all mystical?" Becky chortled.

"So you're saying he got supercharged with energy while wearing a Bolter suit?" Helen asked. "What does that do to you?"

"It's never been done," Watson said. "Theoretically when he turned the suit off he would resolidify, but where would be a mystery. He could have fallen in the middle of the Pacific, or in the frozen wastelands of Siberia. Of course, there's also the chance that his diffused molecules remained scrambled and he would never reform at all, doomed to remain a collection of disjointed particles floating in the aether."

"What?!"

"Look, it's just a theory. Ying said she couldn't find his signature afterwards."

"He could also be out of range," Ying reminded Watson. "The electro-scans I'm able to conduct from here can only go so far. We don't have to bury Raymond yet. But until he returns, we'll just have to hope for the best. We have more pressing matters to attend to."

"Indeed we do," said another.

Everyone gasped softly hearing the new voice, recognizing it immediately despite rarely hearing it. This man was their boss, their founder, and their guide; helping them from the sidelines, aiding in the science, and making all of their experiments possible. The volt-tech was their magic, first conjured by this great wizard.

"Mr. Tesla?" Arthur asked, feeling flustered and dizzy almost immediately.

Nikola Tesla nodded at the young engineer, the sixty-five-year-old man having walked up to the group from the garage of the Freckle Dump base. Behind the tall, thin, and commanding genius, a fleet of Volt Knight Interceptors flew out of the open doors, having dropped off their troops and their special passenger from New York after picking up Foudre earlier. Cobblewood and Morales discussed the situation with each other in the background, while Tesla decided to let his workers know personally.

"This matter with the Oberschock… it requires desperate measures," Tesla told the workers, agents, and the comms specialist. "They cannot be allowed to attack Paris and cripple our volt-tech. We've worked too hard to maintain peace following the fallout of the war."

"So what are we going to do?" Helen asked.

"We have to engage an all-out defense on open ground, where many people could bear witness. Doing such a brazen act requires the support of the Electrocracy. And that's why I'm here: to represent the Teslanauts on the council."

"Wait, are we actually going…?" Arthur asked, so excited he couldn't finish his sentence.

"Some of you are, yes."

"Going where?" Helen asked, her eyes narrowing with suspicious intrigue.

"To Electropolis, the secret city and home base of the entire Electrocracy!" Arthur said, his usual stammer gone and replaced by a rapid hike in talking speed. "It's the ultimate expression of volt-tech's possibilities, and of what the world could become if volt-tech were standard rather than secret. Flying trains! Teleporting buildings! Automated service and facilities! Perpetual electrical power! Experiments in particle physics and atomic energy! It's a utopia of science and engineering, and we're going to experience it at last!"

"Are we?" Becky asked, one of her eyebrows raised. "If it's so secret that even long-term Teslanauts don't know of it, then I doubt we'll be given permission to see it. The Cleanup Squad is probably on its way as we speak!"

"Initially, I admit, I was only going to permit Arthur and Helen to join us," Tesla sighed. "But as Arthur has already so graciously revealed its existence to the lot of you, I suppose you all can come. I trust you enough to maintain its secrecy."

"*Yes*!" Arthur screamed, throwing his fist down while practically dancing in place. "We're going to the big secret city! We're going to Electro-"

Before he could yell any louder, Tesla quickly grasped Arthur's wristband with his own and channeled some electricity using the lock-picking mechanism on his hand. The shock stunned Arthur in place and silenced him at once, keeping him from revealing more details about their destination. Becky and Helen both laughed at this, and even Ivan cracked a smile.

"I do not wish to find my trust in you unwarranted," Tesla snapped. "Now hurry along. We don't have much time."

The next twelve hours went by like a blur for the young agents and factory workers, but not due to the thrill of experience or anything they did themselves. Tesla, Cobblewood, Helen, Arthur, Becky, Ivan, Ji, Watson, Ying, and a few others boarded Tesla's personal airship meant for international travel, and flew away from the Freckle Dump station before the ship made its way to Electropolis. The airship, dubbed the *White Pigeon*, reached roughly two hundred feet in length, large but not terribly long compared to some real massive aerial cruisers even outside the volt-tech world. However, Tesla's was unique in that, rather than one oval-shaped envelope, it came equipped with three, aligned like an upside down triangle with the gondola attached to the lowermost one. Propellers lined the sides of all three envelopes, allowing greater maneuverability if not a terribly significant increase in velocity. The reason for such a distinctive arrangement though had nothing to do with practicality, or any demonstration of volt-tech capabilities. Instead, it came from a very simple reason: Tesla really liked the number three.

Even in a volt-tech-powered ship, the flight took many hours, to the point that they did not arrive until the next morning. Just when Helen and the rest were certain they figured out the direction they went and therefore had a general idea of where they had traveled, agents from the Cleanup Squad emerged from hiding and wiped the memories of everyone but Tesla and Cobblewood for the duration of the trip. Helen only got a glimpse of their gas-mask covered faces and their perpetually blurred bodies, their image in the physical world somehow distorted and blurred. How did they work? Who were these people? Before she could ask, the agents induced her into a brief nap, and by the time she and the others woke up, the Cleanup Squad was gone, and so were her memories of the flight.

"Oh, you all must have fallen asleep," Cobblewood said shortly, walking down the cabin from the cockpit above. "Get up and get ready. We've arrived at Electropolis."

"We *all* fell asleep?" Ji asked. "That's awfully convenient."

"Mr. Tesla is showing us a city so secret even most of the agents don't know of it," Helen muttered, getting off the hard airship floor and rubbing her eyes. "I suppose it makes sense its location must be kept secret as well."

"No, you all fell asleep at the exact same time until the very moment we arrived," Cobblewood grunted. "That's the story. A miraculous accident, isn't it? Nothing more. Now let's go."

Helen climbed up to the bridge of the *White Pigeon*'s gondola, and looked out the windows at this mysterious place. They appeared to have flown to a misty island, twice the size of Manhattan, composed of rocky cliffs and little vegetation. The lack of plant life made deducing their location in the world difficult; they could easily narrow it down if the island had thick jungle trees or boreal forest or some other way to tell the climate. Despite this, the sheer enormity of the cliffs made the island look spectacular and exotic regardless; they reached thousands of feet into the sky, forming a canyon that cut the island in half. A stream of churning ocean water rested beneath them, having eroded the island and built the cliff sides the ship floated through right then.

And built into the canyon walls itself was Electropolis.

Airships big and small moved in every direction, forming midair traffic like the roads of any city. Vast neighborhoods of houses and other residential structures lined the cliffs, with balconies and porches stepping off into nothing. Midair locomotives picked up passengers at designated train stops before twisting and coiling around with their thrusters. Hover-head machines of varying sizes--some no bigger than a soccer ball and others nearly the size of a truck--painted walls, moved supply crates, repaired structures, and performed all sorts of other busywork. Laboratories bigger than the Pyramids of Giza crowded the industrial district, with countless tendrils of glowing wires pumping insurmountable quantities of power for whatever bold and behemothic experiments took place inside. Smelters provided the necessary building material from ore mined across the island, potentially the reason for the lack of vegetation.

The factories, though, made up the majority of the buildings, fully staffed with both humans and machines forging more technology for this prosperous city. The colossal clouds of smoke formed by their work rose up between the mountainous cliffs, with rows of net-like machines filtering the soot and grime and sending it back down via pipes. As well as allowing them to repurpose this waste into metal slabs or whatever else they needed, this kept the great pillars of smoke from revealing this place's secrets to any passing ships. It merely made the island look like it had a perpetual fog. Other ships, those in the know of the big volt-tech secret, moved with clearance to the cliff-built city through the saltwater river, and picked up cargo that other volt-tech bases could use. Electropolis was a perpetual factory, but based on the potted trees and flowers on the residential district's porches and the giant statues of famous inventors lining the central area, it also seemed a great and luxurious place to live.

"This is… incredible," Arthur gasped, his mouth agape with awe.

"It's truly marvelous," Helen agreed. "To think this is what the world could be like."

"It sure is amazing the progress people are capable of if they put their mind to it," Becky added, nodding. "Who lives here, exactly?"

"An incredible collection of hard working people who have dedicated their lives to volt-tech," Tesla said. "I myself plan to retire here in a few years, making only sporadic appearances to the mainland. Some people, though, live their whole lives here, having been publicly declared dead and freed of the burden of the rest of the world. Electropolis has the most important and intellectual minds on Earth working here for the benefit of mankind."

"Is your former boss here?" Ying asked.

"Are you referring to Edison? Of course he's not. Don't be foolish."

"Well then, who are we talking to?" Helen asked.

"The heads of the organization are in the Electocratic Hall," Tesla said. "Most of them are not scientists, but the usual cursory bureaucrats you'd expect in any government body. They're the sort of people required to run such an organization, however, and the current head minister is a dear friend of mine you might have heard of before."

The *White Pigeon* docked at a station near the center of the city, with the stream dividing the canyon spraying misty seawater with every crash upon the rocks. The group of Teslanauts departed as hover-heads tied down the ship by the gondola and performed maintenance on its hull and propulsion systems. Once the group left the ship, they walked down the footpath leading through Electropolis's commercial district on their way to the government epicenter, the path lining the lower side of the cliff with the shops built into the rock. Elevators led to paths further upwards, with layers of buildings and streets nearly up to the top. Due to the constant cloud cover and the skyscraping cliffs, natural light remained low. Therefore, lamp posts looking similar to gas lamps but obviously powered by electricity lined the paths while every vehicle and machine came adorned with spotlights, making the city's atmosphere akin to late dusk even during midday.

Hundreds of people walked with the Teslanauts through the commercial district, either with them toward the Electrocratic Hall or just buying groceries or other supplies for their homes. Most of the citizens were over fifty years old, having long retired from the rest of the world and making permanent residence here, but a few of them had young protégés, or even children that had lived their whole lives in Electropolis. The residential areas came with fine schools, designated to teach youth about volt-tech and the Electrocracy as well as the basic math and liberal arts.

"They're staring at me," Becky grumbled, trying to ignore the people giving her funny looks as they walked by the group. "Of course these old folks never imagined a Negro in their ideal city of the future."

"Just stay close to us," Ivan told her. "We'll keep you safe."

"Sure, but I'm really looking forward to a time when I don't need y'all to keep me safe."

"We're almost there," Tesla said, walking faster as they entered a plaza with a dome-shaped building the size of an automotive factory in its center. "The Electrocratic Hall is up ahead."

In the docks and landing platforms surrounding the city center, French Volt Knight Interceptors, American southern Proton Ranger biplanes, Russian Watt Cossack sea ships, Turkish Firtina Anka Kusu airships, Chinese Shandianlong dirigibles, and vehicles of many other volt-tech factions landed and unloaded their passengers. The sheer number of people who gathered here today from all over the world underscored the importance and urgency of their situation. They needed to make the right decisions today. The fate of volt-tech, and perhaps the world as a whole, was at stake.

"Long time no see, *monsieurs*!" Jean Michel du Foudre laughed, rushing forward to the Electrocratic Hall as fast as his new mechanical leg allowed. A few other Volt Knights walked beside him to aid their captain should he stumble, but he did not appear to need their assistance.

"Ji, Ying," an older Chinese man, Lei Jainyu, said while bowing his head at his two children. He had a small mustache, a tiny beard, and not a single other hair on his head. "I trust the Teslanauts are treating you well?"

"They are indeed, Father," Ji said, bowing back at the head of the Shandianlong.

"And I'm treating Ji and the others well in return!" Ying said with a smirk.

"*Ya tebya davno ne videl,* Crankovich!" a Watt Cossack agent shouted, laughing heartily at his fellow Russian. Ivan just held his head down, trying to not get noticed further by the agents of the country his family had fled.

"We can exchange pleasantries after we've settled this matter with Oberschock," Tesla murmured, preferring not to waste time intermingling with the other agents. "We have a job to do; that is the only reason we came all this way. It is time for us to convene, agents."

Within the Electrocratic Hall sat a circular diplomatic courtroom, shaped like an arena or an amphitheater, with tiers reaching almost fifty feet up in a half-circle from the front. Each faction had its own section in the seating, with the leader on a podium at the front. The room, modeled after Roman architecture, came adorned with white columns and marble floors, without a speck of grime or smudging of boots to be found. The whole room looked pristine and powerful. Important things were decided here.

Helen, Ji, Ying, Arthur, Becky, Ivan, and Watson moved to the middle rows of the Teslanaut seating area, while Cobblewood, Morales, and other high-ranking officials sat in the front. Tesla stood behind the front podium, waiting impatiently for everyone else to gather so they could begin the discussion. Just to the left of the Teslanauts sat the Volt Knights, with Foudre up on the front row with the rest of his squad of agents. Their leader, Rodrique Bouclier, was an enormous Frenchman with a prominent mustache and muscles that could surely punch a car into a pulp. He stood at the front podium, ready to represent his faction in the Electrocracy. To their right, Lei Jainyu reached his podium while the other Shandianlong agents sat down at their designated seats. Ji and Ying eyed them closely, as if comparing the composure and vibe of their previous faction's agents with their own, before turning their attention to the front of the courtroom.

It took another ten minutes, but finally everyone had gathered, ready to begin discussions. As well as roughly a dozen high-ranking judges sitting at their podiums on the stage with their noses in the air, walking up to the front was an old, portly man in his mid-seventies, with a dark bushy mustache and mutton chops, and a fancy suit and bow tie that bespoke a demeanor of professionalism and distinguishment. This man had done a lot in his life and now resided here, having retired from the rest of the world and made permanent residence in Electropolis.

"Is that…?" Arthur asked, eyes wide and vacant with disbelief.

"Who?" Helen said. "Who is that?"

"No, it can't be… he died years ago!"

"Who died years ago? Your father? Your uncle? King Edward VII? Who are you bloody talking about?"

"George Westinghouse," Tesla greeted the older man, nodding respectfully. "Head Minister of the Electrocracy. It is good to see you again."

"Enough with the formalities, Nikola," the man said gruffly, a brief smile peeking through his thick facial hair. "We've known each other too long for that."

"Mr. Westinghouse's health declined in 1911, and thus he retired from his company," Arthur explained quietly to the others sitting with him. "He died three years later in his home in New York… or at least, that's what everyone thought. He looks perfectly healthy to me!"

"He must have moved here around then, having faked his death to maintain the secret and run the Electrocracy," Watson said. "What a legend. Maybe I oughta fake my death by grabbing too many wires or something!"

"What would you do afterwards?" Becky asked, chuckling at Watson's suggestion. "Hide in a cellar with all your rat friends? Besides, we all know electrocution doesn't kill you. It just makes you stronger."

"Members of the Electrocracy, please be seated," Westinghouse ordered, his voice now loud and booming so that everyone could hear. "Our formal discussion begins now."

At his command, everyone who had not taken a seat proceeded to do so, and then the idle chatter and discussions quieted down. Once silence had at last overtaken the assembly, Westinghouse put his arms behind his back and spoke before the delegates.

"We have recently discovered that a rogue volt-tech organization known as the Oberschock Federation has begun initiating aggressive actions," the old Electrocracy Head Minister began. "So far the damage has been the destruction of the Swiss town of Ausgraben, toppled German railroads right at the French border, and hundreds of lives lost, both civilian and volt-tech agents. And according to our latest information, they intend to carry out a precision strike that could severely jeopardize the volt-tech front. Captain Foudre, First Commanding Officer of the Volt

Knights' Eleventh Regiment, I'm told you have a document you'd like to share?"

"*Oui, monsieur*," Foudre said, pulling out the leather journal from a compartment in his armor. Helen sighed sadly seeing the journal in Foudre's meaty hands, remembering that it had belonged to Raymond's father and thus had sparked his sudden departure.

"Zis journal was uncovered in ze dungeons of the Oberschock Federation's headquarters," Foudre explained. "It belonged to a prisoner by ze name of Francis Calvert, a former Teslanaut and zeir lead foundryman and technical officer. His work was highly sought after by ze Teslanauts' enemies, and so he was relocated to a secret bunker in Europe. However, ze Oberschock Federation found him anyway, captured him, and forced him to build most of zeir machines we have fought so far. One of ze projects they made him build was ze Blitzsturm, a highly advanced power generator. With ze Blitzsturm in tow, zey plan to attack Paris and connect the generator with ze Eiffel Tower, sending powerful electrical coils across all our transmitter towers and overloading zem to ze point of zeir destruction. Volt-tech across ze hemisphere will be severely crippled, and with ze attack on Paris, the war would start once more, with little of ze Electrocracy's capabilities left to rein it in."

Hearing this development, the Electrocracy delegates murmured to each other in surprise, trying to determine what could possibly be done to stop such an assault. Westinghouse held up his hand to silence the crowd, but some of them reacted too strongly to listen.

"Zey would attack our capital city and desecrate our monument for such a horrible cause?!" Bouclier demanded with the ferocity of an angry bear. "We must stop zem with great haste! Our country has seen too much devastation already!"

"We can't stop them without revealing ourselves to the world," Lei Jainyu reminded the leader of the Volt Knights. "The exposure of volt-tech would lead to greater consequences than what the Oberschock Federation could do."

"The Shandianlong representative is correct," one of the judges at the front stated.

"Are you suggesting we let zem attack and do nothing to stop zem?!" Bouclier boomed.

"The range of their attack on the towers will not affect volt-tech everywhere," Lei Jainyu said. "The Shandianlong and Proton Rangers will still be active, as well as some of the other factions in those parts of the world. We can still rein the Oberschock Federation in."

"We cannot let zem attack Paris! We cannot let zem restart ze war! What you suggest is madness!"

"The secret must be maintained!" Lei Jainyu insisted. "The very fact that these people are using volt-tech to attack Paris is proof of that. The world is not ready, and we cannot stop them without betraying the truth."

"I will not let zem set foot into our city at *any* cost! I care about my people, unlike you!"

Immediately the Volt Knight and Shandianlong agents started loudly quarreling, until neither side's arguments could be discerned amidst the verbal chaos. Tesla put his hand to his face, trying to figure out how to calm the crowd, while the other factions watched the French and Chinese agents squabble with both horrified and somewhat bemused eyes. The Teslanauts, sitting right between the two arguing factions, shrunk into their seats awkwardly and waited for the mood to improve.

"Silence, everyone!" Westinghouse demanded. "This situation is too critical for us to bicker amongst ourselves! There are ways to stop Oberschock while maintaining the secret."

"You're not suggesting the Cleanup Squad is capable of wiping an entire city's memory, are you?" Lei Jainyu said. "Even if they could, the damage left over from the fight would take too long to rebuild for them to think nothing happened."

"The Cleanup Squad can handle *anything*," Watson grumbled, slouching on his seat while crossing his arms. He did not like to hear the abilities of his favorite squad so easily dismissed.

"We could potentially evacuate the city before Oberschock arrives, lightening the burden of the Cleanup Squad, but we could not guarantee everyone's departure," Westinghouse said. "The safest way to maintain the secret while stopping them is to fight outside the city, before they reach Paris."

"Zat is what I've been saying!" Bouclier huffed.

"The Paris civilians will still see the battle if it's fought too close, as well as those in smaller surrounding towns," another judge noted. "We would need more cover than mere distance if we are to achieve this."

"Thankfully, that's where my experiments will prove most useful," Tesla said, looking back and forth at Bouclier and Lei Jainyu. "For the last couple of years, I've been working on a device meant just for situations such as this where we must fight in the open but maintain the secret. It's a tropospheric destabilizer that can alter thermals and manipulate hydro molecules across a substantial radius."

"Huh?" Watson asked.

"Is he talking about... a weather-controlling machine?" Arthur asked, whispering to Becky beside him with an impressed smile.

"Yes, obviously," Becky chortled, although whether she understood her boss's advanced word usage or was simply being sarcastic was unclear.

"I've heard about this project of yours, Mr. Tesla," Ying said. "I had thought you had issues garnering enough electrical power for it to function properly. Have you been able to make it work?"

"No, but I will once I get it within range of Oberschock's forces," Tesla assured her. "They'll be kindly carrying enough power with them to ensure the tropospheric destabilizer is functional."

"The Blitzsturm?" Bouclier asked.

"Indeed. I can access the power remotely if we install the device with the right wireless receivers. All we would need to do is get within a few miles of it, and then we could conjure a great thunderstorm to keep ourselves hidden from any nearby civilians."

"He *was* talking about a weather-controlling machine!" Arthur said, grinning and bouncing slightly in his seat with excitement.

"Like I said, it was obvious," Becky snapped with a smirk.

"As impressive as this device sounds, such a plan would only work if Oberschock has the Blitzsturm switched on before they reach Paris," another judge reminded the founder and boss of the Teslanaut faction. "They could wait to do so until they're right at the Eiffel Tower."

"If they know they'll face retaliation, they'll turn it on beforehand to minimize the time between contacting the tower and the shock from emitting," Tesla said. "Especially if we bring enough forces to slow them down."

"There's no guarantee of that, though."

"No, but it is our only chance of stopping Oberschock with a large volt-tech force while maintaining the secret. We will have to take that chance."

"I believe it is time to vote," Westinghouse declared, looking around at the heads of the Electrocracy on stage with him. "This first session is for leaders only. If you would wish for the Electrocracy to evacuate Paris and let Oberschock enact their plan in order to maintain the secret, please raise your hand now."

Lei Jainyu, another few leaders, and six of the judges raised their hands, bringing the total count to fourteen.

"Cowards," Bouclier growled under his breath.

"Now, those who wish for the Electrocracy to attempt to use Tesla's machine for cover and fight Oberschock outside of Paris," Westinghouse continued, "please raise your hand now."

Tesla, Bouclier, the leaders of a few other factions, and the other six judges raised their hands. Once again, the total count was fourteen.

"It appears we have a tie," Westinghouse said. "And as our rules dictate, in the event of a tie, we shall open the vote to everyone present. If you wish for the Electrocracy to evacuate Paris and let Oberschock enact their plan in order to maintain the secret, please raise your hand now."

As well as the original fourteen who had voted for this option previously, many others raised their hands, particularly those in the regions of the world that would be least affected by Oberschock's attack, although that was not unanimous. Westinghouse spent the next few minutes counting each hand, while Tesla inwardly counted them in his head and finished in barely a few seconds.

"One hundred sixteen," Westinghouse finally said, his lips pursed upon seeing so many against his old friend's plan. "Now, those who wish for the Electrocracy to attempt to use Tesla's machine for cover and fight Oberschock outside of Paris, please raise your hand now."

Once again, as well as the original fourteen, many others raised their hands, this time mostly those in the regions that would be *most* affected. Helen, Arthur, Becky, Ivan, and Watson held their hands up, with Becky looking exceptionally ecstatic at the prospect of her voice being heard. Ji and Ying looked at each other for a second, then looked at Lei Jainyu, before finally raising their hands in defiance of their father. They knew this was the right thing to do. Lei Jainyu's eyes narrowed, seeing this as an act of betrayal, but Ji and Ying stood firm in their decision.

"It's settled then," Tesla murmured immediately after Ji and Ying's hands rose, nodding.

"What?" Helen asked, shocked at how their boss knew this already.

the heat of the desert, but now the suit was good as new. Burak had the agents help him get the suit back to tiptop shape in the days leading up to their departure from the Anatolia base, for Raymond had a heck of a run ahead of him.

"We've arrived," Burak stated from the front, stopping the truck along with all the others in their convoy. They had parked near an extravagant mosque, its Byzantine architecture and spires indicating a quite old building going back at least to the fourteenth century. Within, though, the mosque featured some hidden modern additions, ones rather essential for the Firtina Anka Kusu operations.

"Within this mosque is Constantinople's main volt-tech transmission tower," Burak explained to Raymond. "Currently it's turned off due to the Allied troops occupying the city, but we shall briefly switch it back on and let you reactivate your Bolter suit. You'll have to run fast to reach the range of another tower, though, for we can't leave this one on for long without drawing attention."

"Where do I go?" Raymond asked.

"The Bolter suit should let you run across water if the crossing is short enough; otherwise, you'll have to run eastward and circle the entire Black Sea. If you can, though, then simply cross the Bosporus strait which will lead you into Thrace. Then keep running along the coast of the Mediterranean until you reach Venice, and from there you should be able to follow roads until you've made it to Paris. Even with the incredible power of the suit, it will take you at least an hour to run this distance. Are you ready?"

"More than ever. Let's do this."

Burak nodded at Raymond, smiling at the young American. "Goodbye, my friend. I trust you will do the right thing."

"I'll try," Raymond sighed, smiling gratefully at Burak in return. "Thank you for helping me."

"You were your own agent of aid, Raymond. I merely cleared the path for you. Now, go. We must continue our own fight."

A minute later, the Firtina Anka Kusu agents activated the tower, sending a sharp crack through the air and causing a few bolts of electricity to zap in place. Seizing his chance, Raymond flicked the switch on his Bolter suit and, to his relief, activated it once more. With that, he ran faster than ever, clearing the Bosporus strait and reaching Thrace within just a few seconds. He moved, driven by knowing what he had to do, and how to move forward in the Teslanauts. His father had given him this life, and now he had to live it.

***

"I just got a call from our vorkers in Paris," Boltzmann said, having returned from Paris after dropping off the supplies. "Zey have finished installing ze receptors on ze tower. Ve must move now before anyone notices!"

The Oberschock workers finished work on all of their machines and prepped the Eisenzentrum for the trip to Paris a little after noon on the first of May. As they had built the base within an old castle, they had to meticulously remove the entire top section through separating the keeps and chambers from the main base beneath. This required the work of multiple cranes, trucks, and mechanical automatons, but through their labor they managed to get it done within merely a few hours.

"I contacted my factories across the continent yesterday," Stonewell said, walking up to Boltzmann as they stood on the balcony leading into the castle entrance. This time, though, they had no roof above them. "Their machines will soon join us on the way to Paris."

"Zis better vork, Mr. Stonewell," Boltzmann growled. "Ve're risking everything vith zis stunt of yours."

"Your people want retribution, don't they?" Stonewell asked, shrugging with his arms held way out. "This is the best way to get it. Don't worry, you will be well supplied through Stonewell Arms and Ammunitions."

"Your lack of honor for your country is astounding."

"Oh, I'll help my country too," Stonewell assured. "My company will be generous to all the nations. It'll be a nice, long, profitable stalemate. But eventually one of you will get ahead, I'm sure!"

Boltzmann shook his head, hating his alliance with this man but knowing it was the only way his people could have their vengeance. The Allied Powers left his country with nothing, and through Stonewell, Boltzmann would ensure they would never insult his people again. He would burn them right out of their privileged holes, and light a fire that would be seen across the world.

"Eisenzentrum base is ready for departure," Ziegler informed the general, the wiry Austrian engineer wiping the sweat off his face.

"Deploy, now!" Boltzmann barked.

Through the heaving of man-sized levers, a balloon unfolded from a chamber in the center of the base, inflating with hydrogen and helium gas within minutes. As this balloon grew, steel panels unfolded within it to form a sturdy envelope, the thick grid framework allowing it to maintain its shape even at such a size. The castle's entry chambers, the factories, the Blitzsturm, Calvert's laboratory; all of it turned into the gondola of an immense dirigible, expanding beyond the mountainous confines of the castle's foundation. Eisenzentrum was becoming a rigid airship, thousands of feet long, bigger than any flying thing the world had ever seen to this point. Nature created the condor and the eagle, but man created this creature, lording over the skies and scraping against the realm of God.

Finally, Oberschock had fully inflated the balloon and carried the whole base with it. Several smaller dirigibles and a squadron of over thirty triplanes escorted this aerial monster, while dozens of tanks and walker mechs patrolled the ground below. Lower still, the Panzerwurm drilled through the depths of the earth, ensuring the Oberschock Federation had dominion over heaven, earth, and hell.

"To Paris!" Boltzmann roared.

"To war!" Stonewell yelled, grinning from ear to ear.

The malevolent army of machines and men made their trajectory toward their target, crossing the French border within just a few hours. Smaller towns underneath got a glimpse of the planes, tanks, and the giant airship, but fled for cover before they could see the mechs or other obvious volt-tech forces. Not that Oberschock was terribly concerned about secrecy, for if any civilian got in their way, they would more often than not blast them and move on. They had only one quarry in mind.

"Ve're fifty kilometers from ze Eiffel Tower," Boltzmann said, standing on one of the *Eisenzentrum* airship's decks outside the gondola and gazing at the grassy meadows surrounding the French capital. "Ve should expect enemy resistance at any point." With such clear skies and a bright afternoon sun, he got a good glimpse of the meadows, and their aerial fleet that escorted their ship carrying the payload. Even this far out, he could see the tower on the horizon.

"Shall ve turn on ze Blitzsturm, zen?" Ziegler asked.

"No, zat could supercharge vhatever veapons ze enemy brings against us," Boltzmann said. "Ve'll turn it on only when near the tower."

"If I may, General, it vould also supercharge our own veapons."

"If the enemy intends to fight, they could keep us from turning on the Blitzsturm later," Stonewell said. "We must activate it now so we can plow right through their forces and straight to the tower!"

"Such a typical American," Boltzmann grunted. "Alvays so eager to throw caution into ze vind."

"We're well past the point of caution. And as the financier of this operation, I say we maintain our course."

"Very vell, I shall switch on ze Blitzsturm," Ziegler said, running into the cabin of the *Eisenzentrum* airship that used to be the castle foundation.

"Relax, friend," Stonewell said, placing his hand on Boltzmann's shoulder despite it clearly violating the old German general's boundaries. "You're about to get everything you ever wanted! And who do you have to thank for it, huh?"

"Zis brings me little joy," Boltzmann growled, tensing his shoulder from Stonewell's grip. "I've seen enough death to last me several lifetimes. I merely vant my people to regain zeir glory stolen from us by ze Allied Powers."

"Yes, your people regain their glory, Americans lost returning from war regain their purpose, and my father's business is permanently in the black. Everyone wins! I'm really doing a public service here, so you should feel-"

"Hold on," Boltzmann murmured, looking up. "Vhat is zis...?"

"What is what?"

The once clear and sunny weather had visibility darkened in the span of a few minutes. Clouds proceeded to form, growing several shades darker at an unnaturally fast rate. Thunder began to rumble, quietly at first, but growing exponentially louder and sharper. Small bursts of lightning blasted the ground and the sides of the *Eisenzentrum* airship, the flaps of the balloon absorbing the electricity and avoiding damage. And slowly, drops fell from the heavens, initially a mild drizzle, but certain to grow more torrential as time went forward.

"Ve're losing control!" an Oberschock triplane pilot shouted, his aircraft struggling in the wind and temperamental thermals.

"It appears we've angered the Almighty," Stonewell said, shrugging.

"Zis is no natural storm," Boltzmann mused, peering with narrowed eyes at the temperamental elements. "It only started once ve activated ze Blitzsturm. Zis is the vork of something more... antagonistic."

"Are you seriously suggesting...?"

"Enemy forces spotted, two kilometers ahead!" an Oberschock agent shouted, coming out onto the deck from the airship's comms stations. "Ve've picked zem up through our electro-scans!"

Boltzmann got a pair of binoculars from his uniform's chest pocket and peered through the thick storm clouds. Though his aged senses could barely pierce through the fog, he could see the lights from vehicles; first only a few, but growing more and more numerous as the seconds ticked onward. Eventually, the Oberschock general realized his forces would face not only the Teslanauts and the Volt Knights, but also forces from many other volt-tech factions from all around the world. Their actions had seemingly ignited the wrath of the entire Electrocracy.

On one such airship, with three envelopes and a wide gondola below, stood their main enemy, the one Oberschock recognized the most. As the father of volt-tech, this man was infamous, as was his signature ship. Their world knew it well, as did the Obershock leader, and hiding within that ship was a device similar in size and shape of the Blitzsturm, but feeding off its power to create these conditions.

"As I suspected," Boltzmann snarled seeing the *White Pigeon* through the clouds, before putting his binoculars aside. "Zis is Tesla's doing."

"You're being ridiculous!" Stonewell snapped. "No mere man is capable of such a feat!"

"Zere is nothing 'mere' about Nikola Tesla. It vould seem ve have a battle in our sights. I trust ze forces from your factories are up to ze challenge."

"Press forward!" Stonewell roared, pointing ahead as the rain became an all-out downpour. "Do not let those blowhards slow us down!"

Within the gondola of the *White Pigeon*, Tesla and a vast collective of Teslanauts prepared for the upcoming conflict, the ship flying ahead of their fleet of planes and dirigibles. As well as the usual field agents like Helen, Ji, and Watson, he had some factory workers on board, to repair any equipment on the fly and endure against Oberschock's assault for as long as possible. Arthur, Becky, Ivan, and roughly a dozen other factory workers stood by, with Watson pulling double duty if either side needed an extra pair of hands.

"The tropospheric destabilizer is successfully in operation," Tesla said, so calm and cool like he expected nothing else. "The Proton Rangers and Volt Knights will flank Oberschock from each side, while the rest of us will attack from the front. Our goal is to bring down their main airship as quickly as possible; I do not want this conflict to go on any longer than necessary."

"Don't worry, boss!" Watson assured him. "I will direct the lightning from your storm and channel it at Oberschock through my fingertips! The battle will be over before sundown!"

"Considering sundown is at least six hours away, it bloody better be," Helen huffed. "How are we field agents fighting them? I'm not very experienced with piloting any of our vehicles."

"We'll drop off teams of agents to deal with their ground forces," Tesla told her. "I will steer my ship at key targets to ensure we bring down as many of their escorts as we can. The Volt Knights are eagerly picking off stragglers as we speak."

"If any of your equipment gets damaged, we'll be right here to fix it!" Becky added. "Lord, this is the closest I've ever been to field work. I'm looking mighty forward to it!"

"Paris is roughly thirty miles behind us," Tesla said. "Let us ensure they get no closer than ten. We're ready to engage."

"Delta Squadron, advance!" Cobblewood shouted outside from her Teslaplane. Rolling down in sequence, a fleet of the planes flew towards the Oberschock's aerial escorts, firing at them with their disintegrator turrets and flying back out in a wide arc. Oberschock's forces were quick to retaliate, sending a fleet of their triplanes to engage with the Teslanauts, beginning the dogfight between the two forces.

Then again, the Electrocracy had brought much more than the Teslanauts to this fight. "Focus on zeir buzzsaw ships!" Foudre demanded, standing on the deck of an Interceptor and pointing forward. "Keep zem from taking out too much of our airpower!"

Oberschock had, as during the train fight, brought the ships with deflating balloons armed with buzzsaws. This time, though, rather than just one, they had a fleet of over a dozen. After gaining altitude, they all deflated their balloons at once, aiming right at the Interceptors and cutting off their escape route.

"Shoot their turbines!" a Proton Ranger general shouted, standing on a side deck of his factions' main airship. Looking similar to a steamboat, with the tiered decks and chugging smoke towers, it had the envelope of their balloons underneath them rather than above, chugging along the sky like it was the Mississippi River. Their agents, typical of their American southern nature, focused much more on conventional firearms rather than the standard disintegrator beams, albeit with minor volt-tech enhancements that aided with range and power. Quite a few of them also had ten-gallon hats, wanting to remain stylish and proud of their culture even so far from home.

The Proton Rangers' sharpshooters aimed their modified Springfield battle rifles at Oberschock's saw ships, despite being thousands of yards away. While the original gun could be used from this distance normally, it was only under extreme circumstances. However, once the Proton Rangers fired a volley at the saw ships, it became clear their volt-tech enhancements made up for any of the weapons' previous shortcomings. Their rounds blasted toward their target, faster than any standard model, and when they collided with the sawships' propellers, the ensuing burst packed more punch than normally possible. The saw ships, unable to aim with their ruptured turbines, fell past their targets, with only a few hitting Interceptors at all. When their balloons re-inflated, they could not change their course, and thus were quickly brought down by another flyby of the Teslaplane squadron.

"Yeah, that'll learn 'em!" the Proton Ranger general hollered.

"Keep focusing on their airpower!" Cobblewood told her fellow pilots. "We'll have to bring down their escorts if we'll hope to get to the-"

"Watch out!" another pilot shouted.

From the ground thousands of feet below, the Oberschock's tanks and walkers began to fire their howitzers, with the aim of hitting the clusters of enemy air forces and taking them out chunks at a time. These howitzers, modified versions of the German Big Bertha, were normally designed for long-range siege combat, blasting fortified buildings and encampments from miles away. After using volt-tech to turn their four-hundred-twenty millimeter caliber shells into disintegration energy beams, they became much more multifaceted. Anything their energy beams hit would shatter, and thus they could target much more than just stationary buildings.

"Their ground combatants are opening fire!" Cobblewood roared.

"This is our moment," Morales said, throwing down his fist. "Everyone, put on your parachutes. We're going to jump now."

"Volt Knight Interceptors and Royal Shock Brigade planes will protect you," Tesla informed the Marshal. "Helen, Ji, Watson, you are to join him, while Ying will remain in radio contact to relay information. Are you ready?"

"Yes, sir!" Watson said, practically throwing his arm out of his socket with how broadly he moved to salute. "We won't let you down!"

"You just wanna go outside and get struck by lightning," Becky chortled.

"And be one with the gods!" Watson proclaimed. "I want nothing more than Zeus himself to strike me with all his might, caressing my body with his immortal power!"

"You're off your blooming rocker," Helen said, shaking her head with an arched eyebrow.

"You just noticed?" Becky asked.

"The planes have cleared the area," Tesla told the field agents. "Go, now."

As Morales, Helen, Ji, Watson, and several other Teslanauts leapt out of the *White Pigeon* and opened their parachutes, the storm raged on, striking great bolts of nature's electrical fury across the sky, onto the ground, and into the power receptors of volt-tech machines. The forces of the Oberschock Federation, the Teslanauts, the Volt Knights, the Proton Rangers, the Royal Shock Brigade, and the other factions warred, firing shells, destroying vehicles, and bringing down troops.

Europe had not seen such a fight since the last days of the Great War. What the Allied Powers feared the most would come true should the Electrocracy fail to halt Oberschock's advance. The Western Front would once again be engulfed in grueling, horrific combat. And so, the agents fought. They piloted planes, manned mechs, wielded weapons, and blasted bodies, all while the turbulent rain and lightning erupted around them and created a raging decor of chaos.

This was war. This was volt-tech war. This was the ultimate manifestation of the brilliance of science, the mastery of engineering, the fury of ammunition, and the wrath of man. This could not be sustained. This had to be controlled. This had to end, and it had to end today.

"We've landed," Morales told Ying, taking off his parachute and walking on the wet grass with the other agents. His backpack held one of the cubes they turned into various equipment for their missions, this time turned into a radio with speakers that everyone around could hear. "How many enemy combatants are ahead?"

"Twelve tanks and fourteen mechs," Ying reported from the *White Pigeon*. "Their howitzers are focusing on our air power. We won't last much longer against them!"

"Bolters, run up to the howitzers and take out their firing crews," Morales told Watson, Ji, and a few other field agents that had come from other Interceptors. "We need to cripple those weapons."

"Yes, sir," Ji said, turning on his suit and disappearing in a flash of electrical energy. Watson, having already zoomed ahead, ran up to the Oberschock artillery and knocked out the agents manning them, either by slamming their heads on the metal railings or by punching them and sending them flying. By the time Ji had incapacitated the crews of two howitzers, Watson had taken out seven.

"I feel so alive!" the wiry and manic teenager roared. "I don't need to be struck by lightning! I *am* lightning!"

"Good job, friend," Ji cheered to his teammate with a grin. "Your zestful manner is rather infectious, I'll admit."

"They'll man those weapons again soon," Morales warned the agents. "We've got to take them out!"

"I'll handle their reinforcements!" Helen told the Marshal, taking her disintegrator rifle and cocking it before running behind a fallen saw ship for cover. From behind the ruptured steel and smoke, she peered through the stormy clouds and looked out for Oberschock agents running back to the howitzers. With a few shots, she took a few out, all the while heaving a sigh at the loss of life. As someone who had wanted to serve in the army like her brothers, though, she recognized that this was how it worked. These men, like her, risked everything to be here, fighting for their countries while remaining aware of the danger. And like so many others in the last decade, they would lay down their lives for nothing. War was hell, but the Oberschock Federation had let it come to this after the fight had already ended four years ago, and they had to be stopped.

"Now, to destroy the howitzer platforms," Morales said.

"Golly gee, I wish you had the Peacemaker," Watson said.

"I do, too. But alas, this new anti-armor weapon of mine will have to do."

"What in the world do you...?"

Watson trailed off, before his eyes widened and his mouth went agape. With a grunt and a heave, Morales carried what looked like a portable cannon four feet in length, but rather than a fuse, the ignition came from electricity, achieved with the simple pull of the trigger. He had assembled it through separate cubes carried by fellow field agents, just like the Peacemaker from before, but as a ranged weapon, this was a whole different beast.

"And the lads thought *I* carried above my weight," Helen said with a smirk.

"What is that thing?" Watson asked. "I want twelve of them."

"This is a portable rocket launcher," Morales explained. "Work on these had been planned for infantry use for several years, but those plans had stopped since the war ended; or at least, they had outside of volt-tech. After I lost the Peacemaker, I had some factory workers relay their plans for anti-armor weapons, one they could manage to build in such a short time. With the amount of mechs we face, something like this would be quite handy."

"And is it handy?" Helen asked.

"Why don't we find out?" Morales said, holding the rocket launcher to his shoulder and pointing it at one of the howitzers. After squinting to make sure he aimed it correctly, what with the thick rain and clouds making that somewhat difficult to perceive, he pulled the trigger and fired a small missile. Roughly two seconds later, a splash of fire and metal was all that remained of the artillery device, with a wave of heat blasting their awestruck faces.

"That's just swell," Watson gushed, his arms dropped and his eyes alight.

"Yes, very impressive," Ji said, trying to hurry them along. "Now let's get the rest, please!"

While the ground forces focused on dismantling the howitzers, Tesla and his crew aboard the *White Pigeon* had their own problems. Cobblewood and the rest of her squadron defended as best as they could, but several Oberschock triplanes managed to swerve past them and target Tesla's airship. They fired many rounds of bullets and beams before passing by and looping back around, rupturing the gondola and threatening to blow one of the ship's three envelopes should the Teslanauts not thwart their efforts.

"The hull can't take much more of their fire!" Becky warned Tesla through the ship's radio. She and the other two factory workers stood in the lower decks of the *White Pigeon*'s gondola, frantically trying to repair the damage from the inside, while communicating with Tesla through a receptor in the ship's pipeline. "We need to fend those planes off or they'll blow us apart!"

"Agents, man the turrets," Tesla ordered the crewmen standing by him on the bridge. "It appears we'll have to fight back ourselves."

At his command, agents climbed inside the airship's six turrets lining the edges of the gondola, holding spherical counter-air gun emplacements that could fire repeating blasts of disintegrator beams. These could pierce through airplane bodies and riddle them with holes, if they could manage to land a hit. The emplacements could swivel all over, able to fire above and below and at any angle, but the Oberschock triplanes could fly faster than their speed of rotation, so they had to pinpoint their aim to maximize the amount of hits.

"The ship bleeds," Ivan warned the factory workers aboard the *White Pigeon*, stroking the walls of the gondola and feeling its mechanisms from his heart. "We need to heal it before it gives way."

"Working on it!" Becky grunted, twisting a wrench to tighten the bolts onto a ruptured panel while Arthur welded it back into place. The enemy disintegrator beams pummeled the *White Pigeon*'s outer panels; a few more blasts and they would pierce through her entirely. The factory workers had to continue their work to maintain hull integrity for as long as the Oberschock triplanes attacked their ship.

Of course, with the howitzers dismantled by the field agents below, the Teslanaut and Royal Shock Brigade airplanes were now less encumbered to ward off Oberschock's aerial forces. "Bogeys are going down!" Cobblewood roared, performing another aeolian roll with another plane and zapping an enemy triplane between them.

"We may just yet halt their advance," Morales whispered from the ground. Looking back at the other field agents, he then motioned forward to the rest of

Oberschock's ground forces. "Fight on, agents!" he shouted. "Keep up the pressure!"

"Look out!" Helen shouted, pointing up.

Dropping straight from the *Eisenzentrum* airship, a familiar machine made contact with the ground, the impact sending a piercing shockwave into the air and through the dirt. Ready to take action once again, Boltzmann and his *Stahlwolf* mech deployed onto the field, the house-sized four-legged vehicle completely undamaged from the thousand-foot plunge. Staring at the Teslanaut field agents, the old German general looked positively savage; his eyes glowed from the reflection of the howitzer wreckages' fire, and his wrinkled lips opened as if he could taste the prospect of vengeance for his country.

"You vill not defeat us again!" Boltzmann roared. "Zis vorld vill be ours! It is our birthright!"

"Many men throughout history have said those words, and they all suffer the same fate," Morales said gruffly, readying his new rocket launcher. "Maniacs like you never learn. Agents, let's take him down."

Watson used his Bolter suit to seemingly blink from one space to another, appearing just in front of Boltzmann in his mech's open cockpit and punching him in the face. Before Boltzmann could defend himself,

Watson ran off, disappearing into the stormy fog while others attacked from other angles. Helen fired at him with her rifle, but Boltzmann quickly held up the *Stahlwolf*'s redwood trunk-sized arm in front of the cockpit, the thick steel holding strong against the disintegrator beams. Ji placed some of the metal rods from training on both sides of the mech, and he and Watson channeled power with their wristbands to zap the *Stahlwolf* with powerful Blitzsturm-enhanced blasts. All the while, Morales aimed the rocket launcher at one of the mech's four crab-like legs, ready to blow it off and cripple the mechanical beast.

"Impressive toys!" Boltzmann snapped, breaking free from the electrical bonds Ji and Watson used against him. "You vould do vell on ze playground!"

"Enough of your rubbish!" Helen shot back. "Marshal, take care of him!"

Morales fired a rocket at last, but the *Stahlwolf* revealed some more impressive gadgets in its arsenal to counter it. Holding its car-sized hands apart, Boltzmann flicked a switch and channeled an electrical shield between the mech's palms, similar to the three-legged machine Morales and Helen first encountered by Strasbourg. Just as then, the electricity fried the rocket midair, making it explode ten feet away from the mech's cockpit rather than right at it.

"Zis squabble is growing tiresome," Boltzmann grunted. "You remain clueless about vhat you're up against."

"We're winning, aren't we?" Morales said. "The whole Electrocracy is against you. Your forces are outmatched!"

Indeed, it seemed from sheer numbers alone, the forces that opposed the Oberschock Federation had the advantage. Squadrons of maneuverable Teslaplanes twenty strong warded off enemy fighters, while the Royal Shock Brigade planes and Proton Ranger airships pushed back against the dirigibles. Oberschock howitzers were destroyed every minute, with Volt Knight ground forces smashing the tanks and smaller mechs. Even the rocket men, enemies that had been a serious challenge beforehand, got blasted into chunky metallic pieces by the massive quantity of Electrocracy ground forces on them the moment they landed on the ground and transformed. And Paris was still over twenty-five miles behind, with the dark clouds and torrential rain successfully concealing the battle from civilian eyes.

But the Oberschock Federation was still not finished. They still had a fire in their hearts and a steel to their resolve that could not be quelled. Their people had been hurt too badly by the Allied Powers for them to not persist. "Outnumbered, perhaps," Boltzmann said, his voice quiet and yet fierce and resolute. "But certainly not unmatched."

Before Morales could once more fire back in their verbal scuffle, he felt the ground under his boots begin to stir. At first it was a mild tremor, but as the seconds ticked on it grew more and more intense, to the point where it grew difficult for the field agents to remain on their feet. The rumbling now drowned the sound of the thunder and rain, and eventually, like a wake of water, the ground itself began to rise.

"Oh no," Morales whispered.

"Not again..." Helen groaned.

Erupting from the surface like a breaching whale, the Oberschock Federation's greatest weapon once more made itself known. The Panzerwurm rose into the air, higher than any building in the world, and it still kept going, its segmented serpentine body seemingly without end. Its two car-sized drills, rotating around its circular mouth, were further revealed to the ground field agents, who stared in awe from below as this mechanical monster rose like a magical beanstalk from the earth. Now, they could see that these drills were attached to the joints of two rotating wings, folded inward with their tips lining down the sides of its body. Even while folded, these wings still provided lift, with thrusters the size of trucks jettisoning columns of flame and pushing against the confines of gravity. While full-on flight was impossible for such a massive contraption, these wings were what allowed it to rise so high.

At once, the name of Panzerwurm became clear in its intent. While the first part came from the German *panzer*, meaning "tank," the second part had a double-meaning. It obviously referred to its shape resembling that of a worm, but alluding to annelids was not all it conveyed. Their language had another meaning for *wurm*, one that medieval bestiaries knew well to fear: "dragon." And this Panzerwurm was certainly draconic.

"Evacuate!" the Proton Ranger general shouted, noticing the Panzerwurm rapidly approaching the hull of their airship.

The malevolent mechanical monster opened its circular sawblade-ridden mouth under their ship, crunching the two-hundred-foot iron vehicle like it was paper. The Proton Rangers leapt out of the ship with their parachutes on their back, but most of them didn't make it, for the Panzerwurm's revolving wings smashed them in midair before they could clear its vicinity. As the Proton Ranger ship was sliced to bits by the cyclone-like maw of the Panzerwurm, the great leviathan fell back down to the ground, unfolding its thousand-foot sail-like wings and pointing its thrusters downward to slow its descent. It curved its face toward the earth, crashing its metal girth into several planes on the way and bringing them down with it. With one move, the Panzerwurm took out nearly twenty percent of the Electrocracy's aerial forces.

"Sweet Jesus," Morales gasped.

"Fire all weapons!" Tesla roared from the bridge of the *White Pigeon*. "Destroy that abomination!" While normally reserved and stoic, seeing such a horrific creation truly rattled his nerves. The Panzerwurm represented everything he stood against as a scientist, using the marvels of volt-tech not for technological progress or the pursuit of knowledge, but wanton destruction and ruin. It had to be taken out.

Morales fired several rockets at one of the machine's innumerable centipede-like segments, blasting perhaps four or five of its millions of pieces off. The Teslaplanes and Royal Shock Brigade fighters barraged its carapace with volleys of disintegrator beams, shredding through its outer panels but unable to penetrate the dozens of layers cocooning its innards. The Volt Knights flew their Interceptors in close range and fired with their lances, rupturing a few parts of its serpentine body while it dove back down under the earth and readied itself for another attack. Many lightning bolts from the storm also struck the beast, its metal body and enormous size making it a perfect conductor. The Panzerwurm was not indestructible. It was made of ordinary steel panels and reinforced chrome. The problem was the sheer mass of it. It would take the Electrocracy's forces hours of constant fire to bring it to a critical state of disrepair, yet it would take the Panzerwurm only a few minutes to do the same to their entire army.

"Vitness ze fury of our hearts manifest," Boltzmann said, staring in awe at Oberschock's magnum opus with moist eyes. "Bask upon ze monster your actions have created. Zis marvel, zis Panzerwurm, zis is you. Zis is vhat you have done to us. All ve are doing is returning ze favor."

"Enough!" Morales snapped. "Watson, Ji! Bring the general to me."

Watson and Ji flicked on their Bolter suits at their Marshal's command. Watson ran up to the

*Stahlwolf*'s cockpit, snatching Boltzmann right off and carrying him right to Morales' feet, while Ji ran off and then ran back, holding his arm out to knock the old general onto his knees before switching his suit off.

"Please, kill me," Boltzmann said, looking down. "My soul has been forfeit for a long time."

"Killing him would do nothing, Marshal," Helen warned the man who had been so helpful to her in her years in the Teslanauts. "We need to destroy the Panzerwurm, and he might be the key."

"You cannot destroy ze Panzerwurm," Boltzmann declared, still not giving any of the agents the dignity of eye contact. "It vill be ze death of all of us."

Oberschock's beast rose from the earth once more, this time setting its sights on the *White Pigeon*. Tesla had his pilots steer the ship out of the way, tilting it starboard as the Panzerwurm's jagged metal edges just barely scraped against the airship's envelopes. With its body so close, the *White Pigeon*'s gunners fired a volley of disintegrator beams that would level the biggest building in New York or Chicago in seconds. The Panzerwurm lost a large chunk of chrome plating, but it curved downward undeterred, taking down another squadron of Teslaplanes that could not maneuver away in time.

"That thing is gobbling us up something fierce!" Cobblewood roared, flying her plane away. "We're running out of forces real quick here!"

The *Eisenzentrum* airship floated over the battle undeterred, still headed straight toward the Eiffel Tower with the Blitzsturm at the ready. The Teslanauts, Volt Knights, Royal Shock Brigade, and Proton Rangers had their forces nearly halved by the Panzerwurm's two attacks, and despite taking considerable damage the great machine continued to operate at full functionality. The Electrocracy would soon be unable to stop Oberschock from reaching Paris. The war would soon begin once more.

"Can you feel it, Marshal?" Boltzmann asked. "Ze despair? Ze burden of failure? It is almost intoxicating, isn't it? It devours you, leaving you vhithered on ze ground much as it did to us. Embrace it. Embrace your destruction."

Before Morales could angrily shut him up, Boltzmann obliged for him. The old German general collapsed onto the ground, his mouth foaming as the light dimmed from his eyes. He had administered onto himself a lethal dose of mercury bichloride, having taken his own words to heart. The Teslanauts stood still and silent, horrified at what this man had done. War truly left no victors.

"Marshal, his mech!" Ji shouted.

Morales looked up to where the *Stahlwolf* had stood, but to his shock, the house-sized mech was no longer before them. Then, after barely hearing the whirring metal gears in the distance, he turned to his left and saw something extraordinary. The *Stahlwolf* had been commandeered, and its new pilot charged the machine straight toward the Panzerwurm.

"Was that any of us?" Watson asked, so confused by this his mind seemed to short circuit.

"We're all standing right here, you dolt," Ji grumbled. "It's not any of us."

"My God!" Helen gasped, catching a glimpse of the *Stahlwolf*s pilot as it turned. "It's Raymond!"

# Chapter Twenty-One

RAYMOND CALVERT had been running for hours. After the Storm Phoenix agents fed him a nice, rich breakfast of menemen and tea before they departed to Constantinople, a traditional Turkish meal for the morning hours, he had fully recovered from his dehydration and delirium. His energy, as well as his drive, had been restored, and he would not stop until he avenged his father. He had wallowed in self-pity too long. Five years too long, in fact. It was now time to act.

After taking a bit of a breather in the nice Italian villas, he followed the roads until he reached Paris, at which point he had noticed the peculiar storm to the east. Noticing the activity of the Parisian community seemed relatively uneventful this afternoon, and remembering what had happened the last time he had been caught in a Bolter suit in this city, he realized the attack must not have reached Paris yet, and he needed to leave before he got spotted once again. He then ran toward the storm and saw the battle at last, and all the Electrocracy's forces fighting against the Oberschock Federation.

"Whoa," Raymond said, his arms hanging low as he gazed upon the fleet of airships, the squadrons of planes, the blasting of disintegrator beams, and the flashing of electricity from both the weapons and the conjured storm. As well as the Teslaplanes from back at the train fight, he noticed vehicles he had never seen before, such as a unique three-enveloped dirigible, a few more streamlined fighter planes, and the biggest airship he had ever seen carrying what almost looked like the foundation of a castle as its gondola. Projectiles flew, pieces fractured, and people fought, in a panoramic display of aerial combat. It was chaos. Total, unbridled, volt-tech chaos.

The worst, though, was a familiar steel behemoth, one that crashed into planes and airships alike when emerging from the earth. It was a true titan, as demonic as those of classical mythology, but modern, made from metal rather than flesh, and fueled by oil and electricity rather than the divine. Impossible science had brought it together, and it would be equally impossible to take it apart.

That was Raymond's target. When Francis refused to put the Panzerwurm together with Oberschock's plans, Stonewell made him pay for it in blood. Francis died trying to keep it from being built.

Now, Raymond had to finish the job and destroy it, and then go after the man who ordered his death.

This, of course, was crazy. He was one young, inexperienced new agent with mediocre scores in rudimentary training and no prior experience in welding, fighting, or piloting, while the Panzerwurm was a mountainous mass of writhing steel and gyrating fire. But Cobblewood gave him high remarks for his determination, and that's what he needed. He had an idea. He had a ridiculous idea. And he had the determination to get it done.

The first step was to hijack a vehicle, preferably one bigger than a biplane but smaller than an office building. Thankfully, this turned out to be by far the easiest part. Once he noticed the *Stahlwolf* in the middle of the field with its pilot detained by the Teslanaut field agents, he pounced on this opportunity and turned off his Bolter suit right after zooming into the mech's open cockpit. This would do.

Of course, the next step was far more difficult, for Raymond had to actually drive the *Stahlwolf* to his target. To put it bluntly, Raymond had never driven a mech. He had never even driven a regular automobile. He had ridden a pig once at a fair when he was a little kid, and he rode the bumper cars at Coney Island when he was older. That was the extent of his driving experience. But for the good of the mission, Raymond would give it his all. After pushing down a pedal at the foot of the cockpit and pointing every lever forward, Raymond slowly yet defiantly lumbered the mech toward the Panzerwurm, with clouds of steam and diesel smoke trailing not too far behind. He heard some gears within the machine's legs strain, as if held back by cables of which Raymond had no time to figure out their purpose, yet the *Stahlwolf* still moved forward, and that was all Raymond had wanted.

The Panzerwurm had returned to the depths of the earth, but the rumbling and the shifting ground were the telltale signs of its impending reemergence. Kicking the pedal under the cockpit like it was the side of a horse, Raymond gradually moved the *Stahlwolf* to the eye of the rippling dirt. This was the part of the plan that would establish whether the rest of it was anything more than a teenager's crazed delusions of heroism, or the quick and painful death sentence it almost assuredly was instead. Naturally, this brought out the most resistance from both his nerve and his surrounding cohorts. He heard the desperate cries of his field agent friends to fall back, to turn on his Bolter suit and get out of the attack radius of the Panzerwurm while he still could, but he ignored them. This was the only way to get it done. At least, if his hunch was correct.

The ground churned like water in a maelstrom, causing the *Stahlwolf* to nearly tumble, but Raymond moved some control levers that stabilized its four legs. Then his stomach lurched as he sunk into the ground, before he found himself in a valley of jagged metal mountains with slopes of revolving teeth-like blades. But just as he finished going down, he immediately went way up. The Panzerwurm emerged from the ground once more, aiming again at the *White Pigeon* as it ascended, and it took the *Stahlwolf* and its young pilot with it.

Raymond hunkered down in the mech's cockpit, now all too aware of how open and exposed he was. The *Stahlwolf* sunk into the Panzerwurm's gullet, as the spinning teeth and constricting gears shredded it into metallic chunks. Raymond squeezed into his seat as hard as he could, riding it into the Panzerwurm's churning and grinding maw. Taking four metal rods out of his pocket, ones he had kept from his earlier training, Raymond stabbed them into the sides of the *Stahlwolf*'s cockpit, one on each side and two where he sat.

"Done," he said, nodding. "Now, time to get out of-"

Before he could switch on the Bolter suit, the *Stahlwolf* jerked downward, before crunching around Raymond and trapping him inside its crumpled hull. The teeth scraped the outside like chainsaws, while the body of the mech compressed around him. Raymond was now trapped inside the *Stahlwolf*, his ear pushed onto his shoulder, his knee jabbed into his chest, and his mouth caught in the bend of his arm. He couldn't move, and he couldn't breathe, as he felt the chills of mortality embracing his wedged body. Within seconds, he would be crushed and shredded by the Panzerwurm's internal mechanisms.

But adrenaline kicked in. Raymond would not die like this. He had made a promise to his mother that he would come back to her, with or without his father. But even without his father, he would have his vengeance. Justice would be served. Squirming his feet to stand on the shriveled floor of the Stahlwolf's cockpit, he stretched his finger on his left hand, and switched on the Bolter suit.

An instant later, he ran forward. He phased through the Panzerwurm's gears, able to blink past them in one step. That one step, however, ended up the only one he could take. He now fell into the open air. The Bolter suit was useless out here.

The Panzerwurm had already begun to bend toward the ground, the *White Pigeon* having pushed it aside with concussive fire. But Raymond couldn't scream, having been out of breath from his arm being pushed into his mouth when trapped in the *Stahlwolf.* However, this turned out to be beneficial, as that meant he could focus on the mission. After switching off the suit, Raymond spun his body around, desperately trying to ignore how close the ground was behind his back, and pulled out his modified disintegrator pistol from his holster. It was father's last gift to him, and with it, Raymond would give one last gift to his father. Closing one eye and aiming it at the Panzerwurm's whirling mouth above him, Raymond pulled the trigger at last.

The disintegrator beam blasted the *Stahlwolf* inside the Panzerwurm, with the metal rods Raymond had placed inside it conducting the beam's optimized electrical kick. The resulting burst of energy caused the *Stahlwolf* to explode, with the blast taking a portion of the Panzerwurm's neck with it. A hailstorm of metal and jagged pieces fell around Raymond, with only the disconnected head of the mighty beast shielding him from debris. The explosion also dislodged the Panzerwurm's drill-tipped wings, causing the entire front of the machine to collapse, the part that drove the rest of it forward.

Raymond continued to fall, the ground now only fifty feet below. The Panzerwurm's head and wings fell downward as well, ready to crush and bury his body after he broke all his bones from the fall, assuming his racing heart, lack of oxygen, or a random lightning strike didn't kill him first. It was a real race on what would deal the final blow.

Yet before any potential flattening, striking, burying, or breaking, a blur grasped him in midair and ran him aside, before the rest of the world blurred with him, although Raymond did not know if his perspective was merely scrambled by his frazzled mind. He had just been an instant away from death, and now someone pulled him to safety. A second later, the blurring stopped, and Raymond was set onto the wet grass by his rescuer.

"Looks like you were right," Ji said, turning off his own Bolter suit after setting Raymond on the ground. "Using the suit to take someone to safety *does* work."

Raymond collapsed into the muddy ground, needing a moment or twelve to catch his breath.

"It's down!" Ying said through the radio aboard the *White Pigeon*, her words breathless with shock and relief. "The Panzerwurm has been taken out!"

"Refocus containment efforts on their main airship," Tesla ordered. "The advantage is ours once more."

The Panzerwurm lay split and broken on the field, demobilized but not fully destroyed. In order to ensure Oberschock did not salvage its parts and potentially rebuild it, the Electrocracy had to stop them right here and now. Without their main attack dog, though, their main advantage was lost. In one move, Raymond had shifted the battle back to the Electrocracy's favor, but with the large fleet of triplanes and smaller dirigibles still escorting the *Eisenzentrum* airship, the fight was far from over.

"Did you really just...?" Watson asked Raymond, looking at the shattered corpse of the Panzerwurm. He and the other field agents walked up to where Ji had taken Raymond, taking a quick break now that Oberschock's forces were on the run.

"I think he did," Morales said, unable to hide his astonishment.

"All in a day's work," Raymond breathed, slowly leaning back up and getting off the ground.

Ji smirked at Raymond and nodded, appreciating his gumption and resolve. Though Ji still felt mildly betrayed by Raymond abandoning them earlier, he had to admit that his fellow agent really came through when the time was right. This young American had some real spunk to him for sure.

"I'm so relieved you're safe!" Helen said. "I thought you had died, then you came back, then two minutes ago I thought you died again, and yet here you are, still kicking like a good lad! You're a real bloody roller coaster, you know?"

"Good to see you too," Raymond said, chuckling.

"What about your father?" Helen asked, her tone now growing more serious. "Did you find out what happened?"

Raymond nodded, his smile fading. Helen's eyes softened, immediately recognizing what he meant. She had felt that way herself only a few years ago. She knew the emptiness like an old friend.

"We have to board their airship and seize their leaders," Morales informed the field agents. "Only then will this fight be over."

"How are we getting up there, then?" Watson asked.

"Just follow my lead," Raymond said, staring at the ruptured metal corpse of the Panzerwurm underneath the *Eisenzentrum* airship. Its panels sloped high enough to allow Raymond to employ a trick he accidentally learned when first using the Bolter suit in Paris, assuming he really, *really* ran.

"You're going to do something off the rocker again, are you?" Helen asked.

"We all are," Raymond said. "I'm not going to abandon my team again. Let's do this together. You and Morales will have to hold onto us, though."

"Brilliant," Helen sighed.

"I'm pleased to see you taking initiative, Calvert," Morales said. "Lead the way, if you would."

Raymond smiled hearing the Marshal's praise, but then his brow furrowed, and his features stiffened, as he recognized the importance of the task at hand. This was now his reason to be a Teslanaut. Not to find his father; he had learned the answer to that. Instead, it was to follow his father's example and help solve the world's problems. He had given Raymond this opportunity, and he would not squander it.

Looking at the Panzerwurm corpse up front, he moved his head back and forth to pop the little bones inside, and then ran for a few seconds in place, before switching on his Bolter suit and running. The Panzerwurm panels functioned as a ramp, angled at a steep enough slope to send him flying just as when he had accidentally sent himself flying above Notre Dame, only this time it was intentional. Once in the air, he switched off the suit, and held out his hands.

His fingers grasped onto the envelope of the *Eisenzentrum* airship, having been launched high enough to make it up the hundreds of feet where it flew. While he started to slip downward, he managed to just barely grasp the edges of its makeshift gondola before sliding onto its outer decks. He fell flat on his face, but on the metal catwalk of the ship's deck rather than shattered on the ground far down below.

While Raymond's maneuver was not graceful, he did manage to get himself up here. The other two Bolters on his squad followed suit, with Morales holding onto Watson and Helen holding onto Ji. Both Morales' and Helen's hair were frazzled, and they both shook slightly from the sheer velocity, but at last, the team had successfully assembled on board the *Eisenzentrum*.

"They've destroyed the Panzerwurm?!" Stonewell snapped, staring down at the wreckage from the bridge of Oberschock's main airship. "You promised me an unstoppable machine!"

"A momentary setback," Ziegler insisted. "Ve shall proceed to Paris as normal."

"Without our main weapon?"

"Zis ship is heavily armed. Her cannons are keeping the Electrocracy's ships at bay. *That* is our main veapon, not some mindless mechanical beast."

"You better be right," Stonewell snarled. "I've risked everything for this. We *will* get to Paris and we *will* unleash the Blitzsturm. I will not let my father or the company he gave me down."

"You're already letting him down."

Stonewell's whole body tensed hearing that voice, his mind barely able to think of a response due to shock and fury. Shakily turning his head, he looked over toward the entrance to the bridge, to what had once been the entryway to the Castle of Eisenzentrum, but was now attached to the steel supports of their airship. A few Oberschock guards lay motionless in the walkway leading to the bridge, having been shocked by electrical attacks. The ones who attacked them stood before Stonewell: five Teslanaut agents, including one Marshal, and one stubborn pest of a new recruit.

"How much does it take to kill you?" Stonewell snapped at Raymond. "Ziegler, take care of them."

Ziegler happily obliged, the Austrian engineer pulling a few levers on the straps of his metal backpack to extend his three spindly mechanical arms. Helen, Ji, Watson, and Morales fired at him with their disintegrator rifles, but Ziegler used his arms to swing around the bridge and vault over the metal walkways. As the four Teslanauts focused their attention on Ziegler, the remaining agent, Raymond, ignored the engineer. Instead, he slowly and assuredly stepped toward Stonewell, holding both hands onto his father's specialized disintegrator pistol.

"You think your father would have wanted this?" Stonewell demanded. "To see you kill a man just to avenge him?"

"Better that than being a robber baron," Raymond shot back. "Your plan would send millions of soldiers still weary from the last war to their deaths, all simply to line your pockets. My plan stops that, by stopping you."

"You can't kill me," Stonewell snapped. "You never fought in the war. You don't have what it takes to take a man's life."

Ziegler swung one of his mechanical arms at Ji's ankles, tripping him before swinging away to avoid further shots from Helen and Watson. Then, after landing directly in front of the other agents, he pulled more levers on his backpack to reveal six more arms, one on each side of the three previous limbs. Rather than rigid spines, these ended with tiny disintegrator pistols, meaning he now had many different ways to attack from many different angles.

"Oh, geez!" Watson shrieked, Ziegler's new gadgets further triggering his arachnophobia.

"Get to cover!" Morales ordered the other agents.

Ziegler opened fire on the Teslanauts, who quickly scrambled out of the way to avoid the flurry of shots. Knowing they had to take action, Ji backed away as far as he could, turned on his Bolter suit, and took a small step forward, zooming sixty feet in one instant. Just before he reached Ziegler, he turned off the suit with his fist held out, the impact dislodging one of the new limbs and sending it hurtling to the floor of the bridge.

"I never fought in war, you're right," Raymond said to Stonewell as his friends continued fighting Ziegler behind him. "And I hope I never will. Humanity has limitless potential; I've realized that with my time here. That's what Mr. Tesla wants. We can build machines and create inventions for the betterment of each other. War stifles that. War is a blight upon humanity."

"It is also inevitable," Stonewell coldly reminded Raymond. "You think it ended with the armistices? War will return, and it will be worse than ever. As long as there's at least two factions in the world, there will always be conflict. All I'm doing is capitalizing on human nature."

Raymond hated this. He hated hearing this piece of filth talk. He hated that this man lived while his father died. Grunting, he lifted up his pistol and pointed it at Stonewell, his grip shaky, but his stare firm. He had his last gift from his father, and he had the one who killed his father ten feet in front of him. All he had to do was pull the trigger.

"Like I said," Stonewell said, staring down the barrel of Raymond's gun. "Human nature."

Helen blasted another one of Ziegler's mechanical limbs off of his pack, but he still had four more left. The limbs could twist and contort enough to focus on all four of the agents at once, regardless of their direction, and it was only a matter of time before one of the Teslanauts could not evade Ziegler's fire any longer.

"We bring this person down, and I'll fire a rocket inside the gondola," Morales said. "I don't know if it will do much against a vessel this big, but we've got to try while we're here."

"Fire the rocket while we're inside?!" Ji shouted.

"If it's what it takes to bring it down."

"I reckon you should think of an alternative, just in case!" Helen snapped. "I would like to see Brimsby Manor again, thank you!"

"Slippery little mongrels, ze lot of you!" Ziegler hissed. "No matter. I vill still cut you down."

Raymond's grip shook further as he held the gun at Stonewell, feeling every muscle in his fingers that would lead to the simple action of pressing the trigger solidify in place. It would be so simple. All he had to do was lightly push down a single digit on his left hand, like a baby holding a toy. But the sheer weight of the action kept him from moving. Even thinking about moving his muscles took considerable effort in his current state.

Stonewell was right. He couldn't do it. He could not take a life, even of a man he thought deserved it. He had not been broken by war like millions of others merely a few years older than him. Machines?

Absolutely. Vehicles? As long as their drivers were safe. But people? Other flesh-and-blood human beings like himself? Destroying them was going too far.

Maybe, though, he simply needed a different target.

Thinking this, Raymond moved his gun a few inches to the left. His teeth clenched within pursed lips, he fired at last. The lone disintegrator beam whizzed past Stonewell's head and then hit the control panel behind him, the electrical properties of the blast frying the circuitry within. Immediately the chorus of fire from the airship's turrets quietened, leaving only sparse and soft blasts.

"Ze electrical receptors of turrets three through nine have been compromised!" Ziegler cried, retracting his mechanical limbs and heading over to attempt to fix the control panel. "His blast ruptured ze vires!"

"How long do you need to repair them?" Stonewell demanded.

"Three minutes, at ze most."

"Get to it, then! We've still got enemy ships in our-"

Another blast from Raymond's gun hit the other end of the control panel, sending out another spray of sparks and a further silencing of cannon fire.

"Zere goes turrets ten through twelve!" Ziegler roared. "It vill take another six minutes to-"

"I don't care about the panels!" Stonewell screamed. "Just take care of that little sh-"

Yet another blast ruptured the cockpit of the *Eisenzentrum* airship, but this time it did not come from Raymond's specialized pistol. Instead, it came from the turrets of the *White Pigeon*, the Teslanaut flagship now capitalizing on Oberschock's inability to return fire.

"It saddens me that it has come to this, but they have accepted no other option," Tesla sighed from the bridge of his ship. "Bring it down."

"Turrets are fully primed and tuned to maximum levels!" Becky said, wiping the sweat off of her brow while tossing her wrench in the air. "Oberschock won't be hitting the jazz clubs anymore after we're done with them!"

"Fire your lances, Volt Knights!" Foudre ordered, leading a brigade of armor-clad agents aboard a fleet of Interceptors surrounding the enemy. "Show zem what zey get for messing with our glorious country!"

At the command of their captains, the *White Pigeon* unloaded its cannons on the Oberschock airship, rupturing the gondola and sending chunks of its castle foundation flying. Even with the continual thunder from the Blitzsturm-generated weather, the explosions from the attack could be heard for miles around. Further parts of the *Eisenzentrum* caught fire, which would surely mix with the hydrogen in the ship's envelope and combust within seconds.

"Abandon ship!" Ziegler shouted, running off.

"Where are you going?!" Stonewell exploded.

"It's over, you madman!" the Austrian engineer said, quickly taking a parachute and running away from the cockpit. "Ve've lost!"

"How are we gonna get out of here?!" Helen asked, crouching in place as the fire started to spread, with some spouts of flame reaching dangerously close to the top.

Raymond took his father's gun and fired it at the cockpit window, the disintegrator beam shattering the glass with only one shot. Noticing the *White Pigeon* only seventy feet or so in front, he hatched a plan only slightly less crazy than the one that killed the Panzerwurm. "Bolters, grab a person and follow me!" he ordered.

"Follow you where?!" Morales demanded.

Raymond answered not by telling the Marshal, but by demonstrating. The Brooklyn teenager seized his non-Bolter passenger and ran out of the cockpit and into the open air, managing to barely make the distance between the two airships. After landing on the outside decks of the *White Pigeon*, the other two Bolters on his team followed his lead, just as the flames within the *Eisenzentrum* reached the hydrogen-filled envelope.

After a tsunami of fire and heat that washed over the agents and nearly charred them on the spot, the massive dirigible slowly fell to the French meadows below, roaring like a dying beast as it descended. Consumed by the inferno, the last great vessel of the Oberschock Federation crashed and burned, its thousands-foot carcass shattered and spread across the plains outside Paris.

"Good riddance," Helen snapped. "Now, let's shimmy on out of-"

Another, *much* larger explosion from the fallen airship interrupted her, reaching so high that the White Pigeon was thrown off course. Tesla's ship tilted and blew hundreds of feet to the starboard in only a few seconds, with only quick reflexes of grabbing the metal railings keeping the agents from plummeting off the sides of the outer deck. The cloud from this second explosion towered for miles, before arching down like a giant mushroom. The light briefly absorbed all other sources, making everything surrounding the fire pitch black, with the agents able to feel the intense heat in their very bones. Such an enormous, fiery cloud shook the Teslanauts to their core, reminding them in full wide-eyed glory how capable volt-tech was of unimaginable destruction.

"What was *that*?!" Watson shrieked, although no one could hear him through their ringing ears.

As his vision returned, Raymond looked over at where the *Eisenzentrum* airship had fallen, now seeing only a few stones and pieces of metal from the castle's original foundation. He wondered if rain from the storm would put out the blazing fire, but he eventually realized the storm had stopped, with the only clouds coming from the giant explosion. Did it blow all the other clouds away?

However, Raymond then realized what that burst was at last. It was the last masterpiece his father had made. The Blitzsturm, the greatest power source the world had ever seen, built by the genius mind of Francis Calvert, was destroyed. And after seeing the damage it wrought, Raymond had to admit, it was for the best.

"Everyone all right?" Morales asked.

"Just dandy," Watson chuckled wearily, his eyes wide with both excitement and panic.

Raymond nodded at Helen and Morales, the two people that Ji and Watson had brought over from the *Eisenzentrum* as they fled. Then, Raymond turned over to the person he had brought along himself, who gazed out at the blazing fields with rage quieter but just as furious as in the prior airship.

"All this," Stonewell sighed, his shoulders shaking as he looked away from the Teslanauts who saved his life. "All this work I've done... all for nothing. You should have let me die."

Raymond shrugged one shoulder and stepped over to Oberschock's financier, placing his hand on the man's shoulder just as mockingly as Stonewell did to him when showing him his father's corpse. "Your father would have been proud," he said. "You threw your country aside and threatened to end the peace we had fought so hard for all for the sake of profits like a good little warmonger. I'm sure he would have done the same thing."

"Don't test me, kid," Stonewell growled. "The world is broken. I only exploited an opportunity. The Central Powers may be gone, but their people live, and they will remember what we've done to them. Even without my aid, they'll come back sooner or later."

"But you won't," Raymond declared. "Where do we send this fellow, Marshal? Does the Electrocracy have a high security volt-tech prison?"

"Oh, I'm sure the U.S. government would love to deal with him themselves," Morales said. "They have special consequences for those guilty of treason."

The sun finally peered through the clouds of dust created by the Blitzsturm's explosion, shining on the fields outside Paris and the broken corpses of tanks, mechs, and airships littering the area. The great burst could clearly be seen for miles around, and without the storm created by Tesla's tropospheric machine with the Blitzsturm's power there was nothing to veil it for now.

"Everyone can see that," Ji said, pointing at the fading but still apparent mushroom cloud. "Not just in Paris; I bet people all the way in Berlin can see it too. How do we hide something this big?"

"Cleanup Squad?" Raymond suggested.

"You're not seriously suggesting that they dispose of all this wreckage and wipe the memories of that many-"

"The Cleanup Squad can handle *anything*," Watson assured Ji. "Trust me. The biggest story in the Paris newspapers tomorrow will be a bad review for a new gourmet restaurant. You can put money on that."

# Chapter Twenty-Two

WATSON, DESPITE his manic tendencies and bizarre logic, turned out to be spot-on. Less than an hour after the Electrocracy's forces successfully halted Oberschock's advance, the Cleanup Squad arrived via a convoy of nearly two dozen black trucks. Out of these trucks stepped over a hundred agents, all clad in gasmasks and armor that distorted the light around them to make them appear perpetually blurred, a feature that clearly also applied to their trucks based on the fact that they seemed to appear out of thin air. The Squad cleared all the rubble with broom-sized handheld devices that looked like a mix of a disintegrator gun and a vacuum cleaner, making it crumble and disintegrate into nothing, then they got back into their trucks and split up to cover the towns whose residents could have seen the Blitzsturm's explosion. Their silent and rapid efficiency was unnerving, making them seem eerily inhuman in nature. They simply showed up, did their job, and left, all without saying a word or communicating anything to anyone else. The secret had to persist.

The day after the battle, the Electrocracy sent out negotiating parties to the surviving Oberschock leaders, before successfully making them sign additional armistices to ensure no further conflict. While the American, British, and French governments still wanted to punish the people of Germany, Austria, Hungary, and the others for their actions in the war, that was out of the Electrocracy's control. On the volt-tech side of things, it appeared the Oberschock Federation would halt their actions and officially disband. However uncertain or uneasy, peace had been maintained.

Stonewell was taken back to America while remaining under constant surveillance by the Teslanauts. He would be tried by the regular government, as his crimes had to be made public to ensure his name would be forever tarnished. While the volt-tech parts would obviously remain secret, his factories all across Europe and his transactions with former Central Power forces were very traceable. He had a lot to answer for.

Raymond, meanwhile, returned to the Freckle Dump station along with the others, as it started making its teleportation jumps back toward the United States. The agents returned their gear to their lockers and prepped for the journey home, the base having teleported from Zürich to Paris, from Paris to Copenhagen, then from Copenhagen to Oslo. The remaining jumps would take them back to Iceland, to Greenland, to Canada, and finally back to New York. It would take the rest of the day, but at least they were going back in time zones rather than forward as they had on the journey here.

"So, uhhh, what are you going to do?" Arthur asked Raymond. "Now that you've found out what happened to your dad, are you, uhh…"

"…gonna leave you guys?" Raymond finished. "Not a chance. Now that I learned about volt-tech, I can't go back to the normal world."

"You *could*," Becky reminded him. "The Cleanup Squad could send you right back. Isn't that right, Watson?"

"Aw man, *Le Lézard Ailé Hargneux* only got one star!" Watson sighed, reading a copy of the *Le Figaro* newspaper he had bought when the station was in Paris. "I wanted to eat there next time I was in town!"

"Thank you, guys, for helping me through this," Raymond said, placing his hand to his chest. "Really. I needed it. I had no idea what kind of world I was stepping into coming here."

"We all look out for each other," Ivan grunted, his kind and caring words totally at odds with his burly physique and grumpy-looking face. "In fact, we got you something. We heard what happened to your... your, umm-"

"Pet hover-head?" Becky asked, smirking.

"Yes," Ivan muttered, his grumpy face now actually consistent with his mood.

"Wait, you couldn't have rebuilt Sparks, could you have?" Raymond asked, raising his eyebrow. "His parts were in the lab in the Oberschock castle foundation, the one that exploded out in the field when the Blitzstrum was destroyed!"

"Oh no, Sparks is history," Watson assured Raymond. "Every part was vaporized in that explosion. That little machine is gone. Dead as a doornail. It ain't never coming back."

"I appreciate your tact, Watson."

"But we did build you a new one!" Becky said. "It's waiting for you in your locker. We specially made it to be like Sparks; Ivan ripped out the wires himself."

"It was the hardest thing I've ever done in my life," Ivan grumbled. "And my family fled the Soviet Union."

Raymond grinned at his friends, nodding at their thoughtful gesture. Before he could verbally express his gratitude, though, Helen ran up to the group, the accomplished British agent breathing heavily after moving in such a hurry.

"Mr. Tesla... Mr. Tesla wants to talk with you," she huffed, her head pointed to the ground as she caught her breath.

"Who?" Becky asked. "You're not looking at any of us, hon."

"Me, obviously," Watson said, already making his way toward Helen with his head held back and his chest puffed out. "I'm the boss's favorite guy. He probably wants to promote me; he knows I've been gunning for his job ever since I've been here."

"Actually, I was talking to Raymond," Helen said, finally raising her head and looking up at the group, specifically at the Brooklyn teenager.

"Really?" Raymond asked. "What did I do?"

"Any reason you're, uh... so short of breath?" Arthur asked.

"I just came back from Mr. Tesla myself," Helen sighed. "He told me he was very impressed with my efforts out in the field, and he let me know he intends to keep me there for the foreseeable future. I'll be the first woman to have a permanent spot with the Teslanaut field agents!"

"Atta girl!" Becky said, clapping long and loud with a big grin. "Someone needs to show all these boys how it's done!"

"Well, it looks like we'll be seeing a lot of each other then out there, huh?" Raymond said.

"Sure seems that way," Helen said, smiling warmly. "I'm off to write a letter to my family. Crack on, don't keep Mr. Tesla waiting!"

With that, she ran off to the dormitories at the lower level of the base, leaving a bewildered group in her wake. Raymond watched her go for a bit longer than he initially realized, before he felt a hand firmly clasp his shoulder.

"You want a shot at that girl?" Watson said from behind Raymond. "Get yourself some Union Jack undergarments."

"I'll get right on that," Raymond muttered, taking Watson's hand off his shoulder.

After a brief walk around the Freckle Dump base, Raymond eventually found Tesla in a special office nearby the factory, normally locked and empty but currently holding its intended occupant. Plaques and diagrams lined the walls, detailing Tesla's varied experiments throughout the years, from his coils, to his wireless receivers, to some even fancier volt-tech equipment like the mechs and autonomous machines. In the back sat a mirror, with personal grooming items such as hair trimmers and shaving cream, as Tesla valued his appearance. All in all, it was the office of a self-obsessed madman, but one with brilliant ideas and a vision of a future that perhaps could not be but one they should all still strive to accomplish.

"Mr. Calvert," Tesla said, sitting back in his chair with his hands on his desk and his fingers interlaced.

"Yes, Mr. Tesla?" Raymond asked, his voice low and quiet. Not thinking at all, he blurted, "Can I call you Nikola?"

"Absolutely not," Tesla said. "Now, I wanted to talk to you about what you did at the French border."

Raymond nodded slowly, his eyes looking away from the founder and leader of the Teslanauts. He knew this was coming from the moment he took this action, but a part of him hoped that Tesla would laugh it off, compliment Raymond's determination, or some other response that would keep him from getting his memory erased by the Cleanup Squad and dumped back home without remembering any of this, including the fate of his father.

Fat chance of that happening.

"You abandoned your squad and entered the enemy's headquarters alone," Tesla began. "You had orders to stand with your fellow agents and you ignored them. We're a tight unit: a collective of energized particles that flow together as a singular current. Any disruption could jeopardize the whole operation. This was a major offense, and I won't tolerate this kind of behavior."

"I'm so sorry," Raymond sighed, closing his eyes and lowering his head. "I let my obsession about my father get the better of me."

"There was a reason we kept it a secret from you."

"Did you know he was dead?"

"We knew he'd been captured, and he was presumed dead, yes. You, however, provided the confirmation."

"What was your plan, then? Just leave me in the dark forever?"

"When the Oberschock Federation made its presence known, we knew if Mr. Calvert was alive, he would be contained in their headquarters. Our plan was to send more experienced agents to infiltrate the base once their assault had been dealt with. One way or another, you would have found out the truth, Raymond. You just had to keep your impulses in check for a little longer."

Raymond exhaled deeply, knowing that, like pretty much all the time, Tesla was correct. He had made a major error doing what he did, even though at that moment it seemed like the only thing to do. If he were to accomplish good things as a Teslanaut, he needed to maintain professionalism on the job. That is, if this blunder didn't squander his chance of being a Teslanaut any further.

"So, what's going to happen to me?" Raymond asked, his head meekly held close to his shoulders.

"Before I make my decision on that matter, I wanted to ask you a question," Tesla said. "Your father believed you would become a great member of this division. He saw the potential in you when you were merely a boy. Why do you think that is? What is it you think he saw?"

"You're asking me to do a self-assessment?"

"Would you rather I assess you myself?"

"I'm headstrong and determined," Raymond quickly said, very much wanting to avoid Tesla assessing him in his current mood. "I'm eager to learn and aware of my shortcomings, and I want nothing more than to be the best Teslanaut I can be. I know I've got a lot to learn, and I want to learn all I can. I'm not the best with volt-tech, but I have a drive to succeed that would be valuable in your organization. That's how I brought down the Panzerwurm. That's how I saved those agents from the falling train. I take risks, but I get results."

Tesla stared at Raymond through his locked hands, his furrowed eyebrows and crinkled mustache providing little conclusiveness to how he felt about Raymond's analysis.

"At least... that's what I think anyway," Raymond finished, sinking back down into his chair.

Tesla clasped his palms together and looked aside, contemplating the young recruit's answer. As the brilliant scientist and engineer thought further, Raymond became all too aware of his own heartbeat, and how much sweat condensed on the back of his neck. At that moment, the base performed its final jump from the station point in St. John's, Canada, to the one in upstate New York, the electrical energy smothering the station and sending all of the agents' molecules instantly from one point to the next. But by this point, Raymond was so used to the sensation, he was barely cognizant of it. All he focused on now was studying every pore and hair on Tesla's face, anticipating his response like a kid cranking a jack-in-the-box.

"I've received recommendations from a few others that I keep you," Tesla finally said. "After telling me about your actions at the French border, Marshal Morales was quick to add your capabilities as an agent, and your results on the field. And Lei Ji also made sure to inform me of your accomplishments."

"Wait… Lei Ji?" Raymond asked, his brow lifting.

"Yes. He told me that he and his sister are very impressed by what you've done. Ji also told me he looks forward to working with you further, and considering his clout in his former organization, I take his assessment very seriously."

Raymond beamed hearing this, especially after his and Ji's rocky start together in their training and fieldwork.

"I suppose I will honor their recommendations," Tesla finally decided. "I'll admit, your achievements so far have been rather remarkable, and you certainly have potential. I will keep a sharp eye on you, however, to ensure you follow your superior's command from now on."

"I understand," Raymond said, sighing with such relief he felt like he would sink into his chair. "Thank you, Mr. Tesla. I won't let you down."

"I would hope not. Despite the disbanding of the Oberschock Federation, the world is still in chaos. The world needs the Electrocracy's actions more than ever, and we will continue to aid in the shadows with the assistance of volt-tech and the actions of our agents."

"Of course," Raymond said, nodding. "I'm eager to help, Mr. Tesla."

"One more thing before you go," Tesla said. "I already sent out a telegram before we departed Paris. I believe a visitor has come to meet you now that we've returned to New York."

"What do you mean?"

"Ray?"

Raymond's eyes widened hearing that voice behind him. It was from the one he had promised to return to weeks ago, with or without his father. And while he was indeed without his father, that did not mean he was lacking parental relations, and it appeared she knew all along about this secret world. Standing up from the chair with tears in his eyes, Raymond walked over to the doorway leading into Tesla's office and hugged his mother tight.

# About the Author

**MATTHEW DONALD** is the kind of guy dads warn their daughters about because while he might appear nice, he also probably still lives in his mother's basement. But don't worry, he has his own place. He graduated from the University of Northern Colorado in 2014 with a B.A. in English and Creative Writing, and is currently working on a few sequels to Teslanauts in addition to his podcasts The Writ Wit and Paleo Bites. He lives in Centennial, Colorado with his cockatiel, Lyra.

Made in the USA
Monee, IL
17 August 2022